THE TWICE
AND
FUTURE
CAESAR

THE TWICE AND FUTURE CAESAR

A Novel of the Merrimack

R. M. MELUCH

DAW BOOKS, INC.

DONALD A. WOLLHEIM, FOUNDER

375 Hudson Street, New York, NY 10014

ELIZABETH R. WOLLHEIM
SHEILA E. GILBERT
PUBLISHERS

www.dawbooks.com

To Jim,
All my yesterdays.

To Stevan,
All my tomorrows.

Prologue

from *The Myriad*

7 June 2443
U.S. Space Battleship *Merrimack*
Globular Cluster IC9870986 a/k/a the Myriad
Sagittarian Space

THE STAR SPARROW SPRANG with a scathing shriek. The deck heaved. The ship rang behind it.

"Missile away."

Captain Farragut heard a murmured benediction from Jose Maria. He hadn't known he was on the deck. Farragut demanded, "Tracking."

"Tracking, aye. We are on course. Accelerating well. Perfect launch, sir."

Perfect. Ten minutes too late to achieve intercept. "Take us down from redline."

Calli relayed orders to back off *Merrimack*'s tearing speed.

All attention remained on the speeding Star Sparrow. No one on the command deck spoke above a murmur, constantly updating velocities, accelerations, the deficit to intercept. All indicated the attempt to stop the message from reaching Origin was going to fail.

Farragut tried to convince himself that he was wrong, that failure was good. Augustus was right; there was no changing the past. Those innocent beings on board the Arran messenger ship would get away alive. That was the way it would happen. Augustus was never wrong.

Tried to inhale calm.

Augustus was always right.

And still the desperate need to run as if his world depended on it.

Low, professional voices read off dispassionate progress reports of the Star Sparrow, the Arran messenger, the Hive swarms.

Captain Farragut watched the chronometer. Watched the plots creep across the tactical map. The Star Sparrow was dead on its estimates, accelerating precisely as calculated.

The variable was the target.

"You're making a race of it, John," said Calli. "The Arran messenger has not kept a constant speed."

"What's our deficit now?"

"Six minutes."

"Augustus, coordinate a firing sequence with fire control." At thousands of times the speed of light, the moment of contact would be brief in the idiotic extreme. He could not risk the explosion occurring a million miles after impact. Detonation by resonant command may be instantaneous, but the decision and execution was not.

Augustus nodded vacantly.

Farragut requested an update. Waited for the inevitable deficit.

"Target is twenty minutes from the gate. Missile twenty—Whoa."

Farragut's head snapped aside. "Explain 'whoa.'"

"Target is decelerating! Five-minute deficit. Four! Three!"

"Control Room! Fire Control here. At this rate of closure we may overshoot."

"I've got you, John," Augustus assured him from the depths of his altered thoughts. "I'm not slowing this bird till we're there. We aren't there yet."

"*Nineteen-second deficit*! Target still decelerating. Eighteen!" Tactical lost his professional monotone. "Arran messenger turning to line up its approach to the *kzachin*. *Ten-second deficit*. Five seconds. Four."

And a long pause.

"Status," Farragut demanded in the long quiet.

"Deficit holding at four seconds. No."

"No, what?"

Tactical made a fist. Opened it. "Five-second deficit. Six. Target is reaccelerating." Dashed beaded sweat from under his nose. "We're losing it, sir."

Calli demanded coolly, "ETA of target to the gate?"

"Five minutes."

At two minutes, Farragut asked again, "Deficit to intercept?"

"Ten seconds," Jeffrey reported gloomily.

Farragut hesitated, ordered, "Push the missile."

The resonant control signal went out to the Star Sparrow's guidance system. "Balk," Fire control reported.

"Override balk."

"Overriding, aye— Distortion! Missile flame out! Star Sparrow is running dead."

There would be no more acceleration from the Star Sparrow, no course correction. The missile sped on inertia.

"Deficit at fifteen seconds. Sixteen. Climbing." The young specialist turned his eyes up. "We're not going to make it, sir."

This is it.

Barring miracles, it was all over. Done is done. Farragut could only watch and wait out the final minute. Wait—for what?

For nothing, he hoped. John Farragut inhaled deeply. His chest felt full of heavy air, as if a gorgon swarm were sitting on it.

He told himself it would be okay. In fifty-four seconds Augustus would be laughing at him and asking him to explain why he opened fire on an unarmed, manned vessel, and John Farragut would be feeling ridiculous. He never imagined wanting so badly to be ridiculous.

He searched for Jose Maria on deck. Wanted to say to him: Here's to Augustus laughing.

He felt a presence immediately behind him. A touch, a breath on his hair. A kiss on his neck.

And he was angry. A line crossed and never expected. Farragut's hair prickled, face burned. He did not appreciate the gesture, and the timing stunk. It pissed him enough to snap around from the face of the imminent Judgment and demand, "What was *that*?"

Augustus elled his thumb and forefinger against his opposing palm, flipped a quick word in American Sign: *Later.*

John Farragut felt himself go wide-eyed. Tough to scare, he was suddenly profoundly terrified. *Later never comes.*

He stared into bottomless eyes. Crushing the tremor out of his voice, he commanded quietly, "Now, I think."

Because he sensed Augustus had no intention of *ever* explaining that. For all Augustus' talk of the immutability of time, Farragut got the feeling Augustus did not expect one or both of them to be here thirty seconds from now, and *that* had been an end-of-the-world stunt Augustus need not live with for more than thirty seconds.

His eyes were suddenly not blank at all. Always, when plugged in, Augustus' eyes became vacant hollows, the thoughts racing deep inside. This time they looked back, aware, omniscient. The patterner had taken in all, synthesized all the minutiae, and saw what he had not seen before this moment.

Farragut stared at him. *You just recanted!*

Saw the answer in his eyes.

MUNDI TERMINUM ADPROPINQUANTE. Now that we are approaching the end of the world, John Farragut.

Your individual existence is a statistical miracle. We are, each and every one of us, highly improbable, a one-in-a-million event at conception. History turns on a space big enough for angels to dance on. I do stand by inevitability. But inevitability works on a macroscopic scale. Macroscopic events are inevitable. The blizzard will come. But the when, the where, and the unique shape of each snowflake is a function of chaos. One breath out of place, and that one singular snowflake never forms. I mistook us for macroscopic. Intuition is subconscious knowledge, and while logic says changing history is impossible, intuition says there are things beyond my ken; and you are a patterner, John Farragut. You know. You know. And you're right. You are chaos. I won't explain later, because there is no later. There is no earlier. There is no time at all. Simply put, it was miraculous knowing you, and that was good-bye.

So said the eyes. Aloud, Augustus answered with an ironic near smile, "I still think you're an idiot."

But Farragut understood him as clearly as if he'd spoken all of it.

I'm right!

The floor of the world kicked out from under him. This was the end of the world he knew.

Did not want to be right.

He faced forward, terrified now. The countdown fell on cotton ears.

"Arran messenger ten seconds from the gate. Nine. Eight."

There is no later.

"He's accelerating again." The count sped up. "We have four seconds. Three. Two. Messenger at the gate—"

Closed his eyes.

Oh, God, it's done. If it happens, it will be this instant. I won't even know. Either I'm here or I'm not, and I never was.

Breathed.

PART ONE

Labyrinth

COLONEL TR STEELE didn't know where he was. He didn't know who he was or what he was. He had the sense of nearing a surface, which suggested he was under something. It was dark. He wasn't breathing. But he had a heartbeat.

He neared consciousness while they were moving him. Didn't know who *they* were. His eyelids fluttered. He heard, as if through thick gauze, concerned murmurs from the people lifting him. One voice sounded sudden alarm, but Steele couldn't understand the words.

What language was that?

Did I crash?

The last thing Colonel Steele knew, he'd been in the cockpit of his fighter Swift, lining up his approach to dock with the United States Space Battleship *Merrimack*.

And now he wasn't.

He had a sense of time having passed. But how long? Hours? He had a bad feeling that it was longer than hours.

How did he get here? Where was here?

Was that voice speaking *Latin?*

Oh, hell, he was sinking back into red-black nothingness.

Where was the *Merrimack?*

And where the hell was Kerry Blue?

* * * * *

5 January 2448
U.S. Space Battleship *Merrimack*
Indra Aleph Star System
Perseid Space

The universe was all wrong.

Rumor had it that Flight Sergeant Kerry Blue had married the Old Man.

Yeah, right. A flight sergeant married to a full bird colonel? Not in this man's Fleet Marine. Flight Sergeant Shasher Wyatt wasn't idiot enough to believe that squid story. And the idea of Kerry Blue married to anyone? In what universe?

But how then to explain how Kerry Blue went from anybody's port in a storm to sleeping alone in her own pod?

Kerry Blue was pretty. Okay, fine, she was what passed for pretty on a space battleship patrolling the edge of nowhere. The longer *Merrimack* stayed out here at the galactic rim, the prettier Kerry Blue got. She had it all over those perfect lindas in the dreambox for being real. But you could have one of those dream babes anytime—anytime you were off duty. You couldn't have Kerry Blue anymore, anytime, at all. That hurt. And for some stupid reason it made her more wantable.

And then there was Cain Salvador—*Lieutenant* Cain Salvador, if you can believe that—acting like her daddy with a shotgun. You touch Kerry Blue on pain of, well, pain. The rumor was that Cain had been best man at the supposed wedding. But just ask him if that was true and Acting Wing Commander Cain Salvador would order you to do something anatomically unacceptable involving a . . . well, anyway. Cain was not the problem. The Kerry Blue of old could get around any chaperone God ever invented. The problem was that Kerry Blue didn't want to get around Cain. She really did act like she was holding a docking beacon for the one man who wasn't on board. And when Kerry Blue fixed on one guy, the rest of you lot were so not screwed.

So the only ball Flight Sergeant Shasher Wyatt got to play with Kerry Blue involved a hoop.

It was Team Alpha versus Team Baker in the starboard maintenance hangar. The Bakers were swabbing the deck with the Alphas, who were not tall.

Alpha Six, Kerry Blue, jumped for the basketball.

So did Geneva Rhine, Alpha Three, the one they called Rhino. Rhino was an upholstered boulder with a cute elfin face. Rhino slammed into Kerry Blue like—well, not like a charging sugarplum fairy. And Rhino and Blue were on the same team. Just the sound could knock the air out of you.

Shasher Wyatt winced.

Kerry Blue came down from the jump, breathless and ball-less. Her feet missed the deck. She landed on her back and rolled. Shasher Wyatt staggered. An alarm clanged.

The status panel flashed red. Shasher Wyatt was over Kerry Blue, trying to help her up. He fell too.

Other Marines on the court in the maintenance bay staggered. The ship shivered. The deck heaved. There was a sound like rocks crushing. The ship's energy shell buzzed.

Whatever *Merrimack* allowed you to feel wasn't anything close to whatever really hit her. The real sounds were muted way down to something that wouldn't blast your eardrums out.

The tremor in the deck was just the smallest suggestion of what had actually hit the space battleship.

The tremor suggested that *Merrimack* had just been nuked.

Right now the ship's auto-defense program would be turning the *Mack* on her central axis faster than your brain synapses could fire, shifting her attitude and raising full shields to cover the engine vents.

Over the loud com the Dingo's voice sounded: "All hands. Siege stations."

Siege status locked the ship up until the command staff could find out exactly what they were dealing with.

Everyone hated sieges. No one—not the navvies, not the Fleet Marines, not the ship's dogs—no one liked a defensive fight. You just wanted to get out there and blow something up. Nothing flew under siege. The Marine Wing's fighter craft were locked down in the hangar bay. Nothing to do but stampede with the rest of the team to the projectile gun blisters and wait for something to open up.

Up ahead of Shasher Wyatt, Kerry Blue was racing Dak Shepard to get to the hatchway of gun bay twenty-five first. She was going to lose that race. Dak used to be a linebacker. But instead of squashing her at the hatchway, Dak grabbed her, shoulders and ass, and launched her into the gun blister ahead of him.

Shasher was last man in. Climbed onto his gun.

Of course the foxtrotting gun ports were buttoned shut. That meant the torpedo tubes would also be shut and the missiles clamped down inside the ship's inertial shell.

The only guns operable at the moment would be the battleship's energy weapons. Those were for the Navy shooters. The Fleet Marines with their projectile weapons had no trade. Got to stare at the blast covers. The monitors didn't show nothin'. Had to wonder if they were broken.

So here was Team Alpha, twiddling their thumbs.

None of them twiddled well.

And there's Kerry Blue seated at her gun next to Shasher. He watched her thigh move as her heels tapped. Heard her muttering, "*C'mon c'mon c'mon.*"

Shasher didn't say anything. No one wants to hear the new guy talk. Shasher had just come over from the Battery. Always wanted to fly. Not flying now.

Here in the gun bay was Dak Shepard, Alpha Two. Solid guy. Dak was a brick. Swam like a brick. He was all muscle, even to his brain. Dog devoted. Dog friendly. Doesn't drool, but he sweats. You can't call him stupid. Okay, fine, you can, but you really want Dak on your team.

Carly Delgado was in the four slot. Strong, hard, tough, bad as a hornet. Bony. Fast. Plays with knives. That little fist swings around like a rock on the end of a whip, and Shasher Wyatt wakes up in the ship's hospital. Why don't you just spar with a bobcat next time, Shasher?

Kerry and Carly are both kickers when they don't have weapons on them, which is rare. Carly's always got a blade on her.

Carly hangs tight with Twitch Fuentes. Twitch looks dangerous, and he can be. But that dark-eyed squint and frown is just his face in at-ease position. Flat planes of heavy bones, brown skin, black hair, broad build. Quiet. After five tours you'd think Twitch would talk but he don't. He understands Americanese as well as anyone else in the team. Shasher guessed Twitch just got so used to not talking he just doesn't do it. Afraid of sounding dumb.

Then there's Geneva Rhine, the Rhino. Rhino likes being a Marine. Don't like being a girl at all. Has a red X tattooed between her eyebrows and tattoos on her knuckles DNFW, as in Do Not Foxtrot With. Rhino hates Romans. Don't we all? But Rhino *hates* Romans.

Not here in the gun bay with the rest of the Alphas was Flight Leader

Cain Salvador. Lieutenant Cain Salvador now. Cain was probably on the command deck. That's where Colonel Steele would be, if Colonel Steele was here.

Merrimack was operating at the back of the Outback, at the edge of the galaxy, where it wouldn't do to have a half battalion of Fleet Marines under the command of a mere rate. It would take two months or more to whistle a real officer out here from Earth. So *they*—the "they" who made those decisions—*they* had gone and field-promoted Cain.

Nothing was right in the universe. Colonel TR Steele should be up there on the command deck, and Cain Salvador—*Flight Leader* Cain Salvador—should be in here in gun bay twenty-five with the rest of us Alphas.

Should be was another way of saying *ain't*.

The buzz of the ship's energy guns vibrated the gun bay.

There's Kerry Blue kicking her heels like a squirmy child. "Well, *someone's* got trade."

"Ain't us, *chica linda*," said Carly Delgado.

"I think they're just shooting in the dark," Shasher Wyatt said.

Dak Shepard: "Can't *we* do that?"

"I'm with Shash," Kerry Blue said. "Know what I'm not hearing?"

Dak and Carly called it at the same time: "Incoming fire."

Listened to the ship's beam gunners raking surrounding space with concentrated hellfire. Didn't sound as though they connected with anything.

"Helm. Take us to FTL."

"FTL, aye."

At the captain's order the space battleship jumped out of normal space to faster than light.

The stars disappeared.

"Change course, random vector."

The pilot acknowledged. "Random vector, aye."

"Jump down to sublight."

"Sublight, aye."

The stars reappeared in the *Merrimack*'s portholes.

"Position of the bogey!" Captain Carmel demanded.

Tactical reported, "Bogey does not register on the tactical screen. Bogey does not appear to be in normal space."

Merrimack's attacker had apparently dropped out of FTL to take its shots and immediately jumped back to FTL space. There was no knowing where the enemy was in FTL space. But here in normal space *Merrimack* was a sitting target.

The captain said, "Dingo, I want to be somewhere else."

The ship's XO, Stuart Ryan, was a lean, hard-strung man from the land of Oz, eager as a wild dog. Dingo Ryan gave the orders, "FTL jump. Random vector."

"FTL, aye. Random vector, aye."

Traveling FTL was dangerous inside a planetary system, but *Merrimack* had collision avoidance programmed into her otherwise random choices to prevent her from crashing through anything massive. Not that she couldn't survive a collision with just about anything short of a black hole.

Safe again at FTL, Calli Carmel rounded on Tactical like a hissing swan. "Tactical! Identify bogey."

The ship's systems would have got a read on the hostile plot in the instant of its appearance while in normal space. Tactical had since had time to process the data.

Marcander Vincent at the tactical station reported, "Bogey reads like a Roman Accipiter. Negative hull identifiers. But it posted a Roman flag."

"Helm. Change course. Random vector."

No one could track a plot moving FTL. But technology never stood still, and Calli Carmel took no chances when dealing with Romans. She assumed *Merrimack* was being tracked even while traveling in FTL space.

"Random course change, aye," the pilot responded.

Calli looked to the tactical station. "Mister Vincent. Was the bogey sending IFF?"

"Negative IFF."

"Negative transmissions while the plot was sublight," the com tech added.

"Dingo. Lock us down."

"Helm. Systems. Full lockdown."

Her XO gave the orders to make it happen. In full lockdown, *Merrimack* was almost invulnerable. The list of threats that could fit through that "almost" was getting longer by the year. *Merrimack* was still a grand ship, but not a new one.

"Lockdown full. Aye."

"Return us to normal space, a thousand klicks from our original position."

"Space normal, aye." The pilot gave the galactic coordinates of the space battleship's new position.

"Stand at full alert," Calli ordered.

And waited for their attacker to come back around for another strike.

Dingo Ryan came to her side. "What do you think?" he muttered.

Calli gave her head a small shake. Really didn't know. "Nothing's right about this."

Dingo glanced to a porthole. You never saw your attacker. But you really couldn't help looking.

"Where is he?"

In the waiting, the ship began a low thumping from within. You felt it through the decks—Marines 'cussing. This percussion number was their own war dance. The Bull Mastiffs of the 89th Battalion wanted out to hunt.

The bogey had shown a Roman flag.

Calli: "Com."

"Com. Aye."

"Give me my direct res link to Numa."

"Res link open. On your com, Captain."

Caesar Numa Pompeii took Calli's hail immediately. Without greeting, the voice of Caesar himself sounded from the captain's com. "What do you have?"

There were no gaps in his transmission. That was telling.

Dingo mouthed without sound, *He's traveling sublight.*

Calli nodded silent acknowledgment. Spoke into the com, "Why did you jump me?"

"Captain Carmel?" Numa sounded innocent. Truly. Not pretending.

Calli told him, "I just took a thousand megaton tap from your Accipiter."

Caesar Numa's voice returned a quiet rumble. "Not mine. Kill it. Then find the nest and kill that."

Calli didn't take orders from the Roman emperor. But she welcomed permission to open fire on a Roman-flagged vessel. That permission betrayed Caesar's desperation to exterminate the subversives.

Caesar Numa didn't ask where Calli was. He would already know, the instant she'd hailed him on the resonator.

Rome had the technology to locate the source of a resonant pulse. The United States Naval Fleet didn't.

The res link went dead without a signoff. Unless Calli had Romulus in custody, Numa, the emperor of Rome, had no time for her.

Calli turned to her XO. "That Accipiter can't be alone."

Dingo gave a quick nod. He also smelled a rival predator here. "There's a hidden outpost or a mothership close by. Got to be. We got lucky flushing out that Accipiter."

"*Lucky* never happens in my presence," Calli said.

Lucky usually meant you didn't understand the situation. *Lucky* meant you were being set up.

"It *looks* like we're close to what we're hunting for," Calli said. "I don't trust the look."

No one ever just happened to run into anyone between stars. And this chance encounter felt altogether wrong.

Calli posed her problem to the XO. "Why did the Accipiter hit us?"

Dingo Ryan didn't understand the question. "Sir?"

"What did the Accipiter gain by attacking us? He knows we're shielded. All he did by shooting at us was give away his presence. Why would he reveal himself? And how did he know we were here?"

"Numa knows we're here," Commander Ryan said.

"Numa knows *now*. He didn't know where we were until I resonated him. Why is there a short-range Roman attack craft out here and why did it hit us?"

"Sir, we're in this star system hunting for a Romulid outpost. Is it too big a stretch to think we finally *found* one?"

"Yes. It is. You know it is. If those are Romulii in that Accipiter, then we didn't find them. They came out and flashed us."

Dingo Ryan covered his eyes and gave a growling snarl.

The war drumming from down decks was getting louder. The Marines pounded, stomping on the bulkheads and ductwork. The sound reverberated through the ship. *BOOM pom pom pom BOOM pom pom pom.*

Captain Carmel finally ordered, "Mr. Ryan. Throw a bucket of water on my dogs. They're not going outside."

Four months after Caesar Numa ejected *Merrimack* from the Zoen star system at the galactic edge, the U.S. space battleship still patrolled the galactic Outback. This was not American space. The Perseid arm of the galaxy was dominated by colonies of the Pacific Rim nations of Earth. The United States had no colonies here.

Merrimack's company and crew of 1145 hands made her the largest U.S. presence in Perseid space.

The Perseid arm of the galaxy had been a festering ground for Romulus and his rabid followers, the Romulii, even before his public rise to power. Romulus had founded most of the Roman colonies in Perseid space while his father Caesar Magnus was still alive.

After Romulus' meteoric rise and meteoric fall, his followers were still fanatics. More than ever. The Romulii became an underground subversive faction of the Roman Empire, disloyal to the legitimate Caesar Numa Pompeii.

The United States was not an ally of Rome or its current emperor, Numa. Between Romulus and Numa, Numa was the lesser of two evils. It had been Caesar Romulus who declared war on the United States of America two years ago. The U.S. didn't want to see that Caesar back in power.

Romulus was missing.

War's end had left Romulus in Caesar Numa's custody, incapacitated, and existing in an induced coma on the Roman capital world Palatine under heavy guard.

At some time between then and now, Romulus' rabid followers had spirited their comatose leader away from Numa's custody. Worst guess had him way out here in Perseid space, being rehabilitated in preparation to bring him back to power.

A healthy Romulus could mobilize worlds. Romulus had been adored. Still was.

That Romulus might be alive and recovering in Perseid space was a nightmare that must never see daylight.

So the Joint Chiefs had not ordered *Merrimack* back to Near Space.

Captain Carmel ordered, "Launch Argus."

Argus, named for the mythical hundred-eyed giant, was a flotilla of drone scouts controlled by the Wraith—Specialist Tim Raytheon—the ship's chief V-jock and drone wrangler. Wraith was young, bony, and pale. He received a rejuv three times a year to keep his reaction times sharp.

Dingo Ryan ordered, "Mister Raytheon, turn over some rocks in this system. You're looking for just about anything. You know what belongs and what doesn't."

"Aye, aye, sir."

The drone flotilla Argus deployed with no more noise than the hissing of missiles through their launch tubes.

As the drones dispersed, Commander Ryan moved to Calli's side. "It's a big search area, Captain," he said quietly.

The rough dimension of the Indra Aleph star system was 500 billion cubic astronomical units.

"It is that, Mister Ryan," Calli allowed.

But it was smaller than infinity. By galactic measure, *Merrimack* was just about stepping on the Romulid lair.

Dingo said, "I'm surprised Romulus' followers don't have him in a labyrinth."

Romulus was beloved by his fanatics for his dangerous and twisted sense of entertainment. Calli's brows lifted. A labyrinth did sound like Rom's sort of fun.

She said at last, "Is there anything to say they don't?"

2

12 Ianuarius 2448
Asteroid 543
Indra Shwa Zed Star System
Perseid Space

THE CRAMPED GRIMY CORRIDOR looked like it used to be white. The lights buzzed within dirty fixtures. Flickered on and off. Something yellow-green dripped off a moldering ceiling that was so low that Nox had to crouch. The drops sizzled on hitting the concrete floor and gave off a sickly sweet vapor. A dark bloody brown crust dried around the fallen drops. Flat, pincered bugs the size of flounders with serrate legs clung to the peeling walls on either side of him. Their mouthparts clacked.

Then the passageway opened to a wide high chamber, and Nox saw in it what he was meant to see: In the floor, a pit. From the ceiling, a pendulum.

Perched over the doorway hunched a molting, raggy-winged, one-eyed raven with a croaking caw and a viciously barbed beak.

Almost none of it was real.

Nox pulled his monoc down over his right eye. The filtered lens on the monoc showed him only what was really there—just a plain metal chamber. No monster bugs, no blood, no pendulum. There really was something sticky on the floor, but it was clear. The raven was nothing but a caw.

Nox walked through the swinging pendulum.

Overly complicated, nonsensical squidsquat. Nox would name this defensive program Jackass Quest, except that he was here to assassinate a Caesar. And a lot of the *merda* in here could really kill him.

Sensors implanted in Nox's eyes were sending readings up to the ship for his guide, Cinna, to process and direct him where to go. The patterner Cinna, codenamed Chessman for this mission, saw through Nox's sensor implants. The implants sent more than visual images. And it wasn't just Nox's sensors sending the patterner information.

The Chessman was seeing through the sensors that all his brothers carried, seven of them, crawling through this maze. Plugged into the ship's vast data bank in patterner mode, Cinna could process all the input at once.

"Nemo. Pit," the Chessman warned.

"I see it," Nox said. "What do you want me to do with it?"

"Don't fall in," said the Chessman.

"Jump off a cliff, O Best Beloved," Nox said back.

"This looks like a game I played," one of Nox's brothers said.

Another answered, "I think this *is* a game I played."

"Gurdanjan's Dungeon," said another.

"That's the one."

This program was set up to deter, distract, disguise, and destroy. This dungeon was meant to really kill them. Playfully.

This was what happened when you put gamers in charge of security. They built in layers of overly elaborate, impractical, and outright frivolous obstacles, when what they really needed were heavily armed guards with orders to shoot to kill.

The *gaminess* of this place had all the hallmarks of the Romulii.

A lofty, no nonsense voice that had to be Nicanor's sounded. "Chessman, can we just shut down the game generator so we can all see what we are doing?"

"We could. If one of you shows me where the generator is," the Chessman responded, and went on just as calmly, "Ogre. Run. To your right. Fast."

Nox heard heavy breathing over the link. Had to be Ogre. Running.

The call signs were confusing Nox. The only call signs Nox knew instantly were Nemo—that was his call sign—and Chessman—that was Cinna, the patterner. Chessman was Nox's navigator in here, his lifeline.

And Scimitar. Nox knew the call sign Scimitar. Scimitar was the whole squad. If Chessman called Scimitar that meant all the brothers and it was an emergency. Nox listened for that one. If Chessman called Scimitar, they were probably running for their lives.

Chessman: "Loki. Walk softly. You have a human being directly under you, one level down."

A whisper, probably Loki, sounded, "Can I shoot down?"

The Chessman: "Don't."

The presence of human guards meant the defenders were serious about guarding something, not just playing games. The presence of human guards also meant it was going to be a son of a bitch getting out of here alive.

The man who sent the Ninth Circle in here was not desperately concerned with their getting out alive. Just in their completing the objective: Kill Romulus.

Caesar Numa couldn't openly order a hit on his predecessor. So Numa had secretly conscripted the most feared and vicious pirate band in civilized space, arranged their very conspicuous deaths, and placed a patterner in their squad.

The brothers were privateers without a marque. Officially they didn't work for Caesar. Officially they were the disgraced dead.

There was a high chance of actually dying in here. They knew that coming in.

The voice of the Chessman sounded in Nox's ear: "Nemo, Paladin. Ignore the falling rocks."

Nox fell, screaming, with a feeling of being crushed and buried alive. His voice came out amazingly loud for having rocks caving in his chest. Nox gasped, "Chessman, is this a tactile illusion?"

"It is. Get up and walk."

It took all Nox's will and strength. He didn't even feel his limbs moving. He just imagined walking. Then suddenly he lurched out of the illusion and staggered. And breathed.

His brother Pallas, code-named Paladin, was standing over him. "You all right?"

"I'm superluminary," Nox snarled, gulping air.

The patterner's calm voice directed, "Nemo. See the iron maiden."

"I see it, Chessman."

"Open it."

Nox hesitated. "What's inside?"

"I won't know until you open it."

Nox's tolerance for gore was getting lower and lower. He swallowed hard. His hand quivered a bit as he grabbed the handle of the iron maiden's lid and pulled it open.

The iron maiden was viciously spiked on the inside but Nox found no victim impaled there.

There was no back part to the torture device at all.

Beyond the open lid stretched a quiet, antiseptic corridor with walls of calm sage green.

The Chessman instructed, "Nemo. Paladin. Advance."

"Are you sure, Chessman?" Nox asked, not trusting his eyes. Nox was a terrorist. The very idea of an iron maiden terrified him.

"Reasonably sure." Cinna's soft voice sounded maddeningly calm.

Nightmares loomed at the back of Nox's consciousness, threatening to paralyze him. He force-marched himself through the opening of the iron maiden, his back tensed, anticipating invisible spikes closing around him like jaws.

But he felt only a soft tiled floor under his foot, just like what he saw. Behind him he felt only Pallas following close as a tail.

Pleasant diffuse lighting shone from the white ceiling of the corridor. White noise drifted in from somewhere. "We're in," said Nox. "I think."

It looked like the game stopped here. Everything around Nox looked, smelled, felt sane and real.

"Move quickly," the Chessman said. "You have set off a silent alarm. Whatever they send against you now will be real. And probably human."

Nox and Pallas were wearing personal fields, which protected them against projectiles and energy weapons, but there were other ways to be killed.

Chessman: "Move."

Nox yanked at the first side door he came to. It opened easily. He stood in the doorframe, staring.

"What am I looking at, Chessman?"

It looked like a hospital room. A man floated unconscious in a tank of pink medical gel.

"Is this real?"

"Yes. He's real."

"You found him!" one of the brothers cried over the link.

"No," Nox said. This wasn't Romulus.

This man was white. You could see that even through the pink gel. He was naked and he was blond. Romulus was bronze-skinned and he had dark hair. Romulus was also younger than this man. "This is the wrong guy," Nox said.

"Are you sure?" one of his brothers asked over the com. "They could have given Romulus a new body."

"Well they're not jolly likely to give him *this* body," said Nox.

This man was what Americans called big, but he was not what Romans considered big. This man was only about Nox's height, but broader, more muscular with heavier bones. His skin was a paler shade of Caucasian than Nox's. His hair a whiter shade of blond. This man was older than Nox.

It was not the body of a Caesar.

Nox did a double take. He hadn't recognized the man at first because the figure was pasty and inanimate and shrouded in pink gel. This unconscious body held none of the energy and defiant fire that made the man the gladiator he was.

Nox had seen him on the imperial broadcasts during the war.

"Chessman, are you seeing this? Do you know this guy?"

"I do. I don't care. It's not the target. Keep going."

Nox broke into a trot down the corridor, throwing doors open on the right side, Pallas was already opening doors on the left side. The rooms were scientific chambers where *medici* could work undisturbed by the insanity of this fortress's substantial moat. There were no *medici* in the rooms now.

Suddenly Nox saw where he wanted to go—the door up ahead with the crest on its lintel in black and gold. Julian colors. "That's it!"

The Chessman spoke, not the words Nox expected. "Scimitar. Scimitar."

"NO!"

Scimitar was the code name for the whole squad. It signaled dire emergency.

"Fall back. Get out. Get out. Scimitar. Scimitar. Get out."

3

AUDIBLE ALARMS SOUNDED NOW. Nox could scarcely hear Cinna's soft voice over them.

"Nemo! Paladin! Get out of there!"

Instead, Nox charged ahead to the imperially crested door. The door was locked. The lock demanded a retinal scan. Nox was not giving that thing his eyeball.

He threw himself at the door, shoulder first. "No. We're *here*. We came here to—" He stopped talking. Better not say why he was here. He hurled himself at the door again. "We came here for a reason. Get me through this door!"

Chessman: "Nemo. Fall back! We'll do it later! You need to get out of there!"

Nox threw his weight against the door. The door didn't feel stout. And with another heave, it gave way. Nox staggered into the chamber.

Came to an abrupt stop.

Pallas ploughed into his back and stopped.

"Merda," Nox said.

Five other voices sounded in their coms. *"What?"*

Nox couldn't say it.

Pallas could. "He's *gone!*"

Nox and Pallas were in a room that was part sickbay and part royal chamber. The walls were hung with royal trappings in black and gold. An oak wreath hung over an empty pallet where a patient had recently lain.

The life-support equipment had been left behind.

A top sheet appeared half-dragged off the pallet, as it might if it clung to someone who'd got up and walked under his own power.

Nox whirled about-face to run away. Collided with Pallas.

Abruptly a heavy metal barrier slid across the doorway with deep thunks of locking mechanisms.

The voice of the Chessman sounded in their ears, "Nemo! Paladin! You got yourselves bottled. Go vertical."

Nox and Pallas looked up. "How?"

The ceiling was high and smooth. There was a vent up there, but it was smaller than Nox's head. Nox didn't see any other egress from this room.

A gurgle sounded from the floor drain.

Pallas, blanched. "*Nego.*" No.

The gurgle from the floor sounded closer. It was coming from a drain no bigger around than Nox's fist.

And suddenly water jetted up from the opening with bone-breaking force.

"Oh no no no," Pallas murmured, lips gone ashen. Water pounded the ceiling and rained down.

Nox had thought they were done with games. With Romulus the games never stopped.

"Is this a tactile illusion, Chessman?" Nox asked, hopeful.

"No."

Pallas bounced off the walls, his boots splashing in the rising water.

Nox roared at the air. "Get us out of here!"

Red lights shone on both Nox's and Pallas' displacement collars. Jammers were operating. There would be no displacing out of here.

Chessman: "Get yourselves on the roof for Santa Claus."

Santa Claus was a physical pick up and grab. *Santa Claus* required Nox and Pallas to get to the asteroid's surface.

The Chessman calmly gave directions to each of the brothers where to go.

Nox and Pallas were locked underground and nearly under water.

A murmur sounded, right next to Nox, so soft Nox scarcely heard it. "*Frater*, I don't want to go this way."

"We're not!" Nox said decisively, one of his better attempts at a bald lie.

Water swirled around Nox's shins. Pallas tried to take a step, splashed forward and fell, face under. He emerged sputtering.

Water shot up in a solid pillar from the floor. It hammered at the ceiling, spraying the whole chamber with hard rain. The water level on the floor rose steadily. Pallas climbed onto the pallet.

Nox waded to him, his legs dragging heavily in the rising flood. Pallas reached down and helped Nox up onto the mattress, which was getting soggy.

"Chessman!" Nox bellowed.

Cinna's voice sounded calm. "In the ceiling there is a vertical shaft intersecting with a horizontal cross duct. The horizontal duct is far too small for human passage, but the vertical stack is wide enough for you to chimney up."

The hard spray from the spouting water had everything wet. Nox's and Pallas' faces dripped.

Nox spat water off his lips. "Yeah? The vent to get at it is far too small too!"

"Widen it," Chessman said.

Widen it. Right.

The ceiling was too high for either Nox or Pallas to reach the vent, even standing on the pallet.

Nox dragged gauntlets onto his wet hands. Pallas fished a hammer claw out of his pack. Pallas boosted Nox up on his shoulders. Pallas teetered on the spongy mattress.

And the lights failed.

Nox roared wordless noise. He pushed his palms against the ceiling to steady their tottering human column in the wet darkness.

A light blossomed from below. Pallas had stuck a glow dot on his own shoulder. Pallas reached up and pressed one onto Nox's back as well.

Nox pulled the cover off the vent and threw it away to the side. Too scared and angry to say anything, he reached down an open palm. The handle of the hammer claw slapped firmly into Nox's waiting glove.

Nox swung the claw at the rim of the small vent. *Widen it. Widen it.* The hammer strike clinked. Nox tried not to scream. "Chessman! It's metal!"

The Chessman, insanely calm, said, "Nemo. It's ductwork. Not armor. It's thin."

Nox forced panic back and realized yes, the barrier did have a thin feel to it. He beat holes into it until he could pry the metal back into razor-edged rolls. He could see at last there really was a shaft up there, maybe a meter wide. Air moved against Nox's face. Water swirled at his thighs.

Under him, Pallas was blowing bubbles on the water surface. "Hurry."

Nox slid the hammer claw into the horizontal duct. He placed gloved hands on the cut edges, and poised to hoist himself up. Pallas got a palm under one of Nox's boots and gave him a push. Nox scrambled up through the jagged hole. He planted one boot on either side of the opening in the horizontal duct.

Down below, Pallas was up to his nose in churning water.

Nox set the small of his back against one wall of the vertical shaft and lifted one boot, sole out, to press hard against the opposite wall. When he was pressing hard enough to hold himself up between boot sole and back, he brought the other boot up. He planted his gauntleted palms on the wall behind him and started to chimney up the shaft. He moved his gloved palms up, then his back up. One foot. The other foot. Quickly. Hands. Back. Step. Step. Hands. Back. Step. Step. Hands—

—slipped. Nox's body folded up like a jackknife as he dropped into Pallas coming up beneath him. He met no resistance. He just swept Pallas along with his descent, and they both plunged into the rising water in a cloud of bubbles, down and down. Nox couldn't see. His leg brushed against the floor. The pounding inrush from the drain surrounded him with solid noise.

He dragged off his gauntlets and kicked up. He found the ceiling. The water was up to the top. There was no room to breathe.

Where was the vent? He'd lost it. He couldn't see. He had no sense of where he was. The mattress should've been under him and wasn't. Which way?

He needed to breathe *now*.

Felt a rough grip and a yank sideways. Then hands under his ass gave him a mighty shove. Pallas launched him up through the vent. Nox caught the sides of the opening and he gasped. Immediately he hauled himself up. He planted his back and feet against the walls of the shaft and chimneyed up again, fast, pressing *hard*.

The water had stopped rising. It stayed flush with the level of the ceiling. There had to be a flotation cutoff switch.

He heard a gasp directly below him. Pallas had found air. Nox heard him coming up beneath him.

Nox ascended as fast as he dared, pressing hard with the small of his back and his boot soles.

The voice of the Chessman: "Nemo. Stop. Paladin stop. Nemo. Open the hatch."

"Hatch?"

"Behind and above your head."

Maintaining pressure between his back and boots Nox craned his neck awkwardly to find the hatch. He lifted his arms to get at it. Fumbled to open it.

And lost purchase between his back and feet. Came down on Pallas. Hard.

A grunt underneath him.

Pallas had his head bowed, ready for it this time. Pallas was braced and holding fast.

Quickly Nox reached for the access hatchway. He grasped the frame and pulled himself up and off of Pallas. He slither-crawled head first through the opening and spilled out to a cloister-sized chamber.

It looked like the living quarters of a *medicus*, but empty. The inhabitant had packed up and gone. Not a panic flight either. The room was orderly. The *medicus* had performed his resurrection and left.

Chessman: "Nemo. Paladin. Move into the corridor and turn left. Quickly. Incoming hostiles."

Superfluous to identify the incoming plots as hostile. Everything in the known universe was hostile to them.

Nox didn't hear his other five brothers on the com anymore. They must've got back to the ship already. Nox hoped that was why he wasn't hearing them anymore.

Nox and Pallas climbed a ladder up a fire shaft to the asteroid surface. Pallas lifted the hatch.

He howled at the cutting cold. Nox and Pallas were wet. Bitter air sliced down the shaft as fire alarms shrieked. With the opening of the fire hatch, the defenders knew exactly where Nox and Pallas were.

Nox climbed to the surface.

Overhead was perfect black. Ice crystals blew across the frozen ground with scraping sounds. Red heat lamps gave off a lurid glow and not a hell of a lot of heat. It was a jagged landscape. The air was thin, held down to the asteroid by a low, energy barrier.

High above that, a physical umbrella dome stretched horizon to flat horizon.

No spacecraft was showing. The umbrella dome was still way up there, shimmering, intact.

Nox lifted his arms, useless. He roared at the blank, artificial sky. "They beached us!"

He hurled epithets.

The calm voice of the Chessman sounded: "Run."

Nox shut up and ran.

With a roar like a mountain crumbling, the ice pack up ahead divided before an invisible plow.

A slash of light appeared like a door into the black void. A ramp lowered from nothingness. Pallas raced up.

Buzzing flashes surrounded Nox, several paces behind. Defensive guns periscoped up from the ground. Their beams glanced off Nox's personal field.

The ramp to the ship was lifting away, the slash of light narrowing.

Nox dove into the light. The ramp rose up, just catching Nox and rolling him aboard. The hatch sealed shut.

Nox rolled to a stop.

The ship's energy gathered underneath him. He could feel it through the warm deck.

The pirate ship sprang, crashing straight up through the asteroid's dome, ripping open the sky.

Then all the stars shining in the viewports disappeared.

In an instant, the pirate ship *Bagheera* was traveling FTL.

Nox lay on his back on the deck, palms over his ears, which felt cold enough to fall off. *Made it!*

Faunus' laughter boomed. "Weren't sure you were going to join us, *frateri!*"

Pallas smiled, but Nox didn't see anything funny. His frozen clothing was thawing. He rasped, "Why did we go in at all! Why didn't we just blow the whole idiot maze up!"

Nicanor spoke crisply, "Because then we wouldn't know that we *completely missed the target!* Romulus got away."

Nox stayed on his back, catching his breath, unfreezing his lungs.

Cinna came down from the control room.

Cinna had been cultivated from the same genetic base as the rest of Nox's Roman-bred brothers, but Cinna was younger. He looked smoother. His irises were opaque black disks. The implanted cables of a patterner hung loose from the back of his neck and his forearms. He wasn't operating as a patterner at the moment. "Did anyone get hit?"

"No," said Pallas.

"No," Orissus growled.

"No," said Nox.

Cinna stalked across the deck, tearing off his com set. An angry young archangel. His finger pointed down at Nox on the deck. "What do you mean *no?* Nox, what is *that?*"

Nox stared back at Cinna, puzzled. He turned his head and followed Cinna's gaze backward, over his own shoulder. There was some blood on the deck. His. Nox's brow knotted. He frowned, confused. "Unclench, Little Brother." Nox pushed himself off the deck and stood up. "I got scratched." Probably from the metal edges of the vent he'd enlarged. He hadn't felt it. He kind of remembered the ripping at his haz suit as he'd fallen through.

"Oh—" Cinna softly swore up blue flames.

"What?" said Nox. "Am I dead?" Thought he was kidding.

Cinna spoke tightly, "Pretty much."

4

CINNA SEIZED NOX by the torn suit and hauled him into the ship's medical compartment.

Formerly an ambassadorial craft, the pirate ship *Bagheera* was a Xerxes type spacecraft. It carried excellent diagnostic equipment, but this was an exotic problem. Cinna needed to jury-rig the analyzers to look for microbombs.

The other six brothers crowded at the chamber hatch, waiting for the prognosis. They were keeping their distance, and they had their personal fields activated. Some microbombs were programmed to detonate under standard detection procedures.

Cinna pronounced, grim. "We didn't escape."

The brothers exchanged uncertain glances. Of course they'd escaped. All eight of them were here.

Galeo fidgeted with his neat red goatee. "What's the problem?"

"Nanites."

Leo drew back sharply. He backed into Orissus and Nicanor who shoved him forward again.

Leo had a positive horror of nanites. Leo saw nanites under the bed, in every drop of water. The others ragged him mercilessly about it. Leo recovered in a moment and gave an annoyed laugh. "No, really, Cinna. What is it?"

"Nanites," said Cinna.

"Verily?" Galeo tried to scoff.

Cinna glared at him. Cinna was always serious.

Nox, from the exam table, said, "I'm fine. See? No raving. No visions."

Romulus' nanites only affected Romulus. And his sister Claudia. The nanites had really slammed Claudia.

These nanites weren't doing anything. "They screwed up," Nox said.

"Do not underestimate the Romulii," Cinna said. "Just because they are a bit insane, doesn't mean they aren't very, very clever."

"So are we," said Nox. *A bit insane and very, very clever.* "We'll get through this."

"I don't think we will."

Coming from Cinna, that was a death sentence.

"Why did the nanites target me?" Nox asked. "Is it because I wasn't born Roman?"

"No. Because you're the one who got who got himself scratched in the dungeon," Cinna said.

Nox craned to look over his shoulder at the scratches on his back. Hell, they didn't even feel infected. "Why didn't these things just kill me immediately and be done with it?"

"That's an interesting question," Cinna said. "It needs answering."

"He's a Trojan Horse," Leo said.

"Yes," Cinna said. "I believe he is."

A graveled voice sounded from the back of the group. Orissus: "Get him out of here."

Nox said, "Maybe I'm not the right carrier. That's why the nanites aren't doing anything."

"They're doing something," Cinna said.

"What can we do for Nox?" That was Nicanor. Stuffy martinet Nicanor. Nox suddenly loved the hell out of him.

Pallas suggested, "Numa has the resources to help Nox if he wants to."

Graveyard snorts all around. Even Nox snorted.

"We can't go to Caesar," Faunus said. "We failed our mission. We didn't kill Romulus. *Merda*, we didn't even *find* Romulus."

"Numa Pompeii won't let anything with nanites near him. He'd kill all of us first," Nicanor said. "Or, more simple, just order us to die."

"Am I contagious?" Nox asked.

The brothers were keeping their distance. Leo was standing just about in the next solar system.

"Somewhat," Cinna said.

"How what?" Nox yelped. "Which what!"

"I'm not sure," Cinna said. "Those scratches are how the nanites got inside you. What they're doing now, I don't know."

Cinna reached behind his back for the cables implanted in his spine. He plugged them into the base of his skull. His face relaxed. His irises, already black, looked like hollow pits. He connected the cables in his forearms, then made a last connection with a port to *Bagheera*'s data array.

He was only in for a moment. Then he pulled all the connections apart. He announced, "Do not kiss Nox good-bye."

Nox took a breath of relief. "You mean I'm going to live?"

Cinna reworded for his brothers, "I mean don't anyone kiss Nox when you say good-bye to him."

"Oh, *merda*."

They would be saying good-bye. From a distance.

Leo asked, from out in the corridor, "What are you going to do, Nox?"

Words stuck in Nox's throat. How was he to know the answer to that? "You mean besides crying like a little girl? I HAVE NO IDEA!"

Cinna was watching the instrument readouts. He made an ominous little sound in his throat.

"What?" Nox snapped.

"Give Nox a strong sedative," Cinna ordered Pallas.

"Tequila," Nox requested.

"Something faster acting than that. Pallas, haste. We need to slow Nox's pulse—fast. The nanites are circulating. And they're oscillating."

"I'm guessing that's bad," Nox said.

Cinna waited until after Pallas administered an intradermal sedative to respond. "It's . . . ominous. Something will happen when all the oscillators sync-up."

The sedative was already slowing Nox's blood circulation. Nox asked fuzzily, "What happens if they sync?"

"There's no *if*. Synchronization is a mathematical certainty. Each oscillator affects all the others. When two oscillators with different periods pulse at the same time, they lock together in the same rhythm and they do *not* fall out of step with each other. Eventually, all the oscillators *will* sync-up with one another. Then it's not good. We could be in danger."

"What about *me*?" said Nox.

"You?" said Cinna. "No question. You're done."

"Keep them from syncing!" Pallas cried. Those were words Nox tried to say, but he was too slow to form them.

"I can't," Cinna said. "They're mingling in Nox's bloodstream. They're in different phases now, but every time one pulses in the vicinity of another, they lock step. It's a symmetrical bond. Sooner or later all the oscillators will pulse together."

"So what happens when they are all synced?"

"I'm pretty sure they blow up."

"Get them out!" Nox cried.

Cinna's hesitation was disturbing. When he spoke, it was worse. "We don't have the equipment to extract nanites."

Nanite extractors were exotic specialized equipment. *Bagheera* was created to be an ambassadorial ship and, though it was exceptionally well supplied, it didn't carry anything like nano-synthesis equipment.

"And we have damn little time. While Nox stays on board, we are all in danger."

Nox asked in a drugged calm, eyes swimming up to Cinna's beautiful face, "Are we pitching Nox out the air lock, Little Brother?"

Cinna turned his opaque gaze down to Nox. "That *is* the plan. Yes."

Orissus brought a life pod to the medical compartment. Nox obediently rolled into the thin-membraned sac. He thought to ask, "Why am I doing this?"

Cinna closed the sac three quarters of the way around him. He left it open over Nox's face.

Nox's brothers, in full containment suits with personal fields activated, carried the life pod to the air lock. Leo wasn't one of the pallbearers. Leo opened the air lock and stepped way aside to let the bearers step through.

The brothers placed Nox in the air lock. The last person Nox saw was Pallas, who nodded encouragingly, stupidly clinging to hope. "It'll be okay."

The life sac closed over Nox's face. It was dark in here. One of his brothers had given him a bottle of tequila. Nox hugged it like a teddy bear.

He felt a pressure change with the air lock shutting, sealing him off.

He knew when the air lock opened. His life pod lost contact with the deck. He heard the swish of expelled air. And that was the end of external sound. His life pod ballooned out, stretched taut.

He floated, weightless, alone with his own breathing, his own pulse, and the soft whisper of the air circulator.

There was no light. Dammit, they hadn't given him a light. Nox floated against the smooth confines of the life pod. He touched against one side, and slowly bounced to the other side.

This isn't a life pod. It's a body bag.

He'd been tossed into the vastest of all oceans. The pressure was minimal. He felt puffy. Heat distributed unevenly, forming uncomfortable cooling eddies around him.

The membrane that separated him from eternity seemed so fragile. It felt as if it might tear at a thought.

How long do I have? He'd asked that before being cast outboard.

Cinna had answered. *Best you not know.*

His heart beat slowly. That was the drugs. It was hard to panic with a heartbeat this slow. All his little oscillators were joining up and flashing together in greater numbers. He felt his own exhalation through his nostrils against his upper lip.

He would have liked some sound. Music. A voice link. Someone to talk to. They'd sent him out with a com tuned to the international emergency channel, but no one was talking to him.

He heard his sluggish pulse brush at his eardrum. Sounded like little pairs of breaths.

He smelled his own fear. Claustrophobia crept through him in the black heart of infinity.

He gave a slow-motion kick in protest.

A noise formed in his throat. It would have been a scream if he had the energy.

Bagheera lurked, dark, cloaked in perfect stealth, monitoring the tiny life pod from a distance.

Bagheera didn't carry the facilities to clean the nanites out of Nox, but as Cinna told his brothers, "Someone out here *does*."

The U.S. Space Battleship *Merrimack* carried a hospital bigger than that of most terrestrial cities. *Merrimack* had nanite scrubbers.

Normally hunting anything in space was like trying to find a needle in a pine forest. But Cinna knew where *Merrimack* had been a few terrestrial days ago. *Merrimack* gave away her position when she sent Caesar a resonant hail.

Merrimack was nearby, astronomically speaking. Not a coincidence. The Americans were hunting the same installation the brothers had just found.

With the lifepod in tow, *Bagheera* raced at threshold velocity to *Merrimack*'s last known position. Cinna gambled that he would find *Merrimack* still in the Indra Aleph star system, wandering in the wrong pine forest.

And here she was, cruising at sublight velocity. But even now, the space battleship was gathering in her drone scouts, perhaps making ready to leave.

Merrimack was a big plot with a distinctive shape. There was only one other spacecraft like her. Her upper and lower sails were swept back like fletching on an arrow. *Merrimack*'s wings were not wings for flying, though they gave an impression of flight. *Merrimack* had wings like a building had wings. *Merrimack* was as aerodynamic as a skyscraper.

The pirate ship set Nox's life pod adrift across the *Merrimack*'s path with a white flag and an SOS beacon.

Cinna murmured a benediction into the void. "Good hunting."

✳ ✳ ✳ ✳ ✳

12 January 2448
U.S. Space Battleship *Merrimack*
Indra Aleph Star System
Perseid Space

Merrimack moved at sublight speed through the Indra Aleph system. Her drones had turned over a lot of rocks, searching for the one Romulus was hiding under. There was still more space to cover, but Captain Carmel was starting to think the Roman had thrown her a bone.

"I've been played. Dingo. Bring in the drones and get us back on our previous course."

"Aye, aye, Captain."

The drones were coming in when Tactical sang out, "Bogey! Directly in our path."

"Evade."

The pilot threw the space battleship into an immediate reverse. *Merrimack*'s inertial shell kept everything that was inside her from flying out through her nose. Even so, you felt the heave.

Calli absorbed the import of the word *directly*.

Directly in a battleship's path signaled intent.

Calli announced over the loud com: "Battle stations." Then to her command crew, "Tactical. Identify the object."

"Shit!" Tactical cried.

Doubting that the object was literally excrement, Captain Carmel said with restrained irritation, "A statement with more content, if you please, Mister Vincent."

"Object is a life pod. With a life in it."

The com tech reported: "I have an SOS on the common band. Interstellar standard."

The sensor tech reported: "The SOS is transmitting from the life pod, sir. The pod is showing a white flag."

Calli felt her face go slack for an instant, astonished.

Someone had tossed a life pod in her path, like a baby in a basket.

"Who else is out here? Where is the Accipiter?"

Tactical reported, "Negative sightings."

The sensor tech added, "No readings of spacecraft other than our drones. No sign of a shipwreck that ought to go with that life pod."

"It must be from the Accipiter," Dingo said.

Calli frowned. She had her arms crossed, her eyes narrowed. "The life pod is sending an SOS. We can't ignore it."

"It's a trap, sir," Dingo said.

"*That* is clear. What's unclear is what to do with it. It's a trap into which we must step. We cannot act like—" She hesitated to speak it. "—pirates."

Dingo Ryan: "Signals!"

"Signals, aye."

"What ship is the life pod registered to?"

Embedded in any life craft's SOS sounder was a code that identified the life craft's mothership.

The signals specialist ran down the code. "Life pod's signal traces back to *Bernini*. That ship is no longer extant."

"Then tell me what kind of ship *Bernini* was when it existed," Calli said.

There was a pause and a hitch while the specialist ran the query twice. "Pacific Consortium make, Xerxes model. Italian-flagged ambassadorial craft. Reported stolen."

The words hit the command deck like a grenade.

The signals specialist kept reading, "Destroyed in 'forty-seven. That was last year."

Yes. Most of us saw that happy event.

The Xerxes class ship hadn't been called *Bernini* then. The pirates who hijacked the Italian ambassadorial craft *Bernini* rechristened it *Bagheera*.

"Can't be," Dingo said. "We saw that ship die."

"We did," Calli said. As much as anyone could really see anything out here. You were dependent on sensors to tell you what you saw.

Bernini/Bagheera died a very showy death with a lot of credible witnesses to verify it, including Caesar Numa's own patterner.

Dingo Ryan suggested, "The pirates must have ballasted their life pods sometime earlier."

Calli shook her head. "You actually think this is a life pod that someone picked up at a surplus outlet?"

"You're right," Dingo backed away from his suggestion. "That doesn't explain what this life pod is doing appearing suddenly in the middle of nowhere with a live person inside."

"This is not the middle of nowhere," Calli told Dingo. "It's *right in front of us.*"

Dingo said, "Trap."

Calli nodded. No question. "Trap."

Someone behind her—had to be one of the Marine guards flanking the hatch—blurted, "Sir! What if it's Colonel Steele?"

All personnel on deck stirred. Colonel TR Steele had been the commander of *Merrimack's* half battalion of Fleet Marines. He'd vanished months ago. In fact he vanished the same day the pirate ship *Bagheera* died.

Calli had never realized just how vital that man was to this ship until she didn't have him. She felt a massive amount of surprised hope rise suddenly on her command deck. Everyone wanted to believe it was Colonel Steele.

Calli felt a chill. "It's not," she said, dead firm.

I should shoot it. White flag be damned. That pod was registered to a pirate ship.

She could make a bomb-proof case in front of a board of inquiry as to why she blew away a lifeboat signaling an SOS and showing a white flag.

"Targeting!"

"Targeting, aye." Targeting sounded nervous.

"Get me a lock on the life pod."

"Lock, aye."

"Fire Control."

"Fire Control, aye." Fire control sounded frightened.

"Send the trigger up here."

"Aye, sir." Fire control sounded relieved. "You have the trigger, sir."

Calli regarded the light on her console, indicating the armed trigger. The safety was on. For now. "Com."

"Com, aye."

"Get me on the universal human distress channel."

"Channel open, aye. On your console, Captain."

Captain Carmel spoke, "Inhabitant of the life pod, identify yourself."

She listened to a long stretch of dead silence. Then a sluggish voice came back in Americanese, "Pirate, ma'am."

A few sharp intakes of breath sounded around the close-packed stations on deck.

Calli returned, "Don't ma'am me, I'm not your mama."

Not too articulate, the voice went on, "I know who you are, Empress Calli."

"Then you know I don't need to honor a white flag for a pirate. How stoned are you to identify yourself as a pirate?"

"I'm already dead, ma'am."

Calli looked to the sensor specialist to confirm the dead status. The young man tilted his hand one way then the other to say *really close.*

"Your pod is failing," Calli said into the com.

"I noticed that," the voice returned, sluggishly dry. "I am also riddled with nanites. My exploding nanites are programmed to go off when my oscillating nanites synchronize. Something like that."

Calli and Dingo exchanged silent stares.

Dingo spoke into the com, "Have your own lot get you out of your fix, pirate."

The pirate's diction was getting sloppier, "Don' have the right equipment. Can spot 'em. Can't get 'em out. You're the only ship might could maybe help me. My name used to be John Farragut."

Calli reeled away from the com as if she'd been spat in the face.

The voice from the com slurred onward, "An' I've seen Adamas."

Calli motioned toward the com tech, her finger slicing across her throat.

"We're mute, sir," said the com tech.

"Scan! Scan everything!" Calli ordered aloud. "Tactical! *Is there anything else out there?*"

"Negative spacecraft," Tactical came back. "Unless it's a Xerxes. And I will bet all our lives there is a Xerxes very close to us right now."

A Xerxes type ship could make itself register as part of the vacuum. The pirate ship *Bagheera* was a Xerxes type ship.

"Gunners. Fire Control. You are clear to fire if you *think* you have a target other than the life pod."

Her hand formed itself into a fist. *This is a huge hoax. But I'm hooked. The pirate knows it.*

If the Farragut didn't do it, the Adamas part did.

Adamas was the Latin word for steel.

The pirate had seen TR Steele.

Do I believe him?

I see the bait. I see the hook. Can I afford not to bite?

There had been unsubstantiated reports of attacks by the pirate band known as the Ninth Circle since their spectacular deaths last year.

This man was claiming to be one of the Ninth Circle. He was claiming to be John Knox Farragut Junior—the younger brother of the famous Admiral John Alexander Farragut, former captain of the *Merrimack*.

But how to know for sure? Who was she really talking to? It was someone playing to her hopes that TR Steele, the commander of her Fleet Marines, was still alive.

"Com!"

The com tech nodded when the mute was off again.

Calli said experimentally into the com, "I have you in my sights and the trigger in my hand, John John."

The weak voice groaned. "Oh, just shoot me. I'm cold."

Startled, Captain Carmel snapped to the com tech. "Cut com."

"Aye, aye, sir. We are silent."

Calli crossed the deck with sharp, agitated strides. "He's for real." The pirate's reaction to the name John John sealed it beyond any doubt.

Calli announced to all hands on the command platform, "Nothing the pirate said is to leave this deck!"

There was a chorus of aye, aye, sirs.

Dingo warned, "He's still a Trojan horse, Captain."

"Of course he's a Trojan horse!" Captain Carmel said. "And I am not bringing him aboard."

✳ ✳ ✳ ✳ ✳

Nox waited in the cold darkness for the return voice. Or the kill shot. One or the other. Just get on with it.

He couldn't stay awake. He couldn't seem to breathe. He was dreaming with his eyes open—ugly black gray clouds swirled in the perfect black, punctuated by sparking flashes. Where were those coming from? He wondered if those were his oscillating nanites. Flashing.

He floated up against one side of the life pod and stayed pressed there. There was the aneurysm in the membrane. He was using up his oxygen in here. The life pod's rebreathers were overwhelmed and the carbon dioxide was building up. And Empress Calli had gone silent.

Nox shut his eyes.

It was a good try, O my brothers.

5

12 Ianuarius 2448
Bagheera
Indra Aleph Star System
Perseid Space

CINNA WATCHED THE MONITORS. Pallas and Faunus crowded him, earnestly helping him watch. Faunus said, "They're not picking him up. Why aren't they picking him up?"

Cinna had told his brothers that *Merrimack* would pick Nox up. It was frightening to see a patterner make a mistake.

"Go get him!" Pallas cried.

"No," Cinna said softly. "We can't."

The patterner was rattled.

I really thought they would pick him up.

He blinked.

Nox was still cold, but he was breathing pure oxygen. And he wasn't in the life pod. A light was on. He was in a metal compartment.

He tried to rise, but that didn't happen. He was strapped down. There was a drone medic inside this compartment. Through a porthole he saw the American space battleship. Her running lights defined her majestic shape. *Merrimack*. The Americans hadn't brought Nox on board. They'd taken him into some much smaller, more expendable craft. He didn't hear any other people on board. He guessed the Yanks weren't going to risk him blowing up inside their battleship. But the drone medic hovering over him wore the Red Cross. *Merrimack* was trying to save him.

How 'bout that?

Nox lost consciousness.

Woke again. He was in a different chamber now, comfortably warm. The biggest difference was the ambient sounds. It was noisy here. Lots of clanging, hissing, voices, banging footsteps, engines. All those sounds, some close by, some a lot farther off. He wasn't in the small craft anymore.

He was on the *Merrimack*.

That could only mean *it worked*! The Americans wouldn't have brought him aboard if he weren't free of nanites.

I'm alive. He laughed out loud. He was going to live.

He tried to crank his head around. Couldn't. He couldn't really lift it either. He was mostly immobilized.

He was tied down. They also had a partial nerve lock on him. That was redundant. So were the shackles. Physical shackles. That was primitive. But then this boat had been known to carry swords.

He was going to live—until the Yanks sucked the intel out of him. Then they would execute him for so many murders.

He strained to look to his left. He could just see the Marine guards posted at the hatch. They were big men, dripping two-hundred-proof hatred. Only thanks to their training they weren't mauling Nox into little strands of shredded pirate. One was a square-built, mean-faced brown guy, the other a fleshy boulder of a black guy. They called each other Twitch and Dak.

The compartment hatch opened. The Marine guards snapped to rigid attention.

A long tall white swan in Navy blue undress uniform swept in. Four bars and a star on her cuff. That was a captain.

She sent the Marine guards out. She kept herself three meters away from Nox.

This had to be Captain Callista Carmel. Nox had heard of her. Who hadn't?

"Empress Calli," Nox said. His voice came out scratchy.

"That is not my title."

It was what they called her in Rome. It was kind of a joke.

Nox had seen pictures. In person she was a you-can't-be-serious, swallow-your-tongue kind of stunning. She could be a stunt double for Helen of Troy. But Calli Carmel only launched one ship. She could flatten Troy for herself without backup.

Nox cleared his throat. "What'd you do to me?"

"Besides save your life?"

"You took my badges." His scars and braids he meant.

"I will not have your mother see you like that when she visits you on death row. Tell me about Adamas. Or was that just a line you threw out there to make us pick you up?"

"I couldn't make that up," Nox said. "It was great bait, so I used it. I really did see Adamas. Last I heard he was a Colonel on *Merrimack*. I couldn't believe it when I saw him . . . where I saw him."

"And where exactly is that?"

"In the place you're looking for."

"What am I looking for?" Calli asked.

"It's a Romulid medical facility embedded in an asteroid in a high tilt orbit around Indra Shwa Zed. The rock is coated in ice, so it looks like a comet. The shield dome is shattered. The facility is underground. It's a rat maze and it has a really stupid game program guarding it."

"Where did you get the nanites?"

"Got scratched."

"Where?"

"On my back."

"Where did you get the scratch on your back?"

"In the facility."

"Where in the facility?"

"I honestly don't know. Did I mention it was a maze? The Romulii have your Colonel Steele in there. Or a dead ringer of him."

"How dead was the ringer?"

"I think he was alive. I didn't look close. He was in a pink tank. You know that medical gel?"

Calli Carmel gave an annoyed-looking nod. She would know exactly what a pink tank was—from the inside out.

Nox said, "Adamas wasn't why I was there."

"What were you doing in this installation?"

"Trying to kill Romulus."

"Why?"

Oh, merda, *that's a good question since I'm supposedly not working for* Caesar Numa. "I'm a psychotic terrorist. Don't you pick up the news broadcasts?"

"Did you kill him?"

"Kill who? Romulus? No. He got away."

"He got away how?"

"No idea."

"Under his own power?"

"Ma'am, here's what I saw." Nox described the chamber precisely for her—the Julian colors, the royal tapestries, the empty pallet, the life-support equipment, and the sheet.

"It looked like Romulus walked out of there. Or the scene was staged to look like he walked. Ma'am, by the time I got there, he was just gone."

"Do not ma'am me. Why did you attack my ship?"

An astonished noise sounded in Nox's throat. Finally he choked out, "We didn't. Wouldn't. Not ever."

"Your Accipiter did."

"I don't have an Accipiter."

"Who attacked me?" Calli demanded.

"Someone stupid with an Accipiter," Nox said, and he was done answering questions. "Is Lieutenant Hamilton on board?"

Captain Carmel walked out.

Merrimack's Intelligence Officer was a lean ferret of a man named Bradley Zolman. He was called just Z.

Z met the captain outside the hatch, frowning. Z had been monitoring the interrogation. He said, "The prisoner dodged your question of why he tried to kill Romulus."

She nodded. "I worded it poorly. Was anything he said true?"

"You need to realize that a brain scan isn't a fact checker," Z explained. "It just tells if the subject is telling the truth as he knows it."

"And?"

"And the prisoner believed everything he said. It's possible your pirate is working for someone who wants you to have all the information on Romulus."

"I know," Calli said, bitter. She knew, but she couldn't quite believe it.

She ordered the ship's Medical Officer to put the prisoner under complete sedation; then she summoned the acting commander of her Marine Wing. "Lieutenant Salvador!"

Cain Salvador reported and snapped to stiff attention. "Aye, sir!"

"Full restraints on the prisoner. Quarantine him in a Space Patrol Torpedo boat hard-docked to the ship. Three Marine guards outside the air lock at all times, a drone guard and a drone monitor on the inside of the Spit boat."

"Aye, aye, sir," Cain said. "Sir?"

"What is it, Lieutenant?"

Cain asked, "Since the pirate is officially dead, can we . . . hurt him a little?"

"I cannot allow torture," Captain Carmel told Cain. "But neither do you need to carry him like a box of apples."

"Potatoes?"

Calli hesitated. "No mashing, boiling, peeling, or planting."

Cain Salvador brightened. "Aye, sir. Sir? Do you know who that pirate looks like?"

"No," the captain said—hard—like Cain Salvador better just forget he ever thought that thought. "He does not."

Flight Sergeant Geneva Rhine took her watch with Dak Shepard and Twitch Fuentes standing guard outside the hatch of the Spit boat, SPT 1, in which the unconscious prisoner had been isolated. Rhino suggested to Lieutenant Cain Salvador something accidental involving the prisoner and the Spit boat's life-support system.

"Don't go there, Rhino," Cain said. "You're a soldier, not a sniveling Roman assassin."

To an all-American mutt like Cain Salvador all Romans sniveled. All Romans were assassins.

Cain added, "Soldiers kill. They don't murder."

"It's not murder if you're doing it for your country," Rhino said. "The guy's a traitor to the United States."

"That's a fuzzy line. Don't go near it," Cain said. Rhino was tenacious, even for a bulldog. So to be perfectly explicit, Cain told her, "Do not kill without orders."

Rhino whispered between clenched teeth, *"So order me."*

"Flight Sergeant."

When Cain called you by your rank, he was done foxtrotting. Rhino backed down. "Sorry, Cain. You know I hate Romans."

"We all hate Romans," Cain said.

The Roman Empire and the United States of America were close kin. One nation had founded the other, though neither nation could agree which one was the mother country and which the ungrateful traitorous breakaway colony. On board the U.S. space battleship *Merrimack* there was no question.

The prox alarm shrieked. Something was way too close to the *Merrimack*.

The deep thrum of beam generators wound up with the hiss of outgoing fire. The Navy gunners were shooting—all banks from the sound of it. Sounded like a star spray of shots, like you do when you can't see your target.

The Exec's voice on the loud com was calling for siege stations again.

＊ ＊ ＊ ＊ ＊

Part of Calli's mind leaped into clarity, and she was barking. "Shut down! *Reel in the guns!* Lockdown! Execute! Yesterday!"

Her order closed *Merrimack*'s force field to near impenetrable. The order for "yesterday" meant do it faster than you think is possible.

The space battleship's prox alarm kept blaring. A deep buzz sounded from all around.

"Tactical! What is setting off the prox alarm?"

"I don't have a plot," Tactical said.

Dingo pointed up. "I know this sound." The buzzing was all around them.

Calli recognized it too. It was an outside inertial field coming in direct contact with *Merrimack*'s inertial field. "He's not registering on the sensors and he's *on* us," Calli said. "That's a Xerxes."

Dingo called for running lights.

"Lights, aye."

The running lights were used on parade or when coming into a space station.

The external lights shone, visible through the ship's portholes. Calli couldn't see anything out there but the ship *Merrimack* herself and the stars flatly shining.

Tactical said, "I'm not detecting anything."

"Then what is the prox alarm picking up?"

Dingo answered, "It has to be the contact. Something is *on* us. It's touching our inertial field."

"Systems. Locate the contact point."

Systems shook his head. "Negative resolution."

Another alarm sounded. Engineering reported, "Field fault! Enemy is attempting starfish!"

In a starfish maneuver a hostile ship insinuated a thin tendril of energy through an enemy ship's solid force field. Once through the field, the energy tendril could be widened. The enemy could send anything in through the created breach.

Marcander Vincent spoke at the tactical station. "We have a dead pirate ship trying to open us up."

Calli snapped, "Say nothing that is not useful, Mister Vincent. Location of the starfish penetration."

Systems reported, "Field penetration sternside of the Spit boat SPT 1."

A loud bang jolted everyone on the command platform. It sounded as though it came from somewhere inside the ship.

Calli: "Identify that."

Systems: "Unknown event. Source was inside the Spit boat."

"Status of the Spit boat," Calli demanded.

Systems: "SPT 1 is hard docked inside *Merrimack*'s energy field."

"Engineering. Reinforce the field at point of starfish assault."

"Aye, aye, sir!"

Calli turned to her exec. "Commander Ryan. On one mark, this is to happen: Lock the Spit boat's air lock *open*—both hatches. Retract *Merrimack*'s force field from the Spit boat. Cast off the Spit boat. Seal our inertial field solid around *Merrimack*. Execute as soon as you have it coordinated. Don't wait for my go ahead."

Dingo gave a brisk nod and got to it.

Before he could execute, a double crack sounded, like the first sound but louder. Everyone ducked.

Calli: "Is that a hull breach?"

Systems: "Negative. Negative hull breach. But the starfish is progressing. Sixty percent through. I am adding layers at point of assault."

The energy tendril was insinuating through the ship's shifting energy layers, just as gorgons used to do.

Calli couldn't afford to let the pirates get so much as a hair's width through the ship's energy shell. Any opening could allow an antimatter insertion. She didn't know if the pirates carried antimatter, but she knew that the leopard *Bagheera* never left survivors on any vessel it attacked.

A third crack sounded. Loud.

The sound affected nothing but made the technicians flinch.

The bangs almost sounded like displacement—the sound of air closing into the void left by matter abruptly ceasing to occupy a space. It was a sound exactly like a thunderclap.

Systems reported, "Sir. If those are actual displacement claps, you know they're screwed. *Merrimack*'s displacement jammers are on full strength."

No. Calli wasn't sure she knew that. Something else was wrong here.

She heard the Dingo give the command, "Execute Severance."

"Severance, aye. We have separation from SPT 1. Inertial field is solid."

"Status of starfish!" Calli demanded.

He needed to breathe *now*.

"We shed the starfish with the Spit boat. We have negative starfish."

Someone cheered.

Not celebrating yet, Captain Carmel ordered, "Helm. FTL. Random vector. Execute."

"FTL, aye. Random vector."

The ship jumped to FTL space. Made two more random vector changes. Only then did Calli order a return to normal space and ask for the status of the cast-off Spit boat.

Systems reported happily: "SPT 1's air lock is open. Negative inertial field around SPT 1. Sir, we let the vacuum in."

Merrimack returned to the site on high alert, prepared to jump to FTL on an instant's notice.

Calli hailed her drone operator. "Mister Raytheon, confirm that the prisoner on board SPT 1 is dead."

"Negative confirmation," Wraith responded.

Calli felt a chill. It wasn't exactly shock. It was a dread come true. "Mister Raytheon, is that negative confirmation because of a detection failure, or are you telling me the prisoner is still alive?"

"Captain. The prisoner is not on board SPT 1."

"Mister Raytheon, check your detection equipment for malfunction. The prisoner was immobilized in restraints. His body has to be there."

Dingo suggested, "The pirates could have displaced him out of there. Those bangs had the sound of displacements."

"We have jammers on. If they tried to displace him out, then he's dead and really gone."

"They must have done," Dingo said.

Calli nodded. The pirates were ruthless. She hadn't realized it extended to their own brothers.

Still, she assumed nothing. "Mister Raytheon. Send the transmission from the drone monitor up to the tactical station. I want to see exactly what's inside SPT 1."

"Aye, aye, sir. Transmission now available."

Calli and Dingo looked over Marcander Vincent's shoulders at the current readout from inside the Spit boat.

Calli blinked. "Is this real time?"

"Yes, sir."

"They did it," Dingo said. "They killed him."

"There's a landing disk." Marcander Vincent pointed.

The flimsy metal disk the size of a dinner plate lay on the pallet where the prisoner had been strapped down. The straps were still buckled.

"Rzajhin manufacture," Marcander Vincent added.

Rzajhin landing disks were cheap, untraceable, and reliable despite the abuse heaped on them. They were the favorite equipment of smugglers.

"How did they get a landing disk through jammers?" Calli said.

"Two of them."

Dingo pointed. A second landing disk lay on the deck, right next to the pallet.

"They must've missed the first placement," Marcander Vincent said.

"No. They didn't miss." Calli tapped her finger on the image.

Dingo saw what troubled her. The landing disks appeared altogether intact, normal. Their lights were on.

"They're *intact*. Those disks got through our jammers *intact*."

It was tricky enough to get an initial landing disk to a destination without a corresponding disk already in place. Sometimes it took several attempts. The pirates got this one on the first try. Through jammers.

"Mister Vincent, back up this record to the time mark of the first crack we heard. I want to see what happened in there."

The playback from the drone monitor showed first a landing disk appearing inside the Spit boat with the sound of a thunderclap. The disk dropped from the air and came to rest on the deck next to the restrained prisoner, Nox.

At the second thunderclap a tall man with a red goatee and the number 666 tattooed on his brow appeared—alive and well—atop the landing disk. He carried another landing disk and another displacement collar with him. He snapped the extra collar around Nox's neck and slid the extra landing disk underneath him. Then the pirate stepped back onto the landing disk that brought him. The two of them—Nox and the red-bearded pirate— vanished with a bang, leaving only their two landing disks behind them.

"They did it." Dingo sounded unhappily astounded. "They displaced through our inertial screen. *With jammers on.* Alive. How in the hell?"

"Patterner," Calli said.

Cold shock gripped the command platform at the word.

The machine-augmented mind of a patterner could synthesize information to solve complex problems with machine speed and human reason.

Calli felt as if she were exhaling poison. "The pirates of the Ninth Circle are not just alive. *They have a patterner embedded with them.*"

Jaunty Dingo Ryan looked as grim as Calli had ever seen him. "That would mean the pirates are working for Caesar Numa Pompeii."

Calli nodded. "That is what it means."

Inwardly she was reeling. She hadn't wanted to believe it.

This patterner had joined in the same charade that made the U.S. and the rest of civilization think that the Ninth Circle were all dead.

The Ninth Circle were known for leaving no witnesses alive behind them. There was a moment back there when *Merrimack* should have died.

The pirates could have killed everyone on board. They hadn't done so. Because someone was holding their leash.

There was only one power with that kind of reach.

Calli had often hated Numa Pompeii, but this was different. Now she hated Numa for not being the man she thought he was. Numa used to mock her, discount her, scorn her. She had weathered his contempt. She'd proved herself a worthy adversary. *Worthy.* As if Numa were someone whose regard mattered.

It *had* mattered. Numa Pompeii had been formidable. As infuriating as the man was, Calli counted on Numa Pompeii to be *Rome*—to embody all its grandeur, strength, honor, intellect, invention, resourcefulness, its limitless ability to conceive and to do, its civilization, daring and cunning, its overweening pride and arrogance. What had happened to the honor?

Here Numa was using that most squalid of space vermin—pirates. It hurt to find the grand, indomitable *triumphalis*, whom Calli thought she knew, here so desperate that he was rooting in the muck with pirates. Numa Pompeii had been something she wanted to believe in. Disappointment came bitter.

Numa was going to be sorry.

Calli turned her head to the Dingo. "Want to compose my report to the admiralty, Stuart?"

"Not on your life, sir," said the Dingo.

A bright flash from the portholes lit the left side of all the faces on the command platform. Specialists hunched over their stations in a useless reflexive cringe.

"Identify that!" Calli demanded as a clattering noise like thrown pebbles buzzed against the ship's inertial shell.

"Explosion," Marcander Vincent reported from the tactical station. "Our own isolation capsule."

The isolation capsule was the small craft that had first picked up Nox's life pod. The isolation capsule had contained the prisoner Nox while the drone medic extricated the nanites from him. *Merrimack* had left the isolation capsule out in space, with the life pod and the infestation of nanites inside it.

It seemed Nox's oscillating nanites had just achieved synchronicity.

"What took them so long to sync?" Dingo wondered out loud.

"I imagine they've been synced for a while," Calli said. "They've been constructing an explosive."

"Constructing an explosive out of what?"

"Out of the isolation capsule, apparently."

"Captain, what do you want done with the Spit boat?"

SPT 1 had been boarded by a pirate—a pirate with imperial resources. It could not be trusted. The Spit boat needed a nanoscopic scan and flush before it could be allowed back inside *Merrimack*'s inertial shell.

"Take it in tow—half hook only. Initiate a full nano scan on it. Take us at best speed to Indra Shwa Zed."

Dingo Ryan gave the orders to make it all happen, then spoke low, not to question his captain's orders out loud on her own command deck, "The pirate said Romulus was already gone from the facility at Indra Shwa Zed."

"No," Calli said. "What the pirate *said* is he didn't *see* Romulus in the facility."

Not seeing didn't need to mean that Romulus wasn't there.

And Indra Shwa Zed was where the pirate had seen TR Steele.

6

16 January 2448
U.S. Space Battleship *Merrimack*
Asteroid 543
Indra Shwa Zed Star System
Perseid Space

THE ASTEROID LOOKED DEAD. Like any of the
millions of other asteroids in the triple star Indra Shwa system.
The rock was larger than some planets, irregular, pocked with
craters, crusted with ice, and unremarkable until *Merrimack*'s active scanners touched it. Then it erupted.

Beam fire lanced up toward the U.S. space battleship.

Impacts against *Merrimack*'s inertial field shimmered and splintered
into jagged fissures. The sharp cracks faded right back to black except for
those red and green blotches left swimming on your retinas.

Flight Sergeant Kerry Blue sat in her cockpit. Her Swift was locked
down in its launch slot on the starboard flight deck under the force field.
She bayed with the rest of her squadron to be set free.

The Swift pilots were ordered to hold.

Then they were ordered to shut up.

Kerry Blue shut up and watched the flashing lights.

A red serpentine fissure sizzled and healed right above her. A blue-
violet one snaked crosswise. Kerry had been through a few dust ups in her

tours of duty. Never seen anything quite like this. Kinda pretty. Now let us the flock out of here to show the lupes something unpretty.

Kerry opened her com. "What's hitting us?"

"Crab crackers," someone answered. Sounded like the Yurg. "Didn't you read the last bulletin?"

"Yeah," said Kerry—reading.

The boffins could've just given her a data module to plug in behind her ear—like an extra bit of brain. Then she would know right *now* what a crab cracker was. But no, the boffins didn't like unnecessary add-ons in your head when you were piloting.

Kerry read the briefing.

Okay, crab crackers were new Roman weaponry, designed to assault hard targets.

Targets didn't come any harder than the *Mack*.

Another blaze of red and indigo splintered above Kerry's canopy. Made her glance up.

Great big white flash.

She didn't flinch from those anymore.

She returned to reading the briefing.

The crab cracker was intended to disrupt a ship's energy shell. *Merrimack*'s shell was constantly reforming in staggered layers, so the crackers never achieved an actual gap in this crab's shell.

But the one-man fighter Swifts weren't so thickly layered. In the grip of one of these crab crackers, a Swift would be broken to pieces, and Kerry Blue would be breathing vacuum.

And that was why Kerry Blue and Alpha Flight were sitting like a clutch of chicks on mama's wing, waiting for the navvies to take out the crab crackers at the source.

Kerry's monitor showed her the asteroid down there. It was completely black. The Romulid station was underneath that frozen blackness.

The enhanced image on Kerry's tactical display showed her waves of escape craft launching from underground chutes. "They're bugging out!" she yelled to no one.

Couldn't stand it anymore. She turned on her com. "Hey! Somebody with a beam gun! *Shoot the rock!* They're getting away! What are you doing!" She kicked her floor plate, trying to wake someone up down there in the battleship.

As near as Kerry could make out *Merrimack* wasn't picking off the runners. *Mack* wasn't even *trying* to shoot at the escaping spaceships.

Someone else, sounded like Rhino, Alpha Seven, clicked on her com too. "Hey! Navvies! What you doin' with your trigger fingers? Shoot something!"

As if the Navy beam gunners on board *Merrimack* would take orders from a couple of Fleet Marine flight sergeants.

Cain Acting-WinCo-No-Fun-Anymore Salvador called for com silence again.

Kerry Blue sat, staring up from her launch slot on the space battleship's wing. She made real sure her com was off and said lots of things.

And watched the enemy getting away.

The weapon on the asteroid surface belched out energy balls—the crab crackers. Their strikes sizzled against *Merrimack*'s force field in a constant barrage.

Captain Carmel pointed at the source of the barrage on one of *Merrimack*'s tactical displays and ordered, "Take that out."

She meant take it *out*.

Dingo gave the orders. "Engineering."

"Engineering, aye."

"Ready half hook. Target the weapon emplacement."

"Half hook ready, aye. Ground weapon emplacement targeted."

"Deploy half hook."

"Half hook, aye."

A tendril of energy deployed like a lariat down to the asteroid surface. It stabbed into the rock and under the gun emplacement and burrowed beneath it.

"Target acquired."

"Helm. Put us somewhere else."

The space battleship's six engines roared with an abrupt acceleration, sudden enough to physically yank the weapon emplacement out of the rock. The half hook immediately released. The uprooted emplacement flew away in the direction of one of Indra Shwa's suns.

"Status of target," Captain Carmel demanded. She didn't want to see that coming back.

"Hostile weapon is not functioning," Tactical advised.

"Does it have any propulsion system to get itself back?" Calli asked.

"Negative," Tactical reported.

Dingo Ryan added, "That weapon emplacement was never meant to fly. The only way that's ever coming back is if some other spacecraft hooks it and hauls it back."

"Tactical. Monitor that. Helm, take us back to the asteroid."

A thumping in the deck had started low. Got louder. Pushed into Calli's awareness.

The fighter pilots, obeying the order for com silence, had taken to stomping their war dance in their cockpits. Sounded like all of them. *BOOM pom pom pom BOOM pom pom pom.* The Swifts were still in physical contact with the ship, so Calli could actually feel the thumps from here on the command platform.

Calli gave the order. "Mister Ryan. Let my dogs out."

Kerry Blue woulda sang hallelujah except that Kerry Blue couldn't sing. *Merrimack* retracted her energy canopy, and the Swifts were off in four, three, two, YeeeeeeeeeeeeeeeeeeeHA!

The fighter craft screamed off the battleship's wings, coms on. Most all of them yelled, slung out at 53 percent of the speed of light. The inertial field only let you feel a fraction of the g's you were actually pulling, but it was still a rush. The inertial field kept the launch from shooting you out your own aft hole.

Kerry Blue yipped and yelled with the rest of them. Remembering that Reg Monroe used to have a screech that only bats could hear, she gave a couple of yips for Reg.

The voice of Cain Salvador sounded in Kerry Blue's helmet. "Deploy lampreys only. Do not damage the targets. Assume the presence of hostages on board all enemy craft."

Problem with being an instant officer is that your mates forget you aren't one of them anymore, and Kerry Blue sent back, "Been told five times, Cain."

So the Fleet Marine pilots got told for a sixth time: "Arrest all spacecraft. Do not destroy enemy spacecraft."

That was *not* Cain Salvador.

That was the voice of God Almighty this time. Captain Calli Carmel. Kerry joined in the company choir: "Aye, aye, sir!"

*　　　*　　　*

Far below, Roman spacecraft launched from their underground bunkers and ran for the big empty. Kerry Blue wasn't sure what kind of hostage the brass thought the enemy could be holding out here. She was just glad to be out of the can and in the hunt.

Knew she needed to run down the enemy before it got clear of the star system's gravitational pull.

Even the slightest gravitational pull got huge when a ship was trying to jump out of normal spacetime. Inside the gravitation of Indra Shwa's three suns and all their orbital crap, the enemy could only run at sublight velocity. But once out of the gravity sink, your Roman target could jump to FTL. And anything achieving FTL has escaped—gone, you'll never see that fugger again, you lost that one, bucko.

So ram your stick through the gate and catch him before he can get there.

The Swifts carried lampreys for this sortie. The right tool for this job.

Kerry had trained on lampreys. Well, not really. She'd trained in a dream box. Never actually used a real lamprey. But the simulators were usually good for teaching you to get it right the first time.

The lamprey was an energy half hook with an additional physical barb on the end of it. How it was supposed to go: The energy tendril loops the target, inserts microbarbs through the weakest part of the target's energy field and into the hull—not enough to breach the hull and let the vacuum in—just enough to snag and hold and reel him in alive.

Someone who wasn't Kerry Blue wanted these lupes alive.

Problem with lampreys was they had a range just about as long as your nose. You needed to get close to your target. Close enough to sniff him.

And if that don't get your heart pumping, you should report yourself in dead.

Then you haul your catch in—your live catch—and hand off the energy tether to *Merrimack*.

That was how it was supposed to go.

Someone on the com was heeing and hawing like riding a wild bronc. The new guy. Shasher Wyatt. Sounded as though Shasher had snagged something a lot bigger than he was, and it was dragging him around the park. "Yeeaaaaaaahhahaha."

Kerry Blue closed on her own target and launched her first lamprey.

Felt like she was roping a steer—something else she'd never done. "Hooks away!"

Her lamprey stabbed through the transport's shield and latched onto its hull.

"Got him!" she cried, proud of herself for one nanosecond.

The son of a bullfrogger didn't fight the energy tendril. It reversed attitude and rammed her. Head on. She actually *saw* it bounce off the energy field right over her canopy. And then it was swinging around on its tether for another hit. On her stern this time.

Not letting that happen. Kerry jinked. She took the hit on her cowcatcher, the stoutest part of her energy field.

The voice of Cain Salvador sounded in her helmet: "Alpha Six. Drop him! Drop him! Drop him! Green Leader, pick up Alpha Six."

Green Leader was driving Space Torpedo Boat 2. He had the mass for this fight.

Kerry Blue swore. And handed off her catch. "Do I get credit for that?"

Merrimack's tracking officer gave her the vector for another target closer to her size.

Kerry Blue snagged that one and managed the hand-off to *Merrimack*. She was getting the hang of this.

The fleeing spacecraft scattered wide. Tracking was giving Kerry Blue the vector of another plot. Way out there. And getting wayer out fast. "Alpha Six you have trade 90 by 35 by 240. Hurry it up, he's accelerating."

Kerry Blue took up the chase. The target had a big jump on her, but she was faster.

The gap was closing, but gravitation was getting weak out here. Target was speeding up. Any second he was going to jump out of normal space.

Target was almost in range.

Almost meant *not*.

Kerry Blue didn't see how she was going to overtake him. She needed to get him now. Right now. Still not close enough.

Kerry redlined her Swift's engine.

Overload. The Swift balked.

"*No!*"

The target vanished.

The Roman had gone FTL. Out of sight. Out of reach.

Tracking calmly assigned her another target. "Alpha Six. You have trade at 90 by 63 by 180. Do try to bring this one back."

"Can't I just shoot something?" Kerry cried. "Beams work real well in normal space, ya know!"

"Negative beams, Alpha Six. Secure all targets with lampreys. Take them alive."

"*Why?*" Kerry raced after her next target. Just knew she was gonna lose this one too. "Even Caesar Numa says it's okay to kill Romuliis."

Lieutenant Cain Salvador answered that one. "We don't take orders from Caesar."

Real low blow, that one. She wanted to tell Cain where he could shove what.

Kerry Blue unleashed her lamprey at her target. "All I'm saying is— *Got him! Got him! Got him! You Roman brit shick!*" Forgot about all she was saying.

"Com protocol," Control said to no one in particular. Probably meant all of them. Kerry Blue wasn't the only one yelling out here. Swift pilots were notorious that way.

Someone else, sounded like Dak Shepard, shouted, "I got a bead! I got a bead! I don't got a bead! Where am I?"

"Alpha Two, this is Tracking. If your intent is not desertion, reverse course."

"I had a bead," Dak protested, probably reversing course.

"Alpha Three. This is Tracking. What are you doing?"

"Wish I knew, sir."

Alpha Three was Geneva Rhine.

Kerry Blue checked her display. Not sure what she was looking at. Looked like Rhino had a lamprey wrapped completely around her own Swift several times and somehow got the barb stuck in her own arresting gear.

Other voices overlapped.

"Mine!"

"Mine!"

"Get off my target!"

"That's not a target. That's *me* you boon!"

"Grettaaaaaaaaa!"

And you could still hear the new guy leaving the solar system, wailing.

Heard Control assuring Shasher Wyatt that the *Merrimack* would come get him after the fur stopped flying. *Mack* hadn't forgotten him.

Merrimack couldn't possibly forget about him, because Shasher Wyatt was warbling over the open com, a no-breath, "YeeahAHahAHahA-Hahhhh—"

And because Shasher had a twin in the Battery whose legal name was Dumbell Wyatt. Gunner Wyatt would notice if Flight Sergeant Wyatt failed to return from this sortie.

"—ahhhhyahahahahaaaaaaah—"

Kerry Blue delivered her catch to *Merrimack* and hied after the next target.

Who knew there could be this many people stupid enough to back Romulus as ruler of the Roman Empire? "Tracking! Gimme a target!"

And, just like that, there were no more targets. Everyone who was going to run from the asteroid was gone.

On the command platform, Captain Carmel gave the go ahead for the next phase of this raid. She pointed to her Exec. "Fast now."

She needed to get the Marines down there before the remaining enemy could scuttle their equipment.

Dingo Ryan gave the orders rapid fire, all but flogging the company and crew. "Go drones. Go boarders. Secure the facility. Execute!"

Recon drones took point on the landing, Marines hard after them.

Kerry Blue, with the rest of the Alphas, set her Swift down on the asteroid's icy surface and climbed down from her cockpit into the wicked cold thin atmo. Her personal heater kicked in. A respirator gave her a couple of breaths for the sprint.

She followed the drones down one of the facility's emergency escape shafts.

The command crew would be able to watch the boarding through the Marines' gunsights. The gunsights were implanted either side of the Marines' eyes. Kerry Blue didn't even notice the black bars on her temples when she looked in a mirror. The gunsights were just part of her face. The sights followed the focus of the wearer's eyes. The visual output was displayed on *Merrimack*'s tactical monitors.

Six pairs of eyes advanced to the chamber where the pirate Nox claimed to have seen TR Steele.

The Marines hadn't been told about Steele, only that there was a possible hostage situation behind this door, a man suspended in a tank of pink medical gel.

The Marines of Alpha Team burst through the door.

Cursing.

"It's empty!" Alpha Four, Carly Delgado cried. "Say again: The compartment is empty."

The command crew could see that.

Even so, Acting WinCo Cain Salvador demanded over the com, "Completely empty?"

The Alphas looked round and round and up and down to show the command crew the completeness of the empty.

"Four walls, floor and ceiling, nothing else," Carly Delgado reported. "What were we expecting?"

Cain Salvador didn't answer the Marine. He muted the com and spoke aside for only the XO to hear, "Nox lied."

According to the pirate, Colonel Steele was supposed to be in that chamber, suspended in a tank of medical gel.

Flight Sergeant Carly Delgado crouched down. She touched her gloved fingers to the wet floor. She lifted her fingertips close to the gunsights bracketing her eyes to show whoever up there was looking through her eyes. "I have pink gunk."

On the command deck a chill lifted the hair on the back of Captain Carmel's neck. Nox hadn't lied. There really had been a pink tank in that chamber.

Steele had been there.

He wasn't there now. Neither was the pink tank.

TR Steele was like John Farragut in a way. Not that Steele had Farragut's flash, exuberance, and blinding charisma. He didn't. TR Steele was earthy, solid, and expressive as granite. Still, he was one of those men whom troops follow eagerly to hell, proud of the privilege. The ship needed him. Captain Carmel would do something about that fraternization skat later, if she ever managed to retrieve him.

Down in the Romulid lair, Alpha Team advanced to a chamber that bore the Roman imperial crest over its lintel. The Marines blasted away the metal door. A point drone pronounced the chamber clear of active booby traps, and the Marines entered.

The life-support equipment was still there. The sheet that Nox had described as "artfully draped" wasn't artful anymore. It was a soggy mess on the floor along with the oak crown. The floor was wet. Overhead was the ragged hole in the ceiling through which Nox had escaped.

The drone accessed the life-support unit's database in the soggy royal chamber. Other drones throughout the facility were gathering all the intelligence they could access.

Captain Carmel asked, "Are there any humans below?"

"None detected so far, sir," the drone wrangler reported.

Cain Salvador answered for her Marine units. "None so far."

None. A feeling like a sudden temperature drop gripped the command deck.

Dingo's wide eyes met the captain's gaze. "We're cactus," Dingo said.

"Get my Marines out of there, Stuart."

Wraith, the drone driver, was already yelping, "The facility's central data bank is erasing itself!"

A self-destruct protocol was underway.

Calli Carmel: "Drones, carry on. Men, out!"

Dingo: "Command to Company. Evac! Evac! Drop everything. Get out of there, *yesterday.*"

7

THE COUNTDOWN WAS SILENT. Wraith gave voice to it. "Thirty. Twenty-nine."

Seconds to the facility's self-destruction.

Kerry Blue counted her footfalls up the ladder rungs. Everyone's displacement collar showed red—not functioning. Do not miss a handhold or you kill yourself and everyone below you.

Kerry flew up the shaft. Knew she wasn't gonna make it. Even if she reached her Swift, she still had to get in it and get spaceborne.

Fifteen. Fourteen. Thirteen.

Kerry Blue reached the top hatch. "I'm gonna die."

"I ain't." Guy below her—Dak Shepard—gave her a boost up and out.

Cold. Her respirator froze up. No air. Not that she was going to do too much more inhaling anyway. Ran.

Ten. Nine.

She found her Swift. Scrambled onto the wing. Dropped into the cockpit.

Five. Four.

Slammed the canopy shut over her. Inhaled.

Engine already running. Lifting off.

Three. Two.

Rising. Not fast enough.

A motion made her look up.

And there was *Merrimack*, huge, getting huger, like a falling building.

One.

The voice of Control: "All small craft. Go topside. Get yourselves in our blast shadow."

Kerry Blue rising. The ground was rising with her. The rock surface bulged.

Kerry pushed the stick and hauled her crate up and over the top of *Merrimack*'s beautiful hulking shielded mass.

The asteroid cracked and exploded. The energy shell around *Merrimack*'s belly and her bottom sail took the blast.

Kerry Blue and the Marine Swifts clustered around the *Merrimack*'s towering topsail while boulders the size of Bermuda hurtled up and past them.

✳ ✳ ✳ ✳ ✳

17 Ianuarius 2448
Bagheera
Perseid Space

"You did *what?*"

Caesar Numa, in all his fuming vastness, appeared as a virtual presence across the light-years. He looked and sounded as if he were right here on board the pirate Xerxes *Bagheera*. Looked ready to murder Cinna and Nox.

Cinna answered, "I went to the Americans."

"You went to the United States Space Battleship *Merrimack!*"

"Yes, Caesar," Cinna said.

Numa menaced the patterner. "Why did I ever think you were a good idea?"

Cinna said, "That information is not in a data bank I can access."

"If I think for a moment you are trying to be comical—"

Numa let the threat hang unfinished. *Don't promise. Just do.*

"It was my idea," Nox said. "I did it."

Nox. There was another bad idea. "Of course you did!"

"We couldn't get to Romulus in the facility," Nox said. "So we sent in someone who could."

"You sent the bloody *Merrimack!*"

"Yes, Caesar."

Numa had given the pirates orders to hunt down and kill Romulus any way they could. It had been slightly resourceful of them to send *Mer-*

rimack against the Romulid facility. But the move was not without consequences. "You're supposed to be dead! You betrayed your existence to the civilized galaxy!"

"There've been sightings of us *everywhere* since we died. Lots of people see us, Caesar. We're the galactic Big Foot. This is just one more crank sighting."

"Callista Carmel saw you!" Numa bellowed. "You talked to her!"

"So 'Empress Calli' says she saw me. So what? She's not a credible witness against Caesar. Everyone expects her to accuse you of bad things."

That was true actually. Anything Calli Carmel said against Caesar Numa Pompeii could easily be dismissed as empty malice. Nox had a point.

This young man was too devious ever to have been a Farragut.

At war's end Numa Pompeii thought he had Romulus securely in custody. In retrospect, Numa should not have taken Romulus into custody at all. At the time it had been imperative that Numa not be connected with Romulus' death. The imperative was looking like an Olympian mistake now.

Numa should have just murdered Romulus as soon as the LEN Red Cross delivered him back to Palatine. Caesar Numa should have marched aboard the spaceship, taken a sword to the asp's neck and walked out with his head.

Should have. Should have. Should have. The idea of Romulus existing in a living hell had been irresistible. Numa should have resisted and taken the political fallout.

"You never actually saw Romulus."

"No, Caesar," Nox affirmed.

Numa exhaled a huff. "They let you find the facility."

Nox's face went slack for a moment. "*Let?* With respect, Caesar, you call that *letting?*"

"You were meant to see the empty chamber."

"What makes Caesar think so?"

"Because you *saw it.*"

Numa watched the dawn come to Cinna's face—a little slow on the uptake for a patterner, Numa thought. But then Cinna wasn't plugged into patterner mode right now.

"We were meant to be the first witnesses," Cinna explained to Nox. "We're the Marys."

"We're the what?" Nox still didn't get it.

Cinna said, "The sheet, half-dragged off the pallet, was draped like an artist's depiction of the shroud left behind at Christ's tomb. We're meant to believe Romulus walked. The Romulii left the life support behind. That's supposed to tell us that Romulus doesn't need it. The Romulii want us to think he is risen without actually showing him to us."

"Not showing him could mean they actually failed," Nox said.

"They didn't fail," Caesar said. "You are wearing a sword."

"Yes, Caesar," Nox said. Sounded confused.

"Fall on it."

There was the briefest pause. One couldn't truly call it a hesitation. It was an instant just long enough for Nox to absorb the command. His eyes went dead. He drew his sword. He set the hilt against a bulkhead, the sword point angled up. He positioned the point, gauging the angle to his midriff. One of those things you need to get right on the first attempt. His face was pasty.

"Stop."

Nox's hand fluttered. The sword clattered to the pirate ship's deck. Nox came to pale attention. His voice lacked strength. "I am yours to command, Caesar."

Numa's voice reverberated. "Yes, you are."

Numa pointed a stout, heavily ringed forefinger at Cinna's image. "Find Romulus. Kill him. Bring me his head."

✳ ✳ ✳ ✳ ✳

17 January 2448
U.S. Space Battleship *Merrimack*
Perseid Space

All the Fleet Marines and their spacecraft and all the drones returning to *Merrimack* from the Romulid installation needed to be scanned down to the molecule.

The Swift pilots bided their time in an outboard isolation chamber by tallying up their scores from the raid.

They were blowing raspberries at Alpha Three, the Rhino.

Geneva Rhine was the most rabid Roman hater in the whole Wing. Her score for that sortie was zero.

"Zee Roh." The Yurg used his whole mouth to pronounce the number.

He used his whole body too. The Yurg was a long, tall white guy with orangutan arms. Yurg circled his long arms into a great hoop. "A big empty round nothing."

Rhino sat with her head hanging low. She'd been a crack shot against the alien attack orbs back at Planet Zoe. Here, against her most detested enemy, the Romans? Nothin'. She stunk.

Her hair was held back in a stubby ponytail that stuck straight up now. She talked at her feet. "Yeah, I got it. I got it."

"A ROUND number," said Shasher Wyatt.

"Yeah. That one. Right." Rhino nodded. Her ponytail bobbed.

She'd got her lamprey wrapped around her own Swift and needed rescuing herself. She could not have done worse if she'd tried.

Not if she'd *tried*.

✳ ✳ ✳ ✳ ✳

2 February 2448
U.S. Space Battleship *Merrimack*
Perseid Space

"Captain Carmel," the com tech said. "The Self is on your harmonic."

Calli was motionless for several long moments. The com tech was about to repeat himself.

Calli tuned her resonator to the exclusive harmonic that linked her to the ruler of half the known galaxy. "Numa."

Without salutation, Caesar Numa Pompeii said, "Where is Jose Maria de Cordillera?"

Of all things Caesar might have said to her, she hadn't expected that. She tried not to show surprise. "I don't know."

"Did you part ways after you left the Zoen system?"

"I don't know where *Don* Cordillera is," Calli said.

She shut off the resonator and turned to her exec. "Where is Jose Maria?"

"In his cabin, I should think," Dingo Ryan said.

✳ ✳ ✳ ✳ ✳

Doctor Jose Maria Rafael Meridia de Cordillera was not in his cabin. His dog was there, but Calli found *Don* Cordillera in the lab with the xenobiologists, Doctors Weng and Sidowski.

Weng and Ski came to sloppy attention. The captain waved them back to as they were.

Rome no longer recognized Jose Maria as a political neutral. He had taken refuge with the U.S. battleship. His racing ship *Mercedes* was hangared inside *Merrimack's* port side cargo hold.

Jose Maria was aging grandly. The white streaks were broad now in his long black hair. His hair was held back with a silver clasp his late wife had given him. He was the master swordsman on *Merrimack*. The former captain of the *Merrimack* was famous for putting swords on spaceships.

The swords hadn't been used in anger since the extermination of the Hive, but they were still popular for exercise.

"Caesar asked after you, Jose Maria."

"I am not surprised, fair Captain. Am I putting you in a difficult position?"

"Not ever."

Weng and Ski were both xenobiologists. Jose Maria was a Nobel Laureate in microbiology. He had the records from the Romulid installation open and on display.

Calli regarded the many displays.

"Are the Romulii working on biologics?" Calli asked.

"Of a sort," Jose Maria said.

Doctor Weng wagged his head, mystified. "Where did the Romulii get the money for this kind of installation?" He sounded envious. It wasn't as if *Merrimack* didn't carry leading edge equipment.

Doctor Sidowski answered, "Evangelicals get limitless funds. Romulus is a god, you know."

Weng: "Romulus was a loon."

Romulus had spent most of the reign of Caesar Magnus in exile in Perseid space. There he'd siphoned off every available imperial resource for his own projects. At the time no one would say no to the son of Caesar Magnus. And the colonists in the far arm of the galaxy didn't *want* to say no to him. Romulus threw money around.

Ski: "And never mind the money, how did the loon attract the talent? He has the best scientists and inventors on his team."

Weng: "Second only to ourselves."

Ski: "We only got a partial download of the loon's data bank, but this stuff is *amazing*."

"Romulus always could amaze," Calli said.

In his reign, Romulus had declared war on the United States. He'd thrown off the Subjugation. He was audacious. He lived like an Olympian— an Olympian god, not an Olympic athlete. No one wanted a meek Caesar.

"What did you find amazing in the recovered data?" Calli asked.

Weng hesitated. "I'm not sure some of this stuff is real."

"Why? What did you find?"

"It looks like—" Weng started, got stuck, as if what he was about to say was weird and past belief.

Ski: "Go ahead and say it."

Weng: "They constructed a patterner."

"The Romulii did?" Calli asked. "No. You're right, Doctor Weng. The Romulii would never."

"Why?" Jose Maria asked. "Why would they never?"

Weng: "Romulii loathe patterners."

Ski: "A patterner brought Romulus down."

"*I* and a patterner brought Romulus down," said Jose Maria. "What can be more powerful than the weapon that brought your god low? The Romulii not only *would* make a patterner, I postulate they *must* make one."

"The plus side of that is that patterners tend to think for themselves and to not love their makers," Calli said. "Did we capture or kill anyone from the facility who has cables hanging out of his neck?"

"No," Weng said. "And I *did* check every prisoner in the ships we captured. The patterner got away."

Ski: "If one ever existed."

"I am convinced that a Romulid patterner does exist," Jose Maria told Calli. "Captured records indicate that the Romulii modified a Xerxes to accommodate a patterner."

Ski: "We didn't see a Xerxes leaving the asteroid."

Weng: "Well, we wouldn't, now would we?"

A Xerxes type ship was known for its perfect stealth. You never detected them.

"Xerxes technology is proprietary, closely guarded, and self-defensive," Jose Maria said. "Xerxes ships turn notoriously lethal when one tries to reverse engineer them. That said, I do not believe it is beyond the resourcefulness of the Romulii to fit Striker capabilities onto a lawfully acquired Xerxes without provoking its self-defense mechanism."

Weng: "Never mind the ship. They would need a live person to make into a patterner."

Ski: "A live person with special requirements. High intellect. Physical vigor."

"*Most* Romans fit those requirements," Calli said. Rome bred its citizens for brains, beauty, and brawn. "They could use just about anyone for their victim."

Ski stammered unintelligibly. Doctor Sidowski became famously inarticulate around Calli Carmel.

Weng answered, hedging, "Uh, sir. We're getting to the unbelievable part here. Doctor Sidowski thinks he might maybe have an idea of who the Romulii might be using as their base human being to construct a patterner."

Ski blurted, "No. I don't *think*. We *know* exactly who they're using."

Weng: "We're reasonably sure we know who they might have tried to use."

Ski: "You won't believe this, Captain."

"Just give me the report," Calli said.

Weng and Ski went silent.

Jose Maria said, "The evidence is as compelling as it is unbelievable."

Calli was already impatient and irritated. Suddenly she was alarmed. "What? Are you telling me they're using *Colonel Steele?*"

"No, fair Captain."

✷ ✷ ✷ ✷ ✷

Awareness.

No sense of time passing.

His last memory had been of madness.

It was still there, the madness. It stabbed, flickering, on and off. A torturing impulse, quickly snuffed. It flared back to life. Difficult to think straight. Impossible. Mind screaming. Make it stop.

The ghost came and went.

He wasn't where he had been. He'd been on the papal balcony in the Vatican on Earth.

Father's bloody ghost was suddenly right here.

Gone. Here. Gone.

Romulus sat up slowly. Opened his mouth and tried to speak. Stopped. Dry.

He could not form and hold a single complete thought. He couldn't talk.

Someone was there with a water bottle. Romulus took a sip from it. Sputtered. The bottle fell through his fingers. Splashed at his bare feet. Another water bottle was quickly in his hands, someone helping him hold it.

A voice reached him in his pit of madness. "Caesar. You have nanites in you. They are torturing you. You need to help us cure you."

He saw the cables in his forearms. Felt them behind his neck.

The voice went on. "We can't get the nanites out of you. You are the only being in the cosmos who can."

What? Tried to speak. Didn't get a sound out.

Father's bloody corpse was right there. Then an instant of peace. Immediately the torture returned. Maddening. What were these people saying to him?

"Forgive us, Caesar. All will become clear in a moment."

Romulus tried to speak. *I don't understand.*

Cables made their connections.

Let there be light.

He knew.

Knew.

Everything.

Knowing horrified.

Aghast, violated, mutilated. And yet.

A galaxy of data formed into patterns.

It was all there. Then a tortured stab from the nanites blinded every other thought.

Romulus knew what this meant. What these men wanted him to do.

The *medici* couldn't remove the nanites from him. They could only interrupt them for a moment at a time, then the nanites came back.

It would take a patterner to remove the nanites from Romulus.

So they'd made one.

Me.

Nanites in his brain triggered the hallucinations and the intense pain. Every time the *medici*'s nanites neutralized the demon ones, other nanites resurrected the demons. The demons were difficult to detect. Upon observation, the demon nanites returned a status of nonexistence.

The patterner Romulus knew his enemy now. He knew where the tools he needed were and how to use them. The *medici* had provided an interface for him to build a cure for himself. He followed the imperative before he could let himself feel outrage for what he'd become.

Get the nanites out. First.

Screaming pain stabbed him.

An instant of clarity.

Jagged flashes reared again, stabbing, scattering his thoughts.

He assembled a program and fed it into his neural network.

Clarity returned. Extended into moments. His breaths evened.

Expectant faces hovered around him.

Romulus was going to demand their names, but he already knew them.

He'd already decided not to kill them. He recognized what they were trying to do.

They'd made him a god.

It hurt, godhood.

He unplugged the cables and inhaled without pain. Without *much* pain. He had a throbbing headache. A rehydrator hissed in his arm.

Nerve and muscle stimulators had kept him from atrophying during his long sleep. His body was toned and sleek as an athlete's.

He straightened his short tunic and set his shoulders proudly back. The faces around him were anxious, amazed, adoring. Terrified.

Then, as a single being with one ringing, passionate voice, all the *medici* saluted him: "Hail, Caesar!"

PART TWO

Orpheus in the

Underworld

8

2 Februarius 2448
Romulid Carrier *Sidonus*
Perseid Space

ROMULUS SEARCHED HIS mind for the *medici's* names. He'd just had them. He didn't remember them now. A moment ago he'd known everything.

Knowing faded. He'd been omniscient just a heartbeat before now. He'd had answers. The answers escaped.

He took a few breaths. His mind was clear. So what happened to everything he just knew?

He remembered—only because he'd learned about patterners years ago—that whatever knowledge he acquired while he was in patterner mode didn't stay with him. He retained only fragments after he disconnected. Old knowledge he did retain. And he knew that he'd just come out of an induced coma.

"How long?" Romulus asked. His voice croaked.

"A year, Caesar."

"What happened to me?"

"Nanites. Specifically programmed."

"From where?"

"The patterner Augustus."

Romulus shook his head. That couldn't be right. "Augustus is dead."

He remembered that. Farragut shot Augustus in the war. "Augustus was dead before this happened to me."

"True, Caesar. But before that, Augustus created nanites programmed specifically to target you. He passed them to someone else to deliver to the Vatican. The nanites lay dormant, waiting for you to touch them."

"And his accomplice was?"

"Jose Maria Rafael Meridia de Cordillera."

"Ah. The saintly Terra Rican. I shall want him dead," Romulus said, as if making a to-do list. "A saintly death. The war?"

"Over. As soon as you fell."

"We were victorious," Romulus assumed.

The voice was careful. "No, Caesar."

"We *lost!*" Romulus started forward. Nearly blacked out. He caught himself.

"No, Caesar. We didn't lose. The war just . . . stopped."

"We control Earth?" Romulus asked. He braced himself for the worst.

And got it. "No, Caesar."

"My troops?"

"Our armed forces have withdrawn from Earth. But there are still a million true Romans on planet who can be called to duty."

"Who is administering my Empire?"

"Numa Pompeii."

Of course it would be Numa. "He presides over the Senate?"

There was a pained pause.

"He styles himself Caesar," said the lead *medicus*. His name was Xavier. Xavier coughed. He added belatedly, "Caesar."

"Well," Romulus said, more to himself than to anyone else.

Xavier said, "We needed to rescue you from Numa's custody to bring you here."

"And where is here?"

"On board your loyal carrier *Sidonus*. Headed to Near Space."

"Headed to Near Space from where?"

"We—we loyal followers of the true Caesar—we had an installation in Perseid space. We were raided by a United States space battleship. We got you out only just in time. This is not the reception we intended for you."

Romulus' brow knotted. "Why are the United States attacking Roman soil if the war is over?"

"The United States don't recognize us as the true Rome. Anyone openly loyal to you has been branded traitor and subversive. That makes us a legitimate target under their kangaroo international law."

"The only law is Rome," Romulus said.

"Many Romans don't recognize us as the true Rome. They mistakenly follow Numa Pompeii."

"They will be educated," Romulus said. And his next breath brought the most important question, the question to which they must not be without the right answer. "Where is Claudia?"

✳ ✳ ✳ ✳ ✳

2 Februarius 2448
Roman Battlefort *Gladiator*
Perseid Space
FTL

Caesar Numa Pompeii's colossal mobile palace, Fortress Aeyrie, raced back to Near Space at threshold velocity. Caesar wasn't in it.

Numa Pompeii fled the gaudy trappings, silk sheets, and hovering servants to take point in his warship, *Gladiator*.

Gladiator was a battlefort, stark, solid, brutal. On board it, Numa wore ancient battle dress. It was uncomfortable. The Empire was at peace. Numa Pompeii was at war.

He rued the loss of Romulus. Not a loss as in a death. The death of Romulus would be a happy event. No, this was the kind of loss that meant no one whose job it was to know could tell Caesar Almighty where the mad traitor Romulus was.

As much as Numa wanted to dismiss Romulus as a cartoon clown unworthy of his imperial attention, the cold fact was that Romulus had a rabid following. Romulus' name could mobilize hundreds of millions of people. Even comatose, Romulus was dividing Numa's Empire.

War unites. I rule a peace.

Once a nation attained peace, dissatisfaction settled in quickly. Romulus had run Rome like a pyramid scheme. Conquests kept cash flowing to pay his bottomless pit of debt. Now Numa was to blame for every fault and inconvenience in the Empire because he was at the helm *now*. It was left for him to restore power and water and communication services to all the colonies. One is never thanked for such things. The service is simply expected.

When Romulus had declared war on the United States of America, Numa had thought him mad. The move was looking brilliant now. Rome really needed to be at war. Deadly enemies were what held people together. Once the outside threats were gone, the people started on each other. And then they'd come after their leader.

The tedium of postwar rebuilding cast a golden glow over memories of Rome ascendant. Romans longed for the old days and might think to resurrect the man who could bring it all back.

Numa had been two steps behind Romulus at every turn.

Enough!

He drove his fist into the bulkhead and sent a giant bronze scarab cricket flying and buzzing.

Numa calmed himself. Fortunately, he knew Romulus' Achilles heel.

"Where is Claudia?" Numa demanded of his adjutant.

"With respect, Caesar, who cares?"

"Romulus does. *Ergo*, I do. Romulus loves Claudia as much as he loves himself. And for those of you not paying attention, that is a vast amount of love." He thundered to shake Mount Olympus, "*Find Claudia!*"

✳ ✳ ✳ ✳ ✳

TR Steele opened his eyes. He saw Roman eagles over him and reached for a weapon that wasn't on him. Tried to reach. His arms were shackled.

The face moved into view over him. Steele tried not to gasp. His hands formed themselves into fists.

The voice sounded, a loathed mellow baritone.

"Rest, gladiator. You are not ready for the arena. You will go in the ring. You will fight. Yes, I saw that. I can read your face. And you're wrong. You will fight, Adamas, or I shall have your wife killed."

Steele felt his face go slack in shock. He couldn't hide it.

The voice went on. "I know that secret. Know this, Adamas. Unless you fight in the arena, I will have the same loyal Roman who delivered you to me execute your wife. Is her name really Kerry Blue? I thought that was a breed of dog."

✳ ✳ ✳ ✳ ✳

15 March 2448
U.S. Space Battleship *Merrimack*
Perseid Space
FTL

Kerry Blue. Flying solo. They called her the Blue Widow because most people didn't believe the Old Man could still be alive. Kerry Blue said he was.

Kerry Blue's hair was brown. Ought to be some kind of lyrical poetic color name for it, but it was just brown. Like mice or wood ashes. Real poetry. It brushed the tops of her wide shoulders when she wore it loose, which wasn't often enough.

Breasts. She had them. Not big, but there. Cain Salvador was too aware that they were there under that girene green jumpsuit.

She had a long waist, hips that flared out girl-style, and a tight ass with girl upholstery Cain shouldn't even be thinking about.

Kerry had strong legs, with a feminine version of muscles that were just too fetching and cute to be called muscles if you want to be honest about it. She had a loose walk, as light on her feet as a Marine can be in jump boots.

Kerry Blue had more suitors than Penelope, even though she hadn't a clue who Penelope was. Cain Salvador had been entrusted with keeping the troops in line. Cain was acting CO of the half bat on board this boat. Cain Salvador was desperate to get Colonel Steele back. Steele may as well have ordered the wolf to walk Red Riding Hood to grandma's house.

Cain revered Steele like a father. Loved him like a brother.

Cain watched over Kerry Blue with the true-blue ferocity of the family bull mastiff.

The Old Man trusted Cain to take care of her.

Trouble was, Cain really really really wanted to care for Kerry Blue.

Merrimack was tearing back to Near Space at threshold velocity. No one was saying why. Cain hoped it was war.

Cain had the men running laps around the decks, climbing the sails, top hatch to bottom hatch. He ran them limp. That was the idea. He ran harder than anyone. And still some impulses were immune to exhaustion.

*   *   *

Cain Salvador walked in on Kerry Blue in the hydroponic garden. She was visiting her plant lizard. It lived here.

Her green pet was perched on her shoulder when Cain stepped through the hatch into the soft green compartment. Kerry moved a webby foot off her face to see who came in.

"Oh."

Kerry's cheeks turned bright red. Kerry Blue didn't ever blush.

And how did it suddenly get so frogging hot in here?

"You gonna run us again?" Kerry Blue said. "I'm not doin' it. You can brig me."

"I'm not gonna brig you."

"I'm not running no more laps. I'm not doin' it."

"I'm not making you run laps."

"No? Then what?"

Cain waved his arm around at the fruits and vegetables. "Sometimes I just like to walk through the green shit. Lord Almighty, Blue, why is your weed humming?"

Her plant lizard was singing. Okay, it was yodeling.

"No reason," said Kerry Blue.

Cain stepped in closer. He lifted his hand. To the lizard. "I've never heard it hum."

Kerry's face looked fevered. The lizard was warbling. Cain touched her cheek. The plant lizard's song spiked.

Cain had been watching out for Kerry Blue, warding off guys who tried to line up a docking maneuver. He was getting sick of it. He was giving guys the wave off when it was nothing he hadn't thought about a jillion times for himself.

His throat got thick. "I gotta go."

Kerry Blue scowled. "You know I can say no for myself, Cain."

"Kerry Blue, you never say no."

"I can say yes for myself," Kerry Blue said, hot.

Cain threw up his hands. "Fine." He turned his back on her. Pissed and relieved all at the same time. Tired of guard dogging her. "Fine." He stalked to the hatch.

"Cain?"

He almost didn't hear her for the plant lizard's trilling. Cain turned, snarling, surly, his lip curled. "What?"

"Yes," said Kerry Blue.

✳ ✳ ✳ ✳ ✳

15 Martius 2448
Romulid Carrier *Sidonus*
Near Space

During the months-long crossing from the Perseid arm of the galaxy in to the Orion Starbridge, Romulus sparred with an automaton. The humanoid automaton was programmed not to seriously injure him, but it would cause him damage—reparable damage—when it saw an opening.

That didn't happen much anymore.

Romulus practiced combat with several machine opponents at a time, first in patterner mode, and then without the augmentation.

He wore gauntlets on his forearms and a high, armored collar at the back of his neck to shield his patterner cables from harm. And he didn't like to see the wretched cables anyway. They looked like tentacles. They made him think of that infernal machine creature, Augustus.

By the time the carrier *Sidonus* crossed into Near Space, Romulus was drawing breath easily in his sparring bouts. His thoughts flowed clear. He was mentally sharp. He was physically strong. Agile. Quick. Masterful.

He destroyed his machine opponents.

His skin glistened. Victorious, he turned to ask Claudia how he looked.

And then he remembered what he'd allowed himself to forget for a blessed instant. Claudia was missing. She was likely still suffering hideous torture from the nanites, same as he had.

He felt rage toward the *medici* for not curing her too. But they didn't know where she was.

They should have found her. They should have rescued her too!

Romulus checked his wrath. It didn't serve his interests to murder skilled people who were serving him to the best of their mortal abilities.

They had made him into a patterner, a patterner vastly superior to the old model. Mentally and physically, Romulus was better than ever.

He would need to find Claudia for himself.

✳ ✳ ✳ ✳ ✳

28 Martius 2448
Roman Imperial Palace
Roma Nova, Palatine
Corona Australis star system
Near Space

"Romulus is here!" Palace sentinels shouted. No warning of the approach. Just an announcement of the arrival.

"Shoot him," Caesar Numa Pompeii said.

"He's in a school ship, *Domni*."

That might explain how the ship was permitted to enter Palatine's airspace unchallenged. School ships traveled freely in the Roman Empire. People who menaced children were eviscerated. As this man should be.

"Show me!"

Quickly done. There were hordes of expectant media craft escorting the school ship, all transmitting live feeds. Numa could view from any angle he desired.

The school ship wasn't a fake. It was a real one, filled with real children. The media had received advance notice of its approach. The imperial palace hadn't been given the courtesy.

Raising the shield dome now in the face of children would make Numa look ridiculous.

Nothing to do but let the school ship land at the Capitoline visitors' pad.

The media had already swarmed into place, poised to capture every angle the moment Romulus appeared.

First to appear on the ramp were dancing children.

Romulus himself, gaudily dressed, stepped out with a protective flock of them, who hung on his robes.

Numa roared. "Get a sniper on him."

"Active deflectors in operation. Can't shoot without hitting a child. I'd rather eat a sword than take that shot," said his closest bodyguard, and he looked to Numa as if expecting a go-ahead-and-kill-yourself order.

"Don't fall on your sword," Numa growled.

Law of Armed Conflict forbade using civilians as shields. But the children couldn't technically be called shields here. The children were where they were supposed to be, and the school ship wasn't carrying weapons, unless one counted Romulus. Numa did. But any shot into a crowd of children would be political suicide.

Numa damned Romulus. Damned himself for letting Romulus get this far.

Romulus was on Numa's literal doorstep. Steps. There were one hundred of them, wide, hewn from glistening snowy marble.

Romulus made a long show of ascending with his flock. He picked up a little one who was struggling to make the climb.

At the summit, the monumental palace doors remained shut against him.

Romulus set down his child and turned before the doors to face the thousands who had flocked to the Capitoline to witness history.

Romulus spread his arms wide at the masses, still gathering.

"Friends, Romans, Countrymen, peoples of the civilized Cosmos. Your Caesar liveth."

The crowd gave an oceanic roar.

Inside the palace, Numa's guards and attendants waited, uneasy. His bodyguard asked. "Caesar?"

"Let him rot out there," Numa said.

That idea backfired.

Romulus was a great entertainer. Soon he was leading the children in a singing game. Then the crowd demanded a speech.

Romulus was playing the moment, waiting for the audience to get bigger.

28 March 2448
U.S. Space Battleship *Merrimack*
Port Chalai
Near Space

Merrimack arrived in Near Space via the colossal displacement facility of the Pacific Boomerang. The Boomerang cut kiloparsecs off the journey from the distant Perseid arm of the galaxy to the Orion Starbridge, a/k/a Near Space, where Earth and Palatine and most major worlds were located.

Upon arrival in Port Chalai in Near Space, *Merrimack* was still a week away from Earth. A voyage to Palatine would be even longer.

The command crew watched the resonant newsfeed from the Roman capital world as strange events unfolded.

Thronged by young children, Romulus mounted the palace steps. He looked healthy, energetic. Not at all like a man who had spent over a year in a tortured coma.

He wore billowing sleeves and a high ornate collar.

"See that?" the Intelligence Officer, Bradley Zolman pointed to the close image on *Merrimack*'s tactical display. "He's covering up his patterner's cables."

Zolman drilled deeper into the recording, which captured more than visuals. The deep scan revealed that Romulus was wearing a polymetal collar under that lacey Elizabethan ruff, and polymetal gauntlets under his voluminous sleeves.

Something was missing.

Calli noticed immediately. No one else did. "Where's Claudia?"

"Sir?"

"Why is Romulus making a public appearance at the palace without precious Claudia on his arm? Where is she?"

"That information is need-to-know," the Intelligence Officer said.

"Z?" Calli said. "I need to know."

28 Martius 2448
Roman Imperial Palace
Roma Nova, Palatine
Corona Australis star system
Near Space

At last the towering doors of the imperial palace moved. They hinged outward, so their parting herded a thick lot of children off to the sides.

The crowd noise spiked.

The doors only moved wide enough to frame Numa Pompeii like a picture. They put all the focus on Numa. And kept him from being flanked.

Caesar Numa Pompeii advanced like a rockslide, agile for such a big man. An oak crown wreathed his balding head. His face was craggy. He was not lovely, especially next to Romulus who should have been named Adonis. Numa was, however, striking.

Children clustered close on all sides of Romulus, clinging to his gold cloak.

Romulus didn't salute Caesar Numa Pompeii. He wouldn't. A salute was a literal wish of health and safety.

Romulus turned his back on Numa and addressed the crowd and the cameras.

"People of Rome." The noise fell away. Everyone strained to hear. "We thank citizen Numa Pompeii for his service in the interim. We hope he enjoys his well-earned retirement. I am here."

The cheers and rumbling objections sorted out who was underground insurgent Romulii and who was honored old Roman guard here.

When the noise subsided, Numa said, "Romulus, it's glib and simplistic to think you can just pick up where you left off."

"Is it?" Romulus spoke directly into a camera. "I suppose it is, seeing that things have gone to hell in my absence, but I will overcome. Of course, one can only expect a substitute to do so much, so it's understandable, though regrettable, that the Empire has lost luster from its former glory under your misguidance. Well, there it is. No use sorrowing over it. You only did the best you could. I am here now."

Numa would not speak at Romulus' child-thronged back. Instead he found another cluster of cameras and talked to them. "Romulus, you can't ignore the fact that you are brain-damaged and there is another Caesar in control today."

"An interim figure," Romulus told his camera. "Of course there would be. It's a perfectly ordinary occurrence for a leader in hospital to return to his office without expecting an insurrection while he was mended."

"The Senate voted a new ruler."

"The senile strike again. The vote was criminally premature."

"The vote was over a year ago. You were effectively dead, Romulus. There is no provision in the constitution for resurrection. And it is clear to everyone here that you are still deranged and infested with nanites."

"Numa Pompeii, we will refrain from having you arrested for treason if you return to your lawful place now."

"Romulus, you are as deluded as ever."

Romulus turned to face Numa. Even forced to look up, Romulus radiated power, superiority. "Pompeii, if your next words are not Hail Caesar, you are a traitor to the Empire."

Numa slowly extended his ring to be kissed.

Romulus rested one hand on the shoulder of the child on his immediate left, and he strode down the wide steps, waving to the crowds that parted before him, a strained smile affixed to his face.

5 April 2448
U.S. Space Battleship *Merrimack*
Near Space

A terrestrial week after Romulus' appearance on Palatine, the Romulii raised a Roman flag and Roman eagles on the artificial world orbiting Beta Centauri.

Beta Centauri, like the whole Centauri star system, was a League of Earth Nations protectorate, but the League offered no resistance to the flag raising beyond polite inquiries.

Global emergency alarms sounded across planet Earth. Earth lay within a half-day's striking distance from the Centauri system.

Apparently Beta Centauri was to be the site of Romulus' government in exile.

Merrimack came to high alert.

"Can't we just shoot them?"

The voice sounded from the rear of Calli Carmel's command platform. The XO, Dingo Ryan, contained a snort of laughter.

The Marine standing guard at the hatch was Flight Sergeant Geneva Rhine, the Rhino. Hard-core Roman hater, that one. Calli had a fleeting thought that the Rhino declared too much.

Captain Carmel shook her head. "The LEN haven't invited us to defend them."

"We're a member of LEN," said Dingo.

"We *are?*" someone else said, and several specialists at the closely packed stations of the command deck sniggered into their consoles.

Calli Carmel tended to forget how young these guys were.

She let it go.

And there was something else. Marcander Vincent at Tactical— not a young guy—spotted it. Possibly the only proactive thing Marcander Vincent had ever done in his long lackluster career.

"There's a newly erected structure on Beta Centauri. Big one."

He brought the structure into close view.

Calli said, because John Farragut wasn't here to say it, "Oh, for Jesus."

It was a coliseum.

9

6 April 2448
U.S. Space Battleship *Merrimack*
Earth orbit
Near Space

THERE WAS A SAYING ON *MERRIMACK*: If anything's gonna happen, it'll happen on the Hamster Watch.

The Hamster Watch was what everyone still called the middle watch, the hours during ship's night, even though the Hamster herself, Lieutenant Glenn Hamilton, was no longer aboard. Lieutenant Hamilton had her own command.

"Steele's alive! Steele's alive!"

They were screaming it in the low-lit corridors on all decks of the *Merrimack*, as if she were a college dorm and not a space battleship.

The Romulii had just announced that the gladiator Adamas was returning to the arena.

That woke everyone up.

Flight Sergeant Kerry Blue looked as though she'd been shot.

Acting Wing Commander Cain Salvador looked as though he'd been stabbed.

Captain Carmel stalked up to the command deck in sweatshirt and sweatpants. She waved down the apology of the Officer of the Watch. "Where is he?"

"Beta Centauri. The artificial planet. Possibly on the daylight side.

Colonel Steele's exact location is uncertain. But local news broadcasts say Adamas is headlined to open the games celebrating Romulus' return."

All first watch personnel had been ordered back to sleep. The forecastle was dark again, but no one was sleeping. *Merrimack* was headed to the Centauri system.

The Fleet Marines, netted into their sleep pods, were whispering.

The last time anyone had seen TR Steele was at the extreme galactic edge, near the planet Zoe.

Steele's Swift had been on approach to *Merrimack*. His Swift overshot the landing slot, and his com had gone silent. When his Swift was recovered, Steele wasn't in it. The landing disk inside his Swift indicated that he'd displaced. He was presumed dead.

Suddenly he was here in Near Space. In Roman hands.

"He's not in Roman hands," someone whispered. "He's in Romulid hands."

"Like there's a difference?" Sounded like Dak over on the Y chromosome side of the partition.

"Not to me." Rhino's voice there. "Only good Roman's a dead Roman."

"How did this *happen*?" Kerry Blue squeaked.

"I keep thinking back to the sortie when we lost him, *chica linda*," Carly said. "We scrambled. There wasn't a displacement collar in the Old Man's Swift. Remember that?"

Twitch and Dak nodded to themselves in the dark. They remembered.

Carly flicked a hard look sideways in the direction of Rhino. Not that Carly was able to see Rhino. Carly knew where she was. "Rhino gave him a collar."

Big Rhino sounded crushed. She whispered a wail, "You think I don't know that?" Then suddenly she gasped on a shuddering thought. "Hey! Do you think they were really after *me*?"

"Uh," Shasher Wyatt started awkwardly. "I'm kinda pretty sure the lupes got the guy they were fishing for."

It took the best part of an eon for Kerry Blue to get alone with Cain Salvador.

"He's gonna kill me," Kerry said. Her face was nearly white. Cain had never realized till now that she had a few freckles.

"You'll be okay, Blue."

"*Okay?* I'm gonna be as *not* okay as anyone ever got!"

"He won't hurt you."

Hurt her? Mean like hit her? Not likely. Not ever. Officers don't hit enlisted men. Steele would just walk away, annul the marriage, and set her ashore. He wouldn't talk to her. Wouldn't look at her. Probably even let her keep the ring she kept in her locker.

Yeah. That won't hurt at all.

"What a fog ducking mess."

And that wasn't even the worst of all possible nightmares. What tore her up was that she might never get to see that look of hurt betrayal and disappointment on Thomas Ryder Steele's face.

Thomas was going into a rigged fight to the death in a Roman arena.

15 April 2448
Columbia City, Beta Centauri
Centauri Star System
Near Space

Steele received instructions from a hologram. No Roman felt safe breathing the same air as the legendary Adamas.

"Gladiator," a holoimage of the lanista greeted Steele.

The lanista's eyes were elaborately painted like a figure in an Egyptian tomb. A tomb would be a good place for him.

"Go to hell," Steele said.

"Pay attention, Adamas, if you want to live. And we truly do want you to live, but it's not a given. You need to earn it.

"Your first opponent will be the chimaera. To kill it, you need to stab it in the heart, but that's not possible until you do all of these first—*all* of these. Pay attention."

The hologram's forefinger jutted up. "First. Cut off its tail. Mind you, the tail's teeth are poison."

Steele's scowl deepened. *The tail's teeth?*

The lanista's middle finger flipped up alongside the forefinger. "Second. Cut off one of the goat's horns. Mind you, the horns are poison tipped."

Another finger. "Third: Cut off the goat head."

Another finger. "Fourth: Break the lion's teeth."

Out came the thumb. "Fifth: Slice off a hank of mane."

The other forefinger. "Sixth: Put out an eye.

"Do all those, then you will—" The lanista stopped and revised slyly. "You *might* be able to stab the chimaera in the heart."

Steele said in dull surprise as he realized, "It's programmed."

"Yes. And when I tell you that you can't stab it in the heart until you do all prerequisites, I mean it. Stay alive. We want this to be entertaining. It's the inaugural combat. We're expecting great things of Adamas. If you play a defensive game, the chimaera is programmed to—well, I shouldn't tell you. So look alive, so to say. Tail. Horn. Head. Teeth. Mane. Eye. Heart. Questions?"

"What's a chimaera?"

The holoimage gave an annoyed huff. "You really are ignorant beef, aren't you." He produced another holoimage.

The chimaera was a full-sized lion, except that it had the head of a wickedly horned goat growing out of its left side. And the goat wasn't a tame little milk nanny like *Merrimack* carried in her hold. This was an Asian kind of goat with long curved scimitars for horns. And there was a snake growing out of the chimaera's ass where a lion tail was supposed to be, fanged-end out.

So that was what the lanista meant when he said the tail had poison teeth.

"Any more questions?"

"How far forward can that tail reach?"

"Can't tell you. We don't want this to look *staged*, you know."

The space battleship *Merrimack* arrived at Beta Centauri and took up a geosynchronous orbit above the coliseum. Other spaceships wanted the position. *Merrimack* told them to move.

Far down below, the arena rocked to the pounding chant of *A-da-mas! A-da-mas!* Romulus, arrayed like an opera star in his royal box, joined the chant.

Fountains of fireworks blazed upward. Expectation rose and spread like a contagion.

An iron portcullis rattled up.

A century of towering Roman soldiers marched out in box formation, all arrayed in antique bronze armor. Inside the hollow center of the precision marching block walked one shorter blond man.

The crowd laughed at the excessive guards, and they cheered, stomped, and chanted. "A-da-mas!"

Calli breathed, "Steele!"

"Is it really?" Dingo asked.

Valid question. The lupes might have fashioned a duplicate. They had his DNA.

This man's blue eyes glanced all around, wary and searching.

He looked straight up, where *Merrimack* was, his face grim and determined, as if he knew he was looking someone straight in the eyes. Maybe he could see *Merrimack* as a bright day star through the energy dome. He looked like a man who had been here before.

"That's Steele," Calli said.

The crowd was screeching, throwing flowers.

The box formation marched to a halt.

The box opened. Steele dashed out.

The box closed and marched back to the gate, which opened for them. They left behind a sword in the sand. The iron gate clattered shut.

"Where's his helmet? They didn't give him a helmet!"

"Steele doesn't like helmets," Calli said.

Captain Carmel summoned her Legal Officer to the command deck. "Mister Buchanan. Is Romulus a military target?"

Rob Roy Buchanan told her, "Captain, you may fire on Romulus if you have a clear shot without collaterals."

"Dingo! Do we have a lock on Romulus?"

"Negative, sir. They have a full energy dome over the coliseum with jammers and deflectors on their deflectors. Any inbound shot will go wild."

Acting WinCo Cain Salvador volunteered. "I can take a squadron down. We can get through the dome slow."

"You'll get through dead," said Commander Ryan. Dingo was a hell rider himself. If the Dingo shied off a sortie, it really was a suicide run.

"Then find another way," Captain Carmel ordered. "Get my Marine out of there!"

※ ※ ※ ※ ※

TR Steele didn't like games. Didn't want to be here in this vast bowl surrounded by thousands of cheering Romans.

They'd tricked him out in a short tunic, a Roman breastplate, boots, and a shield. They'd given him a helmet. But he'd pulled that off back in the elevator.

His escort of one hundred bronze-clad baboons left behind a short sword, the *gladius*, when they retreated from the arena. He retrieved it, then walked around the ring, looking for anything useful in the things thrown from the stands.

A heavy metal gate at the edge of the arena rattled up.

The chimaera burst from its cage. It was bigger than he expected. Twice the size of a normal lion.

It charged at him, roaring. Sounded like a real lion. Steele waited for it.

The three-headed beast closed the distance in seconds. Steele held his position until he could smell the animal musk. He felt its heat.

Then he faked left. The lion went toward the motion. Steele reversed and sprang right, toward the goatless side of the chimaera, his sword raised to stab it in the ribs, but in an instant the goat's long curved horns jabbed over the lion's back in a slicing arc, all the way over and around the lion torso. Steele lurched back scarcely in time.

Off balance, he staggered away.

The chimaera turned away. Its snake tail coiled and struck. Only by muscle reflex did Steele catch the bite on his shield. Without thought, he followed through with a sword stroke.

Sheared the serpent head off.

The head fell to the sand, fanged mouth open, angry red eyes glaring.

The attached part of the tail lashed about in a horror show spectacle. It spurted blood like a hose under pressure.

Steele ducked and sprinted to the side.

The monster body turned full round. One gigantic lion forepaw reached for him, its enormous black dagger claws spread wide. Steele jumped inside its reach, throwing his back flat against the monster's hot furry side. It felt alive.

The goat horns came stabbing over the lion's back again. Steele thrust his shield up. Caught the blow square, but one goat horn punched straight through the metal.

And stuck.

The shield's metal frame was caught on the horn's ridges. The goat head lifted, pulling the shield up with it, dragging Steele's arm up. He needed to let go of the shield. Now. Now. The forearm strap held fast. He writhed, drawn up on his toes.

His feet left the ground.

His body stretched long, dragged by his shield, up and backward across the body of the lion and over the top.

The goat head bowed abruptly, furiously *down*. Steele drew his knees in. Just got his feet under him as the goat slammed him into the sand on the other side of the beast. Hard. The impact jammed his shins.

Splintered light glinted before his eyes.

The ridged goat horn was still stuck in his shield. The poisoned tip was right *there*, scraping his breastplate, smoldering.

The goat head wagged.

With all his weight and force Steele wrenched his shield around tight. A great cracking hammered his eardrums. That was the horn snapping. The poisoned end slid off his breastplate and dropped to the sand. The goat head lifted away without him.

Steele immediately twisted round to catch the lion's open jaws on his shield. He countered with his sword, amazed to find it still in his grip, amazed he hadn't killed himself with it while the beast threw him around.

His sword stroke opened up one side of the lion's enormous face and took out one eye. It gave a screeching roar. Steele reverse slashed across the lion's gaping mouth.

Giant teeth flew in a wide scatter. Steele stabbed the lion's other eye and scrambled away. Tried to scramble. His boot soles slid in the sand.

The lion reared. Came down—

On Steele's upthrust sword. The blade plunged deep inside the lion's chest. Brought Steele to his knees. The blood was warm as if the creature were living. The blood was slick.

The sword slipped out of his hand as the lion bucked backward, taking the sword with it.

Steele scrambled to his feet. The thing had to be mortally wounded.

But of course it wasn't alive in the first place, so it wasn't dying.

The monster's whipping tail was still shooting blood in a ridiculous spray. Red drops painted some of the lower seats. The spectators skittered back, laughing and jeering.

Steele circled around the chimaera, keeping away from its reaching forepaws. The blind monster turned with him. It knew where he was.

It followed Steele's every motion as if it could see him. And Steele was getting the horrible idea that the chimaera really could see him.

He noticed it now. The lion head was blind but the damned goat head sticking out of its side was watching him with baleful eyes. Horizontal pupils narrowed at him.

The lanista had warned him that he needed to cut off the goat head before he could kill the beast.

The beast had his bloody sword.

Steele charged around to the lion's hindquarters, seized the lashing, spurting tail and aimed it at the telltale goat's eyes.

The goat head tossed upward, bugling. Steele dove under the lion body, hammered a paw away with his shield, and pulled his sword out of the chimaera's chest. He scrambled clear of angry paws and stood up swinging. He brought his sword down on the goat's neck, hacking it halfway through.

The head flopped down, hanging on its broad tendons. The lion head screamed. Another sword stroke and the goat head fell loose into the sand.

Steele rammed his shield into the lion's face as it turned on him.

The lion reared. Steele danced in under its lifted paws and jabbed his sword into its ribcage. He skipped out to the side. That had to be a kill stroke.

The lion roared and turned with him, still alive and following his every move.

Despair sapped Steele's strength. His limbs felt suddenly thick and sluggish. His shield weighed heavily.

He tried to think. What all did he need to do before he could kill this thing?

Tail. Horn. Goat head. Teeth. Mane. Eye.

Mane. He was missing the mane.

What kind an idiotic requirement was that? Cut off a piece of mane.

He stalked softly to within range. The lion seemed to see him. It lowered its head and hunkered down, lips drawn back.

The lion sprang at him.

Steele dove out of the way. The lion skidded around with a great spray of sand, its head still tracking him.

What the hell? Steele had removed its eyes.

Steele circled wide, looking for an opening.

It was useless.

The lion bellowed, its jaws spread wide, showing lots of jagged broken teeth. Its mammoth paws with their dagger claws sent up clouds of dusty sand as it launched itself into a gallop.

Steele turned and ran. Heard the boos. The chimaera stayed on his trail, unerring, turn for turn.

Steele glanced around the arena for an exit. Became aware of a block of teenaged boys in the ringside stands not booing. They were shouting and gesturing madly as if eager to help him. Fans. They pointed urgently.

To where the severed goat head was still moving, dragging itself across the sand by its remaining horn. The goat's malevolent eyes blinked clear of blood. Watched him.

Even detached, the goat could still see him. Apparently that meant it could show the lion body where to go.

Steele dashed to the severed goat head and hacked its eyes out. Then he found the severed snakehead. Its red eyes watched him. The lion screamed in a sound like terror, and raced him to get to the snake eyes.

Steele got there first. Stomped down on the snake head. Felt it crush it under his boot.

Now the monster was blundering around, blind, lost. Without its goat head and snake tail it was mostly lion now—a lion with a mechanical refusal to die.

It lifted its wide nostrils in the air and snuffled. It cocked its head to listen, then charged in the general direction of Steele.

Steele let the beast come toward him. At the last moment he lunged aside, letting his sword sweep across the beast's neck. He'd dodged too wide. His blade made only a shallow cut in the lion's neck. But a great clump of mane dropped away with the stroke.

That was the last requirement. Cut off a hank of mane. Now he should be able to finish the beast.

He had to stab it in the heart.

He came at the chimaera from the flank and thrust his sword one more time deep into the barrel chest where the heart should be.

He barely kept a grip on his sword as the lion reared roaring, clawing the air.

Steele ran out from under its slashing claws.

The thing wasn't dying. It came after him, head low, nostrils flaring.

You might be able to stab it in the heart, the lanista had said. The lanista had looked sly when he said the word *might*.

Might. What was the trick? Where did a chimaera keep its heart?
Damn it.

This was a game. Steele didn't know how to play games.

He looked to his fans. The boys were making stabbing motions and pointing at something on the ground.

Yeah. He was supposed to stab the thing in the heart. The lanista had told him that.

Realized the lanista hadn't told him what he might stab *with*.

Steele ran to the severed goat head and chopped off the goat's remaining horn as the chimaera shuffled angrily toward him.

Steele should have noticed the burn mark on his breastplate where the first goat horn had scratched it. But he didn't.

He dropped his sword and seized up the goat horn from the sand.

Instantly felt like he'd closed his hand on a molten poker. Pain lanced all the way up to his jaw. Pain like a solid thing. It felt to be pushing behind his eyes.

The horn dropped from his hand.

His palm was wet, red. He thought he glimpsed bone amid the dripping blood.

The chimaera sped up its advance. It came heavily galloping, nodding. It seemed in agony. But it wasn't an animal. It was a Roman manufactured thing.

Steele quickly tried to work his shield off his left forearm. The leather band stuck.

He needed to free up his left hand to hold a sword. Pain had transformed his right hand and arm into one solid burning useless weight.

He scrambled away from the chimaera's charge. It reared, twisted round and pounced at the sand where he had been. The crowd sounds were mocking.

He cursed, losing strength.

Finally he got the damned shield off his left arm.

You *might* be able to stab the chimaera in the heart.

If he could hold a weapon. What weapon? The sword was useless for a kill stroke.

He couldn't think.

He trotted to keep ahead of the shambling chimaera. The boos were growing loud.

Steele looked to the boys. They knew this game. They were trying to tell him something.

His vision blurred. What did they mean?

They were pantomiming. First they pantomimed the goat's curving horns. Then they made stabbing motions.

The boys seemed to think he needed to use the goat horn to stab the lion's heart.

That's what he'd thought. But he couldn't touch the goat horn. Weren't these guys watching this farce?

Steele thrust his bloody palm at them for them to see.

The boys pulled at their hair. Oh great that they were frustrated. They weren't helping. They were trying maybe to help, but he didn't know what they meant.

This was a game. How did you think like a gamer?

Hair. What of hair?

It came back to him—that useless instruction to cut off a hank of mane. It was so useless that it had to have a purpose.

Hair. Mane.

He got it. Maybe.

The lion was hauling itself toward him. Steele flipped his sword around in his left hand and threw it like an overly large knife.

The blade jabbed and stuck in the beast's broad brow.

The crowd loved him again. Steele loathed them.

As the beast pawed to get the sword out of its face, Steele charged past it and grabbed up the thick hank of mane he'd sheared off. He wrapped swaths of mane around each of his palms. Then he ran to one of the severed goat horns. He took a deep breath, shuddered, and closed one mane-padded hand around the goat horn.

No burning penetrated through the thick layer of lion's mane. Steele closed his other wrapped hand around the horn and turned, ready.

The chimaera lumbered toward him. No need to chase it.

As it neared, Steele dodged heavily to one side and plunged the poisoned goat horn between the thing's ribs where its heart ought to be.

The lion body reared straight up, bugling and thrashing. It staggered on its hind legs. Tottered toward Steele, who broke into a run. The monster tripped toward him on two legs, foot over foot, until finally it fell over theatrically in a billow of dusty sand.

Done.

The crowd cheered.

Steele looked to his boy gang. They weren't celebrating. They were gesturing frantically.

Of course no horror show ever ends the first time the monster dies. Something always comes back for a final bite. It was some kind of law.

The crowd sounds changed to cries and gasps.

The chimaera's shattered teeth were melting into black oozing puddles in the sand. Then they were rising, taking shape, moving, growing. Flapping. Steele thought they might be turning into bats. Steele rocked his sword free from the lion's brow, then stabbed at the things forming. Didn't want to see what they were becoming.

There were too many of them.

One bubbled up and took to ragged flight.

The nightmare thing came at him, keening. Steele swung with his sword and batted it away broadside, hard. The ragged creature whistled skyward. And hit the energy barrier.

Steele hadn't known there was an energy barrier between him and the audience, but of course there had to be.

On impact the black creature dissolved in a bright rainbow spray. More of the tarry black things rose from the sand, chittering, flying at him. Steele slashed and swung at them. Didn't want to know what would happen if he let one touch him.

Got them all.

He bent over, his breath rattling.

Slowly he straightened up. He dragged himself to the goat's other poison-tip horn. It was shorter than the one he'd plunged into the monster.

He still had hanks of lion's mane wrapped around his hands. His right hand was a solid mass of pain, lion hair caked to it with his blood.

He picked up the shorter goat horn in his mane-wrapped left hand and threw it at Romulus.

Energy barriers only stopped fast moving objects. The thrown horn passed through the force field. It fell short of the imperial box and dropped into the crowd.

Won an *ooooh* from the crowd, and a sullen smirk from Caesar.

There was a scramble below Caesar's box for the souvenir. Someone came up with the horn. Held it up like a home run ball.

Steele was disappointed that the horn didn't burn the Roman.

Maybe the passing through the barrier neutralized the caustic, or maybe the caustic was effective on Steele alone. Steele couldn't touch it. The Romans could.

The lupes had anticipated everything here. Nothing staged here. Nope. Not a thing.

The crowd didn't care.

Women in front rows were throwing their tops at him. There came down water bottles, flowers, keys.

Dragging his sword, Steele trudged across the ring.

He picked up the severed snake head in his bloody hand and tossed it up before him. He twisted round, gripping his sword hilt in both hands like a baseball bat, and swung for the fences.

The broadside crack sent the snake head sailing up toward the Imperator's box.

The snakehead passed through the energy barrier. Hit Romulus on the cheek.

A great inhalation rose from the crowd. Fell quickly into a stunned hush.

Except for Steele. Steele danced like a street fighter, beckoning with his bloody hand, daring Romulus to come down.

That brought gasps from the crowd.

Then Caesar stood up.

A moan rose and died in the crowd.

The entire civilized part of the galaxy held its breath, except for Steele, battered, and dancing his leaden foot shuffle. Bones showed through his burned palm, beckoning.

Romulus stood rigid like a spear stabbed in place.

Then Romulus moved.

Out came his sword.

Silence shattered into utter tumult.

CAESAR TOOK OFF A GLOVE. Threw it down into the arena. It landed at Steele's shuffling feet.

Steele picked up the glove in his good hand and waved for Romulus to come down. You could see him saying, "Come on. Come on." Couldn't hear him. The noise in the coliseum was like the inside of a spaceship engine.

Captain Carmel watched from the command deck of the *Merrimack*. "That wasn't an accident, that thing getting through Romulus' force field."

"Hell, no," Dingo said. "Do you think Romulus is wearing a homing device in his cheek?"

"Must be," Calli said. No one's aim was that good from that distance. Romulus wanted Steele to hit him. "Romulus is playing Steele."

"Steele can't tell."

"I don't know. He might be able to tell it's staged."

"Captain, I don't think he cares."

They could see Romulus giving orders to an attendant.

One of the iron gates to the bloody arena clattered up. Steele spun and dropped into a defensive posture.

A medibot, showing a red cross, hovered out into the ring. Steele crouched, sword ready in his left hand to fight it off.

Romulus got on a megaphone and pronounced with the voice of Zeus over the noise. "Let the machine mend you, you ass. I will not fight a lamed adversary."

And Romulus signaled for music.

The crowd stomped along with the beat.

The medical automaton hovered toward Steele. Steele swung at it.

A dart from the medibot immobilized him.

The crowd booed.

The boos might have been for Steele attacking the Red Cross or they could be for the bot paralyzing Steele.

Either way, Steele was unable to move until the bot repaired and re-skinned his hand, rehydrated him, and let him go.

The crowd bayed approval.

Steele flexed his right hand, snatched up his sword from the sand and took a swing at the retreating medibot.

He appeared reenergized and eager for a fight.

Up in the imperial box, Romulus threw off his cloak. He was wearing armor underneath. It gleamed like polished bronze. It was probably something harder and lighter. Romulus had come to the games ready for this match.

An attendant offered Romulus a crested helmet. Romulus made a show of refusing it. He touched the oak crown on his dark locks. You had to read his lips to know he said in Latin, "This is my armor."

The music swelled.

Calli called for the status on measures to retrieve Steele from the arena.

"We can't shoot through the dome, sir," Targeting reported. "Can't be done."

"Then take out the dome generators."

Dingo advised, "The generators are protected under their own force fields."

"Then take out the continental power grid," Calli said.

Tactical located the orbiting power plant that serviced the region around the coliseum.

"Target acquired."

"Secure the target," Calli ordered.

Beam fire hummed and hissed from the space battleship. You couldn't see the shot. You saw the orbital power plant exploding.

Down on the planet surface, lights winked out across the continent.

The energy dome over the coliseum didn't even waver. It shone like a ground star.

The Romulii had constructed the coliseum like a space station, self-contained and adamantly shielded.

Everything around it was dark.

Calli crossed her arms. "I may have just shot myself in the career."

"Captain, this is playing out to a script," Dingo said. "Romulus has anticipated everything."

Calli needed to outthink Romulus. That used to be easy. She used to know Romulus.

She didn't know Romulus the patterner.

She caught herself wishing the unthinkable. She wished to hell that Augustus were here.

Romulus strode down the aisle toward the arena, his hands out to either side, accepting all the touches from his people.

Down in the arena, Steele danced like a boxer.

A moving shadow passed over the stands, followed by a roaring. The engine noise was scarcely distinguishable from the crowd noise. Sunlight glinting off something moving fast made everyone look up.

An echelon of U.S. Fleet Marine Swifts had passed over. They were turning around now in arrowhead formation. They came back and executed an airshow roll over the coliseum.

The Swifts fired field disruptors.

The emplaced defenses around the coliseum neutralized the disruptor signals. The flight of Swifts succeeded only in showing their colors.

And that was all they expected to do.

Captain Carmel had sent down the Alphas. Hoped she hadn't made another mistake. The sight of Alpha Flight could put the heart in Steele or it could fatally distract him.

It was a useless stunt in any case. This fight was fixed. Calli knew it. But Steele got to see his wife fly over before he died. And he would die.

Unless it was part of Romulus' playbook, Steele could not survive this contest.

Across the dust and heat shimmer, Steele looked into Romulus' eyes. He saw an inhuman depth and hollowness to them. Steele had seen eyes like that before.

Augustus.

Those were Augustus' eyes when Augustus was plugged into patterner mode. Steele looked for cables. But if Romulus had patterner cables they would be under that bronze collar and those long gauntlets on his forearms.

There was no saluting.

Romulus opened with a wide back swing, which left a huge opening under his raised arm.

Careless, Steele thought, dodging the strike. He thrust into the opening.

And now his sword was moving itself sideways.

That's what it felt like. Wasn't even a clash. Steele's blade was just sliding off in the wrong direction with Romulus' inhumanly fast parry.

Just like that. Fate turned in an instant.

Steele felt soft wet heat lining either edge of the wound opening in his side. The pain lagged behind the cut. Blood was leaving his head.

Then there was the pain.

A hit. Something felt like a hit. But it was a stab in his midriff. Steele couldn't inhale. Couldn't move his diaphragm. Romulus' sword was in it.

And there went the lights.

Steele landed heavily on his back. His head cracked on the ground. He moved his mouth but couldn't form words. Tried to spit. Tried to breathe.

Romulus strutted a wide circle around his fallen opponent soliciting a decision from the crowd. He milked the moment. Held his thumb pointing parallel with the ground, looking to every last one of the spectators, as if their vote counted.

And maybe it did.

The chant unified, became one creature with many heads, demanding, *Vi-ve! Vi-ve!*

They wanted Steele to live.

After an eternity the hand moved.

Thumb up.

Romulus stood over Steele. "I grant you life. I grant you freedom. Go home to your woman, gladiator."

Romulus then turned his face up to the sky. "*Merrimack,* collect your man."

"*Shit!*" Calli cried.

Down on the planet, a Roman medibot was stabbing Red Cross flags into the sand to plot a box around Steele.

Tactical cried, "We have a hole!"

The opening was visible on the tactical display. A shaft had appeared in the arena's protective energy dome, through which a displacement extraction might be possible.

Commander Ryan turned to Calli. "Captain! It's a Trojan horse!"

"*I want the horse!*" Calli cried. "Dingo. Collect Steele the same way we collected Nox. Nothing touches this ship."

Dingo immediately arranged for an isolation capsule to be equipped with a full trauma rig, nanite scanners, and bomb sniffers. The capsule was cast outboard of *Merrimack* and outside of her inertial shell. He called for the ship's Medical Officer to report to the displacement department.

A practicing Riverite, *Merrimack*'s chief Medical Officer Mohsen Shah calmly accepted whatever occurred. But even Mo's river was capable of rapids. It was odd to see a man look serene while moving that quickly.

Mo Shah ran to the displacement department.

In an instant he was down in the arena, standing over Colonel Steele.

Mo Shah was a strange, benign presence on the killing ground, with his unimposing build and beatific face. The bloodthirsty audience greeted his appearance with polite applause.

Mo Shah knelt beside the fallen gladiator, snapped a displacement collar around Steele's neck, and slid a landing disk underneath him. Then he signaled, "*Merrimack*. I am being ready for displacement."

With a thundercrack Doctor Mo Shah and Colonel TR Steele vanished from the arena.

Doctor Shah reported over his com link, "We are being arrived intact in the isolation capsule, Captain."

"Mo! Can you revive Steele?"

"Colonel Steele is not being dead," Mo Shah reported. Then, as impatient as Mo ever got, said, "My patient is requiring all of my attention." Mo's way of saying leave him alone and let him do his job.

Calli clicked off.

A nanite scan had begun the instant Mo Shah and Steele displaced into the isolation capsule.

Dingo Ryan advised quietly, "The nanite scan is clear so far."

Calli nodded, grateful.

The ship's IO, Bradley Zolman, asked, "What if the nanite is programmed to return a null to a sensor?"

"Then we'll see the shape of the nullity," Dingo Ryan assured him. "If there's a nanite in Steele, the scanner will find it."

"I don't think Romulus planted anything on Steele," Calli said.

"Why? *I* would," said Z.

"You get into trouble anticipating the enemy's moves by what you would do," Calli said. "Romulus doesn't think like normal people. What he values are power, glory, and Claudia. Not in that order."

"Then what does Romulus get out of this stunt?"

"That." Calli nodded at the visual feed from the arena.

The crowd was on its collective feet, dancing. Music rocked. Confetti rained. Flower petals fluttered down. A light show dazzled overhead.

Romulus lifted his arms up and wide, collecting the adoration, to chants of *"Romulus Deus!"*

✳ ✳ ✳ ✳ ✳

15 Aprilis 2448
Xerxes
Centauri Star System
Near Space

Romulus returned to his Xerxes ship, energized. He could do anything. The first night of games had been a spectacular success. Only the powerful could afford to be merciful. He had shown his power and his mercy. He had established his omnipotence.

He had left his data spiders here in his Xerxes searching every known database for clues to where Claudia was.

He had to find her quickly. He couldn't bear the thought of her continuing to suffer as he had suffered.

His *medici* had given him tools to extract the nanites from himself. He could restore Claudia to health with those tools. It was only a matter of finding her.

He checked his search engine's progress. The search was complete.

The data spiders had located Claudia's remains.

Romulus staggered back from the console. He couldn't breathe. Couldn't think. He fell to his knees then forward onto his hands. Coughed into the deck.

Everything was colorless, tasteless, useless.

She was gone. He couldn't save her.

Even he could not bring back the dead.

He got up. Steadied himself on his feet. Breathed volcanic breaths.
He could not bring back the dead.
But he could add more dead.

18 April 2448
U.S. Space Battleship *Merrimack*
Centauri Star System
Near Space

Jose Maria de Cordillera, on board the *Merrimack,* received a resonant hail from his home world.

Terra Rica was a rich, lightly populated planet, a private colony
founded by the wealthy Cordillera family from old Spain. Its habitable
zone was wide. Its atmosphere and waterways were famously clean. Terra
Rica was a paradise.

Jose Maria beheld his niece's face on the resonator. AnaLuisa was at
the controls of her sky yacht. Jose Maria had given her the yacht for her
birthday.

Something was wrong with her face. Even as Jose Maria tried to make
out the dark marks on her cheek, they popped and she jerked. In a blink,
the dark spots had doubled their size. So did a crusty patch on the front
of her shirt.

AnaLuisa blinked tears. Her voice was unsteady. "Tio Jose Maria, I,
oh, this is it."

Jose Maria breathed, "*Corazon.*"

AnaLuisa sobbed. "Do not send medical aid. They—these things—
they are not biologic. Do not send anyone. Do not come. Do not let anyone come. Make everyone go. This started ten minutes ago. They are
doubling, I think. Every minute. I think this is Jericho."

There was a white blank instant during which Jose Maria's mind refused to acknowledge the ultimate nightmare. Something that doubled
itself every minute, something as small as a gram, could consume the
world in eighty minutes. The world would cease to support human life
sooner than that.

The Jericho protocol was the procedure for global evacuation in case
of an aggressive contagion.

AnaLuisa gave way to a moment of crying, then steadied herself. "I do not know how it came in. The air filter does not work now. Everything adjacent to a particle turns like this." She pointed to the crusts on her face. Then gave a squeak. The grey scabs popped on her face and doubled.

Jose Maria heard a cracking noise, of something much larger, breaking. He saw AnaLuisa's hair move, lift.

The sky yacht's windscreen had broken. Fresh air was coming into the pilot's cabin.

Contaminated air was swirling out.

"*Corazon*. Halt your forward progress."

AnaLuisa brought the sky yacht to a stationary position in the air.

Jose Maria opened another resonator and signaled the Terra Rican Home Guard. "Geometric contagion. Factor 2. Period sixty seconds. On my authority, Jericho."

"*Don* Cordillera! Are you sure?"

"My sister's child is at point zero. I am sure." Jose Maria gave the Home Guard the coordinates of the sky yacht.

He watched AnaLuisa gasping. Talked to her. Not sure what he was saying. She fumbled for an oxygen mask. Kicked and collapsed over sideways in her harness.

A tap sounded at Jose Maria's cabin hatch with a tentative voice. "Sorry to disturb you *Don* Cordillera. The captain wishes to inform you of emergency broadcasts from Terra Rica. *Don* Cordillera?"

The hatch edged open. The Marine peered in. Saw that Jose Maria de Cordillera was already aware of the emergency.

Jose Maria kept vigil over his niece. She wasn't moving. The contagion doubled eight more times before the Home Guard got a displacement cordon around the sky yacht.

Survivable displacement required three points of correspondence: the beginning point, the destination, and the thing in transit.

Displacement without a destination was annihilation.

Annihilation was required here.

The visual feed went dark the instant the Home Guard displaced the sky yacht, along with the air around it.

The yacht and its infection, beautiful AnaLuisa, and anyone else on board ceased to exist.

The Home Guard called for a planetwide evacuation as they searched for other points of contagion.

Most Terra Ricans kept displacement disks and collars in their home

First Aid kits. They need only request removal to an orbital shelter and wait their turn.

Air traffic control was routing all air/space craft to exit the atmosphere away from the prevailing winds around the site of the contagion in the northern hemisphere.

More points of contagion were detected as they grew from specks to a distinguishable size. Displacement techs targeted them, along with a wide space around them, and displaced them out.

Captain Carmel invited Jose Maria to the space battleship's command deck. *Merrimack* couldn't go to Terra Rica. This gun platform would not be drawn away from Romulus this close to Earth. But Calli put all of *Merrimack*'s resources at *Don* Cordillera's disposal for synthesizing input from Terra Rica's satellite feeds and directing displacement units to sites of contagion in the far star system.

Jose Maria identified hot spots in the planet's atmosphere and relayed the spatial coordinates to the Terra Rican Home Guard for removal.

A satellite located a hot spot on the water—a floating boulder, rolling on the waves. Doubling and splitting. The Home Guard displaced 500 metric tons of water out along with the boulders to make sure they got all of it.

Jose Maria located a cluster in a cloud in the wake of his niece's sky yacht. The Home Guard targeted the cluster and a great volume of cloud around it, and displaced it. A sound like thunder clapped with its vanishing.

Then the emergency channel quieted, except for the minute-by-minute report of negative sightings.

The contagion was possibly eradicated, but the exodus continued. The evacuation mandated by the Jericho protocol was still in effect.

Mathematically, this contagion—it had to be a manufactured nanovirus—could solidify the planet in eighty minutes.

A true calculation of the contagion's progression hinged on more variables, including how many original seeds were present.

To double itself the nanovirus would require contact with an equal mass. A nanite couldn't recreate itself out of nothing.

Another outbreak within a cloud flashed onto the sensors. It was quickly isolated and displaced.

Another mass appeared on the planet surface. It appeared as a great black and silver gray rock. The mass was already large when the Home Guard located it. It lurched, increasing, but not to twice its size. It might be that the interior mass was cannibalizing itself and only the nanites on the surface of the mass actually increased their numbers.

The Home Guard displaced it out. There would be time to study the recordings and determine the infection's exact progression when the emergency was over.

There followed another lull in the sightings. All watchers remained vigilant for other eruptions.

An orbital monitor reported, "Sighting. Forty-one point twenty north by seventy-three point seventy-four west, elevation two kilometers. Station Omega Nine, you are in range. Take it out."

Station Omega Nine displaced the airborne mass.

And waited.

Watching.

Fifteen minutes passed. Another outbreak should have shown up by now.

The monitors of the Home Guard dared exchange a few tentative hopeful grins.

On the command deck of the *Merrimack,* Jose Maria de Cordillera quickly reviewed all the scans from the Terra Rican monitoring stations. He became aware that all his input came from surface scans.

He didn't have a deep scan. Of course a nanite would need to pass through the atmosphere to go deep. It would have left a surface trail downward.

Unless it had been inserted deep to begin with.

Jeffrey, on first watch at the tactical station, spoke. "Captain? Mr. Cordillera? Problem, I think."

Jose Maria saw it. A color change in the northern ocean.

Tactical reported, "I have upward motion."

Everyone on deck could see it now. Something moved below the ocean swirls. Like a leviathan rising.

The entire ocean floor was lifting up, a vast, pocked, silver-black crust. It broke surface, rocked on the waves.

And doubled.

Air pockets burst and the wide masses cracked.

The Terra Rican Home Guard displaced vast swaths of the continental mass and sent them into the void as fast as they could target them.

It was like shoveling an avalanche.

Fragments tumbled between the waves. Doubled.

More rock masses like lava islands floated up to the surface, broke under internal pressure. Fractured. And doubled.

Satellite surveillance was losing visuals.

The air itself was solidifying.

That was the end of using escape ships. There was no clear path out of the atmosphere. Then there was no atmosphere. Evacuation was all by displacement.

And then there was nothing.

Orbital platforms offered supplies to all ships that made it clear to the vacuum. The supply platforms could send oxygen, food, anything the evacuees needed, as soon as they knew that their ship wasn't contaminated.

They knew quickly.

Merrimack watched through the lens of a satellite in wide orbit around Terra Rica, beyond the highest reaches of the ionosphere.

The planet contracted.

"*Madre de Dios,*" Jose Maria breathed, horrified.

Jeffrey at Tactical saw what Jose Maria saw. "Those orbitals aren't safe, sir."

Jose Maria called over the resonator, "Home Guard! All ships, all stations, leave orbit, best speed. Go. If anyone has FTL capability, tell them to jump. Jump now. Get everyone clear of the planet."

All the satellite feeds went dark.

It took nine minutes for a satellite stationed in close orbit around Terra Rica's sun to relay images of the planet's final contraction and its explosion.

19 April 2448
U.S. Space Battleship *Merrimack*
Centauri Star System
Near Space

Rear Admiral John Alexander Farragut took a shuttle from Base Carolina on Earth out to join *Merrimack* in the Centauri system where Jose Maria de Cordillera had taken refuge.

Farragut came to stand by his old friend in his darkest hour. Jose Maria had been sword master on the *Merrimack* back in the days of the Hive threat, when the ship was under John Farragut's command.

Condolences rolled in from all parts of the civilized galaxy.

Like all heads of state, Romulus issued a public statement on the destruction of Terra Rica. He was not a legitimate head of state, and his address was the only one that did not offer solace to the survivors.

Romulus called on the peoples of all the civilized worlds to witness the hubris of the people from the Land of the Rich. The Terra Ricans had created things that ought never be conceived. See them now brought low by their own God-playing.

He said, in epitaph, "Live by the nanite. Die by the nanite."

Calli watched the broadcast. After several stunned moments she said, "He's implying that Terra Rica did this to itself."

"He's not implying," John Farragut said. "He came right out and said it."

No one had identified the contagion as a nanite before Romulus' statement.

Jose Maria said, "The initial particle that began the holocaust appeared inside the airship I gave to my sister's child for her birthday. How does a nanite get from wherever it was manufactured into a moving vessel in the air without first contaminating everything around it?"

"A patterner with a grudge figured out a delivery system," Farragut said.

Jose Maria nodded. "This was not a laboratory accident. This contagion did not get loose. It was planted. And it is my fault."

John Farragut lifted a hand as if stopping a bus. "You had me right up till that last part. Don't get all Catholic on me now, Jose Maria. It's not your fault. Don't you believe it."

"But I do believe it, young admiral. I delivered the nanites that tortured Romulus and his sister."

"Those nanites wouldn't've done a damned thing to Romulus if he hadn't'a killed his own daddy. So you go say your Hail Marys and take a bath in holy water and get back in the game. I can't stop this monster without you. *Get up.* I need you."

Jose Maria bowed his head. Smiled weakly. A tear slid down the side of his nose. "Sir."

"Good. You can help Targeting get us a lock on Romulus."

"Is the man then a lawful military target?"

"I'm pushing for it. Make sure we're ready when that call comes down."

✳ ✳ ✳ ✳ ✳

The isolation capsule that contained TR Steele and Doctor Mohsen Shah had been pronounced free of any contagion, nanite, or threat. The Intelligence Officer, Colonel Bradley Zolman refused to allow it into *Merrimack*'s dock.

Captain Carmel took her IO discreetly aside. "Z. You're borderline insubordinate. Why?"

"Isn't it obvious, sir?"

"No. That capsule and my men are clean. They've been scanned for every known threat. *You* scanned them. You're thorough."

"Every *known* threat," Z repeated back at her. "It has to be that Romulus has created something new. Something we can't detect. Why else would he send Steele and the doctor back if they weren't rigged?"

"Because he *can*. Romulus doesn't have any interest in destroying *Merrimack*. He just wanted to go into the ring and play gladiator against Adamas. Now either find a booby trap on that isolation capsule or let my officers board."

Colonel TR Steele advanced from the dock and came to stiff attention before his captain. His eyes focused a million miles past her, as if he expected to be shot.

Captain Carmel said coldly, "Your court martial will wait until the present crisis passes, Colonel Steele. Z, bring this Marine up to speed."

Then the captain turned her back on him, and quit the dock.

Kerry Blue. In officer's country. Looking for Colonel Steele. No idea what she was going say when she saw that man face-to-face. Her CO. Her husband. Was there anything to say?

I cheated on you with your best friend. I thought you were dead.

She felt as if there were a burrowing animal loose in her gut. Her face burned. Then it felt like ice.

She'd known he wasn't dead. Deep down, she'd known.

Shouldn't say anything.

What if it got back to him somehow else? About her and Cain.

She froze up altogether as the voice sounded at her back.

"You're out of bounds, Flight Sergeant."

She inhaled quick. Forgot how to exhale. Wanted to throw up. She turned. The face she so desperately wanted and so dreaded to see. Eyes like blue ice. He knew. Oh, he knew.

That look said it all. His face was stone. Betrayed, pissed off, angry, disappointed stone. Kerry Blue felt herself turn white. Opened her mouth to say something difficult.

"Thomas, I—"

Up went Steele's forefinger. "Don't."

"But—"

He stopped her. Whole palm up now. Didn't want to hear it.

Her world shredded around her.

TR Steele spoke, a low growl, and this would be the last word on it. "Kerry Blue, I know who I married."

✳ ✳ ✳ ✳ ✳

19 Aprilis 2448
Xerxes
Centauri Star System
Near Space

Romulus brooded, pacing long strides, restless inside his fortress Xerxes.

Woe to Terra Rica!

It wasn't enough, destroying Terra Rica. It wasn't nearly enough. It didn't bring Claudia back.

Claudia was still dead.

Done was done.

He threw back his head and screamed to the universe, *"NO!"*

Hands shaking, eyes blurred with tears, he plugged into patterner mode. The leads rattled as he made the final connections behind his neck. There must be an answer in the vast information available to him.

The barrage of knowledge struck. He staggered, fell to his knees, almost too angry to see the patterns.

Clarity came to him as a double-edged blade.

The fact remained: Romulus could not bring back the dead.

But there was another question he hadn't seen before, and it had an answer.

I can make her not to have died.

I will move heaven and Earth and all the worlds in between. I will move space and time! My will be done!

11

TIME TRAVEL WAS A FACT. The Xi tablet was testament to that—a twenty-billion-year-old artifact in a fifteen-billion-year-old universe. Time travel was possible. It was only left for Romulus to bend it to his will.

The Xi tablet had been found on a dead world in a star system not distant from Earth, 82 Eridani III.

"Where is the Xi tablet now?" Romulus asked his search engine on board his Xerxes.

The Xerxes responded, "The Smithsonian."

So the Yanks had the Xi tablet.

"Assemble for my review all resources relating to the Xi tablet. Include tangential references."

He paced animatedly as he waited.

The Xi tablet had gone back in time. How?

The Xerxes quickly assembled the responsive data into one repository. As a patterner Romulus could sift through all the information and identify significant connections.

Sometimes the motion of a single molecule made a difference, and its amplifications rippled out across the stars.

All data paths converged to a critical point: an instant in time when a rift existed and then ceased to be.

It had happened in the galactic Deep End, inside a globular cluster of over a million stars, designation IC9870986.

The Myriad.

*   *   *

The Xi tablet originated on an alien world inside the Myriad cluster. Somehow, the Xi tablet ended up on 82 Eridani III—a quarter of the way across the galaxy—billions of years before the tablet was ever formed.

Now the Myriad was falling into itself, feeding a black hole from which no information escaped.

Something was locked inside that black hole that could not exist in this reality. Romulus needed to pinpoint the instant and place where time broke.

And get himself there.

Romulus unplugged his cables. Quitting patterner mode was always an unsettling, stomach-lurching downshift. His thoughts tumbled.

His search told him he was missing information. It also told him where that information was housed.

The United States Space Battleship *Merrimack* had been in the Myriad when something triggered the globular cluster's collapse.

Romulus contacted a human attendant. "We have a loyalist on the *Merrimack,* do we not?"

"Yes, Caesar. She's a Flight Sergeant in the U.S. Fleet Marine."

"Can she mine a database?"

"She is Roman, Caesar."

Of course.

"Get me all the records from *Merrimack* created during *Merrimack*'s maneuvers in the globular cluster Myriad in 2443."

"It shall be done, Caesar."

Romulus plugged back into his data bank. There was something else he'd marked while he was prowling the huge store of information. He hadn't been looking for it. He was surprised to find it.

He disconnected, almost laughing.

Numa Pompeii has a patterner!

Romulus smiled through a throbbing headache.

And a Farragut.

Everything was happening for a reason. This was destiny.

Gods were not ruled by Creation.

✳ ✳ ✳ ✳ ✳

20 Aprilis 2448
Bagheera
Centauri Star System
Near Space

On board the pirate ship *Bagheera*, Orissus growled, "Cinna, do something with him!"

Nox looked left and right. No one else in this compartment but Cinna and Orissus.

Orissus was talking about him, Nox.

"What?" Nox said.

Orissus snarled. "What do you mean *what?* Art thou mad?"

"He is," Cinna told Orissus. Mad, Cinna meant.

"I am?" Nox said. "Why do you think so?"

"Night terrors," Cinna said. "You've been having them. Hysterical screaming for five minutes then you go back to sleep."

"*He* goes back to sleep!" Orissus shouted. "*I* don't!"

"Sorry," Nox mumbled and moved apart to a compartment where no one was. This chamber used to be the ambassador's office.

Nox didn't so much sit down as he crumpled to the deck.

He pulled a dagger.

What is a conscience and can I cut it out?

He found tears on his face. "Am I dying, *Bagheera?*"

The ship heard him. Advised him that it did not understand the question. *Bagheera* told Nox the question was ambiguous, as all things that live can be said to be dying. "Please restate query," the ship said.

"Forget it," Nox said.

"Query deleted," *Bagheera* said.

Bagheera operated in full stealth, orbiting the artificial world of Beta Centauri, where Romulus was celebrating his return.

Numa Pompeii wanted his assassins close to Romulus.

Nox got up from the deck. He dyed his hair, his skin, and his eyes brown. He displaced down to the planet. He could see the coliseum from here. Could hear the crowd.

The games hadn't paused in mourning for the tragedy at Terra Rica. The flag over the coliseum flew at full staff.

Nox had known a Terra Rican, a famous one. Jose Maria de Cordillera.

Very important, so naturally he'd been a guest at Chief Justice John Knox Farragut Senior's house. Nox remembered *Don* Cordillera as a gracious man. Nox would've liked Jose Maria if he hadn't been such a good friend of that other man named John Farragut.

Nox wasn't mourning Terra Rica either. Not a lot. Most of the people had got out. They lost everything, but they got out. The loss was mostly a whole lot of expensive real estate owned by a few overprivileged people.

Nox had grown up overprivileged. He didn't really pity them.

The coliseum on Beta Centauri was filled to climbing-room-only, even though Romulus wasn't there in person. Romulus had flooded the arena and was staging sea battles in it. There were live sharks in the water.

Nox fell into a tavern to watch the battles on the monitors, drink a lot, and lose money.

He walked out of the tavern late.

As he was losing consciousness, he hoped that these were his brothers snatching him off the street and bundling him into the back of a transport.

No such deal.

When he was hauled out of the transport, Nox was either still really really drunk and having hallucinations or he actually was in the presence of Romulus, Caesar Pretender of the Roman Empire.

Nox stumbled as he was pushed into the Presence.

Romulus Julius was the finest looking man that bioengineers could possibly design. His deep brown eyes and full indulgent mouth stopped just short of being sybaritic. His build was athletic. He looked butch and lordly, even dressed up in that big lacy Elizabethan collar and those voluminous sleeves with lace cuffs.

Romulus greeted Nox, "*Ave.*"

Nox was not intimidated by emperors. His own father was a Zeusly being, and Nox currently took orders directly from Caesar Numa Pompeii. Nox wasn't in a groveling mood for this guy.

Guards scanned Nox for weapons. They took his daggers, then they withdrew, leaving Nox facing Romulus.

Nox looked left and right, then squinted at Romulus. It seemed impossible that they should be alone together. There had to be a force field between them, but he couldn't see its shimmer. "Did you know I have orders to assassinate you?"

Romulus said, "And did you know that you are about to get blinded on the road to Damascus?"

For a moment Nox feared he was about to have his eyes gouged out. But Nox had a Bible-thumping father, so he recognized the reference.

Saul of Tarsus had been blinded by the glory of the true God on the road to Damascus and transformed from Christian-killing Roman zealot into epistle-writing Christian zealot.

So Nox was about to receive a revelation.

Romulus said, "I want Cinna."

"No," Nox said.

"I intend no harm. I need Cinna alive and well. He needs me. *You* need me."

"Do I?"

"How do I say it in Americanese: You been done wrong. Very wrong, Nox Antonius."

Something reverberated inside Nox. His face felt hot. It tore Nox up to correct Romulus, "That's not my name."

Antonius, Nox's Roman family name, had been stripped from him. He was outcast now. He was no one.

"I am Caesar, and you are who I say you are, Nox Antonius."

The sound of his Roman name filled Nox with a warmth like a hot drink to one too cold even to shiver.

Romulus went on, "You were not made *damnati* under a legitimate Caesar."

Oh, the snake in Eden wasn't this seductive.

Romulus said, "I need your patterner."

That woke Nox up cold from his pretty, pretty dream. "No. I won't betray my brothers." He spread his arms, offering himself. "Do your worst."

"I tell you I mean Cinna only the best. We have a bond. Cinna and I."

Romulus unlaced his wide collar and pushed up his full sleeves.

Patterner cables extended from Romulus' neck and forearms.

Afraid he was gawking, Nox cried, "Can't be!"

"Am," said Romulus, calmly smoothing his sleeves back down. "Now, I shall tell you what you believe happened on the morning you hazed Cinna."

"I know what happened," Nox said. "I was there." Didn't want to relive it.

"Do not interrupt. On that morning, you and your squad took Cinna to the top of Widow's Edge. You told him to jump off the cliff. It was a ritual hazing. Of course Cinna jumped. The net that was meant to catch him failed to deploy. The incident was caught on satellite surveillance. Funny that a satellite camera just happened to be focused on Widow's Edge at the precise moment on the single instance that the net *ever* failed."

Nox nodded, sour. "Funny."

"For Cinna's supposed death, you and your squad were drummed out of Legio Persus, stripped of your Roman citizenship, and declared *damnati*. Cinna was salvaged from the bottom of the cliff and fashioned into a patterner. Or that's what you believe."

Nox's throat was tight. He squeezed out words. "That's pretty much what happened."

"No. You're wrong. The failure of the net to deploy was not an accident."

"I know," Nox said wearily. And *merda*, tears were pushing their way out. "Some jackaster jammed a rock in the net mechanism for the hell of it." He had to sniffle. That was weak.

Romulus said, "The rock was definitely jammed in there, but no, it was not the random act of a vandal. It was the very deliberate act of a slave named Baucus on orders from his master, Numa Pompeii."

Wet eyelids opened wide. *"Caesar Numa?"*

"Pretender Numa. That criminal slug is not Caesar."

Romulus was speaking terrible, amazing things. "Numa required a young Roman of unquestioned loyalty. Cinna's willingness to take the fatal step proved that he valued honor over life. Numa needed Cinna to appear to die so Numa wouldn't be caught carving up one of his own loyal citizens. And Numa also wanted you—you specifically, Nox Antonius—to take the blame for Cinna's death."

"Me?"

Nox had been no one remarkable back then. Just another ephebe, a young new soldier in Legio Persus. Okay, that was what Nox wanted to think he was. Nox was different. He'd been born in America. He'd been born a Farragut.

Romulus went on. "Squads are always formed in eights. Tell me how was it that there happened to be an opening in your squad for Cinna?"

Nox opened his mouth. He couldn't say it. And he got the idea that Romulus already knew. Nox's squad had numbered seven because Rubeus Tunica Antonius had been stung by a sand needle. Rubeus Tunica hadn't felt it. The brothers hadn't known it happened until Rubeus failed to wake up and the *medici* found the sand needle in his foot.

"Remarkable that your brother Rubeus Tunica didn't feel the sting," Romulus said. "Sand needles are ungodly painful."

Nox was stunned. He knew he was supposed to ask the next question. "Why didn't Rubeus Tunica feel the needle?"

"Anesthetic."

"*Why?*"

"Because it was murder."

Nox sputtered. "*Why?*"

"To create an opening in your squad to fit in a new ephebe to be hazed. Are you not picking up the *pattern* here yet? *Your* squad, Nox Antonius. Yours. Numa wanted *you* out. Because you used to be John Farragut's brother."

Nox appreciated the past tense. He still cringed at the name. "Why not just kill me!"

"Too late. You were already Roman. Numa never wanted you to have Roman citizenship, and he couldn't renounce your citizenship once it had been bestowed *by me*. You came to Rome *in my reign*.

"Numa maneuvered you into a circumstance to have you drummed out of the Empire—my Empire—in disgrace. The same stroke also gave him a loyal, young, and nearly dead Roman to fashion into a patterner. Did you not think it odd that Cinna survived that fall at all let alone that he survived in any state to be made into a logical mastermind?"

Nox couldn't answer. It had seemed unbelievable. But it had happened, so that had been the end of disbelieving.

And a satellite just happening to record Cinna's jump—*that* had always gnawed at him. There was something cosmically unfair about that.

Romulus was telling him now that the satellite had been positioned there specifically to record that instant when Cinna went over the edge.

Nox recognized his cue to ask the question. His throat was dry. He cleared it. Rasped, "How did Cinna survive?"

"There was an arrester hook from another satellite prepositioned and standing by to keep the jumper's skull from hitting the ground. Numa expected you to run home to the United States and pick up your life as John Knox Farragut Junior."

With a chill, Nox remembered the option had been offered to him.

"But instead of running away home, you stood damnation with the rest of your squad. I admire that. And then you got creative. You attempted to acquire the specs to a Xerxes class ship."

Attempt? "I did acquire them."

"Amazingly easy, wasn't it?"

Nox drew in a breath. "Yes," he whispered, cold. His skin felt to be crawling.

"You must know you only acquired those specs with imperial knowledge and permission. When you actually succeeded in hijacking a Xerxes—astonishing fact, that—Numa made you his own tool. And he inserted his patterner back into your damned squad to monitor you. Oh. About that. Have a care for your brother. Cinna has a resonant off switch. He doesn't know it. He is programmed not to be able to detect it. Numa could have terminated Cinna at any moment."

Nox felt cold. "Can he? Terminate Cinna?"

"Not any more. I took the liberty of whiting out the trigger harmonic."

A resonant harmonic and its complement canceled each other out.

"Cinna should have been able to figure out this plot, but Cinna is hard-coded not to be able to see it. But you, Nox Antonius, you should have known that Numa would not send a patterner into the field with a band of outlaws without a means to shut him off."

Nox couldn't talk. Yes, he should have known.

"You are a dedicated man," Romulus said. "I am not asking you to break your vow to serve Rome. But you must recognize that you are not actually serving Rome now. You're serving Numa. Not the same thing at all. He used you. I notice that once he brought you and your brothers under his command he never restored your citizenship, your *gens*, your name. You and your brothers are all still *damnati*. How does that feel?"

Nox was reeling as from body blow after body blow after head shot. He felt about to vomit.

Romulus hit him again with another question. "Do you like your life?"

The question landed like an upper cut.

Winded, in blinding pain, Nox fish-mouthed, open and shut. He pictured all the men he'd murdered. He choked out, "No."

"Ever wish you could do it all over differently?"

Nox coughed. Blurted, "Only when I'm breathing. You know we do! Wishing is useless *merda*! You can't change what is!"

"I can," Romulus said.

Nox stared at him.

"I can change what is. I can change what was."

"Are you offering to restore our citizenship?"

"I can do better. I can make it so you never lost it. Get Cinna in on this interview."

"This is a trap."

"Of course it's a trap. You want to be in it. It serves you. It serves your brothers. It serves me. It serves Rome."

"Why does a patterner need another patterner?"

Romulus smiled. "I am told that there is something to be said in favor of redundance. As you might guess, there is no margin for error on this quest of mine."

Not sure at all, Nox contacted Cinna.

Cinna consented to come.

And Romulus spun them a dream. A life in which Cinna didn't fall, and the brothers were not driven out of Rome, and the Ninth Circle never formed.

It required Romulus to go back in time.

Nox watched Cinna getting angry. Finally Cinna interrupted Romulus. "You're suggesting it can be done. It can't."

"I told him that," Nox said.

"You're not a patterner," Romulus told Nox.

"*I* am," said Cinna. "It can't be done. It would be a time loop. If I go back and prevent myself from becoming a patterner, then how do I know how to go back? It's a paradox. You are full of shit."

"You are not a patterner at the moment. You're not connected. You're speaking as a simple man without all the information."

A tremor. A hesitation. "I could be," Cinna allowed. "I am listening, *domni*."

"I have located a break point. Something happened then and there. A definite break in temporal continuity. The universe pulled the figurative blinds on it."

"Meaning what?" Cinna said. "Literally?"

"There is a star system where a time break occurred. A black hole masked over the break."

"The Myriad," Nox heard himself saying.

"Yes. You would have heard of it," Romulus said.

Well, yeah, John Alexander Farragut exists at the center of the universe, so why not, Nox thought. Refrained from saying that part aloud.

Instead Nox said, "You think that when the Arran spaceship went through the Rim Gate in the Myriad it changed something other than forming the black hole."

"I know it did. If I get to that break point in 2443 then I can rewrite everything going forward."

"If you get back to—!" Nox lost control. He was shouting at Romulus. "That's the whole colossal trick, isn't it? HOW DO YOU GO BACK IN TIME?"

"I recognize your inability to grasp the concept. I will be tolerant," Romulus said. "When the Arran went through the Rim Gate, the Rim Gate collapsed. But the back door is still open. The other end of that wormhole is still there. It's in the 82 Eridani system, near a planet known as Xi."

"It's there? You mean no one else *noticed?*"

"The wormhole in the 82 Eridani system is a known oddity. There is a LEN observation station positioned near it, left over from a study that ran out of funding. The LEN sent a probe into the Xi gate. The probe ceased registering the instant it entered the anomaly. Organizations who fund such things don't like it when their funding disappears into unreadable holes. The observation station is still there, observing nothing."

"I will go through the wormhole at 82 Eridani and come out in 2443. Events flowing forward from the seventh of June 2443 will fall differently. Numa will not become Caesar, and he will not cause a slave to jam a rock into the mechanism in the cliff. You, Cinna, will not fall from Widow's Edge. You will not be butchered into a patterner. You and your brothers will not be drummed out in disgrace and disowned. You will be honorable Romans in *my* Empire."

There was no expression on Cinna's face but for tears streaming from his eyes. "Caesar, that is a lovely fairy tale, but I know you won't succeed because you are here talking to me now. If you tried, you failed."

"The fact that we are talking now means only that I haven't done it yet in this time stream. Once I go, this conversation will exist only as a memory of mine. The events of the past five years will persist like a phantom limb of mine that's been removed. Your life will have had a different course. Your nightmare will never materialize. You will have the proverbial clean slate."

Romulus offered a data reservoir to Cinna. "View this as only you can."

Cinna regarded the data reservoir as he might a poison pill.

Romulus saw his fear. "Have you something to lose?"

Cinna plugged in.

Nox saw Cinna's eyes get that empty look of a patterner adrift in an ocean of information. Cinna murmured as from a great depth, "It's a game of moebius chess. Dangerous."

"Dangerous," Nox echoed, for Romulus to note.

"Then we play carefully," Romulus said.

"How will Cinna get you back in time if he never becomes a patterner? Cinna?"

"Don't speak to him," Romulus said. "Your words are glaciers."

Cinna reached behind his head and unplugged his cables. He bent over. Looked like he might be sick. Cinna spoke thickly toward the floor, "This is conceivable. Brother, we want to do this."

Nox was suddenly trembling, caught between impossible hope and certain terror.

Romulus said, "You have been hideously used by the man pretending to be Imperator of Rome. I shan't hold your honor hostage to your cooperation. You are honorable Romans. I will publically restore your status. Contingent on nothing. I know you hesitate to foreswear an allegiance already sworn, but the fact is you were my men first. You became Numa's men under a fraud. You are still my men. I already have your oaths. I shall set things right.

"That instant in time you so desperately want back? You shall have it."

Nox stared at him in awe and wonder. Romulus owned him now.

"Greater than this," Romulus went on. "When I succeed, Rome will not surrender to the U.S. *The Subjugation will never happen.*"

The Subjugation was only the most humiliating, devastating event in Roman history. When the shredded remains of Roman might walked under racked spears, placing themselves under U.S. command.

Did he really have the power to change that?

Romulus was asking, "What do you say?"

Nox found his voice. "I exist to defend Rome. Everywhere. Always."

12

21 April 2448

WHILE THE REST OF THE civilized galaxy offered support to the survivors of Terra Rica, Romulus held court on Beta Centauri, presiding over the games that celebrated his return.

Romulus opened the next day's games by exonerating the pirates of the Ninth Circle.

He voided the order of condemnation and made their excommunication a nullity. It never happened.

Romulus claimed that all their reported atrocities had been committed by direct order of Numa Pompeii and so rested on Numa's head. Romulus solemnly returned the brothers' names onto the *deme* rolls one by one. He included Nox Antonius.

Calli had tried to tell John Farragut that his younger brother was working for Numa Pompeii. Farragut hadn't wanted to believe it.

He believed it now.

He had just got back from the Centauri system to his office on Earth when the news hit.

"Get me fucking Numa Pompeii on the resonator!"

He startled the whole floor of Base Carolina. You never heard that kind of language out of Rear Admiral John Farragut. Most of the base personnel had never seen him angry. Farragut emerged from his office like an old-style missile hauling itself up a silo. He stormed up the corridor in a wrath-of-Achilles kind of mad to his aide's office.

The whites of Farragut's blue eyes flared, impatient.

The aide said, "Finding him, sir. Numa is not in the imperial palace on Palatine."

"Then where's *Gladiator*?"

"Checking, sir. Okay, the Roman battlefort *Gladiator* is—" Paused to make sure. "In Centauri space. Not answering hails."

✳ ✳ ✳ ✳ ✳

21 Aprilis 2448
Roman Battlefort *Gladiator*
Centauri Star System
Near Space

Caesar Numa Pompeii reclined in the dining chamber of his Roman battlefort *Gladiator* when his exec hailed him over the intercom, *"Domni."*

Numa responded immediately. "Tell me that little ground rodent is dead."

Gladiator was orbiting Beta Centauri, guns ready, waiting for Romulus to show himself one more time. It would be his last appearance ever.

"Negative, *domni*," said Portia Arrianus. "Rear Admiral Farragut demands an audience."

"How does one imagine that Caesar takes calls from an American two-star admiral?"

"He's here, *domni*."

"Here? *Merrimack* is in the Centauri system?"

"No, *domni*. Rear Admiral Farragut arrived on a shuttle. He's docked."

"He's on *Gladiator*? Who let that happen?"

"Domni, it's John Farragut."

As she said it, the roar rose from belowdecks. "Numa!"

John Farragut was *here*.

Numa blinked. "Does he have a sword?"

"I've been advised that he stabbed it into the dock, *domni*."

Heavy, stomping footfalls could be heard, rising from the lower levels.

"What degree of force do you authorize to repel him?" Portia Arrianus requested.

"None. I can take care of myself."

Another bellow. Nearer. "Numa!" Sounded like Farragut was headed to the command deck.

"Here," Numa called wearily from his ship's dining chamber.

Farragut entered the chamber like ball lightning. "Numa, you bastard."

Numa waited, a patient, immobile pile of boulders. "My title is Caesar, you vulgar American hill jack. This ship is Roman territory."

"Rome doesn't have permission to be in this star system," Farragut said. "Centaurus is a LEN protectorate."

"And you're not wearing LEN green," Numa countered. "Don't pretend to be acting for the League of Earth Nations. You have no business here. And I am only here to collect my garbage."

"Where is my brother?"

Numa opened his broad empty hands. "I've lost him. I think he may have turncoated. Again. That is what he is good at."

John Farragut charged in with a fist. Felt the crack, a couple bones giving way. His. Fire lanced up his arm. He felt it in the roots of his teeth.

Farragut was not a small man, but Numa Pompeii was a landmark.

"Broke your hand?" Numa asked mildly.

"Eh—yeah. I think so," Farragut said. His arm felt molten.

Numa pointed to his own jaw. "Titanium."

"Ah." Farragut nodded. Thought he mighta shattered an arm bone. He'd hit Numa hard.

Numa said, "I believe Romulus has seduced your brother and my patterner as well."

"Oh. Good one," Farragut said with a grimace of a smile, eyes watering.

"Do you want the attention of a *medicus*?"

"No," Farragut said. Should've known better. He had a titanium jaw himself. Then, "This really does hurt like a son of a beech tree."

He'd maybe exploded his elbow.

Jewels and gold flashed as Numa snapped his thick fingers. Farragut hadn't noticed the attendant standing by. Numa filled any space he occupied.

At the snap, the attendant produced a medical automaton from a cabinet concealed under the bar.

As the pain washed away from Farragut's arm, his thoughts returned to order. It just now caught up with him exactly what Numa had said. "Your *patterner* changed sides?"

"It appears so." Numa gave a quick glance to the liquor rack. An invitation.

Farragut gave a minute nod.

Numa poured a short Kentucky bourbon for Farragut. Napoleon Brandy for himself.

"They tried to tell me you had one. I didn't believe it. How could you even think of having another patterner created? Numa, did you ever *know* Augustus?"

"I did. And I did install a failsafe in Cinna." He took a long breath and sighed.

Farragut guessed. "It failed."

Numa nodded. "It did. Romulus has a better patterner."

"Romulus *is* a better patterner," Farragut amended.

"No," Numa said. "I heard that tale. I don't believe that sham."

"No. Listen. It's true. Romulus really is a patterner. He's settling scores. He's acting like a madman."

Numa gave a harrumph, a bonfire settling. "That is not an act."

❋ ❋ ❋ ❋ ❋

28 Aprilis 2448
Xerxes
Centauri Star System
Near Space

A Xerxes type ship was programmed to repel or destroy unauthorized boarders. One needed to be introduced in order to gain entrance. Romulus introduced Cinna to his own Xerxes.

Cinna, Nox, and the other brothers of the Ninth Circle still lived on board their own stolen Xerxes, *Bagheera*. They had been exonerated of all their crimes, but they weren't really welcome anywhere.

They would not be pariahs for much longer.

Cinna helped Romulus prepare his Xerxes for his journey that would change everything.

"Once you enter the time gate at 82 Eridani, you will not exist here, Caesar. No one can detect you inside the wormhole, and you won't be able to navigate. You will feel no motion. The sensors will detect nothing of your surroundings. *Merrimack*'s records of Fleet Marines who went through the wormhole indicate it can be extremely unnerving. The episode should last at most a week by your ship's chronometer. But it may be quicker, so stay ready.

"You will come out at the end without warning. The date will be the seventh of June 2443 by the terrestrial calendar. You will instantly meet the Arran messenger ship at the Rim Gate at the edge of the Myriad."

Romulus scowled. "Meet?"

"Collide with," Cinna revised. "It's important that you enter the wormhole with your inertial field already formed into a wide concave surface. The Xerxes' energy shell is designed to slip past objects. We need you to hammer the Arran and move its wreckage away from the wormhole. No piece of the shattered Arran messenger can be allowed to get past you. Nothing must enter the Rim Gate."

"I accept your recommendation," Romulus said.

Cinna then presented Romulus with a heavy slab of lead, the size of a book. "Take this with you. It's your key."

Romulus recognized the artifact from his own research. It was the Xi tablet.

The Xi tablet had been engraved in the Myriad and sent back to 82 Eridani through the same wormhole Romulus was about to travel.

"The Xi tablet knows the way home," Cinna said. "The instant you arrive, history will diverge from what is logged in your data bank. Don't look for the black hole. It will never form.

"*Merrimack* will be nine terrestrial hours away from your position, but she will observe your arrival via the space buoy stationed outside the Rim Gate. You will be in full stealth, but *Merrimack* will observe the Arran messenger crashing into something undetectable—your ship's inertial field."

"Should I destroy the observer buoy?" Romulus asked. He knew the answer. Just wanted to hear it confirmed.

"I advise against it. The image of the Arran's destruction will already be sent. Save your ammunition and give the Yanks no more clues to your presence. The more secret your actions, the less deviation there will be to events as you expect them to unfold. And your ship is lightly armed."

Xerxes ships were built for flight, not fight.

"The more munitions you carry, the lower your threshold velocity. I'm not sure what the right balance should be."

Romulus waved the problem away. "My Xerxes' firepower matters not. I will soon be moving fleets and Legions."

Cinna nodded. "Look for two Roman Legion carriers converging on the

Myriad as you arrive. Their resonant harmonics, signal codes, names of their command personnel, and everything else about them is in your data bank."

"I shall take command of the Legions," Romulus said.

"The patterner Augustus will be flying on point, piloting a Striker. You have the historical record of Augustus' trajectory in your ship's data bank. That trajectory might change as events develop. Secure Augustus' Striker before he can read the new pattern. You have his resonant harmonic."

"If I ping him, I will know exactly where he is," Romulus said.

"Yes. And Augustus will know that someone pinged him, but he won't know who or where you are."

Romulus said, "I will be the only being in the known universe who can get a location on the source of a resonant transmission."

Cinna demurred. "The Hive. Don't forget the Hive. And possibly Constantine Siculus. He's still alive in your target time frame."

Constantine Siculus was a historical monster, who had tried to make himself Caesar. He was dead now.

"Constantine should die sooner," Cinna said. "He knows the Hive harmonics. I think Constantine should be a priority target. At least as important as securing Augustus."

"I recognize the need to remove Constantine," Romulus said. "The problem is that Constantine will be way out in the Deep End of the galaxy when I arrive. He will be nowhere near the Myriad. His lair is months away in the wrong direction from anywhere I want to go. I'm thinking of using a drone to take him out. Assassins are just not to be trusted."

"I'm with you there, Caesar. I've fabricated an appropriate assassin missile for you to deploy against that megalomaniac. Erase Constantine from the game board early. You must be the only one in possession of the Hive harmonics."

Romulus twisted an ironic smile. "We got the harmonics from Constantine. Do you think I'm a megalomaniac?"

Cinna didn't hesitate. "Caesar. You have galactic ambition. You have the ability to restore the Empire. You are the man for the hour. I need to get you back to fix the hour. Greatness is required. Save us."

"I shall. My first act will be to save the sixty-four Legions from Constantine's sabotage."

Constantine Siculus, founder of PanGalactic Industries, had designed and manufactured Rome's devastating killer bots. Most Roman ships of war had carried killer bots as part of their arsenal.

Years ago, when Rome refused to hail Constantine Siculus as Caesar, Constantine detonated all the killer bots, everywhere, instantly, with a resonant trigger.

Sixty-four Legion carriers, with their Legions on board, perished in a single pulse. It was a catastrophe without equal in Roman history.

"My first order, when I arrive in the Myriad in 2443, will be to all Legions to pull the res chambers out of every piece of Constantine's Pan-Galactic crap on board their carriers.

"*My* Legions will not die. Under me, Rome will be strong. The Subjugation will never occur. America will be the Roman province as it was founded. The past five years will take a better course by far."

Cinna picked up his things, ready to return to *Bagheera* and send Romulus to his destiny. "May I ask Caesar a question?"

Romulus nodded to allow it.

"Why did you destroy Terra Rica now, when your journey back to the break point will undo everything that's happened since then?"

"For the same reason I restored your citizenship, Cinna Antonius. I acknowledge the astronomical number of variables in this endeavor. There is a slight but real chance of failure. I did those things now so that, in case I fail, you will at least have your honor and I will at least have my revenge on Jose Maria de Cordillera. But I want better than that for us. Much better."

Cinna's eyes widened in awe. He dropped on one knee and bowed his head. "You won't fail, Caesar," Cinna vowed. "I won't let you."

"I know. Let us begin."

Cinna rose and came to rigid attention. "For strength and honor." He turned smartly and marched through the air lock, back to his pirate Xerxes, *Bagheera*.

Romulus secured his own Xerxes' hatch behind him.

"For Claudia," he said.

✳ ✳ ✳ ✳ ✳

28 April 2448
U.S. Space Battleship *Merrimack*
Centauri Star System
Near Space

Jose Maria de Cordillera now lived as a refugee on board *Merrimack*. There were nations that would welcome him, but a space battleship was the only place he could consider inflicting himself on. "I must not make a target of any place that cannot defend itself against Romulus. I am sorry to imperil you, fair Captain."

Captain Carmel wouldn't have the apology. "Lure him here. We want him." She looked like an elegant predator. She sounded hungry. "Something you need to know, *Don* Cordillera. You and Augustus' nanites didn't drive Romulus mad. Romulus has been a heartless, soulless, conscienceless creature for as long as I've known him. And that's a *while*. Rom never had a real grasp of right and wrong. Right was divinely given to him, and wrong never applied to anything he did. Nanites didn't do that to him. He came out of the box that way."

Jose Maria gave a slow nod, but he didn't look convinced.

"The monster said some cryptic things to me," Jose Maria said, a tremor in his quiet voice. "It sounds as if he is attempting time travel. He went out of his way to use the word 'Myriad.' I believe he intends to go back in time and rescue his sister."

"That's a good project for him," Calli said.

"I would be scoffing too, if he were not a patterner."

"Even a patterner can't just hit a reset button and change the past."

"That appears to be precisely his intent."

"Good for him," Calli said. "He can't do it."

Calli then received a hail from the command deck. Dingo Ryan advised, "U.S. shuttle on approach. Rear Admiral John Farragut is requesting a dock."

"He's coming?"

"He's here."

"Stand by to repel boarders!"

Dingo thought it was a joke. Just to be sure asked, "Really, sir?"

When Calli marched into the docking bay, everyone was already at attention. There were too many people in here. Techs, boffins, flight sergeants, gunners, midwatch personnel, the ship's chef. Everyone had found pressing reasons to be at the dock as the rear admiral's shuttle arrived.

The Marine at the hatch announced Calli's entrance. "Captain on deck."

Everyone inhaled.

Captain Carmel surveyed the assembly with a black expression.

Then Rear Admiral John Farragut blew in, found Calli, hauled her into a bear hug, and announced, "I'm hijacking your boat, Cal."

Calli said, "I see that. Why?"

Farragut gave Jose Maria de Cordillera a thumping hug, then swept both him and Captain Carmel inboard from the dock.

"Romulus is fixin' to go back in time."

Calli's eyes rolled to the overhead. "He can't do it." She had to move fast to keep up with Farragut charging up the ramp tunnel.

"Can he not?" Jose Maria asked across Farragut. "Are you sure, fair Captain? Are you absolutely sure?"

"I went to school with Romulus," Calli said. "He believes whatever he wants to believe."

"You did not go to school with Romulus the *patterner*," Jose Maria said.

"He still can't go back in time. No one can."

"The Xi tablet did," Jose Maria said.

Had her there.

"Something for sure triggered that black hole in the Myriad back in forty-three," Farragut added. "We had front row seats at that event."

"Front row?" Jose Maria nearly smiled. "Young Admiral, I understand you jumped onto the stage."

"I *tried*," Farragut said.

"Five years ago we failed to stop the Archon's messenger from going through the Rim Gate," Calli said flatly. "It went. The black hole formed. But *nothing happened to us*. Jose Maria, you saw it."

"I was not there, fair Captain."

"Right. Why did I think you were there? Point is nothing happened. History didn't change. Romulus may as well flap his arms and expect to fly."

"I believe something did change," Jose Maria said. "Were you aware, fair Captain, of a recent break-in at your Smithsonian Institute?"

Calli looked lost. "Does that mean something?"

"Someone took the Xi tablet."

Farragut lifted his gaze heavenward. "Oh, for Jesus. Where is Romulus now?"

"Right now? We don't know," Calli said. "Last verified sighting was at the games here on Beta Centauri two nights ago. Some little goddess has been filling in for him in his imperial box the last two nights."

"He's in motion," Farragut said. "Get him."

"John? He's in a Xerxes. How do we hunt an undetectable ship?"

"We know where he's going."

"We do? You think he's going to the Myriad?" Calli asked. "That's a huge area and a voyage of several months unless he means to storm the Shotgun."

"He's not going to the Myriad," Farragut said. "Not directly. He's fixin' to take the Xi tablet into the Xi gate at 82 Eridani."

"There's still a gate at 82 Eridani? I thought all the wormholes closed. They disappeared when the Arran messenger went through the Rim Gate and the black hole formed. Every wormhole in the Myriad closed."

"The gate at 82 Eridani didn't close," Farragut said. "I just checked."

"It's still open?"

"It's still *there*," Farragut said. He didn't know if it was exactly open or shut.

"Well, good," Calli said. "The gate at 82 Eridani used to connect to the Rim Gate in the Myriad. This is great. Romulus can go in the gate at 82 Eridani. He'll arrive in the ass end of a black hole two thousand parsecs from here in the Myriad. Good place for him. *Requiesce in inferno, fututor.*"

"I'd like to believe that, Cal, but I don't guess that's the scenario Romulus is imagining. There are two patterners planning this venture. I gotta take it seriously."

"Two? Where'd Rom get another patterner?"

"Numa's patterner turned."

"No. He can't have. Who told you that?"

"Numa. *Two* patterners think Romulus is going back in time. I'm running this grounder out. How fast can we get to 82 Eridani?"

"Without breathing hard, two days."

"How 'bout an ETA more like the ranch is burning down."

"Twenty hours."

"Light it."

13

28 April 2448
1500 hours
U.S. Space Battleship *Merrimack*
Centauri Star System
Near Space

CALLI SIGNALED THE COMMAND DECK on her wrist com as she ran to the ladder. "Dingo. 82 Eridani. Threshold velocity."

Farragut felt the familiar coiling sensation of the ship's six mammoth engines winding up for an almighty spring. Heard them running all out. Felt like he belonged here.

"Threshold, aye," Dingo Ryan said, then warned over the com, "A Xerxes type ship has a higher threshold velocity than the *Mack*, if that's what we're racing, Captain."

"Romulus doesn't know there's a race," Calli said.

But he probably had a head start.

Captain Carmel and Rear Admiral Farragut charged onto the command deck, Jose Maria behind them. Calli was already talking. "Is there any launch platform in the stellar neighborhood that can get a Star Sparrow into the 82 Eridani system earlier than we can?"

Tactical responded, "Sirius is close to 82 Eridani."

"No good," Calli said. She knew the place. "Base Sirius doesn't have interstellar missiles. Tactical, get the feed from the LEN observer buoy in the 82 Eridani system."

Farragut murmured appreciation. "Glad you're in the hunt, Cal."

"John, I'm not going to 82 Eridani because I think Romulus has a prayer of going back in time. I'm going there because it puts Romulus in a chokepoint. When he approaches that gate, I'll have a clear shot at him with no collaterals."

"Fair Captain, how do you intend to detect him?" Jose Maria asked.

John Farragut answered. "There's a static condensate cloud in front of the gate. A LEN scientific expedition laid it out years ago. It was meant to show up anything coming *out* of the gate. We were looking for Hive back then. But nothing ever did come out. Romulus will show up the instant he hits the condensate. Even if we don't see the Xerxes directly, there'll be motion in the particles."

"82 Eridani is several light-years away from us," Jose Maria said. "How will the sighting be instantaneous?"

"There's a LEN space buoy still in place," Farragut said. "It observes the condensate field. The LEN's science project ran out of money, but the buoy's still observing, and it's a resonant feed."

"Tactical!" Calli barked.

"Tactical, aye."

"I want the res feed from the 82 Eridani observer buoy on the main tac display, now."

The field around the Xi gate showed as it existed in real time. The gate itself was not visible. The monitor provided a highlight to indicate where the gate was. The condensate appeared as a wide misty field. Nothing moved inside it.

Romulus hadn't passed through it yet. There was still time.

"Romulus must drop down from FTL to approach the gate. When Romulus enters that condensate field, even in a Xerxes, we'll see him," Calli told Jose Maria. Then to Dingo, "Get us in firing range before he shows."

"We're all out, Captain," Dingo said.

"I mean to nail Romulus in real spacetime," Calli declared. "He is *not* going to disappear into that wormhole and die where I can't see him. I need to see the body!"

No one said it out loud, but you could hear the silent *amen*s.

"Captain, how do we connect ordnance with a Xerxes?" Dingo asked. "Targets don't come any slipperier."

"Don't target the Xerc. Target the point in space he must occupy in order to enter the gate. You're right. There'll be no getting a lock on him. We'll detonate something in the exact position he has to be. Dingo. Prep a karit missile. Calculate the optimal launch time and get it out of here."

A karit missile had a higher threshold velocity than did the *Mack*, but the karit also had a shorter range.

"Get a karit there best speed. We can adjust downward for intercept after it arrives in the 82 Eridani star system."

Dingo set the launch in motion. "Aye, aye, sir."

Jose Maria was trying to keep a placid face, but his eyes crushed shut. "This race could be for nothing. Romulus could be through the Eridani gate already."

"No," Calli said. "We would know. There's no disturbance in the condensate in front of the gate. Nothing passed that way. We haven't lost yet."

"Don't intend to lose," Farragut said.

He wished Romulus had already gone through the Xi gate. Then he would know for absolute certain that events were safely fixed in time, not to be changed. John Farragut wanted his past left just the way he remembered it. His marriage to Kathy. The birth of their daughter, Patsy Augusta.

The very notion that any of that could come undone scared him as nothing in the universe could.

We're racing across space on the eve of annihilation, and I just want to stop the boat and talk to my wife and baby girl.

"Wish to God Augustus was here," he said aloud.

Calli flinched. She couldn't have heard right. "Augustus? He was evil."

Farragut wagged his head no. "Nasty, disagreeable intolerant, ruthless. But not evil. Not at all."

"How is ruthlessness not evil?"

"Ruthlessness is not active malevolence," Jose Maria answered. "It is a want of compassion. Nature is merciless too. Augustus was, after a fashion, extraordinarily ethical. There was no hypocrisy in him. No tact either."

"Roger that," said Farragut. "He mighta been constructed from two bodies, but he only ever had one face. I liked him fine when I wasn't fixing to shine his eye socket." He punched his fist into his opposite palm. "No one got under my hide like that son of a she dog. Wish he was here. Status of the karit launch."

Dingo reported, "Coming up on launch window."

"Launch when ready," Calli ordered. "Don't wait for my say so."

"Aye, sir."

There were sneezes less noticeable than a karit's launch. A karit whispered its way out.

"Karit's away." Fire control reported. Then, "Threshold velocity achieved."

"Godspeed," Jose Maria said.

28 April 2448
1800 hours
U.S. Space Battleship *Merrimack*
Near Space
FTL

Farragut paced as if caged.

Augustus had once called him a patterner, because Farragut picked up connections between events without being aware he was doing it. Farragut supposed that meant he should trust his gut.

Not that his gut had a single neuron in it to be a reliable guide, but some background process running in his subconscious right now knew that if he didn't catch Romulus before he hit the gate, then John Farragut had kissed his Kathy and Patsy Augusta good-bye for the last time.

He'd had the same sense of doom back in the Myriad five years ago, chasing the Archon's messenger to the Rim Gate. His subconscious had been wrong that time. That chase had been for nothing. The Archon's messenger went through the gate, and history didn't change.

He was pretty sure it hadn't.

History had better not be changeable. Because *Merrimack* wasn't going to catch Romulus in time. Not with Romulus in a Xerxes with a two-day lead.

Romulus intended to rewrite everything Farragut didn't want rewritten.

Farragut never knew a man could be so happy tied to the ground. He would do anything to defend his ground.

* * *

Hours crawled. Any second Romulus could show up in 82 Eridani. The karit missile was still two hours out. *Merrimack* even farther.

28 April 2448
2330 hours
U.S. Space Battleship *Merrimack*
Near Space
FTL

The ship's chronometer wound up to the Hamster Watch. Ship's night. The time when anything that was going to happen always happened.

Rear Admiral Farragut woke up the commander of his Fleet Marine attachment and ordered him to the squash court. Farragut just needed someone to bash the hard green ball around with. And he was pretty sure TR Steele wasn't sleeping.

Steele reported as summoned.

There was a lot more Farragut here than when he used to be captain of this boat. The rear admiral had got fat and happy Stateside. But he was still quick on the court. Colonel Steele was angry and distracted, slamming the little green ball around with a rage like it had slept with his wife.

Farragut was lining up his serve, talking. Not saying what Steele expected.

"TR, I'm a little fuzzy on how things get done in the Fleet Marines, but in the regular Navy, marriage trumps frat."

The serve whistled clean by. Steele was left staring at the green ball thudding on the deck.

That was game point. All Farragut.

Farragut said, "So unless you forced that girl—you didn't, did you? They'll ask you that in your court martial—then you're righteous. They'll scowl at you something fierce, and if they really want to be brass holes about it they can make you serve on separate boats, but they can't take your fried eggs."

Steele stood in stunned disbelief. Not just at what Farragut said, but that he was saying it.

It could only mean that Rear Admiral Farragut was a mortal man.

Steele never thought a captain, much less a rear admiral, could be a regular guy like the rest of us mutts.

Just another man who'd had his life turned sideways by a woman.

"Now I hear the world may be ending in a couple hours. You have a wife, TR. Go be with her. Whatever else is happening, park it until we know we're all still here."

Colonel TR Steele summoned Flight Sergeant Kerry Blue to the narrow compartment that was his cabin.

She walked in, and the lights seemed brighter, sharper, more cruel.

The air left Steele's lungs.

His Kerry Blue was afraid of him.

"You thought I was dead," Steele heard himself tell her.

What made him say that? He couldn't just let it pass, could he? Why not plunge an icepick into his own gut?

He saw her freeze up. Her face went chalky, her eyes glassy. She was trying real hard to get the lie out there and make everything all right. But she couldn't say it.

Kerry Blue lied like a dog. Dogs can't lie. Dogs are all out there, and so was she. Looking as though she'd been kicked. Mouth open, trying to say something.

Steele's own face had to be a shipwreck. How many times had he seen a Marine come back from leave wearing the same look that had to be pasted on his own stupid face right now? Steele knew the look too well. The Marine returns early. He sees his woman's got a bump, and he's not the guy who put it there. Sometimes they cry. Steele wasn't gonna cry, but he knew he was wearing that god awful look.

And there's Kerry Blue, stark white.

She was afraid of him. Sticks like a knife. Whatever else, her fear hurt.

He wanted to roar at her. Order her out. But he knew she would take all the air out with her, and then he couldn't breathe.

Furious with himself for bringing it on.

You had to go and say that. He'd put it out there for her to confirm or deny: You thought I was dead.

Why did he say that?

He'd left Kerry Blue alone. Not his idea, but he'd done it. Knew damn well he couldn't leave Kerry Blue alone.

Anger turned like a smart missile. Found its true target.

This wasn't some groundside Jody. Steele knew who the traitor was. *The man's got the right name for it.* Rage burned. But Steele couldn't move against one of his own.

Park it, the rear admiral had said.

John Farragut was the same age as Steele. But he seemed a thousand years older and smarter. The rear admiral knew how to order his targets.

Kerry Blue was everything that was real. She was his, and she was here. Now.

He needed to be here for her.

Now.

29 April 2448
0530 Hours
U.S. Space Battleship *Merrimack*
Near Space
FTL

Farragut reappeared on the command deck before the change of the watch.

Captain Carmel looked at him twice. "John. Is that a mouse?"

Farragut touched his cheekbone gingerly. It felt puffy. "Squash ball. Where are we?"

"Karit's coming in pretty on the outer edge of the star system. Unless Romulus appears right *now*, we'll have the luxury of an ambush."

Just as Tactical cried, "Motion in the condensate!"

Luxury and time had run out.

"Confirm identity of target!"

The object was stealthy, but tactical imagers derived the dimensions and angles of the object from its motion inside the condensate.

"It's a Xerxes!"

"Status of karit missile," Calli demanded.

"Karit missile is inside the star system. Target is slowing for approach to the gate. We have a shot."

"Adjust the karit's speed. If we show too soon, we'll spook the target."

"Aye, sir. Karit will drop down from FTL in ten, nine. Target's advance remains steady. Karit will achieve intercept in six. Five."

Farragut braced for the dreaded last second jink when Romulus would escape the trap.

His teeth were clenched. Farragut caught himself leaning in, tense, willing the karit onward to intercept.

"Three. Two."

The explosion lit up the Tactical display. The misty condensate scattered. Got him!

Several techs stood straight up at their stations with a yell. *"Yeah!"*

The live feed from the observation buoy showed the hit. The condensate lit up for miles.

The target's stealth failed as it died, tumbling away from the gate.

Tactical constructed a visual image from sensor readings of the broken object in the darkness.

A stunned disbelief descended on the command platform.

You could make out the leopard spots on the Xerxes' shattered hull.

We shot the wrong Xerxes.

"It's *Bagheera!*" Dingo said.

Farragut turned away. *I just killed my brother.*

He clung to a wild hope that John Junior hadn't been on board the pirate ship.

"Sir! Look to the gate!"

Another motion disturbed the scattered condensate. A shape. Like the last one but distorted.

Another Xerxes had dropped down from FTL. It wore its energy field wide and thick toward its bow like a catcher's mitt.

"Reload! Launch another karit!" Farragut ordered.

Useless order. *Merrimack* was still light-years away from the target.

"Second karit already underway," Calli advised.

Farragut was happily surprised. Shouldn't have been surprised at all. This was the *Merrimack*. Redundance was good. It was very very good.

"Time to intercept," Calli demanded.

Tactical answered, "Negative intercept. Unless the target slows down, we have a five second deficit. Target will be at the gate in ten seconds. Nine. Eight. Time of the karit to the gate is now thirteen seconds. Twelve. Eleven. Intercept deficit holding steady."

Farragut stared at the tactical display as if he could drive the karit missile faster and will Romulus to slow down. But Romulus knew he was being chased now. He would make no mistakes.

Later someone can tell me why I think this matters.

Later. There might not be a later.

Rear Admiral John Farragut waited through the final seconds in perfect dread for nothing to happen. Trying to memorize this moment, the people around him, as if they were all going away.

"Romulus at the gate in five. Four."

The countdown fell on cotton ears.

"Three. Two."

John Farragut meant to keep his eyes wide this time.

"Xerxes at the gate."

Eyes shut. Held his breath.

It was dawn on the eastern seaboard of the United States of America. Kathy was waking up.

Farragut tried to imprint their images on his memory forever—his wife, his daughter—even though he knew he would be home soon and they would be there.

There would be time.

It only felt as if he was waiting for his world to end.

He breathed.

PART THREE

Reichenbach Falls

14

7 June 2443
U.S. Space Battleship *Merrimack*
Globular Cluster IC9870986 a/k/a the Myriad
Sagittarian Space

H E BREATHED.
One cry with several voices sounded. The clearest from Tactical, "He *bounced!*"
"Ho!" from Targeting.

Captain Farragut's eyes flew open.

On the tactical display the Arran messenger ship was not recognizable. Farragut wasn't even sure it was the Arran messenger. It was flat, utterly flat, as if it had collided with something, hard, and now its crumpled mass was caroming straight away from the Rim Gate, its tail pushed into its nose.

Farragut had been braced for the end of his world, as much as anyone can brace himself for such a thing. Now he felt ridiculous for being afraid.

Everything and everyone was still here, just as they were an instant ago. His too beautiful XO Calli Carmel was still on deck. Big-eared young specialist Jeffrey was still at Tactical. His Terra Rican sword master Jose Maria de Cordillera still observed from the rear of the command deck with the Marine guards. And Captain John Farragut's Roman patterner really had just kissed him on the neck on his own command platform in front of God and his command crew.

Farragut's ears felt red and his face burned bright as the Jupiter Monument. He just wanted to vanish into a black hole. No time for it. He forged ahead. He pointed toward Augustus and told one Marine stationed at the hatch, "Brig that man."

The Marine guard snapped to and glared at Augustus, who went quietly.

Farragut could bring the Roman up on charges later. For now he ordered, "All stations. Figure out what happened and tell me what I just saw. And where is my Star Sparrow?"

Tactical: "Star Sparrow is headed toward the Rim Gate on momentum only. Dead missile. Live warhead."

"Detonate that infernal thing," Farragut ordered. "I don't want someone feeding that back at us."

Not that there was anyone out here who could redirect the burned out Star Sparrow.

But something had already happened that was altogether wrong. The Arran messenger hadn't made it through the gate.

It wasn't just that the Arran ship had plowed into an invisible barrier. The Arran messenger didn't have the velocity to crush itself like that. The trajectory of the wreckage suggested a collision with an undetectable object coming out of the gate at extreme speed.

Undetectable? It was as detectable as a bomb. But what was it? Was it still out there?

The Arran had crashed into *something*. The resultant vector carried the flattened Arran straight away from the gate.

Farragut demanded of anyone, "Was the unseen thing a solid traveler or an energy hammer?"

Targeting: "Other than its effect on the Arran, the observer buoy's instruments don't tell us anything at all."

"Did the thing have a mass?"

Tactical: "Can't tell how much of that force was mass and how much was acceleration."

"What was the position of the Arran messenger at the moment of impact?"

"Precisely at the gate."

"Precisely?" Commander Carmel challenged the term.

Tactical stood by his observation. "*Precisely*. I don't think the Arran messenger got a molecule inside the gate. The force—or object or whatever it was—prevented the Arran from entering the *kzachin*."

"Something else out here didn't want the Arran to go back in time," Farragut guessed. He looked to Jose Maria de Cordillera, who gave a very slight sideways nod, allowing the possibility.

"Who else is out here, young Captain?"

"The LEN," Tactical said.

Someone snorted low into his station. Muttered, "My Aunt Ferdinand."

"That hit didn't come from anything Arran. It's nothing LEN, and it's not Hive," Farragut said. "Commander Carmel!"

"Sir."

"Siege stations."

"Aye, sir."

Calli called the ship defenses to full lockdown.

Farragut moved to the rear of the command platform where his stately civilian sword master stood with the Marine guards. "Jose Maria. Any thoughts on what that thing could be?"

Jose Maria de Cordillera looked baffled. "I would consult with Augustus."

Farragut didn't much want to talk to that son of a she dog. Didn't have a choice. "Calli, your boat. I'm fixin' to talk with our resident Roman."

Lieutenant Colonel TR Steele stepped forward, fist clenched, offering to assist with the Latin-Americanese translation.

Farragut waved Steele down and stalked out the hatch.

Colonel Augustus, *Merrimack*'s Intelligence Officer, sat with one foot up on the bench in the brig, one elbow resting on his bent knee, his eyes shut. A pinch showed in his tall flat brow. He didn't rise, didn't open his eyes at the announcement of the captain's entrance.

"You comfortable?" Farragut asked.

"Not ever."

Augustus looked wrung out. There was considerable pain involved with being a patterner.

"Something happened," Augustus guessed without looking up.

"Tell me what just happened," Farragut said.

Augustus held up a hand, to show his cables unplugged and dangling. "I don't have the input to know that, now do I?"

"Then how do you know something significant happened?"

"Because you're *here*—twitching."

"I do not *twitch*. I am looking for the reason why you undercut my authority on my own command deck."

"Is that what I did? I didn't expect to be here now—however one might define the word 'now.' Events might have gone the other way. Then you wouldn't be stomping in my cell."

Farragut was fairly bouncing off the bulks, his boot heels landing heavily.

"You were the one who said things happen once," John Farragut said.

"I changed my mind. Things happened both ways. Or multiple ways. This is not the only reality. It's the one that I'm in right now, and no, it's really not comfortable at all. Will you stop pacing? You can't imagine that something changed when the Arran went through the *kzachin*. You wouldn't be able to recognize a difference." He slumped back with a sigh. "What do you think you saw that shouldn't have happened?"

Farragut said, "The Arran messenger did *not* go through the *kzachin*."

That opened Augustus' eyes. "Unexpected. How did you make intercept?"

"I didn't. Something hammered the Arran away right at the gate. Rabbit punch. Knocked him flat back. I mean flat and I mean back."

"*Pedica* me."

"What?"

"Not possible."

Farragut didn't think that was literally what Augustus had said. But Augustus was right. It hadn't been possible. Farragut replayed the moment in his mind. One second he was listening to the countdown dwindle to nothing, then a shouted "Ho!" from Tactical, a scrambling at all stations, and on the monitor was the image of the flattened Arran wreckage careering away from the gate.

"It was impossible," Farragut said.

"I just told you that. Don't repeat my words back to me. I don't have the patience for it."

"There was a force that didn't register on the space buoy's sensors. We know something was there only because of what it did. It stopped the Arran."

"Intentional?" Augustus asked with his eyes shut.

"You tell me. Looked intentional as a load of buckshot finding its way into a cheating lover from where I was standing. I need you to plug in to Tactical and figure out what really happened."

"No."

"Colonel Augustus?"

Augustus covered his face with his hand. "My head hurts. I don't feel like it. Brig me." He peered out with one eye through the cage of his fingers as if to check his surroundings. Found Farragut was still here, with him, in the brig. Augustus closed his eye, settled back. "Unless it results in the annihilation of the Hive, don't bother me. I feel like death."

He meant that literally. The patterner was dying. Patterners had severely shortened lifespans. Augustus had passed his due date last year.

"It's an order."

"You have no leverage with me, Captain."

"Yeah?" Farragut said. "There was a moment back there when I thought you mighta given a pile of turnips what happened to me."

Augustus sat up. Anger flared in his hollow eyes. "That was when I didn't think we'd be alive to have this conversation."

After a moment, Augustus exhaled a weary breath. He asked, reluctantly, "What was the vector of the unseen force?"

"Straight out of the *kzachin*."

"Something popped out of the *kzachin* at the very instant the Arran messenger was about to enter?"

"That's what I've been telling you. So you tell me, how did the unseen force coming from the other end of this wormhole know there was a messenger ship fixin' to come through the gate right at that moment?"

"Your unseen force hit the messenger at the precise time and exact place to prevent the messenger from going back in time. That speaks of premeditation. Screams it, actually."

The Rim Gate was known to connect to another gate—another *kzachin*—a quarter way across the galaxy and 10 billion years in the past.

"Patterner," said Farragut.

"Origin didn't have patterners ten billion years ago," Augustus said.

"Well, maybe there's a patterner from our future coming back to take the shot at the messenger we couldn't make. You!" Farragut said on a sudden thought. "It's you. In the future, you're fixin' to come back here and stop the Arran messenger from going through the *kzachin*."

"No, I am not. I don't have a future. But as idiotic as your suggestion is, part of it may have merit. You're a patterner, John. Not your intellect. That's an empty squirrel cage. Your base instinct is matching pieces in the background."

"My instinct is saying the unseen force is not my friend."

"You don't think it could be here to save us from the Hive?"

"No. And you don't believe that either."

"I don't. I just thought you might think so."

"I'd sooner think it's here to saddle up the Hive and ride it right over us."

"Controlling the Hive is a dubious ambition, but you're right on one count. One can never go too far wrong imputing malevolent intent to a hidden power."

Augustus closed his eyes and went silent.

Hours ago Farragut had caught Augustus looking down the business end of a sword.

Farragut scolded, "This is an inconvenient time to be contemplating suicide."

"I didn't consider your convenience. May I have my sword back?"

"All the gorgons in the galaxy heading this way, and you're fixin' to desert. I'm at the Alamo here. I order you not to kill yourself."

"Then you risk me joining the other side in the middle of the next gorgon battle, *id est*, not convenient either."

"Why would you do that? Why would you join the gorgons?"

"It wouldn't be my idea. I'm past the point where I'm certain I can resist Hive influence. It would happen because of equipment failure. I'm at the end of my life. I'm past due. And you're hard on your machines."

"Sorry."

"Don't *ever*. I am here to save the Roman Empire from gorgons. Nothing I do has anything to do with you. Be ready to strike me down if I join the other side."

"Figure out what happened here," Farragut ordered.

"I'm in the brig."

Farragut stalked out. He jerked his thumb back over his shoulder as he told the human Marine guard at the hatch, "Unbrig that man."

✳ ✳ ✳ ✳ ✳

7 Iunius 2443
Xerxes
Globular Cluster IC9870986 a/k/a the Myriad
Sagittarian Space

Sooner than Romulus expected, he was here. Amid the barrage of new thoughts and images, Romulus knew immediately that he had arrived.

If he hadn't been plugged into patterner mode, he couldn't have followed the events. Everything happened so fast.

He, in his Xerxes, had emerged from the Rim Gate and crushed the flimsy Arran messenger ship.

Romulus was in the Myriad. Now.

Now was five years in his own past.

To one side of his Xerxes stretched the darkness of open space. To the other, the Myriad star cluster dazzled with the light of three million suns.

Romulus laughed and heard his own laughter echo back at him from the compartment's walls. As predicted, he'd slammed the Arran messenger ship away from the Rim Gate. The first thing he'd needed to do was already done.

He was feeling omnipotent.

He hadn't realized how much doubt he'd been holding in. He shouted for joy, a triumphant "Ha!" He took in great breaths. He was breathing.

"Ha!" He was alive!

"Ha!" He was here!

"Ha!" He was in his own damned past!

Mastery was intoxicating. He shouted to the overhead, as if his voice could carry across the galaxy, "Claudia! I am here!"

She was alive in this time. Far away, but in this existence, alive, *now*. And he could keep her that way. "I AM A GOD!"

He was aware that he'd already changed future history by destroying the Arran messenger. His certainty of coming events would diminish rapidly from now on.

He needed to get things in order here, fast, so he could start the long journey to Near Space, to Palatine and Claudia.

His first priorities were to neutralize Augustus and to take command of the two Legion carriers.

He took a resonant sounding of the immediate stellar vicinity. He sifted what he needed from the crush of data.

First: There was *Merrimack*, nine hours out and closing on the Rim Gate—exactly where she was supposed to be.

But there was something wrong with her. He brought up her image. There were great holes in her physical hull. Only her energy shell was holding her atmosphere in. Her hull looked like—he couldn't believe it— *chewed*. An empty spot gaped under one massive wing. It made her look off balance. *Merrimack* was missing an engine. She was showing five. She should have six.

That damage was not in the historical log.

The damage looked eerily like Hive work. But the Hive shouldn't be here. Not in the year 2443. Not ever.

In Romulus' memory the Hive had never come to the Myriad.

Romulus executed a broader resonant scan. He felt cold even before he sorted out the mashed-up results.

He found the Hive. Sphere upon sphere was converging on the Myriad. That was wrong. This could not be.

The Hive shouldn't be here. The Hive had never been here!

How could his arrival have changed things so drastically already? *Backward* in time. It wasn't possible. He'd *just* got here.

He told himself that it could be explained. That it didn't matter. To hell with *Merrimack*. Romulus needed to find his Legions. That was an immediate priority.

Where were the Legion carriers? There should be two, closing in on the Myriad.

But the two Roman Legion carriers were not on their historical course. They should be *there*, headed toward the Myriad to challenge *Merrimack* for the star cluster.

And Augustus should be ahead of them, flying point in his Striker.

Augustus was not on his historical vector.

Might Augustus have detected the Xerxes and changed course?

No. Romulus had his Xerxes shrouded in perfect stealth. Augustus in the year 2443 would not be able to detect a Xerxes.

Romulus tried to crush down threatening panic.

He hailed the two Legion carriers on their resonant harmonics. He connected with nothing. In desperation he tried to hail Augustus.

Augustus wasn't just off course. He wasn't here.

Neither were the Legion carriers.

There were another sixty-four Legions out here in the Deep End. Were those off course as well?

Romulus had the harmonics of each of those Legions. He hailed them all.

Silence.

The panic he'd been holding at bay washed over him. Terror such as he had never known. His body vibrated. Sickness welled.

Things were different.

Where were the sixty-four Legions?

He tuned into the Imperial Fleet harmonic, the one that had been in effect on this date in history.

The Fleet harmonic was silent. No one was resonating on it.

They changed the harmonic!

No. No. No.

The Roman fleet was using different harmonics *and he didn't have them.*

There were infinitely many resonant harmonics. He could guess forever and not hit on one. This was a disaster.

And lurking in the back of his consciousness was a worse possibility.

The Legions were not using different harmonics.

The Legions didn't exist.

He trembled on a sudden even worse thought. All gods, was Rome still there?

He was lost in infinity.

He folded over to vomit.

He unplugged from patterner mode.

The moment of panic passed. He breathed deeply, clearing away the storm of wrongness.

He needed to focus on the vital goal.

Claudia. Claudia. Claudia.

Where was Claudia?

He held his breath, dizzy.

He cleaned the sick from his mouth. Steadied his breathing.

He turned off his video and entered Claudia's harmonic in the resonator. He knew that one by heart.

Claudia, if you are not there, I am lost.

He waited.

The universe paused.

The voice of his goddess in heaven snapped, "Yes?"

Her bedchamber was in view, but she was not in the picture.

Romulus croaked, "Claudia."

"Yes?" She sounded vexed.

In the long silence a lump thickened in his throat. His eyes misted.

Claudia demanded, "Who is this?"

"Romulus."

"What's wrong? Where is your video?"

He was intentionally not sending any visuals. "I just needed to hear your voice."

She laughed, baffled. "You just left! What is *with* you?"

She came into view.

She looked so young, not yet thirty terrestrial years. No fear in her head. His bright bird of paradise, his vain child. He would indulge her every whim. He should have made her empress when she asked. She need never ask.

He pressed his hand over his pounding heart. She was too beautiful.

She had gilded the tips of her eyelashes. They flashed and glinted with her blinks.

"Did I?" he asked. *I just left?* His stupid other self had just been with her. Had left her vexed. "It seems like an eternity."

She laughed again. "That's very sweet. I forgive you."

He wondered what that wretched Other—his younger *alter ego*—had done to her to need forgiving.

"Then I can go on living," he said.

He clicked off. She was alive. His beacon in this darkness.

He scrambled to get his feet under him.

There was so much he didn't know. He needed to get into a current data bank, one with recent history and current events in it. He needed to tap into a military harmonic.

Whose harmonic did he know other than Claudia's?

It came to him in a flash.

Mine!

Of course he had his own old harmonics. Panic had been making him stupid. *Slow down.* Trembling, he entered his old harmonic into the resonator. Immediately his old database came up.

He could breathe again. *Me. My own idiot self. My stupid useless other self.* He needed to learn the state of the universe as it existed now.

He dove into his alter ego's records. They differed from his own memories.

Yes, Rome was still standing. Barely. Rome and the United States were not currently at war. There had been no Subjugation, but Rome was in an unholy alliance with the United States against the Hive. The remains of the mighty Roman military really were under U.S. command.

By any and all gods, how had that atrocity happened?

He had known he would change the future from the instant he arrived. Wholly unexpected were changes to the past.

His arrival had changed events that occurred before he got here.

The true horror in all this was the failure of his omniscience. Knowledge was power, and he didn't have as much as he thought he did. Things he thought he knew were wrong.

He coughed. Retched.

There was no reason for him to stay a moment longer out here in the Myriad. Augustus was not where he ought to be. The two Roman Legion carriers were not here. And nothing here was vital or strategic—other than the damned Hive.

The center of all power and civilization was in the Orion Starbridge, Near Space, that dense band of stars that spanned the gap between the inner, Sagittarian, arm of the Milky Way's spiral and the outer, Perseid, arm.

Romulus needed to get back to Palatine, the capital world of the Roman Empire, and to Claudia.

The voyage would take him three terrestrial months at threshold velocity.

Merrimack could get there sooner, only because she could use the Fort Dwight David Eisenhower/Fort Theodore Roosevelt Shotgun to cut thousands of light-years off the journey, and Romulus couldn't.

Displacing through the U.S. Shotgun required precise readings of a vessel and its contents. Romulus could not submit himself or his ship to that kind of scrutiny. Using the Shotgun would place him utterly at the mercy of the U.S. displacement technicians. He couldn't trust them. Small displacement mistakes were fatal. Intentional erasure of an unwanted traveler would be all too easy for the Yanks to do.

Romulus would need to take the slow road home, across the Abyss, the thinly starred darkness between galactic arms.

What of his secret weapon? Did he have that?

The Hive harmonics.

He thought he had the harmonics of the Hives. There were two.

He had just assumed the harmonics were still valid. The harmonics would give him control of the Hives.

Control of the Hives would make him invincible.

Without them—

He couldn't even consider being without them.

He plugged into patterner mode. He hesitated to resonate. What would the Hive make of his contact? His whole universe could turn on this butterfly's wing.

He entered the harmonic of the first Hive into the res chamber, but transmitted nothing. He only listened.

He heard, felt, noise. Almost a monotone. Steady as running water. The resonant life pulse of the Hive. It was vast. It was everywhere at once.

Romulus' contact didn't register in the Hive as an alien presence. Romulus was part of their whole.

He was hungry.

He disconnected. It was an unsettling sensation, being connected to the Hive. The entity spanned galaxies. It existed to feed.

Romulus tried the other harmonic.

The second Hive didn't recognize his otherness either. But now the first Hive noticed him, because he was resonating. He was the enemy.

One Hive did not tolerate the existence of the other Hive. The other Hive knew where Romulus was. Wanted him dead.

A Hive could locate the source of a res pulse. Several swarms of the first Hive were already converging on the Myriad.

And Romulus could harness and redirect all of those swarms whenever he wanted.

I am still a god.

15

7 June 2443
U.S. Space Battleship *Merrimack*
Globular Cluster IC9870986 a/k/a the Myriad
Sagittarian Space

THE RACE WAS OVER, but *Merrimack* continued out to the edge of the Myriad. There were hours left before she would arrive at the Rim Gate.

It was on the Hamster Watch, ship's night, that the Hive spheres nearest to *Merrimack* inexplicably changed direction.

The Hamster didn't need to wake up the captain. John Farragut wasn't sleeping. Hamster had to summon him off the basketball court.

John Farragut bounded onto the command deck, still carrying the basketball. Passed it to one of the Marine guards at the hatch.

Before Hamster could announce the captain's arrival on deck, Farragut was asking, "What's their new vector, Hamster?"

"The five closest swarms are converging on *us*."

"And where are we?"

"Still a few hours from the Rim Gate."

"Are we resonating?"

"Negative resonance since we detonated the Star Sparrow."

"Then what makes us suddenly so interesting?"

Glenn Hamilton hesitated. "The spheres changed course toward us, but I'm not sure that means *we* are what's interesting. Something's not right." She tilted her head in a pose of listening.

Farragut picked up the meaning. "It's quiet."

She nodded. "It's quiet."

No Hive sign.

Farragut pulled back the cover from one of the terrariums on the command deck.

Insects became notoriously frantic under Hive resonance. Insects were always the first to announce Hive interest in the ship.

The ant farm was sleeping.

But the Hive spheres had definitely turned toward *Merrimack*, without warning or apparent reason.

"They've learned how to *sneak?*" Glenn Hamilton suggested.

Farragut looked to his IO, who hadn't left the command deck since he'd been sprung from the brig. "Augustus, you're frowning. Speak."

"I'll speak when I have something to say."

Augustus didn't speak for another two hours.

Lieutenant Colonel Steele arrived on the command deck at the turn of the watch, as *Merrimack* neared the *kzachin* known as the Rim Gate.

The primitive sublight Arran messenger ship was hurtling away from the *kzachin* from the force of an apparent impact. The Arran was dead flat.

Merrimack overtook the wreck.

"Get a drone out there," Farragut ordered. "I want a post mortem on the Arran ship. The Arran ought to be carrying trace molecules of the thing that hit it. Tell me what that thing was."

The retrieval was done quickly, but the analysis and report were so long in coming that Farragut sent Augustus down to the lab to find the reason for the delay.

Several departments had sifted through the drone's recordings. All the specialists reported negative findings. Jose Maria de Cordillera was with them, as baffled as any of them.

Jose Maria and Augustus returned to the command deck to report in person.

"There is nothing on the Arran wreckage that doesn't belong to the Arran ship," Augustus said.

"So it had to be an energy beam that struck the Arran," Farragut said.

"Negative. There's no heat signature. No scoring. No melting. My conclusion—Your people don't like it. They are wrong—is that the Arran was struck by an inertial field. It's the only thing that doesn't leave a signature."

"Jose Maria?" Farragut prompted.

"I do not like it. But I have nothing else, young Captain."

"Well, Augustus, that narrows down our actor to either your people or my people."

"I'm all the people Rome has out here," Augustus said. "And my Striker is secure inside your hangar deck. And point of fact, the evidence does not narrow it down to your people or my people. The unidentified force came out of the Rim Gate. We know that the Rim Gate leads to Origin."

"Origin doesn't have that kind of technology," Farragut said. "Donner's home world doesn't have heavy elements. Origin doesn't have FTL capability. There's something else out there. I need to know what it is and whether it will be gunning for my boat next."

Augustus was already shaking his head. "I've been through all the input." He looked drained and ill as he always did when coming down from patterner mode. "I can't find the pattern in that heap."

"You honestly have no idea?"

"I have ideas. They're all trash." Augustus looked deathly. "I'll tell you how messed up I am right now. Your idea about a time traveler coming out this gate from the future instead of from the past is starting to sound plausible."

Augustus suddenly squinted, pinching the bridge of his nose, as if trying to hold his brains in. He said like a postscript, "You have a shadow."

"A what?"

"A dark thing following you. Look for a powered object in *Merrimack*'s wake. It's resonating. Find it nine meters behind the outer edge of *Merrimack*'s inertial shell, straight back in line from the vent."

Farragut turned to his XO. "Calli, find the shadow. What's out there?"

Tactical reported, "Negative readings. Negative presence."

"Negative prox alarm," Farragut noted.

"Something is there," Augustus said. "In complete stealth."

Farragut: "What *is* it?"

Augustus: "Don't know."

"Then how did you know it's there?"

"Because the Hive knows it's there. The nearest Hive swarms are converging on a point nine meters aft of *Merrimack*, not at a point inside the *Merrimack*. That's why your ship's telltales are silent, John Farragut."

That much was true. There was no Hive sign. The ants in their terrarium stayed snug in their holes.

"The Hive swarms are not converging on your ship. They're converging on your shadow."

"And what is my shadow?"

"Not a friend of yours."

Targeting offered, "Astronomically speaking there's an infinitesimal difference between the ship and a point nine meters behind the ship."

"It's a critical difference," Augustus said.

Farragut shook his head, baffled. "Why would the Hive target a point nine meters behind my *Merrimack*?"

"My guess is—and my guesses carry weight—you will find a powered vessel traveling nine meters behind this ship, transmitting a harmonic more interesting to the Hive than anything else. Whatever it's sending is irresistible to gorgons. There are five Hive spheres focused on that point, to the exclusion of all closer targets. The Hive is pursuing your shadow with a special anger."

"Do we know anything about this—" Farragut was not sure what to call this. "—irresistible harmonic?"

"No."

"Then how do you know something is resonating at all?"

"Pay attention. Because of where the Hive spheres are focused."

Farragut told his XO, "Get the Wraith back in the saddle. Up here, on deck."

The ship's drone wrangler was a young vee jock named Raytheon. Everyone called him Wraith.

Wraith reported to the command deck like a tall, skinny, awkward, pasty white mole dragged from its burrow. He carried his vee helmet under his bony arm. He was given a station next to Tactical. Wraith cast nervous glances back to Augustus, who lurked behind Wraith's station.

Wraith received his orders directly from the captain. "Mister Raytheon, I need you to collect a stealth object out there."

Wraith's prominent Adam's apple made a long bob. "Sir? How can I collect the stealth object? I can't detect it."

"Colonel Augustus will tell you where to go."

The Adam's apple yo-yoed. "Aye, sir," Wraith whispered.

Colonel Augustus was plugging into patterner mode. The towering

Roman looked like a grave monument but less cheerful, his haggard face gone slack, black eyes empty.

Even with floodlights, radar, and lidar, nothing showed behind *Merrimack* other than the Wraith's drone. Wraith drove the drone where Augustus guided him.

Augustus used the Hive spheres' infinitesimal changes in vectors to direct Wraith's drone to the exact point of the stealth vessel.

Wraith reached out a wide mechanical claw to the specified point.

Squawked. Astonished to actually close his claw on a solid object. "I got something!" Wraith cried. "I mean, target secured!" He still couldn't detect what he had except by the pressure of the claw's grip.

"Good job! Hold fast, Wraith!" Farragut looked to Augustus. "Merry Christmas!"

Augustus yanked out all his cable connections. Scowled at Farragut. "It's not a gift. Someone tied a raw steak to your leg while you were swimming in shark-infested waters."

"But it's what I need. Someone just gave me a way to lure the Hive away from the planets! Wraith! Pull the thing's res chamber. Read off the harmonic."

Even as he said it, the transmission from the drone went dark and Wraith gave a startled jerk. He lifted his visor.

Farragut: "What just happened?"

Wraith: "The stealth object destructed. It took out my drone with it. There it goes." Wraith pointed at the enhanced image on the Tactical monitor which showed small pieces of wreckage flying in all directions.

"Helping you was not the intent," Augustus told Farragut.

"Mister Raytheon, get another drone out there. Pick up all the pieces of the shadow vessel."

Several drones were dispatched to collect the debris. There was nothing stealthy about the exploded bits, but they required chasing. The explosion had scattered the pieces wide, and there was nothing out there to slow them down.

"Mister Raytheon, can you salvage the shadow vessel's res chamber?"

"Not a chance, sir."

"I have a patterner," Farragut said. "Just find me the pieces of the res chamber."

"I *got* the res chamber, sir," Wraith said. "It's a solid melted glob. And

I got one big piece of the carrier vessel. Here, this piece has a Pacific Consortium mark."

Wraith positioned a robotic claw to present the "big piece" for viewing on the Tactical monitor. The big piece was one centimeter long.

Enlarged, the broken bit clearly showed the Trademark kiwi wearing a bubble helmet—the Pacific Consortium's mark.

"Dead last thing I ever expected," Farragut said, eyebrows lifted toward the overhead.

Calli leaned in toward the image. She looked betrayed. "I had no idea the Pacifics had any presence out this way at all. Much less planting bait on a U.S. battleship during a galactic crisis."

Farragut worked up to a full roar. "Get me the embassy! No, get me someone to shoot at! If I had the power to declare war, I would."

Wraith was squinting, reading the markings from another shard from the scattered remains. "Patent registered in 2446. That explains that."

It made everything clear as squid ink.

Calli Carmel blinked several times. "Today is June the seventh, 2443," she said, not sounding too confident about it.

"Yes, sir. Last I looked, sir," Wraith said. He heard himself sounding disrespectful and stammered, "Sir."

Farragut leaned toward the display. "This thing was made in the future? You're not serious."

Wraith didn't know if that was a real question. He couldn't talk anyway.

Augustus said, "It does seem someone is having conjugal relations with your head. Just because a thing has a date on it doesn't mean it's actually from that year. I wouldn't declare war on the Kiwis just yet."

"You mean they were *framed?*" Calli said.

Augustus shook his head slowly as if it hurt to move. "As frame-ups go, this is tenuous. It assumes we were meant to find that piece of debris. I don't believe we were."

"Then what? What was the intent?" Farragut asked.

"In this case, I'm inclined to follow my idiot's original thought."

Augustus' idiot? "Me," Farragut said. "You've come over to my side."

Augustus nodded. "When you've eliminated the possible, you're either missing a fact or you've misinterpreted the evidence. *That* is a real patent date."

Farragut was just absorbing the shock when Tactical sang out, "Hive spheres have changed course."

"Where? When?"

Tactical: "They changed the moment the stealth object destructed. It wasn't obvious right away. At these distances the angular differences are next to nothing. But it's definite. I confirmed it twice."

"Where are the spheres headed now?"

"Back the way they were. Toward the nearest inhabited planets."

Augustus announced, "I'm going outside."

Farragut frowned. He was not accustomed to his officers giving themselves orders. But he ought to expect it from Augustus by now.

Farragut turned to Augustus. His scowl relaxed, and he made a covert gesture. He mumbled, barely audible, "Nose."

Augustus touched the back of one finger to his nostrils and brought away blood. He muttered. "*Foutu.* I'm still going outside."

"Augustus. Something out there is armed."

"So am I. And I am not an unshielded Kiwi. Let me out, then take your ship to siege stations."

Augustus had always been spectacularly insubordinate. He wouldn't be for much longer.

Farragut accompanied Augustus to the dock where the Roman Striker crouched like an angry red and black wasp.

A Roman Striker was a very long range, fast attack craft, tightly constructed around its pilot, a patterner. There was a living compartment in the Striker positioned just aft of the cockpit. The living space was high enough for a six foot eight Roman to lift his arms over his head and wide enough for him to lie down.

The living compartment in Augustus' Striker was almost empty now. Augustus had moved most of his personal stuff over to the torpedo storage bay on board *Merrimack,* where he was billeted. In addition to his medical supplies, Augustus had offloaded rich tapestries, climbing plants set in Grecian urns, an elaborately carved Roman couch, a three-legged table, and a full-sized replica of the Winged Victory from the Louvre. John Farragut wasn't sure how Augustus could ever get all that stuff back into this little ship.

Augustus didn't intend to move it back. He wasn't going to need it.

Augustus turned in parting. This could be it.

"You look like hell," Farragut said.

"I am not out here to survive. I already said good-bye to you. So." Augustus climbed into his Striker and pulled the hatch shut.

Romulus tried to come down from his towering rage. He'd intended to turn *Merrimack* into a plague ship, dogged by ravening gorgons, unwelcome at any planet or station.

But somehow *Merrimack* had detected and destroyed Romulus' resonant tail.

Romulus had burned a serpent's tooth missile and a res chamber for nothing. Worse than nothing.

Merrimack should not have been able to detect the serpent's tooth. *Merrimack* didn't have stealth technology in the year 2443, much less the technology to see through advanced stealth.

Things were not making sense.

Romulus plugged into patterner mode to sort through the confusing input. He accessed the records of all events that occurred since his arrival, and then he tapped into his younger self's database, current today.

There he found Augustus.

Augustus was *here*. In the Myriad.

Romulus felt a hard smile spreading across his face.

Augustus was on *Merrimack*.

Now, how to get Augustus out of *Merrimack* without betraying any more information about himself? That was the problem. *Merrimack* was a fortress.

Then, miraculously, like lamb to slaughter, a small craft launched from *Merrimack*. It showed red and black—Flavian colors. A wicked little ship, with scarcely enough room inside to change your mind.

Romulus had to laugh out loud.

That was a patterner's Striker. Augustus was coming to him.

"Captain. Your Roman deserted."

"Say again."

Marcander Vincent had replaced Jeffrey at the tactical station. He reported, "Roman Striker is off the grid. Gone. Quit. Out of here."

"Did the Striker jump to FTL?"

"Negative."

Farragut had a very high tolerance for his barely competent over-age third-string tactician. But he needed his A team right now.

"Mister Vincent, have Jeffrey report to the command deck. Then confine yourself to quarters. Someone else, locate Colonel Augustus' Striker."

✳ ✳ ✳ ✳ ✳

Romulus stood, poised in grandeur over his captive. He meant to strike Augustus with awe when he woke up.

But Augustus wasn't waking up.

Romulus' Xerxes had absorbed the Striker into an energy hook, shut down its engine, and reeled the little ship inside the Xerxes' hold. It took up all the available space.

Augustus arrived unconscious in his cockpit. His skin was cold. He was near to death.

Romulus was a superior patterner, so he knew that nothing he'd done had put Augustus into this state.

Augustus was already dying on his own.

Merda. These earlier patterners didn't last long. They ran hot and needed a pharmacy full of sick-making chemicals to keep them alive—all the things that nanites did for the advanced patterner Romulus. Romulus didn't have those antique chemicals. Augustus was end of life. Threat of stroke was imminent. If Augustus stroked out, then he was free. Even Romulus couldn't mend him. Romulus would be all the king's horses and all the king's men.

Augustus looked maddeningly placid.

Romulus shouted at him, "You will live!"

Augustus' eyelids fluttered. He gave a faint smile, as if at private joke. "Make me." He exhaled like a sigh.

His heartbeat ebbed.

"Oh, no, you don't! You do not walk away from your debt. You owe me! You owe me excruciating agony!"

Augustus' body was not functioning.

"No!"

Romulus could stop the progress of the degeneration if he acted quickly.

Augustus must live and recover just enough to suffer hideously.

Quickly Romulus isolated a batch of his own nanites and configured them to cycle through their restoration routine only once then self-extinguish.

Desperate, Romulus injected the restorative nanites into his worst enemy.

Augustus flatlined.

Romulus kicked him. "Live, you son of a mutant whore!"

16

CONSCIOUSNESS FLICKERED IN AND OUT. Held. A baritone voice from above sounded sweetly menacing.

"Augustus. How do you feel?"

Augustus didn't answer.

"You feel well," Romulus answered for him. "Except hungry, I expect."

Thirsty actually. Augustus was trembling with dehydration. Would not confirm hunger. Did not want to imagine what Romulus would feed him. He couldn't move.

Augustus didn't want to show attention to Romulus, but he needed input. He opened his eyes.

Romulus was setting out medieval instruments, none too clean. Not what Augustus ever thought to bring on an interstellar voyage.

Romulus looked older, filled out. And cabled. *He means for me to believe someone made him into a patterner.*

That was unthinkable. Yet here he was thinking it. Romulus a patterner? Preposterous—that was a word that had waited a long time for someone to fit into it so perfectly. Romulus and recent events were preposterous.

Augustus had caught glimpses of extraordinary things while the Xerxes' medical equipment dragged him back to life. Augustus had thought it a wild dream while it was happening.

Medical monitors displayed his vital signs. They betrayed his low-level apprehension. Romulus didn't appear to like the readings.

Of course, Romulus didn't want apprehension. He would want fear. Romulus would want blind horror.

This Romulus was a handsome man. Beautiful actually, with thick dark locks, full lips, athletic build. He was older than he ought to be by a handful of years at an age when a year mattered. He wore a high collar and gauntlets.

"They say the waiting is the worst part," Romulus said. "No. It is not. But it's part. Where there's life, there's horror."

Romulus was manufacturing blood. He made a show of the transparent bags filling up. "You're going to need a lot of it."

Romulus had cut Augustus' cable connections to prevent him from going into patterner mode. A little late, perhaps. Augustus' own background processes had recorded what he'd missed while he was unconscious. He retained only a fraction of the information he'd been exposed to. Just what was most startling and most necessary.

He could tell that Romulus was picking up a wrongness here. Augustus was too calm, too interested in something other than Romulus.

Augustus forced his heart to speed up. He drew shallow breaths in an imitation of terror.

Romulus should be able to detect the charade. But he didn't. Romulus' strengths had always been his magnetism, cunning, and creativity. Not his power of reason. He was calculating, for sure. But he forced answers to suit his wants.

Augustus needed to keep himself from falling into the same trap, underestimating his opponent. He acknowledged that his opponent was powerful. Augustus had an inferior situation. He must outplay a determined, dangerous man with a superior arsenal.

✳ ✳ ✳ ✳ ✳

"Striker! Back on the grid!" Jeffery announced at Tactical. "Five by thirty by eight!"

Commander Carmel took a step forward, mouth open, staring at the Tactical display. There was Augustus' black and red Striker, suddenly in sensor view.

Captain Farragut was already barking, "FTL jump! Random destination. Execute yesterday. Displacement jammers—"

Just as a *bang* like a displacement thunderclap sounded from down decks.

Merrimack jumped. Calli got on the intercom. "Displacement Department. This is Command. Engage displacement jammers. Identify that sound."

The displacement specialist answered, "Displacement Department, aye. I heard it, Commander. Didn't come from the D department. The sound came from down decks. In the direction of the torpedo storage bays."

"You're telling me a torpedo blew inboard?"

Even as she said it, she knew it couldn't be true. The sound had been a simple crack, not a ship-gutting explosion.

The displacement tech said, "I have no information on the arsenal, sir."

The arsenal weighed in: "Negative detonation of onboard ordnance."

"Command. This is Displacement. That noise definitely had the sound of a displacement event. But we did not initiate any displacement action."

"Displacement. This is Command. Do we have jammers on?"

"Negative jammers in effect at the time of the event. Jammers are engaged now."

Calli looked at the captain. "John, that *sounded* like a displacement event."

Farragut ordered, "Sapper protocol."

Calli on the loud com: "Sapper protocol. All hands, Sapper protocol."

Sapper protocol meant bomb on board.

✳ ✳ ✳ ✳ ✳

Lieutenant Colonel Steele deployed his Marines shipwide. Alpha Team charged to the lower decks, where the displacement sound had originated.

First thing necessary to effect displacement was to establish a working landing disk at the destination point. The displacement event on board *Merrimack* had to be the insertion of that initial landing disk. And you had to assume the payload was going to be a bomb. Getting an initial landing disk in place failed a lot. You could hope this one failed to arrive functional.

You never counted on it.

The Fleet Marines needed to find the landing disk and neutralize it. Yesterday.

Flight Sergeant Twitch Fuentes hauled open hatches as Flight Sergeants Kerry Blue and Carly Delgado scrambled through compartments in the arsenal. Lieutenant Hazard Sewell, who was tall, yanked the covers off high vents and checked the overhead ducts. Little Reg Monroe hooked up deck grates, and the new guy, Cole Darby, got stuck fishing underneath them.

This was when you found out just how big *Merrimack* was.

Scary that the Old Man wasn't bellowing at them to move faster. Meant he knew his dogs were moving flat out.

Means we're gonna die.

Kerry Blue pulled up a round dish from under a rack. It didn't look like any standard LD, but it might be some foreign make. She held it up high. Yelled, "What's this?"

"That's a dogfood bowl, *chica.*"

The dog itself was out somewhere searching for the LD.

Hazard Sewell barked, "We're clear here. Move. Move. Move."

The team piled out through the hatchway, tagged the compartment as clear, and they ran to the next area, eyes up, looking at the overhead piping, the air returns, the water and waste conduits, the bunches of power cables. A hostile landing disk might end up anywhere. Sometimes these things displaced into a solid bulk, but that made a completely different sound. This displacement crack had a horribly clean sound to it. The payload could arrive on it at any next heartbeat.

It was well known that the true proper position for the Sapper protocol was on your knees, eyes tight shut, holding your breath, fingers in your ears, braced for the blast. It was every bit as effective as what they were doing now.

Captain Farragut was down decks with the rest of the hands searching for an LD. Commander Carmel, on the command deck, relayed a report from Systems. "Captain! I am advised that *Merrimack* is ninety kilos more massive than she was before the displacement event."

Farragut yelled into his wrist com. "Roger that, Cal!" And he changed direction, charging toward the torpedo storage bay.

Ninety kilos sounded about right for a very tall, solidly built Roman strung with cables.

Augustus, overly tall for a U.S. space battleship's accommodations, was billeted in a torpedo rack room. Farragut yanked open the hatch to torpedo rack room six.

The rack room looked bigger without torpedoes. The ordnance had all been spent. Left were Augustus' personal belongings—elegant carpets and tapestries, the Roman canopy, the marble winged victory. And Augustus.

Augustus stood there, without a landing disk, clear-eyed, intact, and giving orders. "Captain Farragut, adjust your jammers. Mix them up. Yesterday. You're not safe. And jump to FTL. Change vector."

Farragut, not too proud to comply with a reasonable idea insubordinately expressed, relayed the instructions to his XO before he demanded, "How did you get here?"

"I displaced. Readjust your jammers. Again. I don't trust your lackeys to get it right."

Farragut gave the orders to his XO over his wrist com, then faced Augustus. "Will there be anything else, Colonel?"

"John Farragut, you don't know what you're up against."

"Follow me to the command deck and enlighten me." Captain Farragut led the way, running.

Augustus' voice sounded behind him, "You are nostril deep in *merda*."

"And you?"

"Way over my head in it. Do you know what came out of that wormhole?" John Farragut. Impatient. "Worm?"

"Big one. Romulus. Caesar Romulus."

Farragut glanced back over his shoulder, scowling at Augustus.

Augustus looked rested. There was a clarity to this being's eyes that Augustus never had. The Augustus whom Farragut knew had the haggard face of a terminal drunk. This could not possibly be Augustus.

But it could only be Augustus.

Farragut flew up the ladders and stormed through the hatch between Marine guards onto the command platform.

"Captain on deck," Commander Carmel announced.

Heads turned. Augustus entered close behind the captain.

Instantly, Calli had a hand on her sidearm. So did the Marines flanking the hatchway.

"Don't shoot the Roman," Farragut said.

Calli made eye contact with the captain. "Sir, that's not Augustus."

Farragut waved her down. "It's way too Augustus." And to Augustus, "How did you get here without a landing disk. Without a *collar*." Farragut just now noticed that vital part was missing as well.

Augustus answered, "The ship out there—the one you can't detect—has a sophisticated displacement chamber."

"What's his fire power?"

"Minimal. It's a not a battleship. It's a fortress of solitude. It's small, about the size of a U.S. Long Range Shuttle or a townhouse. It's stealthy, and it was built in the year 2448. You're about to ask if I'm from the future. I am not. But Caesar Romulus is."

"*Caesar* Romulus," Farragut echoed.

"Romulus is Caesar in the year 2448. Today, in 2443, he's only Caesar Magnus' megalomaniac son. Ask your XO about him."

"Romulus," Calli blurted. "Romulus Julius?"

"The same."

"He's not Caesar," Calli said.

"Not *today*."

"Not *ever*," Calli said. And to Farragut, "But the megalomania part is right there."

Farragut said, "Augustus, my *Merrimack* can't pick that ship out of the vacuum. How do I see him? What's he fixin' to hit me with?"

"You *can't* detect him. Not with any of your equipment, but Romulus doesn't have significant firepower. You caught a break there. He has a box of pencils."

"Stealthy pencils," Farragut said.

"They are stealthy, and they're fast. They're called serpent's teeth. His strongest weapon is his ability to displace through jammers without standard equipment. I need to adjust your jammers."

Farragut stepped aside for him to get at the controls. "Go."

That went against protocol, allowing a Roman officer, newly returned from hostile control and custody, to manipulate the ship's defenses. Farragut made quick decisions when he needed to, and he sensed he couldn't delay for a heartbeat here.

"Did *you* displace through jammers?" Calli demanded of Augustus.

"I did not. You failed to have your jammers engaged while I was outside. That was stupid. And you should have skipped town the instant I disappeared. Romulus can displace without three-way correspondence. He needs only the advanced sending station—which his ship has. It works." Augustus was living proof of that.

"And Romulus can get through our jammers," Calli said.

"Not *now*." Augustus had just scrambled the jammer sequence.

"And he's supposed to be from the year 2446?" Farragut asked. He had a tough time with that idea.

"2448 actually."

"The date on the missile fragment we have says 2446."

"That's just the patent registration date. Romulus came from five years in the future. He's lost his looks."

That last was nothing Farragut cared to hear. Augustus liked young men and seldom censored his observations.

"Romulus has better sensors. He has my Striker."

"What's his displacement range?"

"I would move your ship again."

Calli advised, "We are traveling FTL, and the ship has been making random vector changes every two or three seconds, sir."

Farragut acknowledged with a quick nod.

"And your so-called Caesar Romulus does not have your Striker, Augustus," Calli went on. "It's right there." She pointed toward the Tactical display.

The Tactical display gave a visual image to the object lurking in the perfect black. Augustus' red and black Striker tumbled end over end, its hatches open to the vacuum.

"Ah. He spat it out," Augustus said. "Don't retrieve it."

"Wasn't thinking of it," Farragut said.

Calli: "Captain, Romulus can't be behind this. He's not that smart."

"He has an enhanced mind and a huge data library," Augustus answered. "He was always clever. He's five years older than the Romulus you know. He knows how to surround himself with devoted smart people."

"Did you bring any of that huge data library back with you, Colonel Augustus?" Calli asked. She sounded as though she expected a no.

"Bits of it. Accidentally. The interesting bits. Romulus is a patterner."

Any shred of credence fell off Calli's face. "Colonel Augustus, how *exactly* did you allow yourself to be captured?"

"By being unconscious. I woke up in the Xerxes' infirmary. I didn't know Romulus brought my Striker inboard until I tried to access it."

"Access it. You mean Romulus didn't have you in restraints?" Calli said.

"He did. I have an internal connection with my Striker. It allows for silent remote access to my Striker's controls. It's silent unless someone is listening for tachyon clicks. I ordered my Striker to come. I didn't know quite how close it was. Turned out to be inside the Xerxes. I could hear it ripping up the deck clamps. Romulus ran out of the infirmary. Presumably to deal with it."

"He left you alone?" Calli said. "Really."

"In restraints, yes. My Striker's thrashing tripped a fire emergency status. Patients in an infirmary are only ever restrained for their own safety. And a Xerxes exists to keep its inhabitants safe. Under a fire emergency the patient restraints auto-release. Keeps the patients from burning alive if their caregivers are incapacitated. Surprised *me* well enough. I went straight for the displacement chamber."

Farragut turned to his XO. "Calli, get us out of here. Point us at Fort Ike."

Calli issued the necessary commands.

A soft voice sounded from the rear of the command platform. Jose Maria de Cordillera. "Young Captain? Should we not do something to bar the Rim Gate against the Hive? Might gorgons travel through the wormhole? Might they devour the Earth long before we can be born?"

"Not an issue," Augustus said.

"How is that not an issue?" Farragut asked. "I want to be born."

"Because it's an imperative to Romulus," Augustus said. "One of the pieces of information I tripped over and retained. Romulus has the right equipment and the intention to seal the Rim Gate against anything coming or going. He wants that wormhole shut for eternity. Let him do it. We can go now."

"We're all that stands between the gorgons and the living worlds in this system," Farragut said.

"Billions of gorgons will be here inside the month. We're no match," Calli said. "John, you know that."

He did know. It was tearing him up. The gorgons would destroy the beautiful, living planet, Arra.

"Holy Jesus, I do not like running from a battlefield."

Jose Maria offered, "Philip the Second said he retreated like the ram—backing up in order to hit harder."

Sounded great.

Except that's not what I'm doing here. I'm chewed and whipped and empty and delivering eighty-one dead to their mamas. And when the erks get my Mer-rimack *stitched back together, I still got nothing to stand against this monster.*

And what's possible and what's true are just not lining up anymore.

"Sir?" A specialist asked. "Are we gonna die?"

Expected the captain to say something like, "Not without a fight."

He said, absolutely, "No."

That's why men followed John Farragut.

He turned to his XO. "Fort Ike. Best speed."

"Aye, aye, sir."

✳ ✳ ✳ ✳ ✳

Romulus watched *Merrimack* leap to her FTL escape. She was gone. Augustus had got away.

Romulus had only himself to blame.

Had he learned nothing? He badly wanted to press the chase to recapture Augustus, to make Augustus pay for his future crimes. But it wasn't a chase anymore. It would be a hunt.

And Augustus might be dead already.

Romulus couldn't count on it. He had *just* managed to jettison the patterner's Striker before it could rip up his Xerxes from the inside.

Augustus' Striker drifted now, detectable by standard sensors, its hatches open to space.

The Striker was an antique vessel, custom-conformed to its antique pilot. Romulus could destroy it. But he was reluctant to burn another serpent's tooth. He sorely regretted not carrying a bigger arsenal. He had expected to have two Legion carriers at his disposal by now.

Romulus' prescience was a rapidly diminishing reservoir. Already *Merrimack* could be reporting his existence to the powers in Near Space. Would anyone believe there were two of him?

Romulus recognized his worst mistake had come while he'd revived Augustus. Augustus had brief, accidental exposure to knowledge he should never have. Romulus should have just let Augustus die.

It was vital that Augustus not have the Hive harmonics. An Augustus able to control the Hive would be the end of everything. Romulus was afraid to find out what Augustus had seen. Afraid. But he had to know.

With profound dread he tapped into his data banks to see what Augustus' mind had touched.

Did Augustus have the Hive harmonics?

He did not.

Romulus confirmed it twice. Augustus had not accessed information on resonance.

Romulus disconnected from patterner mode, shaking. He brushed moisture from his upper lip. He'd narrowly escaped complete disaster there. He should not be making these kinds of missteps.

Prioritize. Stay disciplined.

Before leaving the Myriad, Romulus launched the assassin missile, which Cinna had prepared, to seek and destroy that megalomaniac Constantine Siculus on Planet Zero, deep in the Deep End of the galaxy.

Constantine Siculus was the only other person in existence in the year 2443 who knew the Hive harmonics and how to determine a location of a resonant pulse. That information must belong to Romulus alone.

It would take months for the assassin missile to connect with its target, but it would be done. Constantine would die.

Augustus' Striker remained as an unaddressed problem. Romulus didn't dare leave it behind intact. But he didn't want to spend any of his ammunition on it.

He knew how he could secure the ship without destroying it himself.

He floated a spider drone into the derelict Striker to place a new interface on top of the patterner's interface. Should Augustus attempt to take remote resonant control of his Striker, the new interface would rewrite Augustus' programming and rupture every synapse in his brain.

That was a good contingency measure.

It wasn't enough.

Augustus was smart. He may be antique and evil, but Romulus shouldn't underestimate Augustus' cunning. Augustus—or anyone—might take the Striker in physical tow.

So Romulus floated a remora into the Striker, where it concealed itself inside the navigation system, to wait—forever if need be—for its trigger. Should the Striker ever drop out of FTL in Near Space territory, the remora would resonate the irresistible harmonic. Ravenous gorgons would announce the Striker's arrival. By then Romulus would have a proper arsenal with which to destroy the Striker, if the Hive hadn't finished it off first.

Now there was one last task Romulus needed to perform before he set off for Near Space and civilization—block and mask the Rim Gate. Nothing must pass through that wormhole ever again. Romulus and Cinna had devised the perfect barrier.

Once Romulus positioned the barrier, he was done here. He turned his Xerxes toward Palatine.

Merrimack, taking her shortcut through the U.S. Shotgun, would reach Near Space before him. There was nothing for it. Romulus would get there. In time.

The Empire needed Romulus.

Rome. Claudia. I come.

17

10 June 2443
U.S. Space Battleship *Merrimack*
Sagittarian Space
FTL

FLIGHT SERGEANT DAK SHEPARD sat up. He wasn't wearing clothes. Didn't know this compartment. It was cold. The lights were dim. He didn't want to be here.

Last he remembered, he was swabbing melted gorgons off the deck after the last gorgon battle. No. Wait. He'd finished doing that. He remembered eating pretzels. He'd heard a cicada. A barking dog. Saw Kerry Blue's eyes get real round.

He'd got real dizzy, as if all the blood was rushing out of his head. Last thing he'd heard was little Reg Monroe screaming that way high ice-pick-in-the-ear shriek she had.

Now he was here. Missed a whole lot of what happened in between there and here.

Didn't know where they'd stuck him. This wasn't the ship's hospital. Wasn't the brig, either, but it was real gloomy. Looked the way he imagined a morgue would.

He swung his legs over the side of the pallet. Set bare feet on the deck grates. *Yi-ya!* It was cold. Heart of greta cold.

He found a sheet. Just lying there. He pulled it around himself, then pushed through the hatch to a corridor.

Not a part of the ship he normally saw.

A navvy fluids tech turned, stared. Dak expected some comment like "nice toga," but the navvy got all hunched over and hustled away like he'd seen a zombie.

Dak found a reflective surface. Nope. He was not a zombie. Just a naked man clutching a sheet.

Not sure where he was in the ship. Didn't want to get caught checking the bull's-eye like a rookie to find what deck he was on.

Finally someone came, walking straight toward him. Short guy. Older. Balding. White coat. No shoulders.

It was Mo Shah. The Riverite doctor.

Mo stopped, eyed Dak head to really cold toes, then said kindly, "Be coming with me, please." Mo took Dak's arm.

Nice man, Mo. There were folks on board Dak liked better, but for out-and-out nice, you gotta go with the Mo. And Mo's hand was warm.

Mo Shah guided Dak through the labyrinth of corridors and shafts to the nice warm, bright hospital section in the ship's main fuselage. Dak made Mo lead the way up the ladders. Didn't want anyone looking up his toga.

Mack carried a big hospital. Medics and techs and Marines and everyone including the ship's dogs clustered around—at a distance—staring as Mo and Dak came through. Dak wondered if he should balance a ball on his nose for them.

And here's Lieutenant Colonel Steele and Captain Farragut. God and God Almighty. Dak froze a moment, torn between coming to attention and holding onto his sheet. Tent Hut! And oh, crud, there goes the sheet.

All eyes wandered off to the sides. A quick nod down from the captain—his eyes way off that way—gave Dak leave to retrieve the sheet. Dak dove for it.

A screech shot up like a sonic bomb from behind all the tall people up front.

"DAK!"

Dak cringed, grasping his sheet around him. "Oh, Reggie girl! The ears!"

Lieutenant Colonel Steele looked thunderstruck. Dak didn't know the Old Man's face could make that expression.

The captain was looking kinda real surprised too. Captain's face never hid anything.

"Dak." The captain didn't sound sure. "It's Dak Shepard, isn't it?"

Dak nodded. Cap'n knew everyone's name.

"How are you, son?"

"Uh." Had to think about that one. "Okay. Nekked, sir. Cold. I had a real greta of a nightmare."

"How did you come to be in this state, son?"

Dak's teeth were chattering. "I dunno. Can I get some clothes?"

Captain said softly, "Mo, see to the Marine."

Right after he ordered everyone back to their stations, Captain Farragut sought out the one person who hadn't been in the hospital staring at Dak.

Augustus, about as long as a torpedo, lay in a rack, an ornate Roman tapestry pulled across him for a blanket. He didn't rise at the captain's entrance. Didn't open his eyes. It was normal for Augustus to sleep most of the day.

Farragut said, "Something you want to report, Augustus?"

Eyes stayed shut. "I brought one of your Marines back to life."

"Yes," Farragut said. "Was it just the one?"

There had been eighty-one dead in static cold storage on the space battleship. Eighty now.

"The flight sergeant was the only one I could repair," Augustus said. "He was still fresh when they put him in the preserver. And his was a simple wound."

Yes. Of course. Beheading was simple.

One of the hard-shelled, pincered kind of monster—the kind called a can opener—had killed Flight Sergeant Shepard. Simply.

"I thought Rome didn't have the technology for that kind of resurrection," Farragut said.

"Rome doesn't. Romulus does. I came across the procedure in Romulus' data bank. The knowledge was interesting. It stayed with me after I disconnected. Thought I'd try it."

"You experimented on my Marine?"

"I sense disapproval. It wasn't as though I was going to kill him. Should I put him back the way I found him? Is he not all right? He struck me as rather peculiar."

Augustus had restored the Marine just fine. Dak had a lot of great qualities, but intellect was not one of them.

"Can you re-sus the others?" Farragut asked.

"The others are overdone. And you assume they want to be brought back."

"I do assume," Farragut said.

"I do not."

Augustus had been brought back from the dead. Never was happy about it.

✳ ✳ ✳ ✳ ✳

Marines in the forecastle stood up and applauded Dak's entrance right before Taps.

The Yurg gave Dak's head a tug, making sure it was on tight.

"What was it like?" Gunner Shasher Wyatt asked.

"I don't wanna do it again," Flight Sergeant Dak Shepard said. Then he saw Kerry Blue, and he gave a hopeful grin. "Welcome a man back from the dead?"

"Uh." Kerry Blue took a step backward. "I don't do zombies."

Lieutenant Hazard Sewell stepped down from officers' country to welcome Dak back to life.

"Where are we, sir?" Dak asked. "Where'd all the stars go?"

No stars meant they were traveling FTL.

"We're halfway home."

"You mean we left the Myriad?"

"Feels like a retreat," Flight Leader Hazard Sewell said. Southern gentleman Hazard Sewell took retreats personally.

"That's because it's a retreat, sir," Carly Delgado said, sour. She was sitting on the edge of Dak's sleep pod in the rack. She flicked her switchblade into the cracks between deck grates at her feet.

There was a League of Earth Nations ship still operating back there inside the star cluster Myriad. The international ship was one of the big round geodesic kind that everyone called a LEN golf ball. It was orbiting the planet Arra, taking on all the refugees it could. The LEN were doing good work, and righteous proud of it they were, too. They let *Merrimack* know it. Flight Sergeant Taher had been standing guard at the hatch to the command platform when some Lennie official from the golf ball called *Merrimack* coward over the com and tried to *order* Captain Farragut to get back there and pick up refugees.

"Cap'n told 'em we're chewed," Taher said. "Told 'em we're out of hard ordnance, and we're carrying eighty-one dead."

"That many?" Kerry Blue said.

"Wow," Reggie said, real soft.

"Yeah," Taher said. "The Lennie says back, 'Then you have eighty-one open sleep pods, do you not?'"

Big Richard gave a kind of gurgle. "What'd the captain say to *that?*"

"I don't know those words," Taher said. "Anyway, it's down to eighty now. Can't count Dak anymore."

"I'm not sleeping with no alien," Dak said.

Taher's head ducked down. His eyebrows stayed up where they were. "*What?*"

Cole Darby patted Dak's beefy shoulder. "We won't let the aliens get your sleep pod, Dak."

"They're not getting my C-rats neither."

"They can have mine," said Menendez.

"I was told the Arrans can't digest anything we have to eat," Reg Monroe said. "We would need to carry food for the aliens too, if we took them aboard. Their molecules are built wrong. Is that true?"

"Yeah, there's something like that," Kerry Blue said. "I couldn't eat anything when I was on world."

Tattoo was sounding over the loud com: "TAPS, TAPS, lights out, all hands turn into their rack, no movement about the decks Taa-AAAPS."

The she-men withdrew to the double x chromosomed side of the forecastle. The forecastle went dark.

You could still hear your mates rustling in their pods.

"Where are the Romans?" someone whispered.

"What do you want with 'em?"

"Shoot 'em."

"I thought there were Romans out here." The voice sounded like Big Richard's.

There had been rumors of a massive buildup of Romans in the Deep End. Sixty-four Legions. That was the number you always heard.

"Hope they're doin' better than we are." That sounded like Shasher Wyatt.

"They're Romans! I hope they all get eaten." That also sounded like Shasher Wyatt. So it had to be Shasher's twin, Dumbell. "Do you think we taste like chicken?"

Dak told them to shut up.

✳ ✳ ✳ ✳ ✳

22 June 2443
U.S. Space Battleship *Merrimack*
Perseid Space

Grunt work. It's what you do with seven hundred and twenty Marines when they weren't fighting. You tried to fill their every waking moment and leave 'em too spent to dream. They always, always, had something in reserve.

And some things never change. There's Kerry Blue making some navvy very happy in the maintenance shed. And tearing the hell out of every dream Lieutenant Colonel TR Steele wasn't allowed to have.

What was it about Kerry Blue that shot his brain out the air lock? She was nobody's vision of immortal beauty. Nothing out of the ordinary about her face, except that it turned him to slush. She looked friendly. Her hair was brown. Breasts, yes. Two present, but not the first things Steele saw. Hips and ass—maybe he saw those first. It was her loose-jointed, unsoldierly hi-there walk that was going to land him in Leavenworth. He couldn't even call it a come on. It was the way Kerry Blue got herself from here to there whether anyone was looking or not. When she climbed over an obstacle, it wasn't smooth, but it was, well, easy. Kerry Blue was easy. Her voice was definitely a she-voice. Not particularly sweet. It was bright and a little bit scratchy, and the sound of it hollowed Steele right out.

She was a screamer. An ecstatic screamer. You always know what Kerry's doing. Just not who. Not Steele. Not ever.

Apparently she was over that asshole Cowboy. She'd had way too much help getting over that asshole Cowboy.

Steele bellowed at Flight Sergeant Kerry Blue to get back into uniform and get her work done. He added more tasks, not sure they even needed doing. Anything to keep Kerry Blue occupied in some activity other than what she did best—break TR Steele's heart.

He wanted her more than he wanted his next breath.

Why was there no air to be had whenever she left a compartment?

And whose idiot idea was it to allow women in the Fleet Marine anyway?

As for the navvy who'd been helping Kerry get over that asshole Cowboy, Steele wanted him dead. The navvy wasn't in Steele's chain of command, so Steele couldn't skin him. That guy had run like a rabbit, and Steele tried not to look at him. Didn't want to be able to recognize him.

Steele turned his eyes to the overhead while Flight Sergeant Kerry Blue zipped and snapped. "Sir?" she said, like gearing up for a question.

Steele grunted for her to go ahead.

"Do you think Augustus could bring Cowboy back from the dead? You know, like he did Dak?"

Steele felt his whole head burn. Why didn't she just plunge a dagger into his chest? He roared at her to go carry out her orders.

He stalked away, breaths heaving as though he'd just come out of the ring after twelve rounds with King Kong Goliath. His head was on fire. He heard a roaring.

Bring Cowboy back?

I wanted him dead! I want him to stay dead!

TR Steele hated Cowboy.

Because Kerry Blue loved him. She loved Cowboy, and she'd just stepped on Steele's guilt for wishing one of his own men dead.

Steele was dizzy with rage.

Could Augustus bring Cowboy back from the dead?

He didn't remember deciding to come here. But Steele found himself here, standing at the monster's hatch.

Steele didn't tap for admittance. He pounded with the bottom of his fist to announce himself, then let himself into the lair of the loathed Roman cyborg Augustus.

Augustus was horizontal in his rack. The man looked like a hungry snake amid a lot of gaudy Roman stuff that glittered like gold.

One eye opened. This was some mythical creature you sell your soul to. Augustus commented languidly, "You?"

This visit was unexpected.

Unexpected on Steele's part too. And, just to be a shit, Steele answered back, "No." *This is not me.*

Augustus didn't speak again. It was Steele's move.

No way out now. Just say what he came for. "It's about Flight Sergeant Jaime Carver."

"I don't know this man."

"You heard of him. They called him Cowboy. He died right before you came aboard. He's in the morgue."

"Oh. That mess," Augustus said. "I know the one."

Steele wanted to retreat. Wanted to go take a shower. It was as if this creature's glance left a slime on him. And Steele didn't even want what he was about to ask for.

He came here out of guilt for wanting Kerry Blue. Out of guilt for wanting Cowboy dead because Kerry Blue loved him.

Steele had wanted Cowboy dead. And now Cowboy was dead.

He was my soldier.

Cowboy had done it to himself. That was a fact. Still, Steele heard himself asking, choking, "Can you bring Cowboy back from the dead like you did Flight Sergeant Shepard?"

Augustus moved, like a snake shifting its coils. He exhaled as if going to sleep. He closed his eyes, dismissive, and said, "I can't ungrind meat."

* * * * *

28 June 2443
U.S. Space Battleship *Merrimack*
Perseid Space

The voyage to Fort Eisenhower dragged on. From Fort Ike the two megaklick jump to Fort Roosevelt would take less than a heartbeat. Getting to Fort Ike was taking a lifetime.

With no gorgons to kill, a man gets restless.

Flight Sergeant Cole Darby. The Darb. In for a routine physical.

Doctor Mohsen Shah glanced at his patient. Glanced again. Looked startled. As startled as the serene Riverite ever got. "How has your nose come to being so?"

"What?" said Cole Darby. As if nothing whatsoever could be wrong.

"Your nose is being flat."

"It is being smelling just fine, Mo." Darb gave a sniff. "Smells nice in here. Smells green."

Mo Shah kept the ship's hospital smelling of chlorophyll.

Mo inspected the nose. "The cartilage is being crushed."

Cole Darby shrugged. "So I look like Dak."

Cole Darby had been in a fight. Fighting will get you in deep shiatsu on board a Navy ship.

Mo asked, "Who won the fight?"

"The guy with the straight nose."

Mo gave a sigh. And let the issue roll. Count on a Riverite to let it roll. The physician said, "I am needing to be mending your nose."

"Do you have to?" Cole Darby asked. "I like this look." He checked his profile in the mirror as far as he could. His eyes slid all the way sideways. His normally straight Anglo nose had gone altogether snubby. "Do I look like a street king or what?"

"It is indeed being a face that is belonging in the brig." Mo agreed. "The Navy is wanting its Fleet Marines to be performing at optimal capacity. That is including breathing."

"Fine. Fine. Fine." Cole Darby was doomed to carry a face that could strike terror in the hearts of baby bunnies, but only for their first six weeks. "Fix my honking nose."

❋ ❋ ❋ ❋ ❋

1 July 2443
U.S. Space Battleship *Merrimack*
Sagittarian Space

Something was not right on John Farragut's ship. A secret. A secret known to a lot of people, but not to him, and he was the captain. Farragut asked his XO, "Do you know what's afoot?"

"I've got it covered, sir."

"I'd like to know exactly what you have covered, Mister Carmel."

Calli pressed her full lips into a line. Confessed. "They've decorated the Og, sir."

Took a couple moments for all the implications to sink in. The surly chief, Ogden Bannerman, would never stand for any kind of "decoration," whatever that meant. Farragut realized, "He's asleep on duty."

Calli nodded.

"You woke him?"

Calli pouted, shut her eyes with a serious shake of her head that said, *Not on a bet.*

Another realization, "You decorated him?"

Calli nodded, desperate not to smile.

"Write him up?"

"Just waiting till he wakes up, sir."

"Well," said Farragut, resigned. "Let's see him."

* * *

The Og was a piece of work. This was serious.

The Chief had fallen asleep in his chair. So heavy a sleep you might have thought he was dead except for the snoring.

For that much stuff to be hanging on him meant the Chief had been there a long time. From the looks of it he had been visited by every navvy and Marine on board the space battleship.

Christmas ornaments and earrings hung from all parts of his clothing, and he was strung three times round with Ramadan lights—which were the same thing as Christmas lights except that these came out of Sabrina Ali's locker. There was a dreidel in his ear.

It was amazing what the crew had squirreled away in those little lockers. Chalk. There was always chalk on any ship of war. What else would one use to write messages on one's bombs? Someone had chalked the Og's brambling brows blue.

The string of formal spoons had to have come from Chef Zack, who kept a close eye on his cutlery. There was also a popcorn garland, and a garland of all the spare/lost buttons on board *Merrimack*, and crown of braided garlic over locks of cornsilk hair.

Company and crew had stuffed socks inside the Og's shirt to give him breasts. There was a flanged leather skirt of Roman ceremonial armor draped half round the Og's waist. There was too much Og for it to go all the way around.

"Where'd he get the Roman kilt?" Farragut whispered.

Calli gave a significant look. The answer was obvious, but still a surprise. Only one person on board had a set of Roman ceremonial armor.

Farragut blinked, surprised. "Damn."

The Og woke bellowing. You could hear the thunder throughout the ship. Threatening all with the brig, castration, cat-o-nine-tails, keel-hauling. Chief Ogden Bannerman was going to bring every last one of you dogs up on charges. You'll have to come to me to get your crap back and when you do—

In the sudden silence, you could guess that Chief Ogden Bannerman had found the captain's stars on his collar.

✳ ✳ ✳ ✳ ✳

4 July 2443
U.S. Space Battleship *Merrimack*
Sagittarian Space

Company and crew were performing a percussive version of the 1812 Overture on the ship. Any tool and any solid surface could be conscripted into the orchestra.

Colonel Augustus glared at Captain Farragut. He had been doing it since he entered the Officers' Mess and took up a barstool next to the captain.

Farragut finally demanded, "What?"

"Romulus remembers a Subjugation," Augustus said. It had the sound of something that had been festering for a while.

"Subjugation? What's that?"

Augustus' brows drew together. Farragut read an unspoken *As if you didn't know* on Augustus' face. Augustus said, "Roman Legions marching under crossed spears. There's defeat, and then there's degradation. Subjugation happens when you crush and humiliate your enemy."

"Nothing like that ever happened on my watch."

"It did in Romulus' timeline."

"You're looking at me like it's my fault."

"You ordered it."

"Pretty sure I didn't."

Softly, "You really don't know?"

"There's a lot I don't know. What in particular's got you looking at me like I killed your dog?"

The look in Augustus' black eyes was all hatred.

"Sixty-four Roman Legions are gone."

"What do you mean *gone?*"

5 July 2443
U.S. Space Battleship *Merrimack*
Sagittarian Space

"Sir?"

It was *her* voice. Steele turned mechanically.

Kerry Blue there. "Thank you for asking Augustus about Cowboy."

Steele felt himself turning to glue. Steele didn't know how she'd found out that he'd asked Augustus for help. That Roman ghoul must have told her. The man was not a man. Augustus was a natural sadist.

Steele had only asked Augustus to revive Cowboy to clear his own conscience. Because Steele had wanted Cowboy dead.

Cowboy was dead. Why was Kerry Blue still hanging her heart on that worthless ass?

Steele growled at her. "I didn't do it for you. I did it for his widow."

Kerry Blue's freckles got very noticeable. Her face had gone to chalk. She looked like he'd just shot her.

Her voice came out thin. "His what?"

Part of him wanted to shout at her, call her a slut. But he was an officer. Rules of frat said he had no right thinking about what she did in her free time. He was blundering like a jilted, out of line moose.

"Cowboy's wife," he snarled at her. "His pregnant wife!"

✳ ✳ ✳ ✳ ✳

5 Quintilis 2443
Xerxes
The Abyss

Like sailing ships of old, spaceships took time to cross the vastness between shores. Even traveling faster than light it took months just to cross the explored part of the galaxy.

As Romulus' ship crept back toward civilization—crossing the thinly starred region known as the Abyss that stretched between the Sagittarian arm of the galaxy and Near Space—he marked the points so far where the anticipated reality had branched off in different directions. They were small things, most of them. But he, of all people, knew that small things— nano-sized things—could make exponential changes in a pattern.

Merrimack had been exactly where she was supposed to be, but *Merrimack* had a sister ship, *Monitor*. Where was *Monitor*?

He found her where he thought she should be. *Monitor* was operating in Near Space, close to Earth. There was supposed to be a Roman mole on *Monitor*, serving as a command officer. Romulus couldn't find a record of the mole on board. He couldn't find any record of the man at all. Jorge Medina never existed. That was frightening.

Romulus would not allow himself to be frightened. Uncertainty was a fact of existence. He was a patterner. He would adjust.

What hadn't changed: Romulus' younger self was already gathering loyal followers who would one day call themselves Romulii. He remembered doing that. His younger alter ego was recruiting Legions in Perseid space in his own name without his father's knowledge. One of the smartest things he'd ever done. He had done a lot of things right. Those Legions were still intact and loyal to him. Romulus could use those.

Magnus didn't know about the Perseid Legions, so that useless old man hadn't flushed those brave souls down the Hive's maw with the other sixty-four Legions.

I am the only one in the galaxy alive today who knows there are two Hives.

I am only one who knows the Hive harmonics.

I am the only one who knows what makes the irresistible harmonic irresistible.

Very well, there was Constantine Siculus remaining at large. Constantine also knew the Hive harmonics. But Constantine was not long for this universe. The assassin missile was on its way hubward, to Constantine's distant lair.

Romulus was the only man alive who knew that resonating the complement of a Hive harmonic exterminated the entire Hive. He knew that because it had been done in the future.

And Romulus knew how to calculate the harmonic of the succeeding Hive generation that hatched after its parent Hive died. He'd got that algorithm from a mole on board *Merrimack*.

His mole wasn't on board *Merrimack* in this timeline. Her name was Geneva Rhine. She had given him all of *Merrimack*'s historical logs. But it seemed now that the records that Geneva Rhine gave him in 2448 were not an entirely accurate record of events here and now in the year 2443.

Romulus recognized that his current existence must be a parallel universe, not just a fork in the universe he had known. Events predating his arrival had changed. The idea was terrifying.

He had no time for terror. He needed to account for the differences.

What do people in this year in this universe know of me?

They knew that Romulus was Caesar Magnus' natural son. Leadership in the Roman Empire was not hereditary. But the Empire ran on patronage. The son of Caesar commanded attention. Romulus' status as son of

Caesar gave him a usable allowance and produced a tendency in people to say yes to him.

No one refused Romulus credit. He needn't tap his own existing funds, which was good, because his alter ego might notice the expenditures.

Romulus was still months away from Near Space, but resonance was immediate and everywhere. Resonance knew no spatial distance. Romulus could make transactions and issue orders to Near Space from his Xerxes just as easily as he could from the palace in Nova Roma on Palatine. He need only avoid attracting the notice of his other self. His journey was long, but Romulus had work to do and he didn't need to be on Palatine to get started.

❋ ❋ ❋ ❋ ❋

8 July 2443
U.S. Space Battleship *Merrimack*
Fort Dwight David Eisenhower
Edge of Sagittarian Space

Merrimack's crew and half bat of Fleet Marines looked out the portals as the space battleship sublighted for her approach to Fort Eisenhower.

Merrimack always got a festive welcome at Ike.

Not this time.

The assembled space stations that comprised the fort were dark. No flags. No concert over the fort's channel. There was no light show. Few lights at all. Just reds and greens to tell *Merrimack* where the space lanes were, and the controller's matter-of-fact voice telling her where to go.

It filled the ship with unease.

Everyone knew that the Hive was advancing. But the first spheres, moving at their top speed, wouldn't be here at the space fort for another six years. It seemed a little soon to start mourning. Farragut couldn't even call his ship's reception subdued. It was hostile.

Should the Hive go unchecked, these space stations would be the first U.S. settlements in line to be eaten. National defense needed to find a way to turn back the Hive. Meanwhile they formulated plans to evacuate the fort.

There was already a long line of ships queued up to get into the Shotgun and back to Near Space, and back to Earth.

Lieutenant Colonel Steele could count on Farragut to treat his dogs right. But the captain was a little slow in calling for liberty this time. Steele sought him out at the change of the watch. "Captain, are my men getting any R and R?"

"Not here, TR."

Steele withheld an expression of disapproval. The Fleet Marines always got liberty at the space forts. They really needed it now. The soldiers were battle-scarred and in mourning. They'd taken to leaving notes and candy on their dead friends' preservation pods.

Marines bounced back quickly if you let them out to play. They lived fast, played hard, and then they were ready for the next fight.

Steele saw them gazing toward the lights in the portholes, hopeful as dogs holding their leashes in their mouths.

Farragut must have heard Steele gearing up for a protest, because he said, "You don't want to let your dogs ashore here, TR. This is grim. You're not hearing the com chat."

It had got ugly. Com pundits were demanding that *Merrimack* go back and help the planets in the Myriad battle the Hive invasion. The voices were calling on all stations in Fort Ike not to let *Merrimack* personnel debark at their facilities.

Fort Dwight David Eisenhower issued its own statement advising that any space station found turning away U.S. soldiers must detach and depart from the space fort at once under its own power. The Shotgun was forbidden to it.

Farragut told Steele, "Ike is no place to walk your dogs. Mine either. Wait till we get to Fort Ted. I'm fixin' to push us to the head of this line into the Shotgun. Don't much care whose head I gotta kick. We'll be there."

"Sir?" Steele began, then waited for permission to speak further.

"Go ahead, TR."

"This is a U.S. fort."

Fort Ike was a huge trading post, operating under the protection of the United States military. Its international constellation of space stations depended on the Shotgun for commercial traffic.

"Why are we letting the LEN say anything at all?" Steele asked.

"We're a member of the LEN," Farragut said.

Steele drew in his chin. "We *are?*"

For allies, you really just wanted to shoot them.

Steele then asked, "Permission to go ashore, sir?"

"Purpose?"

"Foraging."

"Go. Make it fast. Watch your back."

Steele collected LEN glowers in Fort Ike. To hell with them. He was on a mission. He saw what the captain was talking about. Too many refugees here. Too much LEN.

He completed his objective and returned to *Merrimack* chased by slugs.

Steele felt all the eyes on him as he stepped into the forecastle. He'd rather be going into battle than face this lot with this news.

"Are we getting out of the can, sir?" a Marine asked. Sounded like Shasher Wyatt. Might've been his twin, Dumbell.

At least Steele's dogs didn't look all that hopeful this time, so he wouldn't be disappointing them bitterly.

They had eyes. They could see what was out the portholes.

Steele gave one quick shake of his head. "Cap'n says the party's at Fort Ted."

His eyes flicked toward a porthole, to the darkness outside.

He spoke without looking at anyone. "Flight Sergeant Blue. Report to hydroponics at 2045." And he was out through the hatch.

Kerry Blue's eyes got big. She exchanged stares with her mates. Her voice came out pitched way high. "What now? What did I *do*?"

Hydroponics? She thought quickly. What could be in hydroponics? "Oh, shitska. He's gonna make me beach my lizard plant!"

"Aw, no!" little Reg cried. "You don't really think so."

"What else could it be?"

Kerry had got the lizard plant on the planet Arra. The ruler of the world gave it to her. It was a sweet little guy—the lizard plant was. The Archon was okay too.

"The Old Man can't make me set my little guy ashore, can he?"

Big fat long pause.

Icky Iverson blurted, "He might."

Really might. What else could he want with her in hydroponics? "What time is it now?"

"You got seven minutes, *chica*."

"I gotta go."

Kerry Blue ran up decks, shot up the ladders, hauled herself through the hatch into the moist brightness of hydroponics. Inhaled to announce herself.

Steele wasn't here yet.

Kerry Blue was alone with the vegetation. The large compartment was misty and warm, filled with light and oxygen.

A light weight settled on her shoulder. A webby foot touched her cheek. Her lizard plant crooned in her ear.

Poor little guy was gonna be the only one of its kind. She'd wished ever since they'd left Arra that she'd brought a friend for it. She was lucky to have this one. A wobble started in her throat. Steele was going to take her big-eyed green friend away.

At 2045 hours the hatch opened. Kerry Blue came to attention.

Kerry's lizard plant climbed to the top of her head. It was quivering wildly.

Yeah, the Old Man could be a real scary guy. Kerry stood rigid.

Steele advanced stiffly up the row, carrying a bunch of leaves in one big hand. Funny how red Steele looked under the cool lights.

He set the green leafy bunch down in a row of lettuce under the nearest sprinkler. Grunted. "Here."

Within the bunch of leaves, two round soulful eyes opened. The tightly wrapped leaves relaxed in a motion like a sigh. Now Kerry could see the tail, the legs.

"Oh!" She couldn't talk, too joyful. She gushed, "How? How did you do this!"

"LEN's been bitchin' at us to take on refugees. I took one."

Kerry's lizard plant leaned so far over Kerry's face it teetered and had to set one webby foot on her nose to catch its balance. The lizard plant was quivering. Then it jumped down into the lettuce with the new guy.

Steele had turned stiffly about face and was marching out. He was at the hatch.

Kerry cried at his back. "Sir! Thank you! Thank you so much!"

A snarl. A grunt without looking back. He was out.

The two lizard plants crooned at each other, singing and chortling. And okay, *that* was a giggle. Kerry had to laugh.

She wished Steele had stayed to see this. But what the hell. The man's got a heart of brick.

18

9 July 2443
U.S. Space Battleship *Merrimack*
Fort Dwight David Eisenhower
Sagittarian Space

Q UICKER THAN ANYONE EVER EXPECTED,
the order came down from the XO for all hands to assume whole
ship displacement stations.

No one was sure who Farragut had charmed, threatened, or promised
what, but *Merrimack* was given the next space lane into the Shotgun. The
ship would be in Near Space in no time.

9 July 2443
U.S. Space Battleship *Merrimack*
Fort Theodore Roosevelt
Beta Aurigae star system
Near Space

Merrimack arrived in Fort Roosevelt the same instant she left Fort
Eisenhower.

Unwrapped from her displacement shroud, *Merrimack* made a guided
approach into the wide collection of space stations that formed Fort Theodore Roosevelt. The lights were on. The flags were out.

As *Merrimack* traveled the space lanes among the stations, skyrockets, fanfare, and fountains of lights met her. You could see people crowding the clear ports of all the stations to wave and salute the battered space battleship. There was music piping across the Fort's channel.

Merrimack had her running lights on. The company and crew could see the space battleship's ragged, beaten reflection in the shiny surfaces of the stations' clear ports. People were taking pictures of her. They cheered her and gripped friendly fists like encouraging a champion boxer to get up.

Space stations vied with one another for how many Bulldogs and Merrimackers they could host. Gotta love a place that don't let you buy your own drinks.

Fort Ted had the facilities to repair *Mack*. The station's maintenance hangar had a new engine manufactured, ready and standing by for installation. Senior Engineer Kit Kittering looked as if she'd got a pony for Christmas.

The twin suns of Beta Aurigae were wrapped together tighter than Mercury and the Sun, and they orbited each other a lot faster. All Marines and navvies had filters implanted in their eyes, or they would all be blind from staring at the suns going round and round.

There was a red dwarf component of this star system, too, but at 330 astronomical units out you couldn't see it, even if there hadn't been all the fortress lights washing out the view.

A miasma of escaped air from the many stations gave the Fort a slight atmosphere. It glowed a bit, like a city in fog.

Inside the space stations, the locals made the visiting Marines feel right at home.

Kerry Blue, unleashed, went pub hopping with her team.

Liberty was granted on approved stations. The Marines made the rounds, bar to bar, station to station. They didn't go to Mad Bear O's. Too many officers. The Fleet Marines gathered at places like The Five Chariots, MorePork, and, of course, Boobook's under the sign of a rather astonished looking owl.

Kerry Blue and Team Alpha had to visit Squid Station. Just had to. There was no place to get a drink in Squidville, but the Vwakikikikik—"squids" to their friends—were always good for a laugh. It was always a surprise when funniness translated across alien genomes. Humor didn't always translate among human tribes, so it was outright weird to connect with absolute aliens.

The squids were even funnier now with the new language module. The patterner Augustus had rewritten the whole interface. Never realized how many shades of meaning were missing in the old one until you listened using the new one.

Merrimack had a dedicated xenolinguist on board. You would've thought he might have noticed the shortcomings in the old translator. Apparently it was slow work for an unenhanced brain, and Doctor Patrick Hamilton had other things to do. Didn't stop him from trying to find flaws in the new language module.

He didn't find any.

In the Squid Station, more properly Vwakikikikik Station (Yeah, like squids were ever proper), transparent tunnels through the water gave visiting humans dry, oxygenated paths to stroll among the residents. You had to wear the Vwakikikikik language module to understand what the squids were saying. Sometimes it was better not to know.

Vwakikikikik Station was pretty in a blue sort of way. The red, yellow, and white corals were beautiful, but dumb as lava. The long waving lavender, yellow, pink, and green seaweeds were very intelligent. Someone had dubbed those "Sargassons." The name stuck.

Sargassons insured the survival and spread of their species across the cosmos by being colorful and decorative in countless aquariums of many alien species across Near Space.

Unlike Sargassons, squids didn't have much use for serenity. The squids would sneak up on you in your pedestrian tunnel at a stealthy glide through the veils of purple, blue, and green seaweed and reefs of brilliant coral, then, abruptly, they splatted themselves against the transparent walkway with a loud *thwuck!* of their suckers, which was squidese for "gotcha!"

Squids cackled like crumpling metal when they made people jump.

Squids recognized human faces. In fact, they recognized faces better than Kerry Blue did. So the squids all noticed there was a new guy in Team Alpha, Cole Darby. The Darb was carrying an octopus. He'd bought it from a vendor on the main station of Fort Ted. Now he was lugging it around in a globe.

Well, you'd've thought the Darb had brought a puppy. The squids were all squeaking and bubbling over the adorable little thing.

Squids did a large import trade in terrestrial octopi. (That's *octopuses* if you're a red-blooded American who refuses to use Latin plurals, thank you very much.) Most humans assumed the Vwakikikikik were eating the octopuses. Not so. The octopuses were beloved pets to the squids, like dogs to man. On the watery planet Vwakikikikikkk, octopus was squid's best friend. And while the octopuses were edible, the Vwakikikikik found the very suggestion heinous.

The Vwakikikikik asked after Cowboy Carver. Everybody loved Cowboy, and the squids were really sad to learn of his passing. Then some large mouth went and let drop that Flight Sergeant Cole Darby was Cowboy Carver's replacement.

Thick moment.

Darb—who turned out to be a real smart guy though not the bravest—handed over the puppy. Okay it was the octopus. Darb pushed the globe through the tunnel membrane and into the water for the squids to hold.

The squids were charmed. They ballasted the globe and passed the octopus around, bubbling. They were thrilled pink—literally—that they were allowed to keep it.

Cole Darby was no Cowboy Carver, but he was okay.

The Alphas got to reminiscing with the squids about Cowboy Carver.

There was the time Cowboy had done a male stripper act in the pedestrian tunnel. One squid turned vivid pink and curled its tentacles into quivering loops on the watery side of the tunnel membrane. Then a squid official came jetting over. The officious one informed Cowboy that his courtship had been accepted. The official had Cowboy—hell, it had all of them—convinced that the betrothal was a binding Vwakikikikik contract and that Vwakikikikik station had the sovereign status of an embassy, so squid law was THE law here.

Cowboy had gone and got himself married.

A junior squid pushed scuba gear through the passageway's membrane and into the dry pedestrian tunnel. Told Cowboy he could gear up and pass through the membrane to consummate the union.

Cowboy ran screaming to the nearest displacement facility and back to *Merrimack*. Never saw any man move that fast and that loud.

Old Man Steele threw Cowboy in the brig, and Cowboy was happy to be there.

The squids, who knew how to run a prank all the way home, signaled *Merrimack* and offered to post Cowboy's bail. Steele had very woodenly informed the Vwakikikikik that there was no bail in the military. The squids told the Old Man to "unstuff." No one ever saw TR Steele turn so red.

Kerry Blue's belly hurt from laughing. She returned to the *Merrimack* at the last possible moment, nicely buzzed. She didn't hate Cowboy so much anymore.

She went to the forecastle. The Old Man was right there, waiting for her. Glowering.

"What?" Kerry Blue said.

Steele's eyes bugged out fit to explode.

Kerry rephrased, "What, *sir?*"

Then she remembered what she'd done. She'd really done it too.

Lieutenant Colonel Steele and Lieutenant Glenn Hamilton were sanitizing the lockers of the dead company and crew before sending the contents home to their grieving families.

Cowboy's locker hung open.

There was some money in there, intact, but everything else was ash.

"What happened here?" Steele's ears were some kind of crimson.

Kerry Blue said, "It's sanitized, ain't it?"

"This wasn't yours!"

Kerry Blue choked. "*No?*"

That red teddy for sure didn't fit Cowboy. Kerry Blue said, "You'da done it if I hadn't. Sir."

Kerry Blue was pretty sure that Steele didn't want Cowboy's family to see the stuff she'd burned.

Kerry Blue pulled a photo chit from one of her pockets. She'd been carrying it around. Wanted to trash it real bad. Kept trying to but hadn't been able to go through with it. She gave it to Steele now, glad to be rid of it. "*This* ain't mine."

When you squeezed the chit, it gave you a life-sized holo of a pregnant woman, beaming as though she'd done something really important.

Steele looked as if he were about to atomize Kerry Blue. He probably would have, but the Hamster spoke first, like the final word. "Thank you, Flight Sergeant."

The Hamster was all right. No wonder the captain was sweet on her.

✳ ✳ ✳ ✳ ✳

Captain Farragut informed his Intelligence Officer that he needed a way to counter the perfect stealth of Romulus' spacecraft.

Augustus found few leads. "That ship type is currently under development by the Pacific Consortium."

"Under development?" Farragut said.

"It hasn't been built yet."

"Romulus is piloting one now. Did he steal the prototype?"

"The prototype hasn't been built yet. The ship in development is not even called Xerxes yet."

Augustus only knew it would be called Xerxes because he'd been aboard it.

The Pacific Consortium's actual manufacturing facility was way out in Perseid space, but the Pacifics had a presence here in Fort Roosevelt.

Captain Farragut took a shuttle to the Pacific Consortium's station to advise the local representatives of a credible threat to their development facility in Perseid space.

"There's a terrorist using Pacific research against the United States."

Consortium officials demanded that Farragut identify the terrorist.

Farragut told them he couldn't provide that. The truth would sound like a perverse joke. He requested that the Pacific Rim coalition accept U.S. assistance in defending against attempts to steal Pacific technology.

The interview turned from frosty to bitter arctic.

Farragut guessed he couldn't blame them. He heard himself talking a fine line between lunatic and very bad industrial spy.

"Exactly what do you suppose we are developing, Captain Farragut?"

"Y'all are manufacturing a full-stealth spacecraft. You're fixing to call it a Xerxes. It can't be seen for lookin' at it. It won't register on sensors. It's the fastest ship of its mass. It's meant to be an ambassadorial craft."

Farragut was briskly escorted to the air lock.

At least they didn't space him. He was pretty sure they wanted to.

Immediately following that episode, the U.S. State Department contacted Captain Farragut, demanding to know what he'd said to so piss off America's closest allies. And had Captain Farragut ever heard of "chain of command."

Farragut was not a secretive man. He was a "see the target, acquire the target, secure the target" kind of guy. He supposed it sounded bad, his asking for information on trade secrets.

Rear Admiral Mishindi's voice came over the com with greater volume than Farragut had ever heard out of him. "*What weren't you thinking!*"

Trying to explain it just made him sound a little bit crackers. Farragut was still on the interview when breaking news lit up all the space repeaters. The Pacific Consortium's development center in Perseid space had blown up.

The Pacific Consortium was now screaming at the U.S.

Rear Admiral Mishindi looked ready to ream his formerly favorite ship captain. "Well, John. You've created a diplomatic incident. Is this what you were going for?"

"This here is sorta actually the incident I was trying to get in front of, sir," Farragut said.

Mishindi demanded that Farragut's Intelligence Officer be put on the com at once.

"Colonel Augustus," Mishindi began tightly. "Are your people involved in the sabotage of the Pacific Consortium's facility?"

Augustus didn't call the rear admiral "Sir." He didn't bother looking at Mishindi at all. "My particular people, no. But I cannot, will not, answer for Romulus' people."

"*Romulus?*" Rear Admiral Mishindi blinked as if a fastball just got past him. "Romulus son of Magnus? Romulus is a bit player. Forget Romulus!"

"At your peril," said Augustus and walked away from the com.

Mishindi's eyes flared very white in his dark face. "Captain Farragut. You do know that you may send that thing back to Palatine any time."

That thing. Augustus.

"I do know, sir. It's what he wants. It would be a mistake. I need him."

Captain Farragut searched for Colonel Augustus. Found him at last in the brig. Farragut frowned, puzzled. "Why are you here?"

"I figured it's where you'd want me."

Farragut leaned against the hatchway. "I thought about it. Augustus, are we sure it was Romulus who blew up the Pacifics' development center? Romulus can't have got to Perseid space from the Myriad that fast, can he?"

"Romulus doesn't need to be in Perseid space. He only needed to order the hit. He has dangerous friends in Perseid space, it would seem."

"So answer me this: Did Romulus just make his own future-built ship cease to exist?"

"The classic paradox doesn't seem to be playing out that way," Augustus said. "But we'll know soon enough."

"How?"

"When Romulus meets Romulus."

＊ ＊ ＊ ＊ ＊

3 September 2443
Xerxes
Roma Nova, Palatine
Corona Australis star system
Near Space

At last. At long last. Romulus arrived inside the Lambda Coronae Australis star system, where lay Palatine, capital world of the Roman Empire.

His Xerxes breeched Palatine airspace undetected. His ship's descent over the capital city of Nova Roma triggered no alarms. He set down in a park near the Capitoline Hill. No one heard or saw a thing.

Security picked up his approach on foot to the palace. All the sensors recognized him and let him pass.

He was climbing the one hundred wide snowy steps to the palace on the Capitoline when he saw her.

She waited at the top. A vision. Auburn hair. Stature of a goddess. Soft. Fierce. Haughty. She took his breath away.

He paused on the steps to steady himself against the force of emotion that swept over him. The enormity of what he'd done to get here caught up with him.

Her image shimmered through the mist that sprang to his eyes. Emotion thickened his throat. She was here. He had arrived.

She saw him.

Amazement crossed Claudia's face with a tentative smile as he mounted the stairs. "Look at you!"

She knew him. Even with five years on him, she knew him.

Romulus climbed the rest of the hundred steps to her, effortlessly. He felt winged. He reached the top. He stood over her. Breathed in the cloud of her scent, her warmth. She was here. He was here. He'd done it. He had moved space and time. He was here.

Her wide dark eyes moved, taking in all of him.

His voice came out thick. "How do I look?"

Her gaze met his. "Formidable."

Her mouth stayed open, marveling, smiling. He offered her his arm. She slipped her little hand into the crook of his elbow and fell into step beside him. She would be able to feel the hard gauntlet under his sleeve, concealing his patterner's cables.

He felt her living presence beside him. He was lord of the universe.

She kept stealing glances up at him as he escorted her inside the palace. Against all facts, she knew him. Changed as he was, she knew him.

So did his alter ego.

Young Romulus had caught a glimpse of him in the forecourt. Young Romulus came bounding inside to see himself in the atrium. The alter ego knew exactly who he was. The young alter ego looked dazzled.

Romulus, the god, faced the younger being who called himself Romulus now in this *Anno Domini* 2443.

Was I ever such a feckless idiot? This face that I used to see in the mirror gazes back at me now with star-struck wonder.

"So this is what I become," said the alter ego, grinning, amazed.

That is what I was? I could just die.

No use waiting another moment. The sooner done, the less confusion. Romulus the patterner, the god, needed to know right now, once and for dead certain, what would happen. It was the old time-travel conundrum.

"Let us have this done."

Patterner Romulus, newly arrived from *Anno Domini* 2448, drew his weapon here in 2443 and shot his younger self in the head.

19

THE ALTER EGO WAS DEAD.

Romulus the patterner lived. He'd been certain that he would. Everything he'd seen so far told him this was a parallel universe, not a fork in the one he'd left behind.

Claudia screamed. Wholly expected.

The palace guards had their weapons out, not sure where to point them. The guards didn't know what they'd seen. What to do. There was a dead Romulus. There was a live Romulus.

"Put those away," the living Romulus ordered. He turned his back on the guns, holstered his sidearm, and took Claudia in his arms. "That!" He sneered at the dead man. "That thing is nothing. I am the one who loves you more than any man ever loved anything or anyone. You are empress of my universe. Sweet Claudia, grieve not for that."

The word *empress* reached through her terror and grief. He knew it would.

Romulus pulled an eraser from his sleeve, turned it on the fallen body of the alter ego, and atomized the remains. Claudia squeaked. A guard ordered uselessly, "Hold!"

Another guard pulled the trigger of his weapon.

The guard's weapon didn't fire. It recognized the target as Caesar's son. Everyone heard the damning tone of machine refusal. The weapon spoke: "Target denied."

The guard who'd tried to fire on Romulus turned white. Said awkwardly, apologetic, "*Domni.*"

Romulus ignored the guard's existence, as if it were a trivial thing, the attempt to kill him. It was good that everyone saw the weapon refusing to fire on him. The man could vanish later if Romulus was still vexed. For now Romulus gave all his attention to Claudia. "Do you still want blue diamonds? For your crown? I think emeralds become you."

The palace guards stared at this authoritarian being who looked and sounded like Romulus, who seemed to have assassinated another Romulus. There was no protocol for this scenario. The palace *guns* thought he was the true son of Caesar and had refused to fire on him.

This Romulus acted as if everything were under control and there were no issues worth his attention.

The captain of the guard blurted, "*Domni!*"

Romulus turned, annoyed. In a normal voice, a bit tired, he said, "What?"

"I beg your pardon. I require—request—some physical readings."

"Why did you not require those earlier? I should break you for letting that imposter into my sister's company. But I recognize that it was a convincing fraud. It even fooled Claudia. Now pay attention and do your duty." Romulus offered himself to be read. "I am who I am."

His DNA, his retinae, his bioelectric signature, and his brain waves all said he was Romulus son of Magnus. There was some oddity in the age of his cells. But things could happen to age a man. Mere age did not change who a man was.

His cables—Romulus called them his prostheses—they were his and none of their concern. "Just verify who I am. My personal business is my own."

The guards posed the challenge questions they had on record. He answered all correctly without hesitation. Until he had enough of it. "You are done. Thou shalt leave now."

This was, irrefutably, Romulus son of Magnus.

One guard blurted, "You just murdered someone."

"Who?" Romulus said faintly. "Whom did I murder? Someone must be dead if I murdered someone. You cannot arrest me for murder until you produce or even identify a victim."

Romulus was known as a games player. If Romulus set a snare, you didn't want to step into it. The guards withdrew.

Romulus turned to Claudia.

Claudia's face was wet. She looked pretty crying. Most women looked grotesque. She sniffled. Her pretty hands gestured over the empty space where had lain that thing she'd mistaken for him, Romulus, her adored brother. She squeaked, "I don't understand."

Romulus cupped her cheek in his palm. "Anything you want is yours. That is all you ever need to know."

He'd always held sway over her. She loved him like a prisoner in love with her captor. He was the lord of her existence, the most powerful being in the universe. She must love him.

Claudia let him guide her inside to a private chamber. He told her, "We need to remove Magnus."

Claudia revived at once, exasperated. "Have I not been telling you so!"

"Yes, beloved. I didn't listen until it was too late."

"Is it too late?"

"Not this time. You were right. You are right. There are things that must happen."

"Marry me," Claudia demanded.

"Yes. That is one."

She threw her arms around him. Kissed him all over his face. Then she pulled back and pummeled his chest with one fist.

"What! *Took!* You! So! *Long!*"

"Oh, my sweet, longer than you know. Come."

He escorted her out of the palace, past the abashed guards. He ordered them to stay at their posts.

His Xerxes sat, invisible on the palace grounds. He introduced Claudia to the Xerxes. She looked nervous. Must've thought he was crazy, talking to vacant air.

Then he led her by the hand up the unseen ramp.

A Xerxes would kill unauthorized borders. Claudia had been introduced. The ship accepted her. Romulus instructed the Xerxes to obey Claudia's every wish and to defend her against all harm.

"These chambers are whatever you command them to be," he told her.

The deck to which they entered appeared now as an ornate terrace overlooking a brilliant, deep blue sea. They could see bright coral, white sand, and colorful fish under the surface.

"Change the appearance as you wish. Only tell it what you want. Just don't try to walk through the cordons. Those mean real walls."

Later in the evening, Romulus and Claudia sat cuddled together in a virtual alpine ski lodge. They watched news bulletins reporting the assassination of Caesar's son, Romulus.

There were interviews with witnesses, but no recordings of the assassination itself.

"What is this?" Claudia pointed at the vid.

"Idiocy," Romulus said. "Let the comments fall like the rain."

Senators were launching their own investigations into the event. They claimed that a being who looked like an older Romulus had murdered Romulus son of Magnus. They wanted to apprehend and charge this imposter with the assassination.

Romulus got up, threw on a toga over his black shirt and black jeans, and pulled on his black riding boots.

"I'm sorry, Claudia. I need to sort out these monkeys. Make the ship entertain you."

"I want to watch the monkeys."

Romulus brought up the program that would transmit the Senate proceedings for her to watch from the safety of the Xerxes.

Romulus presented himself at the midnight meeting in the curia and announced to all the Senators, "I live."

Senator Ventus said at once, "That is not Romulus."

Romulus twisted a smile. "With disrespect, I beg to differ."

Most of the Senators noticed a difference, but the longer one looked at him and heard him speak, the more one became convinced that he had to be Romulus. He remembered private conversations. But it was the inimitable attitude that sealed it.

One of the guards who had checked him in the entryway testified: "He's not a clone. Clones have unique cellular markers. I don't know what witnesses saw, but this is, beyond any doubt, Romulus son of Magnus."

Senator Ventus pointed. "There's something wrong with his neck and arms. I think we should see."

Romulus shamed Ventus. Told him to leave his prostheses out of this.

Senator Quirinius demanded a DNA test be run on Romulus' victim.

"You're beyond ridiculous now. If I killed someone, then you tell me who it is that I killed. You can't. You slander me. I shall seek recourse."

Senator Quirinius' face muscles writhed. "You killed Romulus."

"Bring the corpse."

Quirinius couldn't produce the body. So a group of Senators respectfully summoned Romulus' father into the Curia.

"All rise for Caesar Magnus."

On seeing Romulus, the old man trembled a little.

Romulus looked him level in the eyes. "Do you know who I am?"

Magnus nodded slowly.

"Good. *We* are making a public announcement, Father."

Magnus inquired, guarded, "What do you suppose I will say?"

"Anything you like," Romulus said. "I'll go first."

Romulus announced through all the news services that he would be making a galaxy-shaking announcement.

Watch for it.

A lot of people asked why he didn't just make the announcement.

But the announcement was shaping up to be a major event to be broadcast across civilized space. Romulus didn't give a date or time. *Watch for it.*

It happened on Lieutenant Glenn Hamilton's watch.

Romulus' event opened with enormous fanfare that gave time for most of civilization to wake up, drop everything, and tune in.

Romulus had never been a civic leader, but he was Caesar Magnus' natural son, so he was a celebrity.

Even if you wanted to snub Romulus, the anticipated event was taking on enough momentum that you had to watch just so you knew what everyone else was going to be talking about afterward.

Romulus made his entrance in an arena at an unidentified location, which made one wonder how the audience knew to go there, or if the audience and the arena were even real.

Romulus strode under an arch to the accompaniment of ferocious music that was all brass and triumph and gloria in a rain of cold fire. There was a quick scramble among the news commentators to identify the musical composition.

"That's grand," Calli said. She looked to Jose Maria de Cordillera, who had joined her and the captain on *Merrimack*'s command deck. "What's the music?"

Jose Maria shook his head.

The news commentators were saying it was Romulus' own composition.

The music climbed, labored, from a beaten and broken depth up to a hard fought peak, where it stood up and took flight.

While the galaxy waited for Romulus' appearance, reporters consulted musical critics, who were comparing his work to Beethoven.

Farragut turned around. "Cal, Jose Maria, y'all listen to this classical stuff. Are they blowing smoke up Romulus' stern pipe?"

"He's not Beethoven," Calli said. "The composition is a little over-wrought. But it's not hack work."

Jose Maria said, "I never knew Romulus had music in him."

"Then he stole it," Farragut said.

"You'd think so," Calli allowed. "But I don't know who he could've stolen it *from*. It doesn't sound like anyone else. Maybe Berlioz, but it's better than Berlioz." She looked to Jose Maria.

"It sounds like something Romulus would compose if Romulus was a composer," Jose Maria said. "And apparently he is."

"Sir?" a perplexed technician spoke out of turn from his station. "Who cares?"

Jose Maria answered that. "Megalomania coupled with creative orga-nization of thought on that level is a little frightening. I care."

On a mammoth display behind the podium where Romulus was to give his address, a resonant visual feed began transmitting. The transmis-sion source was identified as the League of Earth Nations ship *Woodland Serenity*. The ship was visible by starlight in the spectacular star cluster called the Myriad.

Then images from the lush planet Arra came into focus. Closer, they revealed tentacled gorgons devastating fields and forests, towns and living beings.

The images engulfed the arena so that even if you were safe on your space battleship, or sitting in Mad Bear O's with your tequila shots watch-ing the show on the screen over the bar, you felt you were about to be eaten alive.

Romulus stepped up to the podium, a tiny island in the chaos.

He lifted his arms at the terrifying images thrashing around him. "Does this surprise you?" Romulus asked his audience. "Did any of you know of this? Does it horrify? I tell you, this is not news. And this is far from the real horror. *This* is the horror."

The images went dark. The music became low and solemn.

"Legio Primus, Adamantine. Legio Secundus, Valorous."

In a grave, heroic voice Romulus named off the Legions of Rome. It was a long list. He named sixty-four, then stopped. The music stopped.

Silence stretched. The questioning crowd waited. Dread was growing claws.

"Romans! Do you have fathers, sons, loved ones in these honored Legions?" Romulus asked. "Where are they now?"

A camera found Caesar Magnus, who was turning gray.

The huge image behind Romulus leaped into a close-up of masses of gorgons in a feeding frenzy.

Romulus turned to his father. "Magnus, tell the people where their Legions are."

John Farragut, on the command deck of his ship, reacted with a jolt. Blurted, "Oh, for Jesus."

Romulus spoke into the cameras. "It fell to me—because your elected leaders failed—to inform the families, to recognize them, and to thank them for their sacrifice. To acknowledge their service and courage."

Romulus made a steady, imperious presence as he revealed Rome's darkest secret. "Sixty-four Roman Legions are dead and no one told *Rome*. Magnus placed the forces of Rome under U.S. command, and look where it got us. The United States fed the best of Rome to the Hive."

"Ho! Foul! Wrong!" Farragut shouted at the display.

Romulus was making it sound as though the U.S. lost those Legions.

"It's not true," Lieutenant Hamilton said. "We never took command of sixty-four Legions. Did we?"

"No," Farragut said.

"It doesn't need to be true," Calli said. "It's what Romulus needs Rome to believe."

Magnus only put Rome's forces under U.S. control *after* the sixty-four Legions fell to the Hive. Romulus was reversing cause and effect. And Rome would willingly believe it, because the truth was unbearable.

Romulus said, "The truth has been kept from you by Magnus and his creature, the Frankenstein monster Augustus."

All eyes on the command deck of *Merrimack* turned to Magnus' patterner, standing at the rear of the platform.

Augustus blinked genuine surprise. "That was well played. He's lining up all his enemies on one side."

Farragut said/asked, "You knew the sixty-four Legions were gone."

"I did. Why do you suppose Magnus gave me to you? It was not my will to be here, taking orders from an American captain. Rome is desperate."

Romulus wasn't done with devious surprises. The background image had changed again to show the great round LEN vessel *Woodland Serenity* taking on refugees from the planet Arra. Then he juxtaposed that with an image of the space battleship *Merrimack* retreating, accompanied by a soundtrack of the LEN crying for the big ship to stop right now and take on refugees. "Come back!"

The image of *Merrimack* shrank very small and vanished in the darkness. You still heard the LEN cries for help.

It was a damning image.

"The United States Space battleship *Merrimack* was there at this imperiled world," Romulus announced to the listening galaxy. "See *Merrimack* run. This is what placing your faith in the United States wins you. Here is the United States in action."

Farragut looked at all the stunned faces of the young specialists on his command deck. He said reasonably, "We can expect villagers with pitchforks at our next port of call, I think."

Romulus wasn't even done.

"The situation is dire." Romulus gazed into the recorders. "But I am here."

Before anyone could say yippee, Romulus held out his hand melodramatically, like a wizard, reaching up toward the heavens, as if he could reach across kiloparsecs to the distant star cluster in the Deep End where horrible aliens ravaged a beautiful world that brave Romans died trying to defend. Romulus pronounced, "I forbid this to go on."

Calli rolled her eyes. "Great. What's he—?"

Gorgons rose from the Arran fields. The monsters lifted into the air, tentacles waving and reaching.

Someone on the command deck made a sound of disgust. "Come *on*. These images have to be faked."

But they weren't.

Shocked reports came over the resonator on official harmonics from the LEN vessel *Woodland Serenity*, which was there in the Myriad. The reports on site validated the incredible images. The League of Nations crew were crying, jubilant. "The Hive is lifting away! *The Hive is lifting away!*"

Farragut said, "Can't be. The Hive never leaves food."

"They are doing so," Augustus observed.

"Actually, we recently saw this behavior in the Hive," Jose Maria said.

Farragut nodded. "Our shadow. That stealth missile Romulus set on our tail. It led the Hive to us. We were the dress rehearsal for this act."

Augustus agreed. "Romulus has another drone out there resonating the irresistible harmonic. He's using it to lead the Hive off the planet."

The gorgons swarmed upward and away. The LEN called it a miracle.

A reporter in the arena where Romulus was putting on his show asked Romulus how he effected the miracle.

Romulus roared back at the questioner. "How did I do it? *Ask others why they did not!* Who *else* has the solution and what are they withholding it for? The highest bidder?"

"He's trying to turn everyone against us," Calli said.

"Trying?" Farragut said. "The crazy man's getting it done."

"That was masterful," Augustus said.

Jeffrey snapped from the tactical station, "And you're praising him!" Added a belated, sheepish, "Sir."

Captain Farragut motioned Jeffrey down. "Deny brilliance in your enemy at your sorrow, son. Colonel Augustus, less praise for the crazy man."

"This is a good thing, isn't it?" Hamster asked carefully. "It means Donner's people will live."

Glenn Hamilton had a place in her heart for the alien archon Donner. "The planet Arra will live. Do we care who played the Pied Piper?"

"It ought to be good," Farragut said.

"It ought to be good," Calli said. "But Hamlin paid dearly for the piper's service."

Immediately after Romulus' public miracle, the Roman Senate convened in the Curia.

The stone rotunda stood opposite the palace on the Capitoline Hill. Romulus hadn't been invited inside the Curia. Romulus wasn't a Senator and had no official place there.

Romulus should have been invited.

The main compartment in his Xerxes looked now like the hanging gardens of Babylon. Romulus sat at a picnic with Claudia on a blanket behind a virtual waterfall. He'd needed to scale back the tactile images a little, because Claudia minded the dampness on her hair.

She fretted over the lack of news from the Curia. Blamed it on their father.

"That useless man!" Claudia cried. "I should like to see him dead!"

"I have seen him dead," Romulus said. "It was a mistake."

"*What?*"

"I will tell you a story." He picked up her hand, kissed it, and replaced it on the blanket. "In time."

"Why are you not angry at these morons!"

"Anger is another face of fear, my sweet. It doesn't serve. This development is inconvenient. Very inconvenient, if these imbeciles are doing what I suspect they're doing. It forces me to use a weapon I would rather not spend yet."

He leaned over to lay his cheek against her hair. She smelled of cinnamon and wood spice.

His brows contracted, thoughtful. "Gaius Julius Caesar." He tried out the sound of the name and found it lacking. "How did that man's name get to be synonymous with kingship for centuries? How did *Caesar* get to be a title? *Caesar* Augustus. *Kaiser* Wilhelm. *Tsar* Nikolai. Caesar! Caesar! Caesar!"

"You shall be Caesar Romulus," Claudia said.

"No. That's just it. Why should I lean on some lesser man's name? I will, henceforth, be Romulus. *The* Romulus. My name shall be ascendant. The name 'Romulus' will eclipse the name 'Caesar.' In the future Romans will speak the name Romulus when they mean God Imperator."

"That is much better," Claudia said, smiling at last.

"Let the Senate name their puny Caesar. I am *the* Romulus. The Senate must confer the imperium upon me."

"They might not be bright enough to give it to you," Claudia said.

"Then I shall just take it."

Most political observers expected a long wait for the Roman Senate to make their decision as to whom should be elevated into Magnus' place as leader of the vast Roman Empire. There would be weeks or months of impressive oratory.

The matter was decided within hours.

Just after Taps sounded at 2105 hours on *Merrimack*, Lieutenant Glenn Hamilton summoned Captain John Farragut and Commander Calli Carmel back to the command platform.

Calli arrived on the command deck first.

Hamster announced, "XO on deck."

Calli stopped dead in the hatchway as she saw the image on the tactical monitor. "Oh. No."

The Roman broadcast showed white smoke pouring from a stack above the Curia.

Calli moved quickly aside because John Farragut arrived like a cannon ball.

"Captain on deck."

"What's with the smoke?" Farragut said. "Did they elect a Pope?"

"Either that or the Curia's on fire, sir," Hamster said.

The bronze-clad doors of the Roman Senate house parted. The Consul Gaius Americanus advanced. Dark, graying, dignified. He carried a crown-sized oak wreath.

"Is that him?" Hamster asked. "Is that who they picked?"

"No," Calli said. "That's who they should've picked. But they didn't."

A large mass remained in shadow behind the Consul Gaius Americanus.

"You mean it's done, Cal? Already?"

Calli nodded. "They just need to finish pushing his ego out through the doors."

"Sir? Who is that?" Glenn Hamilton asked as the mountainous figure stepped out of the shadows to center stage.

"Numa Pompous Ass," Calli Carmel said. "Triumphalis. Big Roman hero."

"Huge Roman hero," Captain Farragut observed.

The triumphalis Numa Pompeii was an Olympic-sized mass of not very pretty. Only as power attracts could Numa Pompeii be called attractive.

Jose Maria de Cordillera arrived on deck. His long hair was wet and his clothes stuck to him. He looked at the tactical monitor and glanced among the officers. "It is done?"

Calli gave a brisk nod. "Rome can be decisive when her feet are on fire."

"Good thing to remember if you're fixin' to go to war with her," Farragut said.

The Roman Senate had named Numa Pompeii the next Imperator of Rome.

Augustus arrived on deck just in time to see Gaius Americanus place the oak crown on Numa Pompeii's thinly haired head, which appeared to have been hewn from a boulder with a broad chisel. Augustus murmured, "Hail, Caesar."

Calli advised Captain Farragut, "Numa is a hard line warmongering glory hound."

Farragut nodded acknowledgment. He turned to his patterner. "Colonel Augustus?"

"Captain Farragut," said the Roman.

John Farragut put out a palm. "Sword."

Augustus quit the command deck.

A very long silence fell in which only the equipment spoke.

Augustus reappeared moments later, armed, in the hatchway. He passed between two wary MPs.

Augustus unbelted his scabbard and passed it to the captain.

Farragut accepted the sword.

"Brig," said Farragut to Augustus. Then, to one of the Marine guards at the hatch, "Yurg, give the colonel company on the way there."

"Aye, aye, Captain. This way, Colonel Augustus."

The com specialist abruptly turned from his station. "Sir. The LEN is making a public plea to Romulus for help."

"The LEN? Help?" Farragut said, off balance. "Why? What's happening? Where?"

"The word from planet Arra is that the Hive swarms are turning around."

"Turning? You mean again?"

"Aye, sir. The gorgons are headed back down to the planet. They're eating everything. Whatever was luring them away before isn't doing it anymore."

"I'm fixin' to take a wild guess here that Romulus might not be all that happy with the election results," Farragut said.

Hamster asked, "Do you really think Romulus actually controls the Hive?"

"He's my first suspect," Farragut said.

Calli nodded. Hers, too.

The com specialist broke in. "Sir. The LEN are begging Romulus to reinstate his protection on the planet. Romulus just told the League rep, 'Go ask Caesar to save them.' That's a quote, sir."

Farragut looked astonished. "Well, there it is. Romulus is using the Hive as a weapon in his own private power grab."

The LEN publicly turned to the new Caesar, Numa Pompeii, for help. As if Caesar Numa Pompeii could have the same power to move the Hive.

In no time, Numa Pompeii made his appearance before the galactic media. He made a show of listening to the LEN pleas, a serious expression set on his craggy face. He nodded like a compassionate god, while behind him, towering holo displays relayed LEN camera images of the gorgons renewing their devastation on the Arran landscape in the wake of Romulus' abandonment. Only Numa didn't call it abandonment. He called it "Romulus' failure."

Numa Pompeii then turned away dramatically, as if he'd seen enough. He made a theatrical upward lifting motion with his broad hands. And as he did, the cameras on distant Arra captured images of the Hive swarms rising into the air, tentacles reaching upward as they left the ground.

The alien plague lifted away, apparently in obedience to Numa Pompeii's command.

LEN officials there on the planet Arra were shown crying with gratitude and relief. They hailed Numa their savior.

Numa allowed time for the media to verify the truth of the images. Caesar Numa Pompeii really was pulling the gorgons away from the planet surface.

Then Numa turned to the cameras with deep disgust and scolded the watching galaxy, "Put not your faith in mad dogs."

20

JOHN FARRAGUT TURNED AWAY from the Tactical
display. He jerked a thumb over his shoulder at the images of Hive
swarms turning at Numa Pompeii's command. "Is that real? Somebody tell me how Numa can be directing the Hive. And from two thousand parsecs away!"

"Numa has the irresistible harmonic," Commander Calli Carmel said.
"Must have."

"So what if he does? How did Numa get a *resonator* all the way across
two thousand parsecs to the Myriad for the gorgons to chase? He doesn't
have any ships out there. How is Numa controlling a resonator from two
thousands parsecs away."

Calli shook her head. Not a clue.

Jose Maria de Cordillera suggested, "Possibly you may find answers in
the brig, young Captain."

Farragut bounded to the hatch. "Commander Carmel has the deck
and the con. Jose Maria, I'd like you with me."

Augustus didn't rise at the captain's entrance into the cell. He spoke
with his eyes shut, motionless as a coiled serpent. "*Ave, Don* Cordillera."

To Farragut Augustus said nothing.

"Who do you belong to?" Farragut demanded.

"Rome," said Augustus.

"Are you Numa's man?"

"Numa Pompeii has made it known that he'd be damned if he ever stooped to using patterners. I don't know if Numa is damned or not, but I won't move against him, given that he's the lawful Imperator."

"I need you to see this." Farragut sat down with a resonator.

A moment passed.

"It requires opening your eyes, Augustus."

The eyes opened.

Farragut replayed the wizard's duel for Augustus, showing first the Hive's renewed assault on the planet Arra in the wake of the election of Numa Pompeii and then the Hive lifting away from the planet at Numa's supposed command.

"How is Numa controlling the Hive from two klarcs away?"

"I was not consulted."

"Might Numa have an agent inside the LEN and on site?" Jose Maria suggested. "There could be someone on board *Woodland Serenity* who can deploy decoys and effect resonance in the Myriad on behalf of Caesar."

"Numa's mind is not a database that I can access," Augustus said. "But it's a well-reasoned guess, *Don* Cordillera. Can I come out of the brig?"

Farragut said, "Not until I know where Numa's Rome stands with the U.S. Need anything in here, Augustus?"

"*Don* Cordillera and a chessboard."

Farragut looked at Jose Maria, who nodded consent.

"Moebius or regular board?"

The shape of the board didn't really matter to these two. They kept all the moves in their heads anyway.

"Moebius," Augustus said. "It's more elegant."

Romulus paced long strides within his Xerxes. He was vibrating with rage. And fear. He'd thought he was past fear.

His secret weapon had betrayed him.

Numa Pompeii should *not* have the irresistible harmonic yet. Not in the year 2443. But Numa did have it. It was yet another deviation from the original timeline as Romulus had lived it.

And now the Roman Senate had declared Numa their Caesar because they thought Numa controlled the Hive. These people did not understand the nature of the enemy.

And they do not understand the power of me.

They required enlightenment.

Romulus would teach these lesser beings what a powerless pretender was Numa Pompeii.

Romulus issued a terse pronouncement. "People of all nations, try to find me when you are ready to kneel."

Immediately, sarcastic media commentators claimed to be quaking in terror. They asked one another: "Anyone kneeling at your location? Not here. You? Let's check in with our affiliate on Mu Cygnus. Any outbreaks of kneeling there?"

"Why, yes, Sal, I have a sighting of kneeling here on Thaleia. Oh. No. Wait. That's a marriage proposal . . . Stand by. . . . Yes. She said yes."

✳ ✳ ✳ ✳ ✳

10 September 2443
Roma Nova, Palatine
Corona Australis star system
Near Space

Upon the ascension of Caesar Numa Pompeii, Magnus was invited to leave the imperial palace. There was a tacit command for him to remove his children with him.

Magnus engaged a freighter to transport his belongings out of the palace and back to his country estate in the green rolling hills outside Nova Roma here on Palatine.

Magnus' son Romulus showed up in person to collect a few things he valued and some things Claudia wanted. The palace had been their home for most of their lives.

Romulus didn't really care to see his father, but Magnus sought Romulus out.

The old man looked sad and unbearably solicitous. The monumental scale of the palace, the thick soaring columns, the vast domed ceiling high overhead, all made Magnus look very, very small. He hadn't been rejuvenated. His own fault. He didn't need to look that frail. If he thought age made him look wise, he was desperately mistaken. He looked beaten.

Caesar Magnus had been responsible for the annihilation of sixty-four Legions. No one recovers from that.

And Magnus took personally the mockery heaped on his child.

Magnus sounded mortally embarrassed. "My son, you cannot expect to ascend so quickly without stumbling. If you would rule, take a step back."

Romulus absorbed the absurdity. This broken man dared give him advice? *If I would rule?* A dangerous glassy-eyed smile slid onto Romulus' face. *I do rule.* Romulus said softly, "I rule an Empire bigger than this galaxy."

✳ ✳ ✳ ✳ ✳

Within days of Numa's miracle, the gorgons in the Myriad inexplicably reversed themselves one more time. Ravenous swarms of them descended back to the surface of the planet Arra. The Hive threat had *not* been neutralized after all.

The League of Earth Nations contacted the new Imperator of Rome, Numa Pompeii. The LEN urgently requested that Numa restore his protection to the planet Arra and to the other worlds within the Myriad star cluster.

The demand, the need for it, caught Numa off guard. He didn't let his confusion show. He improvised. He told the LEN that the reversal of the Hive was the League's fault. The LEN hadn't obeyed his instructions to the letter.

The LEN representatives insisted they had done everything Numa required.

Numa Pompeii clicked off and turned away from the resonator in his battlefort *Gladiator*. "*Merda.*"

"*Domni?*" his exec, Portia Arrianus prompted.

Numa had not yet made any move to take up residence in the imperial palace on Palatine. He had always preferred his battlefort to any ground station.

He told his exec, "Confirm that the LEN decoys in the Myriad are actually resonating on the proper Hive harmonic."

Portia Arrianus promptly entered the irresistible harmonic into her res chamber. She reported, startled, "Nothing, *Domni*. I'm reading nothing on that harmonic. The decoys are not resonating."

"Resonate the irresistible harmonic."

"It's not going, *Domni*."

Numa snarled. "Explain 'It's not going.' Resonant pulses don't *go*. They *are*."

"*Domni*, the harmonic is *not*."

"How does a harmonic vanish?"

"Someone must be resonating on the complement of the harmonic. That's the only way."

It was a known phenomenon. You could interrupt harmonic messages by resonating the complement of the harmonic. Neither harmonic existed at the moment of collision. The tactic was common among jilted lovers.

Numa growled in sudden revelation.

"Get me that pinprick on the resonator. No. Strike that. Set me down in *my* palace."

Numa Pompeii in his vast flesh arrived inside the imperial palace with a displacement thundercrack. He strode across the marble antechamber and prowled all the chambers, his sword drawn, ready for Romulus. He found only Magnus looking withered and forlorn. Packing.

Numa received a resonant hail. He assumed it was Portia Arrianus, and he answered, impatient. "Speak."

No video image accompanied the slow sardonic voice that didn't belong to his executive officer. "Caesar. Save them."

Numa. Voice like an earthquake. "Romulus! You are taking responsibility for the Hive reversal in the Myriad?"

"I'm revealing your impotence in the face of humankind's greatest threat."

"Stop canceling out my harmonic. Otherwise, confess to being humankind's greatest threat yourself."

"The harmonic is all yours," Romulus said blithely. "May it give you joy."

Numa reactivated the irresistible harmonic. It existed again. But there was nothing irresistible about it now. The LEN in the Myriad reported that the gorgons on the planet Arra continued to ravage everything within tentacle reach. Whatever had been distracting the Hive earlier was now gone.

"What did you do, Romulus?" Numa roared into his res com. "*What the hell did you do?*"

"Knowledge is power, *Caesar*. I have it. You do not. Knees," Romulus told Numa. "I am expecting knees."

✳ ✳ ✳ ✳ ✳

No one was kneeling. It was a tragedy, of course, the Hive's renewed descent to the beautiful distant alien world, Arra. But its threat to Earth and Palatine was still remote. Humankind had more than a century in which to prepare for the eventual gorgon invasion of Near Space, time enough to devise a solution. The nations would think of something in that time.

"You don't have a century," Romulus told humankind. "You have until *yesterday*."

The Hive that had existed on the irresistible harmonic was dead. It died the instant Romulus resonated the complement of the Hive harmonic.

When a Hive's harmonic goes silent, the entire Hive dies.

But during its long existence a Hive left behind eggs anywhere it ever found food.

And in the combined presence of food and the absence of its parent Hive, those eggs wakened as a new Hive, resonating a new harmonic.

Romulus had seen that happen in the future. Here, now, he made it happen sooner.

Romulus knew the new harmonic of the successor Hive. He'd got it from *Merrimack*'s future records.

Romulus knew where some eggs of the successor Hive lay buried, strategically located. He'd already seen them hatch five years from now.

And on an airless world a scant twenty light-years from Earth, tentacles broke from ancient bedrock.

✳ ✳ ✳ ✳ ✳

14 September 2443
U.S. Space Battleship *Merrimack*
Fort Theodore Roosevelt
Near Space

John Farragut visited his patterner in the brig. "Augustus, does Romulus have your Striker?"

Augustus had been playing a Spanish guitar. The guitar belonged to Jose Maria. Augustus set the guitar aside on the cot. "I believe not."

"Where is your Striker?" Farragut demanded.

"Last we saw, Romulus chucked it out of his Xerxes. Back in the Myriad."

"Means he might have taken your Striker in tow."

"He didn't," Augustus said. "You know that."

"I do?"

"You should. Towing my ship would obviate his stealth. You would have detected it."

"Did he scuttle it? Your Striker?"

"You would need more input to make that conclusion, and I'm lacking equipment to get any such information."

"Ask your Striker if it's still out there."

Farragut knew that Augustus could contact his ship remotely. Resonance didn't care how far apart you were.

"For what purpose?" Augustus asked.

"Your ship is too valuable and dangerous a piece of equipment to be left floating around."

"So am I," said Augustus, valuable and dangerous. "You don't want me to ping my Striker if it's still in the Myriad."

"Why don't I want that? Because the Hive will detect your Striker receiving the res pulse? I'd like few things better than for the Hive to eat your Striker and get it off the game board."

Saying so, Farragut walked around the moebius chessboard. Moebius chess was like real chess, but it forced you to look at the board differently. It was too easy to make a false move.

This game was still in progress. Farragut had to lean over to see the pieces in the upside down curve. "How does anyone play this?"

"Carefully."

"Does Jose Maria have a chance of winning this game? You're a patterner."

"He does if I don't plug into patterner mode."

Farragut straightened up. "Ask your Striker where it is."

"You'll cost *Don* Cordillera the game."

Farragut crossed his arms in a pose of impatient waiting.

"If you so order," Augustus said. "If I contact my Striker, it could destroy me. Is that what you want?"

"How? Why would your own ship destroy you?"

"It is probable, to a near certainty, that Romulus rigged my Striker to snare my programming in the event that I try to access its control system."

"No. I don't want that," John Farragut growled, taking big strides in the tight compartment. But John Farragut didn't like leaving a loose end of that magnitude that far behind him either.

Merrimack's artificial gravity gave one of its hiccups. Farragut momentarily lost contact with the deck. Gravity restored, he landed without missing a step, long accustomed to his ship's moods.

The strings of the Spanish guitar vibrated an open chord.

The pieces on the chessboard were magnetic and held their positions. Farragut signaled the guard that he was ready to exit the brig.

Augustus spoke at his back. "Tell *Don* Cordillera I have mate in three."

✳ ✳ ✳ ✳ ✳

15 September 2443
Kentucky, USA
Earth
Near Space

His Honor John Knox Farragut Senior, Justice of the Supreme Court of the Commonwealth of Kentucky, took a call from his wife. Mama Farragut told him they had a guest at the house.

Hospitality was a sacred duty, so it didn't matter that the visitor was Roman. Mama Farragut had taken him in, offered refreshment and insisted he stay for dinner. When she found out the visitor was a man of importance, she called her husband in the state capital. Did John Senior want to join them for dinner? The guest's name was Romulus.

Dinner itself was fairly civilized. Nothing of any weight was discussed during the meal. Romulus complimented his hostess.

When the bourbon and cigars came out, the women and children left the room. His Honor kept his work and home life separate. He did not want the mother of his children involved in politics.

The gloves came off. A smile was really just a show of teeth anyway. Romulus and His Honor smiled at each other.

John Junior, who was fourteen—just old enough to be allowed to stay in the room—remained silent, awed, as smiles flashed like razors.

The visitor was audacious. His Honor would have shot the Roman if he weren't a guest.

There were interstellar warrants out on this particular Roman, but you do not abuse guests in your house. You just don't.

Romulus had floated the idea of provincial rule for his host. Justice John Knox Farragut Senior already considered himself the de facto ruler of the Commonwealth of Kentucky. He did not appreciate a Roman offering him what was already his.

At evening's end, His Honor left it to young John John to escort their guest out.

Romulus shocked John Junior to holy hell when he turned at the transport's hatch and told him, "Your eldest brother is overrated, you know. You bear your father's full name. Yet your father doesn't know your worth. When you get tired of being John John, here is my exclusive harmonic." He passed young John a data slip. "It's not turning coat. America was founded as—and still is—a Roman province. The time for deciding is soon. I have seen your heart and it is Roman. *Erroso.*"

The parting word wasn't Latin. It was Greek. John Junior was well educated and recognized the word. Alexander the Great signed his letters so. *Be strong.*

As John Junior went back into the house, breaking news was showing on the receiver.

A state of emergency had been declared on the Near Space planet of 82 Eridani III. Verified reports were coming in of gorgons emerging from the prehistoric ground.

Astronomically speaking, the Hive was now in Earth's backyard.

Experts were scrambling for estimates of when the swarm might arrive on Earth.

21

16 September 2443
U.S. Space Battleship *Merrimack*
Fort Theodore Roosevelt
Near Space

"NEVER," Captain John Farragut declared. "We are not letting the Hive reach Earth. Ever."

On orders from the Admiralty, *Merrimack* blazed out of Fort Theodore Roosevelt toward the 82 Eridani star system. At threshold velocity it would take her over twenty-four hours to get there.

Farragut slid down the ladders to the brig, hauled open the hatch to Augustus' cell, shrugged Augustus' scabbard off his back and threw it at Augustus. "Augustus. Out."

Augustus caught the sheathed sword. Didn't rise. Sullen. "Give me a reason."

"Gorgons. 82 Eridani III."

Augustus was on his feet. His shock looked genuine.

✳ ✳ ✳ ✳ ✳

Merrimack tore up the distance between Fort Ted and 82 Eridani III.

Twenty-four hours was an eternity when you felt you were standing still. Without modification, there was no sense of motion inside a ship's inertial shell. You're punching through space in incomprehensible measures, but you don't know it. You only felt the ship's sudden burbles that leaned you unexpectedly sideways or lifted you up off the deck. Otherwise you felt nothing.

In a dead calm, Navy specialists go stir crazy and Fleet Marines want to murder them. All hands needed to feel like they were getting somewhere.

So *Merrimack*'s environmental systems were modified to make you feel like she was flying. And Lieutenant Colonel Steele put you to work. There were drills and a lot of cleaning. Your Swift better be clean enough to lick. He made you do it, too—lick it. There were machines that could clean things quicker and better, but machines don't mind the waiting.

And there was basketball. There was no life without basketball. Cole Darby hadn't played much before he joined the Fleet Marines. Now it was Wing versus Battery in the maintenance hangar.

This close to threshold velocity, *Mack* gets moodier. Her inertial hiccups turn you sideways and leave you there. Real interesting when you're trying to make a free throw.

Oh, bad luck, Dumbell. The ball fell up.

Lieutenant Colonel Steele kept his Fleet Marines busy when they were on duty. Worry could gnaw a hole through your guts. The Old Man don't want you thinking about how close the gorgons are to Earth. Off duty, you snuck some bad thinking in. *We're standing on the brink of the end of everything.*

Don't think, Darb. Just make this three-pointer—

Up your nose, Shasher Wyatt!

✳ ✳ ✳ ✳ ✳

Six hours before planetfall Taps sounded. Most of *Merrimack*'s personnel hit the rack. They slept if they could, and they'd better give it their best effort. In six hours they'd be back into an unholy burr ball.

TR Steele walked through the aisles of hydroponics. He was in search of light and warmth—and of those two ridiculous lizard plants Kerry Blue was so fond of. Didn't see them. They usually made themselves known. They were the only plants that didn't stay planted. They chortled. They climbed him like a tree. They did ridiculous things.

But he didn't see them now. Wondered if they might have died.

He felt a sting he shouldn't feel. Lots of things die. These two were just plants with legs. And tongues. And tails. And big eyes. And webbed feet.

And Kerry Blue loved them.

The lizard plants were as close as he could get to Kerry Blue now, in this dark hour. And they were gone.

He felt a sense of loss. And foreboding. He was going back into battle in five hours. It weighed on him. The enemy was close to home.

The hatch to the moist green compartment sucked open. Sucked shut. A Marine stepped in. Barefoot, dressed only in tank top and sweat shorts, she tiptoed up the aisle, a bushy lizard plant under either arm.

She didn't see him. The compartment was large, and a clump of what were supposed to be banana trees stood between them. Steele was from Oklahoma. He thought the banana trees were alien.

He stayed motionless. Tried to breathe silently. Saw her between the wide green fronds, her bare arms well-toned, strong in a girly way. She placed the plants in a patch of mint. Her whispered scold carried. "Stay put, you guys!"

She poured water into bowls for them.

Her brown hair was loose on her shoulders.

The sight of her hurt. There was a painful lump in his throat, a burning in his eyes. A raging hard-on down below.

Kerry Blue retreated on tiptoe.

As soon as the hatch sucked shut behind her, the lizard plants pulled themselves out of their trough and scampered for the hatch, trying to follow her. They were the dumbest looking things. And completely useless.

Steele strode over to them. They cowered low. He scooped them up. Put them back in their trough. They hunkered down in their places, goggle eyes staring.

"Stay," he ordered them.

He left hydroponics and went back to his own cabin. He had private quarters in officer's country. He lay in his rack, cursing the desk-commando eunuch who ever thought that putting women in combat was a good idea.

Thoughts churned in the dark. Would it be any better keeping a woman safe at home? No. The enemy just now proved that there was no safe home. The Hive was erupting in quick striking distance of Earth.

He had to face it: He needed Kerry Blue here, with him. Armed and trained in twenty-one scenarios.

✳ ✳ ✳ ✳ ✳

17 September 2443
U.S. Space Battleship *Merrimack*
82 Eridani III
Near Space

An emergency evacuation of the domed settlements on the third planet of the 82 Eridani system was underway as *Merrimack* arrived.

The space battlecruiser *Rio Grande* was already there, her Swifts deployed. The fighter craft fired beam shots on the masses of gorgons as they broke out of the ground and spidered toward the inhabited domes.

"Just why are there so many people on 82 Eridani III?" Calli said, appalled.

John Farragut supposed he was wearing the same stunned expression as his XO.

Merrimack descended low enough to physically see the settlement through her portholes.

There were acres of newly constructed domes on the dark planet. They were physical domes, not energy domes, housing a scientific expedition that made no sense. The domes shone bright white from their interior lights.

Someone with galactic amounts of currency had flushed a lot of it into this world sometimes known as Xi.

A dome flickered to darkness as it broke open.

The domes were equipped with no defenses. They had no stable of spacecraft. The research scientists had been ferried here and left without a means of quick exit.

Swifts strafed the open airless ground. You heard a holy lot of barking on the Marine harmonic. The space battlecruiser *Rio Grande* carried the other half of the 89th battalion—the Bull Mastiffs.

Captain Farragut tried to contact *Rio*'s captain, but Dallas McDaniels was not on board *Rio* at the moment. Captain McDaniels had commandeered a Swift. He was outside shooting gorgons.

Captain Farragut spoke over the Fleet Marine com without identifying himself: "What do you call a Navy Captain at the controls of a Swift?"

A chorus of Fleet Marines answered at once: "Flight risk."

The voice of Captain Dallas McDaniels: "Is that you, John, old son?"

"Ahoy and howdy, Dallas. You started without me. What's your tally?"

"Lost count," Captain McDaniels sent back. "Don't reckon these things died this easy in the Deep End. You have any idea what's causing them to be so amenable to the notion here?"

"No, sir. I do not. And I'm getting unkind looks from my Flight Controller. Pick up channel G."

Captain McDaniels came back on the G harmonic, leaving the Marine harmonic to the Marines: "It's like these gorgons never seen a Swift before."

Which wasn't possible. They both knew it. It was a well-known fact by now that you don't keep secrets from separate members of the Hive. You teach one gorgon, you've taught them all, everywhere, instantly.

"Are these even real gorgons?" Captain McDaniels asked.

"Not sure. Keep it simple. Make 'em die."

"Roger that."

McDaniels signed off, yelling.

John Farragut was getting harsh looks from his XO now. The commander of his Fleet Marines was also frowning.

Calli spoke very very low. "Captain, you're not."

"No." He was not going outside to play with a Swift. "I've got the big guns right here. TR, release the hounds."

"Sir."

Lieutenant Colonel TR Steele left the command platform, roaring for his pilots and gunners to kit up in bunny suits and bubble helmets. And everyone take a sword.

Kerry Blue squawked. "Not flight suits?"

Bunny suits were standard issue spacesuits for ground duty. And swords? No one took a sword on board a Swift.

Reg Monroe: "He's talking to the battery, right?"

Carly Delgado: "No, *chicas*. He's talking to all of us."

Steele: "No one is flying. You're going in on the ground. *Merrimack* will descend to the surface. You will debark best speed. Proceed to the domes with swords at the ready. Escort the civilians to the evacuation vehicles. Secure all displacement equipment behind them."

Kerry saw Lieutenant Hazard Sewell open his mouth, an objection in there. Never got it out.

Steele: "You are not flying. They need fishers inside the domes."

To "fish" was to Fight Inside Someone's House. The Fleet Marines who served on *Merrimack* were masters of wielding sharp metal in tight corridors packed with equal parts gorgons and your very best friendlies.

"You are the experts," Steele told his Bull Mastiffs.

"None better," Lieutenant Hazard Sewell said, and gave an eighty-ninth battalion bark.

Hoo Ra.

When the Marines assembled in full gear at the sail, Lieutenant Colonel Steele spat on Kerry Blue's bubble helmet.

The glob slid off quick and clean. The Old Man looked disappointed.

He could've benched her if she hadn't passed that test. She didn't know why Steele never wanted to send her forward. She was as good as anyone else. Couldn't understand why he hated her.

Steele was kitted up for ground duty too. He was going down with his dogs. He and Farragut were alike that way. Both of 'em led from the front.

Kerry glanced out a portal. The planet was getting real big. *Merrimack* was descending fast.

And we got orders to proceed down the lower sail. Why do they call it a sail? It's a one-hundred-fifty-foot tower slanted back like a shark fin, mostly filled with equipment. And it has a ladder for deploying us lot.

The Fleet Marines filed down in units, Kerry Blue down front with Alpha Team. Waiting on the ladder for the hatch to open. Twitch Fuentes below her, Cole Darby positioned to come down on her head if she didn't move it when it came time to jump.

Hatch open. Everybody out. Kerry Blue jumped.

She landed easy. The gravity wasn't too fierce. She ran to make way for everybody else.

She could see now where *Merrimack* let the Bull Mastiffs out—in the center of a ring of widely spaced domes that housed the settlements.

Kerry looked for Dome E. Couldn't see for the bright white flashes that split the perfect black. She blinked. She had to find Dome E. Or, better yet, just follow Lieutenant Hazard Sewell.

Ran with her team through a rain of sparks.

Whipping gorgon legs sniped at her flank. She hadn't even seen them. A downstroke with her sword made the biting mouths fall away. More mouths moved in. She sliced those off too.

Heard the hiss of a suit leak. One of the mouths got her. Then came that little *fwip* sound as her suit sealed itself.

She stabbed a landing disk as she ran past it. It stuck to her sword point and came with her. She had to kick it off. The Marines had orders to secure *all* displacement gear.

Steele motioned with his sword for Red Squad to split right, and Hazard Sewell led the charge into Dome E. Everybody get inside as fast as you can pack yourselves through the air lock and make way for the evacuees to get out.

Kerry Blue, first thing, pulled the D collar off a civilian, who fought her for it. Kerry won. Told the woman to suit up for dust off.

The woman said she'd rather displace.

"Suit or die. Those are the choices." Kerry slashed the legs off a gorgon that fell from the overhead.

The ground shook. Not good. Makes the civilians scream, and that don't help.

The floor tiles moved, breaking underfoot. Kerry stumbled over the uneven ground, hacking at the tentacles that bloomed up between the broken edges of foundation tiles.

The dome lights failed.

Headlamps on. Made for jarring shadows.

Kerry Blue tried to count her dead. Couldn't verify half her kills. The gorgons disintegrated, and she was left arguing over pools of ooze that really were her kills, not yours, Cole Darby, go get your own. No time to argue. Lots more opportunities. Priority targets were the gorgons that got between the civilians and the exits.

Not feeling as scared as she oughtta be. Reminded herself: Do not under-respect the enemy.

Most of the resident scientists had already suited up for evacuation. Kerry's crew had to clear the gorgons from the exit and then shove refugees out the air lock. Keep 'em moving.

Until you had to stop.

Civilians were whiny and unpredictable and really hard not to cut. Even the smart ones. Especially the smart ones. It was like dressing children, making sure they were ready to go outside in the snow. This geek woman tried to go out the air lock with a big ol' gash in her pressure suit. Told Kerry Blue, "It'll be fine. I don't mind the cold."

"Ma'am? You'll mind the vacuum." Kerry Blue slapped a piece of sealer on the gashed sleeve before the woman could get out there and pop her lungs.

Keep 'em moving.

Green Team was out there on the other side of the lock, clearing a path for the civilians to get to the landers.

They heard something over the com: "We're down here stabbing bilge balloons and babysitting tourists while *Rio's* Wing is flying and shooting. Is that fair?"

Hazard Sewell, right beside her: "We are known for no friendly hacking. You should be flattered, Marine."

Fishing was a real art form. Kerry's company was hard-practiced at fighting in narrow corridors alongside brothers she loved more than her own life.

"I'm flattered, Mister Lieutenant Hazard Sewell, sir," Kerry Blue said as a Swift executed a barrel roll over the dome. "I'd rather be flying!"

She saw Hazard's white face through his crystal-clean bubble helmet, mouthing words for only her to see: *Me too.*

Swarms of gorgons scaled the dome, trying to get in through the top. Kerry could see them moving up there on the translucent panels.

She heard a deep structural groan. Dome E was cracking. Air hissed out. Kerry Blue's suit fluttered in the current.

A glut of gorgons briefly plugged the crack. Then the crack widened, and the whole wad of them fell in, down, and splattered onto the buildings and the running people.

More of them tumbled down in giant clumps.

"Oough!" A gorgon fell through the ceiling, right onto Kerry Blue. Would've killed her in normal gravity. This one dropped her to the broken floor, knocking the breath out of her. She felt the tentacle hits; the thing was biting at her suit.

Suddenly the gorgon sack was melting all over her.

"GRETAAAAAA!" There was Dak with a sword. Master crazy. Severed tentacles and gorgon bits flying this way and the other way. Dark ooze slid down Dak's sleeves.

Kerry jumped to her feet and cut open the next gorgon that came at them. "Tango Yankee, Dak!"

Dak was already away, flailing and yelling like a berserker, "Greta Greta Greta Greta!"

Kerry's team guided the civilians through the dome's air lock. Another squad waited outside to shepherd the people into the waiting life craft.

And *Rio's* Wing was upstairs, flying cover. Lucky them. Their Swifts became dragons in the dark. They scorched bright paths across the black rock.

Many, many whippy legs fled before them.

From way upstairs, *Merrimack* advised that there was no more human life inside Dome E.

Kerry looked up at the dying dome. Air hissed out. Freezing steam glittered in the emergency lights.

There were more gorgons out here. Lots and lots, harassing the landers and trying to get into the other domes.

The gorgons out here were the bloated kind. Under atmospheric pressure gorgon bodies got smaller, compressed to about a meter wide not counting all those snaky tentacles. These gorgons were balloons. Their fanged tentacles were all the same.

A squadron of Swifts from *Rio Grande* approached for another strafing run to burn the refugees' escape route clear of gorgons. The fighters came in real low on the deck.

Kerry would've been moving a lot faster than that if she were flying that close to the ground.

Suddenly a whole mass of gorgons rose up from the rock surface, tentacles clasped to form a living net of themselves. Five of the Swifts pulled up and clear. The last one flew right into the net, and crashed down into the rock. Kerry watched it auger in. A scream. Hers. *"No!"*

There was no explosion.

A mass of dark thrashing bodies piled on top of the Swift.

The pilot could be alive. You could bury a Swift and live if you had the fat part of your energy field—your cowcatcher—deployed right. Kerry Blue knew that real well. The pilot could be alive.

The other Swifts came in screaming, flaming. Gorgons leaped and clutched and burned.

The downed Swift was moving, coming out of the ground, rising in a drunken motion.

Kerry Blue squinted. Didn't look right. The crate wasn't flying. And it didn't have its cowcatcher deployed. It didn't have a force field at all.

The gorgons had it. A mass of tentacles pried the Swift out of the rock. More were pulling at its canopy.

"Hotel One, this is *Rio*. Negative life signs in the downed craft. Secure the crash site."

Secure it meant fry it. You don't let gorgons eat your dead. The Swift's wingman came down blazing and screaming. Melted all the gorgons from the crash site and incinerated the pilot's remains.

*   *   *

As evacuation landers lifted off from 82 Eridani III, *Merrimack's* tactical specialist reported, "Activity on the far side of the planet."

"What activity?" Commander Carmel demanded.

"Gorgon emergence."

Tactical read off the planetary coordinates and brought up an image of gorgons climbing out of the ground.

They spilled out like pebbled lava and crawled over each other, building themselves into a towering mound. Then the mound slipped wide. It looked like a volcano with still more gorgons crawling out of its central crater.

"Get an incendiary down its throat," Farragut ordered. "Cook 'em."

Merrimack circled half round the planet and breathed fire into the crater until the ground stopped crawling.

Steam rolled across the rock and froze.

"Look for escape holes."

"Aye, sir," said Tactical. Then immediately, "There they are."

Tactical fed the coordinates to Targeting and brought the area into view.

More holes formed in the rock several klicks away from the first target, like volcanic vents, spewing live gorgons.

"Burn them, sir?"

"Negative. Wait until they give us a bigger surface target."

Tactical reported yet another vent, bigger, erupting at the planet's pole.

The emerging masses were changing shape. Packing themselves together, building and contracting.

The XO murmured, "John? What do these shapes look like to you?"

"I see it, Cal. Do we have anyone left downstairs!"

"Negative human life down below. We are clear to unleash anything you want on the planet, sir."

Captain Farragut hailed the *Rio Grande*. "Dallas! The enemy are forming up! The gorgons are trying to make spheres! Do not let them organize! Gorgons can achieve FTL in sphere formation. Beams will just scatter them and drive them into hiding to regroup. We need a neutron hose here, and I don't have one."

"*Merrimack*. This is *Rio Grande*. We can oblige, *Merrimack*. Clear orbit. Advise when you are away."

Farragut looked to his exec. "Make sure all our Marines are on board and put us somewhere else, Cal."

The space battleship *Merrimack* jumped to FTL.

The space battlecruiser *Rio Grande* took a neutron hose to the planet 82 Eridani III, returning the long dead world to deadness again.

22

17 September 2443
U.S. Space Battleship *Merrimack*
82 Eridani Star System
Near Space

"WHO'D WE LOSE?" Hazard Sewell asked. "I saw a Swift go down."

"That was Piotr Czerwonykoszula."

"Who?"

"FNG." Cole Darby said. New Guy.

Darb had very recently been an FNG.

Flight Sergeant Czerwonykoszula flew out of *Rio*. Still, he was a Bull Mastiff. One of the 89th.

The Bull Mastiffs sent up a howl for their fallen brother. He was one of us. And next time it could be any one of us.

There wasn't so much as a molecule left of him to send home. Old Man Steele told the family that Piotr Czerwonykoszula took a whole lot of gorgons down with him.

On the voyage home to the Solar System from 82 Eridani, Captain Farragut praised his Fleet Marines. Thanked them. Stood them for a round of drinks—on him personally. And barked the 89th Bull Mastiff salute.

After the toasts, Captain Farragut, Commander Carmel, the civilian *Don* Jose Maria de Cordillera, and the Roman Colonel Augustus stayed behind in the bar—the captain drinking Kentucky bourbon, Calli drinking Mezcal *sin gusano*. Jose Maria still had a bottle of Spanish Rioja left from dinner. Augustus watched ice cubes melt in a glass of seltzer.

They rehashed the battle.

82 Eridani III, planet Xi, was so ancient that its core held no vestigial heat. Yet the living Hive had come out of the rock. Not just rock. Bedrock.

The planet was the multibillion-year-old birthplace of the Arran civilization.

The archon Donner, the leader of the Arran civilization in the Myriad, had been born on Xi. He and his people had come forward in time billions of years through the Rim Gate at the edge of the Myriad.

It was Donner who had first posed the question: Why were there no descendants of his ancient people out here among the stars—people billions of years more advanced than Earthlings? Why hadn't Donner's people colonized the stars?

Their descendants should be out here somewhere.

Now it was apparent what had happened to those people. Before Donner's early civilization could develop faster-than-light travel, the Hive had arrived at 82 Eridani III—planet Xi—and destroyed all life on it.

"Why didn't the Hive destroy all life on Earth at the same time they destroyed 82 Eridani?" Calli asked. "The worlds are close together."

"They are close now," Augustus said. "Earth didn't exist at the time. *Sol* didn't exist at the time. The Solar system is young."

Donner's colonists on planet Arra in the Myriad were all that was left of the ancient Xi civilization. Now their adopted homeworld was under Hive attack.

"Donner was a good dictator," Farragut said into his bourbon.

"Was?" said Calli. "Is he dead?"

"Not last I knew. But he's not exactly a dictator any more. He's overseeing the evacuation of Arra with the LEN."

Farragut scowled into his bourbon. Breathed in. Held it. Hesitated to speak again. "I know I'm billions of years late to the party, but why do I have the feeling that Romulus planted those gorgons on Xi?"

"Because your subconscious is paying attention even if you're not, John Farragut," Augustus said. "Romulus didn't plant the gorgons, but he intentionally woke them up. The money trail for the scientific expedition on Xi leads to an imperial account on Palatine. Romulus set the breakfast table for the buried Hive."

"He's a patterner," Calli said. "How can we possibly battle a patterner from the future?"

"Romulus may be a patterner, but he wasn't made out of patterner material. Patterners are chosen for our integrity, our loyalty, and our intelligence. Romulus is only intelligent. Being a patterner allows him to recognize interconnections and logical outcomes. It doesn't force him to see anything. He can solve complex problems if he has exposure to the required data. He can outmaneuver us. And he should. But he won't. He's delusional. He's *Romulus*."

"And he knows the future," Calli said. "He knows everything we're going to do."

"Again, no. The future changed the instant Romulus arrived in his own past. His future knowledge is actually two sets of mismatched faulty data, neither of which is necessarily true."

Jose Maria: "And do you not think Romulus the patterner can figure that out?"

Calli nodded agreement with Jose Maria. "Romulus should figure that out."

"He should. But he's in love with his own omniscience," Augustus said. "We're blind to our future. That's our advantage."

"We're blind—? Now how in the Sam Hill is that any kind of advantage, Augustus?"

"It keeps you from swinging at a change-up when you're expecting a fast ball, John Farragut. Romulus has false certainties. And because he's Romulus, he will continue to refuse truths he badly wants not to see. That is where he will fall. If he doesn't kill us first."

※ ※ ※ ※ ※

Numa Pompeii issued an Empire-wide mandate from the imperial palace on Palatine for any Roman citizen to kill Romulus on sight wherever he was.

Because military service was a condition for full citizenship, Rome's citizenry was well prepared to carry out the mandate should the opportunity present.

But Romulus had vanished. He was not in Roma Nova. He wasn't even on the planet Palatine.

He reappeared days later on the artificial planet that orbited Beta Centauri. There, Romulus hoisted the imperial flag and his own eagles over the main city. He chose new colors for himself. Red, black, and gold.

He set up his government-in-exile inside the Italian embassy over cries of treason from Roma Nova and polite objections from the League of Earth Nations, whose world it was. Beta Centauri had no national identity. Romulus met no armed resistance. The LEN officials questioned the legality of his action. It wasn't exactly a challenge. More of an inquiry.

The Italian Ambassador claimed to be enjoying lively discussions with his guest.

"He's saying that under duress!" Farragut said. He was more than ready to charge into the Centauri system and free an embassy-full of hostages.

Jose Maria shook his head slowly. "I do not detect any sign of duress from the ambassador, young Captain."

"Calli?" Farragut appealed to his exec. Calli knew Rome. Calli knew Romulus.

"Romulus can be charming. I can believe the discussions are lively," Calli said. "Honestly, John, I don't think we'll be getting an invitation from the LEN to invade Beta Centauri."

"I don't like him there."

"I'm right with you, sir," Calli said.

Beta Centauri was a strategic outpost. Centauri was the closest star system to Earth.

Augustus said it. "It puts Romulus a javelin's throw from Alpha Centauri and within a day's striking distance of Earth."

Lieutenant Colonel Steele, who usually kept quiet on the command platform, broke his silence. "Striking distance? What's Romulus got to strike with? What's he got?"

"I have no information to work with," Augustus said. "He's exceptionally good at keeping secrets."

"Can someone get a bead on Romulus from Centauri orbit? Sniper shot? Get me to Centauri!" Farragut said. "I'll do it."

"Romulus is on Italian soil," Calli said. "Hitting Romulus inside the embassy would be an act of war. Against the wrong country."

✳ ✳ ✳ ✳ ✳

30 September 2443
Italian Embassy
Beta Centauri
Centauri Star System
Near Space

"What is this face?" Claudia demanded. That snapped Romulus back to attention. She'd caught him frowning.

"I can't locate Jose Maria de Cordillera," Romulus said. "He's not where he's supposed to be. But, you know what? I don't need to find him. I just need to torch his world. He needs to watch. Now you're pouting, Empress. Why?"

"I want it."

"Want what, my sweet? You want Terra Rica?"

"Yes. I want Terra Rica for my domain. I don't like it here. There's no society on Beta Centauri."

Claudia was accustomed to the operas and shows, sensations, concerts, grand balls, riotous festivals, lavish routs, races, wealth, culture, and the exquisite beauty of Roma Nova on Palatine.

Romulus considered this. "Destroying the planet does seem a waste of beautiful *terra firma*. Shall I just remove the people?"

"Only the boring ones. I want *Don* Cordillera's family to be my servants."

"I want Jose Maria's family dead," Romulus said.

"Nooo. I want them in splendid livery and waiting on me."

Romulus struggled not to tell her the future he'd rescued her from. She had no idea what agonies that saintly monster Jose Maria meant to put her and him through.

Romulus forced a smile. "You're right. Death is ugly. I don't want ugliness touching you. House Cordillera will live as your servant stable. But *Don* Cordillera needs to die."

"Why?"

For what he would do to you in a vanished future.

He couldn't tell her.

Claudia pulled on his hands as if coaxing him to dance with her. "He would make the most spectacular butler! I want him."

"Then you shall have him," Romulus lied.

✳ ✳ ✳ ✳ ✳

1 October 2443
U.S. Space Battleship *Merrimack*
Earth orbit
Near Space

In a public broadcast from Beta Centauri, Romulus stated that a Roman Imperator had the exclusive right to declare war on behalf of the Empire. Romulus announced his intent to exercise that right.

Calli, watching the transmission from the command deck of *Merrimack*, lifted her hands, baffled, then let them drop, disgusted. "Now he's taking powers he doesn't legally have."

"Like that's never been done," Farragut said.

"Romulus doesn't have the right to make war," Augustus said.

"He says he does," Calli said. "He's invoking the divine right of kings."

"He's not king of anything," Farragut said. "So who is Romulus fixin' to declare war against? Surely not *Rome*. He can't declare against his own Empire, can he?"

Calli said, "A just war, *jus ad bellum*, requires the means and a justifiable reason. He doesn't have it."

She looked to Augustus, who gave the smallest nod of agreement.

An alert came across military channels that Romulus had stepped outside the Italian embassy.

Farragut cried, "Who do we have at Beta Centauri! Anyone got a shot?"

The newsfeed from Beta Centauri showed Romulus, in full antique regalia—bronze cuirass, greaves, and crested helmet—stalking up the street known as "Embassy Row" to the gates of the U.S. embassy on Beta Centauri. He carried a cornel wood spear fitted with a barbarous iron head that had been dipped in what looked like blood.

Embassy guards behind the wrought iron bars watched him approach. They weren't moving as long as Romulus stayed outside the perimeter of their sovereign ground.

Romulus stood outside the gates and announced: "I, Romulus, and the People of Rome declare and make war on the so-called United States of America. To restore Roman honor and might, squandered by false kings. To remove the false government from the soil of the Roman province of America, a degenerate society that doesn't value military prowess in its leadership. To uproot the cancerous decadent tyranny that has taken hold there."

Saying so he hurled the spear between the iron bars of the gate. The spear point stabbed deep into the embassy's stout wooden door.

Captain John Farragut watched the newscast from *Merrimack*'s command platform. A lot of mouths hung open around him.

Farragut looked to his XO, hopeful. "Are we at war?"

"I don't think so," Calli said. She turned to Jose Maria de Cordillera, standing at the back.

Jose Maria shook his head. "I rather think not."

"Shucks," said Farragut.

✳ ✳ ✳ ✳ ✳

Through the porthole in the captain's quarters on *Merrimack*, Earth appeared like a white-veiled jewel in the blackness of space.

Jose Maria de Cordillera sat on the bench and played his guitar.

Augustus lay flat on his back on the deck grates, nursing a headache. He looked dead. It was easy to step on him, especially when the ship's artificial gravity gave one of its burbles.

Farragut mused out loud. "Romulus is a patterner. He has a stealthy ship developed in the future."

Only the guitar spoke for several measures.

"He has a stealthy ship."

"You said that," the floor spoke.

"It stands repeating." Farragut turned his back on the porthole. "Romulus has a stealthy ship. He destroyed that ship's development facility. Why did he do that?"

"Presumably to keep its secrets." Jose Maria stopped playing. "To keep rivals from being constructed. But you know that, young Captain."

"Yes, I know that. That's the point. Is Romulus really overlooking something so all-fired obvious? Or has he taken care of it, and I missed the explosions."

The dawn came to Jose Maria. "You mean redundance is good. Redundance is good."

"Redundance is extraordinary. What did destroying the Consortium's development facility win Romulus? The Pacific Consortium *must* have an offsite backup of all the records they lost when Romulus destroyed the development facility."

"More than one backup," Jose Maria suggested. "Redundance is very, very good. But Romulus is a patterner. He must have noticed that."

From the floor: "Ability to see doesn't make you *look*."

"Thank you for agreeing with me for once, Augustus."

"It is so seldom deserved."

"The Pacifics lost a facility," Farragut went on. "But you *know* they haven't lost any technical knowledge. They know how this Xerxes ship is going to be put together. I need to get it into the Consortium's head that Romulus already has their finished design."

Jose Maria said, "You cannot believe that developing a failsafe today will result in any changes to the ship that Romulus now flies."

"No. But the *Pacifics* need to find a way around their own defenses. They're the only ones who can do it."

The floor spoke. "Your plan of attack, John Farragut?"

"I need someone more diplomatic than I am to explain all that to the Pacific Consortium."

The Pacific Consortium representative received *Don* Jose Maria de Cordillera with all the warmth of a Swiss bank auditor. Jose Maria returned to *Merrimack* too quickly.

"What did they say?" Farragut asked.

"Nothing," Jose Maria said. "I mean that literally."

Farragut stood baffled. Mouth open. Nothing coming out. Then the roar. "They have no idea what they're doing! The Pacifics are creating a ship that can't be seen, can't be tracked, can't be remote-accessed, has no failsafe against being used as a weapon. If that isn't the dumbest godforsaken thing—!" He couldn't believe it.

He really couldn't believe it.

✳ ✳ ✳ ✳ ✳

2 October 2443
Italian Embassy
Beta Centauri

Romulus made his next appearance on a broadcast from inside the Italian embassy on Beta Centauri. He wanted to clarify that he had declared war against the United States of America for herself as a breakaway Roman province but not as a member of the League of Earth Nations. Romulus had no quarrel with the LEN.

Then, to Rome's colony, America, Romulus offered amnesty to any U.S.

citizen who wanted to fight on the right side. There was no shame in being born under unlawful rule. "Make a decision now. Once America loses the war, the Empire has no use for losers. America was founded as a Roman colony. American Romans must join me proudly. I welcome you home."

John Farragut shut off the display. "Romulus won't get any Americans taking up that offer."

Caesar Numa Pompeii was not getting suckered into whatever game Romulus was playing. Romulus had no troops, no territory, no ships. He wasn't even son of Caesar anymore. Romulus stood on borrowed ground, braying.

Numa controlled the Empire's home world and Rome's colonies. Rome's colonies were bled out. Caesar Numa was not about to levy troops from colonies that had already lost sixty-four Legions to the Hive. And for *what?* To combat Romulus' empire of vapor? Romulus needed a fight. Numa did not. The Hive was not a threat to Near Space. Approaching Hive spheres wouldn't reach Near Space for another one hundred years. The Hive would not get any more Roman soldiers than Magnus had already fed to it. Numa could wait Romulus out.

Numa made his own announcement.

"That thing is not Rome. I do not recognize that pretender's delusions of leadership of the Empire. Romulus' organization is not a lawful entity. His declaration of war against the United States has no legal force. A state of war does not exist between the United States of America and the Roman Empire. Romulus, son of criminally inept Magnus, is nothing but a self-employed terrorist."

Marisa Johnson, President of the United States of America, didn't favor Romulus with a quick reaction. Romulus' declarations meant nothing, and his words were beneath Presidential notice. Two days passed before Marisa Johnson issued her own brief statement, tacking it on like an afterthought following statements on the economy and the trade deficit. She addressed her remarks to the American people, not to Romulus or Rome. "We do not recognize Romulus' arbitrary assumption of powers. We do not recognize his status as head of any legitimate State. We do not recognize Romulus' declaration of war against these United States and will not answer it. I have nothing further to say on the topic."

And she fell forward onto her desk, blood pooling under her nose.

✳ ✳ ✳ ✳ ✳

4 October 2443

Merrimack's U.S. flag stood motionless in the vacuum. It didn't look right. You really wanted to see Old Glory wave.

At half-staff, it really didn't look right at all.

The public outcry over the assassination of the American President had been immediate and universal. Even Numa Pompeii's Rome offered sympathy, without recognizing U.S. independence.

No one officially accused Romulus. Not yet. Investigators were still searching for proof of his involvement. They were not finding it. They could only acknowledge that President Johnson's death had been achieved by means of a two-stage weapon. The initial stage had been the delivery of an explosive charge—possibly nitro based—into the President. An aide remembered the President coughing recently. They'd both thought she'd inhaled a gnat in the rose garden. The aide had given the President a glass of water.

The second stage was carried out days later, a detonation of the initial charge by remote trigger. The charge was in her chest.

The investigation and the funeral preparations dominated the news services.

"Just let me know when we're at war," Captain Farragut said.

"Sir? I have something," Tactical reported.

Captain Farragut was the only man on *Merrimack* who could stand Marcander Vincent, and that just barely.

Farragut asked with forced calm, "Define 'something,' Mister Vincent."

"Can't." Marcander Vincent threw images up on several displays.

The tactical displays showed vast black mats, like millions of snakes thrashing in an oil slick. They washed up on a black volcanic shore from out of a wide blue ocean on the daylight side of a world. Clots of the substance were breaking up into stringy mats as they hit the rocks.

"Where are those images coming from?"

Tactical replied, "Twenty-eight degrees north latitude, fifteen degrees west longitude."

"*What planet?*"

"Ours. Here. This is Earth."

Astonished, Farragut asked, "What's the Home Guard say?"

"Nothing from the Home Guard—"

Com interrupted, "Here it comes."

Came the blare that always preceded an emergency broadcast, just as an insectoid shivering broke out on deck.

Crickets in stick cages on the command platform chirped. Ants in their terrariums poured from their holes.

The systems specialist leaned away from his station and retched, and Commander Carmel announced over the loud com: *"Hive sign! Hive!"*

PART FOUR

Total War

23

3 October 2443
U.S. Space Battleship *Merrimack*
Earth
Near Space

NO ONE EXPECTED this battle for another century and a half, if ever. Not here. Not on Earth.

Captain John Farragut wanted to bless the Earth Horizon Guard to kingdom come. The Horizon Guard had managed *not* to detect the gorgons entering Earth's atmosphere. But gorgons were here, washing ashore from the Atlantic Ocean, masses of them. Many were dead, but thousands more, maybe millions more, were still alive. How did they just *sneak* past Earth's defenses?

Merrimack's captive insects on the command platform buzzed in panic.

Farragut asked of anyone on the command platform, "Are there gorgons on my boat?"

"None reported so far," Lieutenant Glenn Hamilton said. She had already initiated a search. "All hands are doing a sweep. The dogs are checking the tight spots."

"The gorgons may not be on board yet, but they know where we are."

That was apparent. The telltales were singing madly.

"Where are they coming *from?*" Glenn cried, frustrated. "We didn't carry them from 82 Eridani, did we?"

"Hell of a thought, Hamster," Farragut said. "Not really possible."

Farragut looked to his patterner, who would shoot him down quick as thinking about it if he made a wrong assumption.

Augustus shook his head slowly, no. "We—your *Merrimack*—did not bring gorgons here. And not from 82 Eridani. 82 Eridani III is thoroughly dead. These Hive cells are displacing from somewhere else."

"Displacing!" Farragut could not have heard right. "There's no precedent for gorgon displacement."

"Then they learned," Augustus said flatly. "We know they can learn. Distance doesn't mean anything to resonance."

"Not to resonance, it doesn't, but distance sure as morning means something to displacement accuracy," Farragut said.

"And that's why this lot are making a sodding mess of themselves," Augustus said.

✳ ✳ ✳ ✳ ✳

Amid the catastrophe, Vice President Sampson Reed was hastily sworn in as President of the United States of America.

It had been a joke, not a funny one, that Marisa Johnson chose Sampson Reed as her vice president as a life insurance policy. No matter how much anyone hated Marisa Johnson, they wouldn't let her come to harm so long as Sampson Reed was waiting in the wings.

Now, President Reed had the Home Guard trying to assess the enemy. Res scans were less than helpful. Like trying to identify the properties of elementary particles, to observe the Hive was to change it.

Because no one had seen the Hive arrive, and gorgons were washing up on the Canary Islands, the fear was that the gorgons were hatching out of the Earth.

Vwakikikikik ships already in Earth's orbit offered to help scout the ocean floor for enemy activity.

Squids were normally as serious as a pool full of preschoolers. Squids did not wage war. They didn't have weapons. But it was in the squids' self-interest to help humanity stop this plague before it could find its way to the squids' watery homeworld, Vwakikikikikkk.

The squids' translucent blue orbs descended from orbit to float and roll on the terrestrial ocean waves. The squids exited their craft through water locks and dove down to the ocean depths.

The pressure meant nothing to them. The salinity was irritating but tolerable. The squids reached the Atlantic floor in minutes.

They felt the seismic disturbances and verified that they were not originating from within the earth. The upheavals were coming from scattered locations in deep water.

Then the squids sighted gorgons at depth.

Tentacles lashed out from black masses of liquid.

Veterans of Hive encounters immediately recognized the ooze as the remains of dead gorgons. Live gorgons sucked the dead ooze, then took notice of the squids.

Merrimack's xenolinguist reported to the command deck to assist in communicating with their squid allies. This was Hamster's husband, Patrick Hamilton.

By the time Doctor Patrick Hamilton made his entrance, Colonel Augustus was already plugged into patterner mode and connected on the com with the squid ship, doing just fine translating subtle shades of Vwakikikikik meanings.

Patrick wasn't needed here after all. Someone forgot to tell him. He hovered at the rear of the platform like a lost glove. His wife didn't look at him. Lieutenant Glenn Hamilton was working.

Augustus queried the Vwakikikikik scouts: Might the gorgons be hatching from the bedrock? They'd done it on 82 Eridani III.

It was a horrifying thought. The squids cast about, searching for anything emerging from the ocean floor. They reported negative signs of eruptions.

At that moment they witnessed a displacement event. A sudden massive expression of ooze burst into existence in the water, swirling with dismembered tentacles. The displacement shock registered on all shore stations. The force would have killed humans that close to the epicenter. The squids flowed with the shock wave.

"*That* was a displacement event," *Merrimack*'s displacement tech confirmed.

"Using what equipment?" Farragut demanded.

Augustus: "The Vwakikikikik report negative equipment. The gorgons are spontaneously displacing. They're not doing a neat job of it."

Great clouds of black ooze plumed and spread on the current. The living monsters sucked in the debris of their dead.

"Displacement. This is Command. Confirm jammers."

"Displacement jammers active, aye."

Nothing was going to displace intact aboard *Merrimack*.

Captain Farragut sent a personal message to the Vwakikikikik ship. Thanked the Vwakikikikik for the recon and strongly advised them to get out of the water and out of the atmosphere, and out of the Solar System. Yesterday.

The Vwakikikikik thanked Captain Farragut for his concern. Squids shot to the surface as if chased by gorgons.

The command crew watched the tactical display in horror as gorgons welled up underneath the rising squids. They weren't rising fast enough. You wanted to help them. "*Swim!*" somebody yelled at the tactical displays.

The Vwakikikikik reached the surface and squeezed themselves inboard their watery ships.

Four of the alien globes waddled into the air and gained altitude. The last orb rose, wallowed, lurched in the air, leaking. Withering. Its membrane was pierced in many places, and the globe was spilling water and squids. Thrashing tentacles reached for them.

Vwakikikikik engineers tried to shore up the ship while others sealed the rents and sliced off grasping gorgon mouths.

"TR. Get some cover out there," Farragut ordered.

Lieutenant Colonel Steele on the loud com: *Scramble. All flights. Scramble.*

And to the erks in the flight hangars Steele sent instructions. "Prep all Swifts for in-atmo action. Close support loads. Torches and short-range edged projectiles. Launch 'em yesterday."

Kerry Blue. Running to her Swift. *Go. Go. Go.*

Climbed onto the wing of her waiting crate, Alpha Six. Vaulted into the open cockpit. Bubble helmet on. Secure. Pulled the harness down around her and clasped it shut.

Her erk gave her harness a good jerk to make sure she was strapped in tight, then gave her bubble helmet a double pat. *Go.*

Kerry pulled her canopy forward. Locked.

Instructions streamed into her helmet com. "Engage one enemy at a time. Negative ricochets. Negative collaterals."

"Yeah yeah yeah. We love our squids," Kerry said, tapping her feet. "Let me out!"

"Alpha Six, your com is live."

Oops.

The elevator shaft descended around her Swift. A butt-slamming lift hauled her Swift abruptly *up*. She was always afraid the top hatch wouldn't slide open fast enough, and she'd be mashed up against it, dead flat. But the overhead opened to the stars. Her crate popped out onto the flight deck atop *Merrimack*'s starboard wing.

The glowing blue, green, and white world shone down below. Warm yellow sun way over that way.

Kerry Blue waited in her launch slot, counting down and revving up. Three. Two. Yeeeeeah!

Marine Swifts catapulted off the topside flight deck, screaming. *This is what we live for.*

The Fleet Marines, the Alphas in particular, took this dust-up personally. Squids were brothers, and they were here defending *our* Earth. Had to rescue them. Just had to.

The erks had hung flamethrowers on the Swifts. Fire worked well on gorgons. Worked on squid membranes too. Be ultra-careful about that while you fry the gorgons off the squid bubble.

They had to get it done fast.

Swifts were notoriously short-ranged in atmo. They carried no coolant. It hotted up fast down here.

Kerry Blue already felt she was cooking just closing on the targets.

Lieutenant Hazard Sewell on the com: "Call your targets. Fire at will. Tallyho. Tallyho. Tallyho."

They were flying in deuces for this sortie. Fighter and wingman. No solos except for Hazard Sewell. He was down here for his eyes, not his guns.

Flight Sergeant Cole Darby stuck to Kerry Blue's tail close enough to give her a baby.

Do not screw up, he told himself. Not just because he really really liked Kerry Blue. But the Old Man would have his nuts in a grinder if Kerry don't come back same way she left.

A long tear appeared in the foundering squid ship. The squids were in trouble. He saw them spilling through the tear in the membrane and falling into the ocean, where there were gorgons waiting for them.

Getting a little frantic, Darb willed the Vwakikikikik: *Hang on!*

Kerry Blue was crazy. She led Darb in *that* close and smeared flaming gorgons all over Darby's canopy. The bits slid off. Darb sheared off sideways to keep up with Blue.

Voice of Dak Shepard: "Greta! Greta! Gretaaah! Come on!"

Another pair of Swifts came in on the deck. Baker Three and Four. The lead crate was shredding gorgons that came up from the water to snap at the Vwakikikikik ship.

In a blink, a mass of tentacles shot high up from the water. Came down with a Swift—Baker Four—in its mouths. Plunged under, down and down, in a pillar of bubbles. The water looked to be boiling.

Kerry Blue: "Who is that?"

Is. She said is. You always say *is* because a Swift's personal field can withstand a nuke. And because you don't want to bury a brother until you see the body.

Cole Darby saw things bobbing up to the surface that ought never be outboard of a Swift.

It was—really *was*—Baker Four, Alun Cochcrys, new guy. This was his first flight in anger.

That's the way it works. If you're gonna get yourself dead, you get that business out of the way fast. That's why Cowboy Carver's death had been such a surprise. Cowboy bought the casino after surviving too much. That fother mucking shum dit should've been immortal by then. Cowboy screwed up in all ways a man could up screw. And now Cole Darby—not Cowboy Carver—was flying Alpha Seven.

After thirteen sorties you were expected not to die. And those thirteen had to be angry sorties. Only sorties where something was trying to kill you counted toward lucky thirteen. Standing patrols didn't count unless you were bounced and survived it.

Alun Cochcrys' prang left Baker Three hanging out here flying solo. Though, really, Baker Three—that was Big Richard—might actually be safer without Cochcrys on his tail.

Alpha One, Lieutenant Hazard Sewell, picked him up. "Baker Three. Baker Three. Baker Three. I have your six."

"Do you have to, sir?" Big Richard sent.

You never really trusted officers at the controls.

Darb couldn't afford to look. Had to keep watch on Alpha Six, Kerry Blue. Kerry Blue turns into a mama wolf when she's protecting her own.

The squids were her compadres. And now there was a Bull Mastiff to avenge.

Kerry Blue was all offense out here. The gorgons were gonna die. It was Darb's duty to keep Kerry Blue alive while she made that happen.

Gorgons swarmed around the leaking squid ship as if there was nothing else to eat in the whole wide ocean.

Control warned the pilots not to fire any ordnance that could ricochet. The moving planes of the ocean surface could take your shots anywhere. And there's an old saying, probably started by archers in the Trojan War: Friendly fire isn't.

So a Swift's guns will balk if you try to fire something that is doomed to ricochet. Your Swift keeps a firing record. Means your crate will rat you out if you try to fire at something you shouldn't.

At last *Merrimack* got a clean skyhook around the Vwakikikikik ship. Made sure there were no gorgons inside the inertial field, then recalled her Swifts and limped the punctured, leaking squid ship to the nearest wet dock on Iceland.

The Spanish navy sent in heavy amphibious craft to hunt down the monsters under the sea.

✳ ✳ ✳ ✳ ✳

5 October 2443
U.S. Space Battleship *Merrimack*
Earth orbit
Near Space

The new President, Sampson Reed, was known as the Continental Shelf for his lantern jaw and Jurassic-scale chin. His thick shock of honey-colored hair and his blindingly white teeth of equine proportions made him a favorite among political cartoonists. President Sampson Reed issued a stern message to Romulus, publically scolding him. "Releasing the Hive on civilians is total war."

Romulus scolded back via broadcast media: "Then why did you do it? Why did you bring the monsters home? This emergency is your most grievous fault. Clean up your own mess."

Captain Farragut turned away from the news display. "Romulus is saying we did this to ourselves."

"That's what I heard," Calli said.

"He's lying, of course," Farragut said.

"Is he?" Calli asked. "Of course?"

"He's not," Augustus said. "Lying. Not entirely. You, the United States, had a hand in bringing this infection to Earth."

"How do you figure that?"

"Your nation is a member of the LEN."

"We are?" a specialist muttered a little too loudly into her console.

Farragut demanded of Augustus, "What has the LEN to do with the arrival of the Hive on Earth?"

"The LEN rescue mission to the Myriad has been displacing Arran biologics to Earth."

John Farragut never displaced anything while in the presence of gorgons. He'd been afraid of the gorgons fouling the displacement. And he'd been afraid of exactly this: teaching the gorgons how to displace. He remembered saying it back in the Deep End: *If the gorgons learn how to displace, this war is over.*

The LEN had taught the Hive the possibility of displacement.

The LEN taught the Hive the location of Earth.

"The Hive followed the evacuees," Augustus said.

"No." Farragut rejected the idea. He didn't even want to think it. It wasn't possible. "These gorgons can't be coming from Arra. There's no safe displacement over that kind of distance. The LEN can't be displacing life from Arra to Earth. It's *two thousand parsecs.*"

"The LEN *are* displacing over distance. Not safely. They lose most of their biologics in transit. Given a choice between probable death in transit and certain death on Arra, the LEN apparently chose desperation measures, without thinking of the consequences."

Farragut cried, "How could even the LEN be stupid enough to let the gorgons get at their displacement equipment!"

"There's no sign that the gorgons are using LEN equipment," Augustus said. "It doesn't look as though the Hive is using equipment at all. They're following the displacement event. One successful displacement in their midst, and they all know how it's done. And they know where to go. They don't need to report back. When one gorgon knows a thing, the entire Hive knows it. The entire Hive knows where Earth is. There's still a very high mortality rate when they displace. But there is an inexhaustible supply of gorgons."

The gorgons were arriving in badly damaged swarms. Even so, too many of them lived.

"I want one hundred percent mortality."

"How does it feel to want, John Farragut?"

The Hive adjusted tactics again.

All at once the gorgons stopped displacing into Earth's ocean. Now they were displacing into the vacuum outside Earth's atmosphere. Now that they weren't displacing into a competing mass of ocean water, more of the gorgons arrived in the Solar System intact. From the vacuum they descended to the planet.

The first swarms to enter Earth's atmosphere from space burned up as bright meteors.

But the Hive adapted again. Too soon the gorgons figured out how to control their descent. Weather satellites picked them up as particulate clouds, until the weather satellites went dark.

"How are they doing that?" Farragut roared at the tactical display of gently descending gorgon swarms. "It's bolognium physics."

"Bolognium holds the universe together," Augustus said.

❋ ❋ ❋ ❋ ❋

18 October 2443
U.S. Space Battleship *Merrimack*
Earth orbit
Near Space

The Hive had come to Earth. It didn't seem real. It was the end of the world.

Merrimack deployed her Swifts in constant rotation.

Flight Sergeant Cole Darby listened to the beam generator winding up all through the middle watch, ship's night, when he was supposed to be sleeping. The forecastle was dark. The pounding of the guns heaving out fragmentation rounds never stopped. The sizzle of God knows what hitting the space battleship's inertial shell hissed and spat at unexpected intervals. Darby was starting to get used to it.

He could hear livestock down in the hold. He'd expected the farm animals to be offloaded now that *Merrimack* was home. But they were still here. It was nice to hear them shuffle and bleat and moo through the middle watch. For no reason that made sense, the animal sounds were calming.

The hatch to the forecastle opened. Cole Darby heard the soft padding of paws and the sound of doggy breathing. Probably one of the hospital's two goldens.

Darb wasn't sure, but he suspected that the MO had the dogs doing rounds, sniffing out stress cases.

Darb unsnapped part of his netting and stuck an arm outside his sleep pod. The padding footfalls quickened, drew near. A velvet muzzle and a cool nose found its way into Darb's palm.

He fell asleep as the guns pounded.

24

23 October 2443
U.S. Space Battleship *Merrimack*
Earth orbit
Near Space

FLIGHT SERGEANT RANZA ESPINOZA hadn't gone into the Myriad with the rest of her company. She'd been beached for being pregnant.

She would've incubated the kid if she'd known the tour was going to be that exciting. She'd missed all the gorgon battles. She got her linebacker figure back in no time and learned how to use a sword.

She was on *Merrimack* now. She'd brought pictures.

The she-men passed the imager around in the forecastle. The imager came around to Kerry Blue.

"Hm," Kerry Blue said.

Ranza had a squid.

Okay, it was a baby boy. That's what Ranza said. The pictures said it was a squid. The child was now in the care of Ranza's mom.

Ranza's mom was already raising Ranza's first two children.

Flight Sergeant Reg Monroe frowned at the photos, dubious. "You figure out what's causing this, Ranza?"

"I'm done," Ranza said. She'd said that the last time. "This is the last one."

Kerry Blue tilted her head to look at a picture sideways. Didn't help. The baby was still kind of squashed looking.

Carly Delgado gave Kerry a shoulder shove. "You ever think about having kids, *chica linda*?"

Kerry gave a snort. "Who would raise them?"

"Ranza's mom."

Ranza had to ask, "So whose chair did I take?"

A pause. Reg Monroe looked as if she were trying to inhale her lips.

Ranza had moved into Alun Cochcrys' spot. Baker Four.

"FNG," Kerry Blue told her. "Gone light speed."

"Aw, fungus," Ranza said. Spat for luck.

New guy. It's always a new guy.

At midrats in the Mess, the Fleet Marines who were not on patrol toasted Alun Cochcrys and all the FNGs. It was a toast to themselves, really. They were all new guys once, and one day—some time in the way, way, way distant future—they would all go light speed.

"What's that mean?" Cole Darby asked. "Gone light speed?"

"Means you're dead, squid for brains," Carly said.

"I know it means you're dead. *Why* does it mean that?"

"Because we never go light speed."

"Got it," Darb said.

Dak Shepard's brow got tight. Said, "Uh. Yeah we do. All the time."

It was Lieutenant Hazard Sewell who had to explain it to Dak. "No. We pass from a state slower than light directly to a state faster than light, but we never exist at the speed of light. If you're traveling at the speed of light, you're drinking your beer with Alun Cochcrys."

It was unlucky to fly in a dead man's crate. And even though Ranza Espinoza was a veteran Swift pilot, she'd never flown against this enemy. Hive wasn't like Romans. She got training in a dreambox. Next morning she would be flying against gorgons for real. In a dead man's Swift.

Her mates were afraid for her. They made sure to trip her, spill coffee on her, drop things on her, push unwary navvies into her, anything to spend all her bad luck before she made her first flight against the Hive.

At reveille on the day of Ranza's first gorgon fight, her wingman, Big Richard, even came over from the xy-chromosome side of the forecastle to pee on her sleep pod.

Ranza was touched. "Aw, you guys are the best."

24 October 2443
U.S. Space Battleship *Merrimack*
Earth orbit
Near Space

The Swifts of Red Squadron made strafing runs over amber waves of grain. They mowed down gorgons with fragmentation rounds.

Gorgons leaped up from the fields and clutched at the Swifts. Cole Darby, flying ass-end Charlie for Alpha Flight, called for help. "I've got a clinger! Somebody hose me off."

"I got you, *hermano*." Kerry Blue, Alpha Six, pulled up and dropped back down behind Cole Darby. Shredded the gorgon off Darb's inertial shell.

Then Alpha Flight sped out of the atmosphere to shed some heat as Baker Flight dove in to their place, screaming and blasting gorgons from the fields.

They heard Ranza yelling over the com, having a good day. "And one! And two! Feed the frags! Come *on!* Hey!"

Baker Three had gone vertical.

Ranza, Baker Four, dutifully stuck to Big Richard's tail, but she squawked all the way. "Where you taking us? Targets are all back down that way!"

"Aren't you a little *warm*, Ranza?" Big Richard asked.

"Oh. Yeah."

Swifts were notoriously short-winded in atmosphere. All Ranza's instruments were redlined, and now that Big Richard mentioned it, she was sweating like pig iron. She followed Baker Three to the roof of the world to cool off.

When the Swifts had spent all their fragmentation rounds, they withdrew to the vacuum. Lieutenant Sewell requested approach vectors to *Merrimack*.

Got the wave off. "Negative approach. Wing, tread water. We have gorgons on board."

"Roger that." Hazard Sewell led his squadrons into high orbit, wide of the civilian lanes.

Merrimack descended into atmo, rolling hot. The gorgons clinging to her energy shell must either bale or burn.

Most of the gorgons clung unto death. They could levitate, but flying in air was not their long suit. It wasn't *Merrimack*'s best feature either. She flew like a building but with less grace. She came down fast. Gorgons stripped off and ignited as *Merrimack* plunged, tumbling and toppling. Fiery gorgon pieces dragged off her.

Chase planes from Earth's Horizon Guard finished off anything that dropped away still intact.

Looking out *Merrimack*'s portholes could get a body nauseated, if one's body was prone to that sort of thing. The deck felt more or less steady underfoot, but the black and yellow-orange view outside revealed that she was spinning and jerking, making instant reversals, and flaming a lot of gorgons.

The ship's six mammoth engines hummed. Gravitation fluctuated.

In the Mess, Jose Maria's wine jumped out of his glass.

"I probably did not need that anyway," he told Augustus as the wine found its way through the deck grates.

Gravitation steadied. As *Merrimack* climbed out of the atmosphere, the stars returned to the portholes, not spinning.

But *Merrimack*'s inertial screen gave a sickening hum. It was the unmistakable sound of gorgons inside the distortion field. Over the loud com the XO announced gorgon insinuation. Swords. All hands. Swords.

Gorgons that had already insinuated into the ship's energy shell before *Mack*'s plunge into atmo escaped the burning. They continued to squeeze themselves through the energy barrier to get at the ship's hull.

Merrimack's Marines were all outboard, either in Swifts or on the ground.

Over the loud com, Captain Farragut called on all available crew to suit up, grab a handheld flamethrower, and step outside to clear the ship's hull of intruders.

Kitted up in bright orange atmospheric suits fitted with rebreathers and headlamps, Colonel Augustus and Jose Maria de Cordillera climbed out an air lock to join the other hull walkers on the hunt for gorgons that had squeezed in through *Merrimack*'s energy shell.

Artificial gravity was slight out here. Walking on the hull was tricky. Space appeared glassy and deep through the energy barrier. The stars twinkled.

The height of the energy shell varied. A layer of attenuated air filled the space between the energy shell and the ship's hull. The thin air would soon be smoky with burning gorgons.

It was difficult to spot the black gorgons against the blackness of space as the impossible creatures contorted and threaded their bodies through the defensive energy layers.

The gorgons took an excruciatingly long time to emerge into the air where you could burn them up or cut them down.

Waiting for a gorgon to drop, Augustus asked Jose Maria de Cordillera via their suit-to-suit link in a conversational voice, "Do you know what a tachyon clicker is?"

Jose Maria answered at once, his focus not leaving the emerging gorgon. "An obsolete, inefficient method of faster than light communication."

"Tachyon messaging does have one virtue that resonance does not," Augustus said.

Jose Maria agreed. "The Hive takes no notice of tachyon clicks. But a tachyon clicker is a relic. No one carries tachyon clickers these days. Whom could you hope to contact, Augustus?"

"Patterners carried clickers in their Strikers."

"Aside from yourself, the only other living patterner is Romulus."

"I don't want to talk to a living patterner. I certainly don't want Romulus. He doesn't have a tachyon clicker."

"Then whom do you hope to contact?"

"My Striker."

Jose Maria hesitated a long time. The ship's lights drew a bright nimbus around his head within his bubble helmet, like a halo of an angel or a martyred saint.

"I must know to whom are you loyal, Augustus."

"Caesar Magnus."

"Magnus is no longer Caesar," Jose Maria said.

Augustus knew that. "Magnus is a broken shell. I resent him. He put me under American command. But he is a good Roman. There is my loyalty. Do you have a tachyon clicker, Doctor Cordillera?"

"A tachyon clicker is appallingly slow and terribly directional, and we left your Striker in the Deep End. It is in the Myriad, is it not?"

"We assume it is there. I should like to know for certain."

"Can you not contact your Striker another way?"

"Not without incurring Hive interest."

Resonance on any harmonic attracted the Hive.

"*Merrimack* may have a tachyon clicker," Jose Maria said. "It would be redundant."

"I know. She has one."

"Then I misunderstand your purpose in asking."

"My purpose is redundance. I have a secret I don't want to die with me."

"Will you be dying soon?"

"Likely. Can you work *Merrimack*'s tachyon clicker?"

"Why do you not just ask our young captain for yourself?"

"I don't want your young captain to know that I want it. You are the sword master on a space battleship. No one will question your interest in antiques."

"There is a reason not to tell the young captain?" Jose Maria asked.

"There is. Here comes a runner. Do you want it?"

A gorgon had insinuated completely through the ship's inertial shell, unnoticed by anyone else, and now moved like a mad shadow across the hull on its many legs.

"Too fast for me. Take it," Jose Maria said. "Here is one more my speed."

Gorgons continued to arrive in the Solar System out of nowhere. Most of them winked into existence high above Earth's ionosphere, then headed down. Many of them arrived dead. Those were eaten by other gorgons who survived the displacement. Others burned in descent through the atmosphere. Ground fire and Swift patrols picked off some of the survivors. That was like tagging individual raindrops.

Too many of the monsters lived to touch Earth and eat whatever was in front of their mouths.

25 October 2443
Xerxes
Earth orbit
Near Space

Romulus had been beating down so many unexpected challenges that it was a surprise when something actually went precisely according to plan. The assassin missile that Cinna had prepared to take out Constantine in the Deep End had finally connected with its target. Constantine was dead.

The resonant verification of the deed drew the immediate attention of the Hive to Romulus' Xerxes. But a quick jump to FTL shook the gorgons off, and Romulus could take a moment to relish his success. That one gnawing concern was finally put to rest.

With Constantine dead, Romulus now had sole knowledge of both Hive harmonics.

26 October 2443
U.S. Battleship *Merrimack*
Earth orbit
Near Space

It was mid watch on the *Merrimack*.

The ship was quiet except for her guns. You didn't even really notice those anymore. You missed them when they were silent.

A loud *crack* of displacement broke the pseudo-quiet.

Hamster flinched. Her eyes shut themselves against the splatter of droplets. Alarms sounded, telling her what was already obvious. Perimeter breach. Displacement event. Inside *Merrimack*.

Gorgon bits splattered all the surfaces of the command platform. The pieces immediately melted into black liquid.

Crew spat residue off their lips and blinked their eyes clear of the stinging ooze.

The captain's voice sounded over the intercom. "Hamster! What are you doing to my boat!"

"Gorgons tried to displace aboard, sir."

"Intact?"

"Oh, *no*, sir. Jammers are working very, very well."

Displacement jammers didn't repel. They disrupted, so the gorgon arrived the farthest state from intact.

"It may have been just one gorgon. I don't think they'll be trying that again." Glenn wanted to clean off her nose, but there wasn't a clean thing anywhere on the command deck with which to wipe. Every surface—deck grate, console, display, crewman, MP, the overhead, lighting instrument, hair, uniform, dog, terrarium—was flecked with black ooze.

Lieutenant Hamilton summoned a squad of Marines to the command platform to clean the deck and bring her a fresh uniform.

26 October 2443
Xerxes
FTL

Romulus, secure inside his Xerxes, knew fear. Thanks to LEN bungling, gorgons had learned to spontaneously displace themselves. The Hive had found its way to Earth. Now, gorgons were coming in swarms of alarming size. They were ravaging grain fields and attacking flocks and wildlife. Romulus never wanted that. He'd only wanted the *threat* of that. Not the reality. This was horrendous.

His most powerful weapon had slipped his control.

How had it come to this? The gorgons' ability to displace themselves came as a shock. There had never been any indication that they could spontaneously displace. Somehow they had learned. And now they were on Earth.

Romulus did not want to rule a dead world.

His assumptions and conclusions were only as good as his input. He'd been lacking critical information. He hadn't noticed the knowledge missing. He assumed he had all of it. Now he knew that he didn't. He was a patterner. He should not be miscalculating.

He'd come here assuming he had complete knowledge of all events in the past. But the past was different from the one he knew. *The past had changed.*

Time was not a line.

He was not prepared for this.

Claudia waltzed into the cabin, breathless and smiling, dressed all in sporty white, and twirling a skinny racquet. "Come play badminton with me and the Oxfords. I don't know who programmed them, but they're cheating."

Her face was shining.

Romulus disconnected from patterner mode, like stepping off a bullet. His thoughts slowed, left him nauseated for a moment. Then he rose and kissed his sister's brow. He spoke thickly. "Give me a moment, my sweet."

He sat down again and reengaged patterning.

Romulus' lightning thoughts returned to his crisis. He processed the ramifications of this gorgon infestation on Earth. He had the ability to destroy the present Hive in an instant. Doing so would save the world— and leave him powerless. Not an acceptable trade.

He must use this turn of events to his advantage.

Hive presence on Earth could give him the opportunity to show his might. And show the inadequacy of the armed forces of the United States.

The U.S. Fleet Marines were fighting the invading cells nonstop. The LEN also. They were losing.

Good.

Meanwhile Romulus could organize protection for his government in exile on Beta Centauri. Beta Centauri could resonate on the Hive harmonic, sending the signal the gorgons emitted when they had exhausted edible targets.

The Hive would sense there was nothing to eat on Beta Centauri, and the gorgons would withdraw. That would show Romulus' power.

He would then devise and distribute protection for his followers on a person-by-person basis.

The rest of humanity on Earth and in Near Space would need to beg. He didn't need their adoration. He could do with their loathing as long as he had their abject mortal dread.

And Romulus still had another weapon in his arsenal. The irresistible harmonic—the harmonic of the second Hive, rival to this one. He could leverage one Hive against the other.

Swarms of the rival Hive had not come to Near Space yet. But they might. And they would, if Romulus needed them to be here.

All was not lost. He realized that now. In fact, the Hive presence on Earth was a good thing. It gave an urgency missing before now.

Earth was out of time. Earth needed a savior. Right now. Even if they hated Romulus, people would beg for their children's sake.

Romulus unplugged his cables and looked at Claudia. He took her hand. She tugged for him to come.

Claudia had not been happy here on Beta Centauri. People outside the Italian embassy acted differently around her. They were as cheerful and funny as if they were perched on a nest of scorpions. So Romulus programmed the Xerxes with exciting settings and populated those settings with spirited, witty people to flatter her, bold courtiers for her to tease, and sassy confidantes for her to talk to. She was happy again. She wanted him to come play.

His first impulse was to continue planning his next moves. But he needed to keep perspective. Claudia wanted to play. This is what it was all for. The Empire, for her.

The universe could wait.

He kissed Claudia's hand. "Lead on. We must trounce those despicable Oxfords."

28 October 2443
U.S. Space Battleship *Merrimack*
Earth orbit
Near Space

Caesar Numa Pompeii had no intention of attending the upcoming funeral services for the United States' fallen President, because Caesar refused to acknowledge the U.S. as a separate nation from Rome.

Neither did Numa offer assistance to Earth in her present invasion crisis, even though Earth was the wellspring of all humanity, the mother world of the Empire, the site of the Eternal City of Rome. Caesar ought to show an interest.

On the command platform of the *Merrimack*, Jose Maria wondered out loud, "Why does Caesar not act?"

Commander Calli Carmel answered. "He is acting. Numa is doing a calculated nothing."

In between the wars, young Calli Carmel had been a student of Numa Pompeii at the Imperial Military Institute. She had always been beneath Numa's notice—a ridiculously pretty distraction in Numa's opinion, who ought to ornament a rich man's arm.

"Numa is doing nothing because he *can*. His predecessor lost *sixty-four Roman Legions* to the Hive. Numa has the power to levy fresh troops from the colonies, but he knows what they've already lost. He still has his Praetorian Guard to defend Palatine in case Palatine comes under attack. But he's not going to spend his own people to defend Earth unless it looks like we're going to fail."

Alone of all places on planet Earth the city of Rome was not under gorgon assault. The city of Rome existed in a bubble of immunity not of Caesar Numa's making, and Numa didn't make the mistake of trying to take credit for that Passover. He would not confess to not having powers that Romulus had.

"Numa can afford to wait."

"We can't," Farragut said. "The Hive is here."

"May I request shore leave, Captain?"

"*Shore leave?* What are you up to, Cal?"

"I'd like to attend President Johnson's funeral."

She was going to kick Caesar Numa in the strength and honor.

The Imperial Information network was bound to carry coverage of President Marisa Johnson's state funeral.

A decorated veteran of Hive combat, and drop-dead stunning to look at, Commander Calli Carmel was able to get an appearance on the galactic mass media. She had a minute.

Calli appeared before a resonator. "President Marisa Johnson was a fearless commander in chief who never caved to extortion. She was a leader who gave her life for her beliefs.

"Today, in contrast, Caesar Numa Pompeii shows his Empire what he's actually made of. See him sitting back and letting others fight for the survival of the cradle of civilization. America may have been founded as a Roman colony, but America has risen above that. Even now, Caesar can depend on America to defend the birthplace of Rome for him. It's a hell of a thing to have delegated to us. But we, these United States, are up to the task. President Johnson's America continues to defend Earth, including Roman soil, regardless of Caesar's failure of will."

She thought her speech went well, but who was she kidding? Numa would make it a point not to listen to her, if he was even aware of her appearance on the galactic news net.

It wasn't Numa who heard her. It was Rome.

Within days, eight Roman colonial worlds announced their intent to secede from the Empire, and dozens more had it under discussion. Rome's colonies had been levied to ruin by Magnus. They'd lost sixty-four Legions without any explanation and without bodies to bury. Now they were shamed by Palatine's failure to control the alien invasion of Earth. Rome's colonial planets demanded home rule.

Caesar Numa Pompeii came out like Moses with a commandment-smashing speech for the ages. Pundits were calling it his Sinai Address. Numa Pompeii had an almighty presence and a deep booming resonant voice. Worlds quaked when he spoke. You weren't sure whether to say Hail Caesar or Amen.

Numa promised that the insurrection of pretender Romulus would be brief. "This is not a civil war. Romulus' followers are not lawful belligerents.

Romulus is a terrorist who wields a weaponized plague. His adherents are a handful of criminals. Romulus is worthy of only our utmost loathing and a quick termination. And any Roman world that attempts to secede from the Empire will reap the fate of Romulus.

"There is one single united Empire of Rome. If you are not with me, you are against me, and make no mistake, I am Rome."

Neither was Numa calling the Hive menace a war. There was no honor in that enemy. He branded the incursion a "wildfire." This enemy consumed everything and left only devastation. Numa called all able Romans forward as firefighters.

Farragut caught a glance pass between his XO and Colonel Augustus. Augustus looked whimsical. Calli was round-eyed.

"What?" Captain Farragut demanded, missing some significance.

"Word choice," Calli said.

"What of it?"

Augustus answered, "'Wildfire' this time. Instead of 'plague.' Fire is much sexier, don't you think?"

"More heroic," Calli said.

Numa's speech went on. "The nations of Earth are inadequate to defend the cradle of humanity. Only the will and might of Rome can prevail. As for our renegade colony, America, we shall put down that rebellion after the wildfire is suppressed. Rule of Earth requires there to be an Earth. Rome, this is your hour. Step forward."

Watching the broadcast finish, Calli had her palms pressed together before her lips as if praying. "I may be sorry I woke that dragon. Numa's Legions will be coming here."

"What Legions?"

"He will have them! Oh, John. Have I just screwed up?"

"Maybe," Farragut said. "But Numa said one thing right. Ownership of Earth requires there to be an Earth. I look forward to beating the *merda* out of him and his Legions when we're done fighting the Hive."

1 November 2443
Near Space

The flags were still at half-staff for President Johnson. The rain of gorgons from above the atmosphere intensified.

The U.S. State Department called out Romulus in a universal broadcast. "We know that Romulus assassinated President Johnson. Romulus must surrender himself and answer for his crime."

Romulus answered publicly, "Assassinated? We didn't assassinate President Johnson. We killed her. Since when is the commander in chief of the armed forces of a nation at war not a military target?"

Shocked that Romulus confessed, the Secretary of State responded directly over a tight beam. "Marisa Johnson *might* have been a legitimate target if the United States were at war. These United States are not at war with Rome, and you, sir, are not a nation. Your kangaroo declaration has no effect. Surrender or be chased down like a common felon."

Romulus took his case to his galactic audience. "People of all worlds. Do not obey those who lead you to slaughter for the purpose of maintaining their own positions. Convince your keepers to stop resisting my rightful rule. Your leaders are killing you. I am here to restore Rome. Protection against the Hive is available for the asking. From me. The Hive respects absolute power. I have that power."

Romulus' offer of protection required the suppliant to make a pilgrimage to Romulus' government in exile on Beta Centauri and submit to a rite of Confirmation in an anointed Roman Catholic church, there to swear on bended knee allegiance to the true Rome and to Rome's true and only Imperator, Romulus *Quem Dei Adorant*.

Romulus Whom Gods Adore.

"The Hive respects absolute power. I have it."

Romulus' protection was not transferable. Half of the protection resided in a holy medal that the suppliant must wear. The medal was useless without the other part of the protection, which was a harmonic substance injected into the suppliant's bloodstream and keyed to one's unique genetic signature. Neither part—the medal nor the injection—was useful without the other. And there was no reading the protective harmonic off of either part. The protection could not be reverse engineered.

Romulus scoffed at the idea of reverse engineering. "I created this protection unasked, and I give it freely, because it is right and proper. No one should be seeking profit from this emergency."

Romulus let it be known that he might be persuaded to lead the pestilence away from certain fields or flocks. He bestowed protection on Vatican City because it was "right and just." Other nations needed to earn that boon.

And because he was benevolent, Romulus would extend protection to a beloved pet brought to him in the arms of a child.

The U.S. State Department warned its citizens that if they traveled to Beta Centauri and swore to Romulus, then they should not come home. Anyone carrying one of Romulus' protective medals would be turned away at the ionosphere.

Even so, pilgrims flocked to Beta Centauri from all the countries of Earth, because the protection actually worked and because no lawful authority had protection to give.

It was extortion. It was hideous. People saw the true face of the monster, and still they journeyed to Beta Centauri, selling their souls to keep their children safe.

The Fleet Marines on *Merrimack* sneered at the turncoats. They called the pilgrims headed to the Centauri system, "horse pants."

"What's with centaurs anyway?" Kerry Blue asked. "Whose bright idea was that? Boxers, briefs, or horse? I mean, can we be serious?"

Cole Darby's brows lifted as far as they would go. "Apparently we cannot."

15 November 2443
Xerxes
Beta Centauri
Near Space

Romulus fashioned a resonator into an earring for Claudia to wear. "It's an amulet," he told her. "Never take it off."

Actually, he made sure she *couldn't* take it off. He didn't trust her not to get bored with it. "If you want a different style, come to me. But know that this one carries inside it all my love."

He injected her with a resonant intradermal. Now, wherever she went, the Hive would mistake her for one of its members and ignore her. She could pass through them in safety. Not that he would ever allow the monsters to come so close to his beloved.

* * * * *

Romulus disappeared from the public eye for a few days. No one knew where he was. You could hope he was dead, but you didn't count on it.

He resurfaced at Terra Rica, where he planted his imperial eagles on the Cordillera estate.

The nation-planet of Terra Rica had few defenses other than goodwill.

Jose Maria de Cordillera, on board *Merrimack*, looked to Captain John Farragut for help. "What can be done?"

Farragut gave a heavy sigh. "Here's where neutrality bites you in the hindquarters, Jose Maria. We can expect righteous indignation and strong words from my government. I don't know what kind of military support I can wrangle for you while Earth is under Hive siege. And you might not want U.S. help anyway. Romulus could decide to displace gorgons to Terra Rica to spite us."

Then Jose Maria received a video. It had been sent to him in care of his niece AnaLuisa on Terra Rica. When the family saw what it was, they forwarded it to Jose Maria on board *Merrimack*. The recording was a cruel fiction starring AnaLuisa. AnaLuisa asked her uncle what it meant.

It had to be fiction.

Jose Maria was afraid it was not.

The video began with his niece AnaLuisa piloting a sky yacht, an advanced kind he'd never heard of. He saw AnaLuisa as if he were taking a resonant call from her. He heard his own voice talking to her over a com.

His niece looked older than she should be. Here she looked old enough to be piloting a sky yacht.

She had motes on her face.

She was speaking to him. She invoked the Jericho Protocol.

Jose Maria watched the chilling story play out. Within hours it was all over. The final scene was a long view from space. Jose Maria's beautiful niece, his beautiful world, was dead.

It was dreadfully realistic.

Jose Maria gave the video to Augustus. He whispered, because he had no voice, "Is this real?"

Augustus answered. "No and yes. Terra Rica is still out there. It's still alive. Today. But the configuration of the background planets and stars in this recording is consistent with a date in *Anno Domini* 2448, which is also consistent with the apparent age of your niece in this recording."

Jose Maria's voice shuddered. "This *will* happen?"

"No. This *already happened* in a future reality."

Jose Maria inhaled, like breathing in knives. "Is there nothing to be done?"

"Stay in the present tense if you're to be of any use to anyone," Augustus said coldly. "In some reality, the destruction of Terra Rica actually happens. But not in *this* reality. And this is the one we have."

Jose Maria stared at the data capsule with dread sorrow.

Captain John Farragut put out his hand. "Let me see that."

Jose Maria gave Farragut the capsule. Farragut threw it into the annihilator.

Jose Maria looked quietly stunned. He spoke resentfully, "That was not yours to destroy."

"I am the master of this vessel," Captain John Farragut said. "Torture devices are subject to summary annihilation, no process, no recourse. Stay with me, Jose Maria. I need you."

Romulus still needed to kill Jose Maria. Horribly. But he couldn't find him. Jose Maria wasn't on Terra Rica.

Romulus had sent the recording of Terra Rica's destruction to the Cordillera family on Terra Rica, but he received no confirmation that it ever got to Jose Maria or that Jose Maria actually viewed it.

Romulus gave the planet Terra Rica to Claudia at her demand.

Terra Rica had light industry and no military. It had a huge export business in pharmaceuticals, and it was a planetary breadbasket. It produced a wealth of natural building materials.

As Romulus desperately hoped, Claudia was disenchanted with it inside a terrestrial day.

With Claudia safely restored to her gilded cage inside the Xerxes, Romulus pointed his ship back toward his power base on Beta Centauri.

While in transit, Romulus escorted Claudia to a recreation of the Anastasis Ball, a well-recorded party that celebrated the emergence of the new Roman Empire in year 2290, when secret Romans broke the Long Silence and revealed their Empire ascendant.

The Xerxes brought the occasion to life. The greatest bands of the day played. It took some intricate programming to keep Claudia from running into the compartment's physical walls as she danced. She changed her dress twelve times. She loved the antique fashions. Shimmering bubbles floated up to the towering ceiling. She caught and released sparkling flits that left her hands dusted with gold. He'd never seen her so happy.

The programmed courtiers were charming to her. Romulus called out a cheeky, insolent rake to the terrace with drawn rapiers. Romulus fought the rake to the ground, had him on his back at swordpoint, waiting for Claudia's mercy. She had none.

✳ ✳ ✳ ✳ ✳

18 November 2443
Kentucky, USA
Earth

Gorgons were difficult to kill. Vacuum didn't kill them, Neither did they crush. They were pressure impervious. They burned slowly.

Gorgons descended on Kentucky. Decimated as they were, clouds of them still got past Earth's Horizon Guard, and they were falling on the Farragut estate.

His Honor John Knox Farragut Senior ran outside with a Colt .45, blaspheming, a dinner napkin still tucked into his collar. He quickly found out that bullets were no good against gorgons. He turned around and came back out with a scythe.

The horses were running.

Mama Farragut bade her eighth-born son, "John John, see to your father."

"He's fine," John Junior said. "He's wearing an adamantine net."

"Gorgons can chew through adamantine," sister Leah said.

"Only if they live long enough," John John said. "His Honor is scary."

The family dogs howled, milling, and whining. They banged at the windows. Leah had orders to lock the dogs indoors. The hounds desperately wanted to get out there and help their master, but they were too slow to survive a gorgon.

"Watch his back for him, John John," Leah said. "Gorgons learn."

"The gorgons are learning to run away," John Junior observed, making no move to go out and help.

The Farraguts' golden Xanthin serpent, which had never been anything other than a sweet furry family pet, coiled itself around His Honor's waist and bit the fanged end off any tentacle that tried to strike its master from behind.

The eldest Farragut daughter paced, pushing herself off the walls, out of her mind with worry. Her mares were screaming. Amanda was going to lose all her foals. She kept from saying that aloud. It would sound small compared to what other people were losing. She kept her foals out of it and wailed, "Where's the Horizon Guard! Where are the U.S. Fleet Marines?"

A roar from the sky brought all the Farraguts out to the porch in time to catch the retreating sterns of a flight of Fleet Marine Swifts, flying so low they flattened the tall grasses in the pastures. The fighter craft fired fragmentation rounds at the gorgons in the fields. They swept wide of Justice Farragut, who took off his hat and waved.

Leah, on the porch, yelled back into the house, "Mama! John sent the Marines!"

John Knox Farragut Junior stood back. He leaned against the door-jamb, his arms crossed, mouth shut.

A second flight of Swifts made a low pass, picking off gorgons.

John sent the Marines. Well, yes, it must be Captain John Alexander Farragut's idea to send in the Marines after seven years away from Earth. Because God knows our State Senator, Catherine Farragut Mays, could have nothing to do with the appearance of Fleet Marines over Kentucky in a crisis. No. It's all John Alexander. Everything is John Alexander.

His Honor, Justice John Knox Farragut Senior, marched in from the field. He was drenched in sweat. He left his scythe at the bottom of the steps, and he climbed up to the wide front porch. He uncoiled the Xanthin serpent from his wide waist and bundled it into Leah's arms. "Brush him out. Give him some water. Some quail eggs after he's cooled down. Good snake." He ruffled the serpent's golden fur.

He moved back out to the edge of the porch to watch the Marine Swifts come down for another pass.

21 November 2443
Kentucky, USA
Earth

Captain John Alexander Farragut never came home from the Battle of Eta Cassiopeia seven years ago. His wife Laura sued for abandonment and he let her carve him up. He never told anyone that the children weren't his, though anyone who could read a calendar knew whose children they weren't.

Captain Farragut took a Fleet Marine Swift into Earth's atmosphere.

Swifts were small fighter craft. Farragut barely fit into the cockpit. He set the little ship down on the old homestead in Kentucky. He would not displace while there were gorgons on world.

The Swift sat in the grass between the ancient oaks. The oaks clung to most of their brown leaves. The old house sprawled with several added wings. It had housed twenty-one children, some of whom came back, and now there were grandchildren.

As the firstborn walked up the front steps to the deep front porch, he heard a sullen adolescent male voice from inside.

"Oh, joy. The hero of Eta Cas is among us."

That was followed by Mama's quick scold, "John John!"

Captain Farragut inwardly winced. They still called his younger brother John John. The sound of it had always grated. John Alexander Farragut didn't think it was right somehow. It was belittling.

But he was not going to fly in here and drop a lot of opinions and leave Mama to clean up the wreckage. Captain Farragut kept his observations to himself. He called the young man "John," then walked into his mother's teary, breathy embrace.

Farraguts from all over swarmed into the old Kentucky home. There were twenty brothers and sisters, a flock of nieces and nephews, and seven years' worth of hugging and crying to fit into a short time.

There was a lull in the Hive activity in the Eastern U.S. for the moment. The Marines had cleared away most of the gorgons from the region. The outbreaks were elsewhere. It wouldn't stay that way. This was only a small space in which to breathe.

In which to finally come home.

An inner archway darkened.

His father.

A frozen moment Captain Farragut had been dreading. He was never sure how this would go. The frozen moment broke. His Honor stomped into the front room with wide-flung arms and a booming how the hell are you, boy! A whomp on the back. A firm hearty shake of his hand. Proud. So proud.

His Honor motioned in the direction of the quiet skies. "You run them out?"

"No, sir. Not yet."

His Honor guided Captain Farragut out of the parlor under a heavy arm. Out of Mama's earshot His Honor said, "Sugar's for your mama. Give me the straight story."

"It's Armageddon," said John Alexander Farragut.

The old man nodded gravely, absorbing that. "We gonna win?"

"If I have anything to say about it. And I do."

"Good man," His Honor said.

Captain John Alexander Farragut found his younger brother, John Junior, packing for a journey.

"You're leaving," Captain Farragut said, surprised.

John Knox Farragut Junior didn't look at his famous brother. "I've learned that the way to get respect around here is not to be here for years on end."

"Where are you going?" Captain Farragut asked, reproach in his voice. "Mama needs you."

"I'm enlisting."

"You're too young."

"Not for a Roman Legion, I'm not."

Crack!

Before he knew what he was doing Captain John Alexander Farragut had hauled off and decked his brother. Remorse was immediate. "Oh, for Jesus. I'm sorry."

He was more than sorry. He was horrified. *I just turned into our father.*

"I never wanted to be that, John."

The words drew a hard smile from John Junior. John John spoke with soft wrath. "You don't need to *be* at all." And he pulled a revolver from behind his back.

With only half a heartbeat to be startled, John Alexander Farragut batted the gun aside, doubled his brother over with a blow to the middle, and stepped on his wrist. He picked up the revolver.

He left John John gasping on the carpet.

Captain Farragut took the revolver out with him. He stalked into the front parlor and informed their father, "I'm going. Keep your blades sharp. It's still the only thing that works against the gorgons. I'll see that you get better top cover here. This shouldn't've happened." He nodded out the window where gorgon scars were visible in the century oaks.

He didn't mention John John pulling a gun on him. Captain Farragut had called his younger brother's bluff. Called it hard. The incident was done. No point shaming the young man over a stupid flash of teenaged temper.

From His Honor, Captain John Alexander Farragut got a great thumping bear hug. He was the firstborn, the captain, the hero. Always and ever the favorite.

John Knox Farragut Junior pulled himself off the floor. When he got his breath back, he stumbled out the back door and stalked up the six-mile-long driveway, past all the century oaks, past the wide horse pastures, toward the front gate of the Farragut estate.

The number of John Farraguts back in that house had reached critical mass. It was impossible to breathe in there. John John felt himself diminishing into nothingness.

He marched, jetting breaths through his nostrils like an angry bull. Brittle fallen leaves crunched underfoot. He didn't know what he was going to do. He'd left his bag behind. He'd left everything.

He wondered how long it would be before anyone noticed he was gone. Would anyone notice? Ever?

He heard the Swift roar to life. He flattened himself against a stout tree trunk to stay out of view. And he didn't want to see it if John did a roll in his Swift over the house.

He didn't know if he'd been completely serious when he said he was joining a Roman Legion. It wasn't the worst idea he'd ever had. America really was a Roman colony, so his thoughts weren't actually treasonous. Romulus had invited him to join the Empire two months ago when he had visited the house.

John Knox Farragut Junior had studied history. He knew about the founding of America, the parts they didn't teach in U.S. schools—that Christopher Columbus and Amerigo Vespucci were Romans. That Thomas Jefferson was a Roman traitor. That the province of America belonged to its Roman founders.

The United States, the nation his father stood for, was in the wrong.

Truths you uncover for yourself are more powerful than what you are hand fed in school. Secrets held power.

The mottos of twenty-five U.S. states and the District of Columbia were in Latin.

America rightfully belonged to Rome. It was a revelation.

Rome never really fell. Rome had gone underground and persisted as a secret society for centuries. It lived in the Catholic Church until Vatican II. The fall of the church was a serious setback. But secret Rome still had a grip on law and the sciences, especially medicine—any discipline conducted in Latin, the language of the Empire.

With the advent of the Internet at the end of the twentieth century, the widely scattered Roman sects regrouped. Latin returned to American schools.

The Internet exploded with sites on which Romans could converse, hiding in plain sight. Loyal Romans were taken for historical reenactors.

At the dawn of the FTL era, an American-based intellectual community founded the planetary colony Palatine in the Lambda Coronae Australis star system. And in the year 2290, Rome revealed herself and declared independence from the United States of America.

The new Rome fought a war of secession against the U.S. and won.

Palatine flourished. The new Rome engaged in a continuing race with its mother world to colonize hospitable planets. The Roman Empire now spread across one sixth of the Milky Way. There would be no reining Rome back in.

The best the U.S. could do was to keep her own independence and colonize more worlds, spreading her presence as wide as Rome's.

All the while, it was Rome's vision and destiny to recapture her birthplace, the terrestrial city of Rome, and to bring her most successful colony, America, under her rule.

Given that America was founded as a Roman colony, what was so terribly wrong with the idea of his joining a Roman Legion? Rome was united for a higher purpose than America's self-serving individualism. John's famous brother had no right to hit him for wanting to be part of something greater.

And there was no evidence that Romulus was sending gorgons to Earth.

John Knox Farragut Junior had come to the end of the eternal driveway of his father's estate.

The elaborate front gates parted at his command.

John stalked out to the country road.

The gates hadn't even closed behind him when a transport dropped straight down from the sky like an elevator without a shaft. A hatch opened.

John Knox Farragut Junior opened his mouth. He meant to say something.

Then there was nothing.

25

22 November 2443
Romulid Government in Exile
Beta Centauri
Near Space

JOHN KNOX FARRAGUT JUNIOR wasn't where he had been a heartbeat ago. In fact, a heartbeat was too long a measure of time to describe what he'd just experienced. Clearly, time had passed, but he hadn't sensed any of it. In one moment, he'd been outside the gate to his father's estate, and now, instantly, he wasn't. A chunk of reality in between then and now was gone.

The chamber was grand, gilt, and ornate, overdone in an Italian Renaissance style. The night sky showed through the skylight in the high, vaulted ceiling. John John recognized a constellation up there—the familiar W of Cassiopeia. But the constellation was wrong. Cassiopeia had her cat at her knee. Cassiopeia's Cat was a star that didn't belong to Cassiopeia when viewed from Earth—because the star known as Cassiopeia's Cat was Earth's star, Sol.

John John wasn't on Earth anymore. He could see Sol in the constellation of Cassiopeia. That meant he was in the Centauri star system.

He had fallen down a very long rabbit hole.

He turned to find someone else with him in the ornate chamber.

This place could only be the Italian embassy on Beta Centauri, because *that* was Caesar Romulus.

Romulus was a physically beautiful human being, lean, athletic. He was dressed all in black here. His shirt had full sleeves and a high collar. A gilded oak leaf crown wreathed his dark curls.

John Junior stared, astonished to be here, alone in presence of the Imperator.

No doubt there would be failsafes in place to insure Romulus' security, but John John wasn't feeling violent. He kept a civilized voice. "You kidnapped me."

"If you don't wish to be here, I can deliver you back to one of the other John Farraguts."

That stung. Before John John could speak, Romulus went on. "You are a valuable, underappreciated man, squandered in your current circumstance. I want you in my Empire."

John John's heart swelled, then collapsed in suspicion. *I'm being used to get to my father and my brother*. He wanted to believe this fairy tale too badly.

He answered in Latin. "Is it your empire, *domni*? I was led to believe that you are mad."

"I have been imprisoned under the most violent torture you can imagine, so, yes, I suppose I was mad for that time. It was a temporary condition, not a character trait. I am well now. I am sane. Ask your other question."

John John wondered if the man was reading his mind. "Do you actually think you're a god?" As soon as the question was out, John John winced. He wanted it back.

But it made Romulus smile. "Between you and me? Not exactly.

"But a galactic empire needs a god. So it shall have one. The unimaginable enormity of the thing demands it. You cannot have a fallible human being at the helm of an entity this vast without factions of every colony challenging every decision the man makes—from what tax he decides to cut to the color of his first lady's dress—as happens in our American colony. People need certainty.

"See how the pretender Numa Pompeii, who styles himself Caesar, struggles for respect. Half measures get one nowhere but cut in half. So I am a god. And you want to be part of something greater than yourself. I want you in my inner circle."

John John wanted to believe this too badly. Common sense told him he was being used to get at his father and his brother. "Why me? Because I'm a Farragut?"

"Because you are a being of great worth. I value you. Your devotion, once earned, is unshakable." He sounded absolutely certain, wholly sincere.

John John stammered, bewildered. "It is. But how can you possibly know that about me?"

"I do know. Did I not tell you? I have seen your heart, and it is Roman." Romulus had told him so, at his father's house. Two months ago.

John John felt something moving inside him, a yearning to belong. Here was recognition of his potential by an astonishing, powerful leader.

"I am sending you to join a Legion." Romulus wasn't even asking him. He was telling John John what was to be.

"A Legion?" John John blurted. "You have a Legion?"

"Multiple Legions. Of course I have. How does one maintain an empire without Legions? Don't believe the propaganda coming out of our province of America. You will receive training in your Legion. Kneel."

There was no room for indecision here. John Knox Farragut Junior had been raised to know that a burning bush has no patience. A leap of faith was required. Uncertainty be damned. And he really had nowhere else to go. He knelt.

Romulus' voice sounded above his head. "From this day forward, be no longer John Knox Farragut Junior. Your name shall be Nox. Nox without the K. Nox as in Night. Your *gens*, your *familia*, shall be mine. I adopt you.

"Rise, Nox Romulus."

18 December 2443
U.S. Space Battleship *Merrimack*
Earth orbit
Near Space

The com tech turned from his console, startled. "Captain. Call from Senator Catherine Mays in Washington."

"Put her on my box."

"You have the Senator, sir."

Captain Farragut spoke into the com, brightly. "Cat!"

His sister's voice came back. Not brightly. "John! What the hell!"

"What?"

"John John!"

"John—?" Captain Farragut felt like he'd stepped out an air lock. Lost. "What about him? Talk to me, Cat. Use verbs. Is John hurt?"

Captain Farragut hadn't thought he'd hit his kid brother quite that hard. He was going to be sick if he'd done him real harm.

"The State Department informed me that John John *renounced his U.S. citizenship!* What the hell happened?"

Cat didn't normally invoke hell, much. It was in order here.

"I—Well, I hit him," Captain Farragut confessed. He left out the part where young John drew a pistol on him first.

"Nobody renounces his citizenship because his big brother hits him!" Cat said. "What's going on!"

"Is it a done deed? I thought it took a while to process those things. Expatriation takes weeks. Months."

"John John told the consulate on Beta Centauri when he made his renunciation that he's not bound to fill out any more forms or jump through any more U.S. hoops. He doesn't recognize U.S. sovereignty. He's sworn to Rome and *Rome recognized him*."

"Rome did? Rome can't. Rome needs to follow procedures. Where's Numa? I can hash this out with Numa."

"John John didn't swear to Numa Pompeii," Catherine said. "He swore to Romulus."

Oh, for Jesus.

25 January 2444

Centauri star system

Near Space

Caesar Numa's Praetorian Guard sublighted in the Centauri star system. The Praetorian Legion carrier descended straight down on the Italian embassy and hovered there, poised to crush it.

Numa demanded that the Italian embassy give up the traitor Romulus to Rome immediately.

But Romulus was not in the Italian embassy. Romulus wasn't in Centauri space at all. He had disappeared and taken his eagles and his red, black, and gold flag with him.

25 January 2444
U.S. Space Battleship *Merrimack*
Earth orbit
Near Space

Captain Farragut shouted at the tactical display. "Where is that weasel?! *He has my brother!*"

He knew as well as anyone that until Romulus came down from FTL and dropped his stealth mode, there could be no knowing where Romulus was.

Farragut's pounding footfalls shook the deck grates as he paced the command platform. "What is Romulus' end game? Augustus?"

Augustus stood in maddening calm, his gaze distant. He might have been watching a sunset. "I cannot pattern a madman. He is subject to misfire. Mister Carmel is your expert on things Romulus. I suggest you consult her."

Calli's head turned sharply.

Commander Calli Carmel had attended the Imperial Military Institute with Romulus and Claudia during the peace.

"I can't 'pattern' a crazy man either. How can Romulus possibly think to do anything without troops? No one can lead Rome without an army."

"Then he has an army," said Augustus.

Farragut came to an abrupt stop as if he'd hit a wall. "*Does* he?"

"He must," said Augustus.

Calli gasped. Her eyes rounded. "He must, *ergo* he *does*."

"Since Romulus is from the future—oh, close your mouth, John Farragut—Romulus came from the future. He will have a whole catalog of people he knows will serve him in the future. He knows where to find those people *now*."

✳ ✳ ✳ ✳

More gorgons displaced into the Solar System and found their way to Earth in damaged masses. The U.S. Fleet Marines flew round the clock patrols, trying to keep the monsters from making landfall. The gorgons were becoming skilled at avoiding *Merrimack* and anything the ground batteries threw at them. Many got through.

Earth was the only Near Space world under Hive attack. None of the United States' Near Space colonies were under gorgon siege.

Two hundred light-years from Earth, Palatine, the capital world of the Roman Empire, was not under Hive attack.

None of Rome's many colonial worlds were under siege, and Rome had almost as many colonies as the U.S.

None of the League of Earth Nations' Near Space colonies showed Hive sign. It could only be that the Hive hadn't identified the other worlds as food sources yet.

Merrimack's withdrawal from the Deep End had left no U.S. military units in the Sagittarius arm of the galaxy. Even the LEN expedition was pulling out of the Myriad and heading home.

The Deep End and the galactic hub now belonged to the Hive.

In the opposite direction—out toward the Perseid arm of the galaxy— there was no Hive presence at all. The Hive hadn't arrived in Perseid space yet. It would take the Hive swarms centuries or even millennia to make that journey.

First, the gorgons would eat their way through Palatine, Earth, and all the planets of Near Space.

Distant Perseid space had been colonized mostly by countries from Earth's Pacific region. The Pacifics had constructed the massive displacement facility called the Boomerang to provide instantaneous travel between Port Chalai in Near Space and Port Campbell in Perseid space. But the Pacific colonies hadn't any trained troops or warships to send home to defend Earth against the Hive. The Pacifics had no enemies.

31 January 2444
U.S. Space Battleship *Merrimack*
Earth orbit
Near Space

Lieutenant Glenn Hamilton, Officer of the Deck on the middle watch, woke up the captain.

"Message from the Admiralty. Port Chalai has fallen to hostile forces."

The captain's fast clanging footfalls sounded on the ladder rungs between decks.

"Captain on deck." The Marine guard announced Farragut as he charged onto the command platform demanding, "What do we know?"

Lieutenant Hamilton moved out of his way. "Hostile forces simultaneously occupied Port Chalai in Near Space and Port Campbell in Perseid Space. They've taken control of the Boomerang."

"Who are 'they?'"

"Waiting confirmation, sir, but they're Romulus' forces."

The port authorities hadn't even had time to get out an SOS. By the time the alert reached Earth, the takeover was done. Images streamed of Romulus' red, black, and gold flags posted on all the space stations in both ports.

Neither Port Chalai in Near Space nor Port Campbell in Perseid Space was a military installation. Both ports were Pacific Rim trading settlements, made up of many peaceful and prosperous space stations.

The Boomerang reduced months of FTL travel between galactic arms into a single instant. Control of the Boomerang would give Romulus a chokehold on all traffic between Near Space and the outer arm of the galaxy.

Captain Farragut stared at the images from Port Chalai on *Merrimack*'s tactical display.

There, at the Near Space terminus of the Boomerang, were three hulking Roman style Legion carriers, painted red, black, and gold. Romulus' colors.

Lieutenant Hamilton: "Sir. I have Rear Admiral Mishindi on your direct com."

Farragut picked up the direct feed. "Sir! This has got to be an illusion! You know Romans always put on a convincing show."

"It's real, John." Rear Admiral Mishindi sounded tired. "Those Legion carriers came through the Boomerang from Port Campbell." Mishindi took a long breath. Sighed. "One may guess they carry Legions."

John Farragut wouldn't have it. "Those ships could be carrying eighty tons of blue peaches for all we know!"

Mishindi gave a strained smile and shook his head. "Apparently Romulus has many devoted followers in Perseid Space. God knows how he had time to recruit them, but he has them."

Time. Time never seemed to be a problem for Romulus.

A low, sardonic voice sounded from the rear of the command deck: "Almost as if there were two of him."

"I didn't ask you to speak, Colonel Augustus."

"Sir."

"Romulus has Legions," Farragut said, trying to make himself believe it. His voice sounded hollow to his own ears. "Does Numa have Legions?"

"That is not known." Rear Admiral Mishindi was looking gray around the edges.

"Numa rules worlds!" Farragut shouted to be heard above the roar of Fleet Marine Swifts launching off *Merrimack*'s wing. The sound reverberated through the whole space battleship. "He's a *dictator* for cryin' tears! It's been— what? Three months since his Sinai Address? He must have something!"

"And he may. But Numa Pompeii doesn't issue public reports of his recruiting and training progress," Rear Admiral Mishindi said. "Numa Pompeii hasn't been sighted for days. Intelligence lost him right after his appearance at Beta Centauri."

It was easy to lose people if they had FTL capability.

"Even if Caesar Numa has the means to challenge Romulus' forces for control of Port Chalai, it's not good for the United States either way—to have Numa or Romulus controlling the only fast supply route between Near Space and the outer arm of the galaxy."

Rear Admiral Mishindi saw Captain Farragut about to speak and cut him off. "Don't even think it, John."

"Send me in!"

"No, John. We can't bleed off resources from the defense of Earth against the Hive to help the Pacifics against Romulus. We are *just* keeping ahead of the gorgons here at home."

Another flight of Swifts was returning to *Merrimack* from a gorgon-slaying sortie. They clunked into their slots on the ship's wings. The hiss of flight elevators and the slamming of hatches echoed through the space battleship's hull.

Farragut shouted over the noise. "I'm not saying help the Pacifics. It's the Pacifics' own fault Romulus took their ports. I'm saying *send me there!* *I'll* take the Boomer and stake a proper flag on both ports!"

Farragut was still major league pissed at the Pacific Consortium for not listening to his warnings about the lack of failsafes in their design of Romulus' Xerxes spacecraft.

Mishindi looked grave. "That is not a realistic scenario."

"It's a real good scenario! Romulus is traveling in a Pacific-made ship! The Pacifics let Romulus get hold of their Xerxes. That fodgorsaken piece of work has made Romulus invincible."

"I know."

And now Romulus had Legions here in Near Space.

✳ ✳ ✳ ✳ ✳

3 February 2444
U.S. Space Battleship *Merrimack*
Earth orbit
Near Space

Captain Farragut woke to the vibration of his wrist com. He squinted at the chronometer, confused. The command deck was hailing him in the middle of the mid watch, his night cycle, yet there were no sounds of emergency. Only the normal ambient bangs, hisses, and booms of a ship at war.

Captain Farragut's voice came out gravelly. "Hamster? What's the emergency?"

"I'm sorry. This is not an emergency, sir." Glenn Hamilton had the prettiest voice. "Not for us. It's a major event. I thought you'd want to know Numa Pompeii's battlefort, the *Gladiator*, sublighted at Port Chalai. He destroyed the Port Chalai terminus of the Boomerang. Romulus won't be getting any more legionaries out of Perseid Space for a very long time."

He was wide awake now. Bolt upright. John Farragut wanted to tell that woman she had just made him a very happy man. Unwise.

Instead: "Roger that. Out."

✳ ✳ ✳ ✳ ✳

5 February 2444
U.S. Space Battleship *Merrimack*
Earth orbit
Near Space

Romulus' three Legion carriers in Near Space had gone FTL. There was no tracking them. They could appear anywhere, anytime, shooting.

Merrimack was on high alert. She couldn't leap to the safety of FTL space. She needed to stay sublight to dispatch and receive her fighter craft and spout flames at masses of gorgons trying to enter Earth's atmosphere.

Captain Farragut found his ship's xenolinguist, Doctor Patrick Hamilton, in his lab, listening intently to sounds in his headphones while observing images of silky mammoths on a display. It was nothing relevant to their current crisis.

Farragut shut Patrick Hamilton's imager off. The mammoths disappeared.

Patrick Hamilton took off his headset. But he didn't stand up. "Yes, Captain?"

"Could the Hive possibly have a language?" Farragut asked.

"You want to talk to it?" Patrick Hamilton asked. Added, belatedly, "Sir?"

Patrick Hamilton was an artistic-looking man, a handful of years younger than Farragut, much more slender, with soft brown hair and soft brown eyes. Women thought Patrick Hamilton attractive until he opened his mouth.

Farragut said, "I'll talk to the Hive if I can feed it misinformation. Or if I can convince it to drop dead."

Patrick wagged his head. "No go. The Hive doesn't have a language Does the Roman cyborg say it does? Then he can just plug in and spit out a full lexicon in five hours like he did in the Myriad '

"I'm not talking to the Roman cyborg right now," Farragut said evenly "And *you* are talking to the captain."

John Farragut was a famously easygoing man, but there were limits.

"Yes, sir," Patrick said, abashed. "I think—I *think*—the Hive is a single entity. I mean the *whole* Hive. All the swarms. All the spheres. Its communication is all internal—the equivalent of a neural network. Think of the reaction of a stomach to food. The body's signal to increase gastric acid isn't language."

"The cyborg might agree with you," Farragut said.

Augustus had said something similar, back in the Myriad. When the Hive had overwhelmed his consciousness, Augustus had called the Hive a gut.

"The signal doesn't *say* anything," Patrick Hamilton said. "Like a whiff of pheromones tells me to chase a hot *linda*. The sensory input triggers a response, but the signal is not part of a language. There's no syntax, no meaning."

If Farragut had hackles, they would be standing straight up now. This man had a perfectly beautiful, fun, smart, capable *linda* wearing his ring. Lieutenant Glenn Hamilton was command-caliber sharp. She was too good for Doctor Hamilton.

Captain Farragut was thinking about Mrs. Hamilton in ways three hundred sixty degrees—a full turn of the screw—wrong.

He forced his focus back to the real topic. "What is the Hive hearing, smelling, or sensing in response to the irresistible harmonic?"

Patrick pouted. "The what?"

This man had not been paying attention.

"There is a resonant harmonic that makes all the gorgons in the stellar area stop whatever they're doing and go chase the resonant source. What's the message?"

"I would ask a xenobiologist," Patrick said.

"I have. I'm asking you now."

"My *guess?* This is no better than a guess. My *guess* is that the resonance *is* the message. It's an IFF. Identification Friend or Foe. If the gorgons go on the offensive when you resonate on that harmonic, you're probably looking at a foe."

"Then what is Romulus giving his people that protects them from Hive interest?"

"Same thing, different gang. It's still Identification Foe or Friend. If the gorgons are sitting down to dinner together, that suggests they're all sending the Friend harmonic."

"Two Hives," Farragut said.

"Yeah. Yes, sir. There are probably two Hives."

✳ ✳ ✳ ✳ ✳

Cole Darby's private journal. Keep Out. This is PRIVATE.

If you think we got no time for gossip just because we're fighting the battle of Armageddon, you'd be wrong. What is life but who is doing who? You think there's a lot of whispering when we're bored? Well, life on the edge ramps it up red hot when your blood's racing and gorgons eat you alive in your dreams.

Lots of action makes for lots of tales. And the rumor mill, it be grinding.

Captain Farragut has a thing for Lieutenant Hamilton. He thinks it's a secret, but undiscovered fog giants in the Andromeda galaxy know about it. The only one who thinks it's a secret is Captain Farragut. He calls her Hamster. Okay, yeah, I know that's her nickname. But that's the thing. Farragut doesn't use nicknames. Glenn Hamilton is the only man-jane on board this whole big boat the captain doesn't call by name.

Truth is, the Hamster's husband is a gwerb. I've seen Doctor Ham give Kerry Blue the dancing eyebrows like he thinks she really really wants him. Kerry Blue just rolls her eyes and walks away. Patrick Hamilton isn't repulsive to look at. Okay, yeah, he is when he flashes that icky sappy come-on baby smile at Kerry Blue. He oughtta know that Blue don't do married men. Not on purpose. And holy mascons on the moon—did she ever go orbital when she found out about Cowboy's wife! Other than that, if you're married, Kerry Blue's not riding. Oh, well, yeah, okay, she'll comfort a man who's just been Jodyed, but that's different.

Most of us Bull Mastiffs think the Hamster ought to beach the gwerb and be with the captain. The captain really deserves to have what he wants. But that would leave a frat charge hanging out there. No getting around that.

* * * * *

6 February 2444
U.S. Space Battleship *Merrimack*
Earth orbit
Near Space

John Farragut sighted Lieutenant Glenn Hamilton on the elevated access walkway that circled the open space below the sail.

When Hamster was on the command deck, in crisp uniform, she looked like a seasoned officer. And so she was.

Here, in soft gray sweats, her brown-red ponytail bouncing behind her, she looked terribly cute. She should not be allowed out of her cabin like that. John Farragut just wanted to grab one of the cables, swing across the gap like Tarzan, seize her, and swing back.

He grabbed hold of a cable.

Hugely bad idea.

He let go of the cable and waited for Glenn to jog around to where he was.

She slowed, paused, jogging in place. Her face was wet with sweat. She sniffed, then greeted him with an almost smile. "Hey."

"Why are you on the loose at this hour?" Farragut asked. It was the evening watch. Hamster should be sleeping.

The smile vanished. "My cabin's crowded."

Glenn and Patrick Hamilton had one of the few conjugal cabins on *Merrimack*.

Anger rose. If Patrick Hamilton had someone else in that cabin instead of his wife . . .

"I'll clear it out for you," Farragut offered. "I've got a brig." He would be more than happy to stuff Patrick in detention. Adultery wasn't a crime, but it was sure as hell against regs.

Glenn shook her head. "The brig won't hold Hot Trixi Allnight."

Something exploded behind Farragut's eyes. He saw sparks.

Patrick was married to the beautiful Glenn Hamilton and yet he was playing around with a programmed imaginary sex donna in a dreambox? Farragut wanted to extend a plank out the air lock and make Patrick Hamilton walk it.

"I can remove Doctor Hamilton from your cabin if you want to sleep in your own rack," Farragut offered. "Happy to do it."

"I don't want to sleep there," Glenn said.

"I'd let you use my cabin, but that would send the wrong message."

Glenn stopped jogging in place. Her face got soft, sad, wistful. Her gaze dropped to their feet. "*Would* it?" she asked.

Too many thoughts and feelings collided into a giant pileup. He stammered. John Farragut never stammered. "Um. Message received. Unable to comply."

Glenn looked away. "I'm sorry. I'm off base."

Farragut was a long time putting words together. Breath stopped in his broad chest.

"If it were only a matter of crawling over broken glass, I'd be there." But there were stars on his shoulders.

Hamster's sudden smile was dizzying. "You have no idea how much I appreciate that, John." She beamed up at him. Wiped her face on her sleeve. "I'm just going to rack out in the hospital. Good night."

"Good night, Glenn."

✳ ✳ ✳ ✳ ✳

11 February 2444
U.S. Space Battleship *Merrimack*
Earth orbit
Near Space

The Marine Wing of the 89th Battalion flew top cover for the ground grunts who were tasked with plumbing gorgon holes in China. Sensors don't pick up gorgons. You gotta jab a probe down there and be ready to kill whatever comes up. Left alone underground long enough, gorgons divided in two.

Lieutenant Colonel TR Steele wanted to brig Kerry Blue so she wouldn't be flying close support over the gorgon holes, but he couldn't come up with an excuse.

At least Kerry Blue wasn't on the ground, doing hole duty.

Steele could not keep her safe. She was a Marine. She was here to stand in harm's way.

What idiot let women serve in the Fleet Marines, anyway?

Kerry Blue existed in the moment. She doesn't anticipate. She's right there, in the right now. She doesn't dream.

Steele dreamed. Things he should never dream about one of his Marines. He couldn't get rid of her. Had no reason to transfer her out. And when he thought of transferring her, he couldn't breathe. Might as well transfer a lung.

She ruled his up, his down, his horizon. He could not keep her safe.

Merrimack's tactical monitors showed images from Guangdong Province on Earth. The gorgons had been mostly neutralized there for the moment, but they'd left the coast devastated. Lieutenant Colonel Steele's Marines were still securing the holes.

Imported rock dragons were used as telltales in the area. Rock dragons wore a crust of silicates on their hides that made them indistinguishable from the ravaged ground. You didn't see the rock dragons until they detached from their rocks and slithered away. They could sense gorgons almost as well as insects could. You see a galloping rock, you know there are gorgons there.

The rocks in Guangdong were quiet for now. LEN soldiers at the space dock helped unload relief packages for the needy residents.

Officials stamped the arriving packages as they were offloaded from the transport for dispersal.

Doctor Patrick Hamilton burst through the hatch onto *Merrimack*'s command deck.

Immediately he shied as the MPs presented weapons.

Doctor Hamilton cringed and babbled and finally got out a word. "Sir!" He looked pale. Offered a language module toward the XO with quaking hand. He flapped his other hand toward the tactical display. "You need to look at that with this turned on."

Here was obviously some kind of xenolinguistical emergency.

Annoyed, Calli nodded for the MPs to allow the civilian-in-uniform to approach.

Commander Carmel took the offered module. She plugged it in behind her ear as she viewed the tactical displays.

She *saw*.

Immediately she was shouting, "Lieutenant Colonel Steele! Get a detail down to Guangdong. Detain those people." She pointed at the officials who were stamping the incoming relief supplies. "Use extreme caution."

Steele dispatched one of his ground units to make the arrests. Only when they were in motion did he ask the XO why.

Calli indicated the stamps, which the officials were using to mark all the incoming boxes and bags of relief supplies.

The stamps were Hanzi characters. Steele couldn't read them.

Calli turned to Patrick. "Doctor Hamilton. Do you want to translate this cluster?"

"Yes, sir. The stamps read: 'Gift of Romulus Imperator.'"

"Oh, hell!" Marcander Vincent at the tactical station blurted. "I must've watched the LEN deliver thousands of tons of food down there! All those bags got stamped with—I thought they were port officials! Everyone thinks—"

Calli gave a single hard nod. "Yes, they do."

Disaster relief. Gift of Romulus Imperator.

Calli covered her eyes. Hated to be played. She should have seen it.

It was a very Romulus sort of stunt.

Calli turned to Patrick Hamilton as if just remembering he was there. She spoke as if she were swallowing a bone. "Thank you, Doctor Hamilton."

She didn't say more, but Patrick heard the unspoken thought anyway: *I guess there might be a reason we have you on board after all.*

✳ ✳ ✳ ✳ ✳

16 February 2444
U.S. Space Battleship *Merrimack*
Earth orbit
Near Space

A disturbance on the low band registered off the scale. It signaled the displacement of a very large mass, very close—close enough to Earth to set off the Horizon Guard alarms.

It happened on Lieutenant Glenn Hamilton's watch. "Identify that," the Hamster demanded.

Tactical: "Spherical object. Two mile diameter."

Marcander Vincent brought up a visual on the tactical display.

A Hive sphere. An entire sphere.

The magnitude of everything that had come before diminished. The enemy were arriving by the millions now.

Glenn Hamilton felt the hope sink out through the deck.

She woke up the ship. "Battle stations!"

26

FLIGHTS OF MARINE SWIFTS banged down on their
landing slips atop *Merrimack*'s wings. Clamps locked them down.
Elevators hauled the fighter craft inboard and brought them
down hard.

A Long Range Shuttle carrying another company of Fleet Marines
from Guangdong Province docked with the space battleship. Fleet Marines stampeded aboard in cadence.

Captain Farragut charged onto the command platform carrying his
shirt, jacket, and boots with him. His scabbard hung from his shoulder.
He dropped the boots as he took in the image on the tactical display.

The colossal sphere lurked in the darkness, just visible by earthshine.
Forbidding. Ice-crusted. Motionless.

Farragut nodded forward. "Where is that?"

Tactical: "Three times Lunar orbit."

"Trajectory?"

"None."

Farragut pulled on a boot. "Is it dead?" He desperately wanted it to be
dead.

"It could be dead," Lieutenant Hamilton said, not convinced. "It *might*
not have survived displacement."

It looked inert.

Then the frozen sphere shrugged. Long fissures gapped in its surface.
Ice flaked off as it expanded. Looked as though it ought to be thundering,
but of course it wasn't making a sound in the vacuum.

Very close focus showed a black serrate appendage breaking through the frozen dead layer. Tactical announced: "That's not a gorgon."

Targeting: "They're razors! We have razors!"

Razors—also called soldiers or can openers—were the harder form of the Hive. Gorgons were the mouths and the stomachs of the Hive. Razors were bigger, hard-shelled, and sharp-clawed. They were the Hive's bodyguards. Razors broke hard targets. Like *Merrimack*.

Commander Carmel arrived on deck just as the sphere contracted, went still, then swelled and ruptured. Black glaciers sheared off and shattered into living pieces flying all directions.

Creatures like monstrous armored beetles, bigger than most men, clawed free of the broken ice and set to eating the food immediately available in the vacuum, which was the remains of their own dead.

Farragut pulled on his other boot, hopping a bit. "Commander Carmel, as soon as all hands are on board, damn that thing to hell."

"Aye, sir. Helm. Bring us in close enough to smell the brimstone."

You could hear Marines shouting out roll call several decks down.

Merrimack advanced. A black-gray wall of ice filled her tactical displays.

They had to get the guns close. Otherwise the Hive would erase tags and foul the trajectories of the loads. Calculating the future position of a target was impossible at any distance. The Hive knew how to evade. "Fire Control, mixed loads. Stand by."

"Mixed loads, aye. Standing by, aye."

Commander Carmel waited until the razors were so close the ship's collision alarms went off.

"Fire Control. Fire when ready. Fire everything."

Kerry Blue heard/felt the ship's guns coil and hiss. The lights dipped. You knew something was massively wrong when that happened. Then came the first sick buzz of something in contact with the ship's inertial shell.

Kerry ducked her head on reflex. Like that was going to help. She turned her eyes upward. "They're coming in."

The XO's voice sounded on the loud com: "All hands. All hands. We have hard hostiles on board."

The Alphas exchanged looks. Kerry Blue had thought the boarders were gorgons. Just assumed gorgons.

There were razors in Near Space?

"Hey Ranza! Did you train for razors?"

"Those the big black shiny ones with the claws?" Ranza gave her sword an experimental swing. The blade made a mighty swooshing sound through the air. "Yeah. Bring 'em."

The hum of insinuation got louder. It sounded like the monsters were everywhere.

No Swifts flew in a Hive storm. Kerry Blue and all the other Marines and crew stood by to repel boarders. The Fleet Marines trained on twenty-one scenarios. This scenario wasn't anyone's favorite.

Lieutenant Hazard Sewell led a charge out to the starboard wing where the Swifts were hangared. The Hive had developed some concept of efficiency. Parts of the ship designed to be opened to the outside were now the enemy's first points of entry.

Hive razors were clawing at the flight elevators.

A wind picked up Kerry Blue's ponytail. There was always some air movement in a ship this size, but this was different. Her ears popped with the pressure change.

"Hull breach!" Kerry said. Sure, everyone else had already figured that out.

The first monsters had pressed themselves through the force field and now pried their way through the ship's hull.

Air spilled out of the ship to fill the gap between the outer hull and the inertial shell.

Kerry Blue ran hard, snarling, teeth clenched. *Schistschistschistschist!*

She burst into the maintenance hangar. Peripheral motion, shiny black, made her swing. Giant claw fell, still clacking.

Kerry Blue kicked, fed the monster its own mouth.

She stomped on a pincered claw. Brilliant. As if she could crush something that could squeeze itself through an inertial field. She stabbed. Sword point still worked.

Sounds of struggle bounced off the bulks, slammed back at her ears. Grunts, sword clashes, clangs. Twitch Fuentes yelling. Not sure if Twitch meant to say something or he was just yelling. Didn't sound right.

Kerry sheared off two claws. The soldier melted.

"Twitch! Where are you?"

Didn't see him.

She heard him. Gargling. Not Twitch's normal strong baritone.

Black carapaces cracked and disintegrated under Kerry's sword strokes as she advanced stomp by stomp. "Twitch!"

Heard him. Speaking in tongues.

"Twitch! Talk! Use words!" Kerry cut off a claw. Another.

"Twitch!"

Twitch was gurgling now. Sounds ricocheted off all the hard surfaces. Up was down. No direction. "Carly! What is that man saying!" Where was Carly, and why wasn't Carly with Twitch?

Kerry Blue was already yelling, *"Medic!"* She knew there'd be need for one by the time a medibot got out here.

Kerry advanced, Cole Darby clearing her six. They came to a maintenance pit. A melee down there.

Twitch emerged from the maintenance pit, head and one shoulder. His face was as white as brown could be, shining with sweat. Planted his elbow on the main deck and pulled himself up from the pit by one arm. Something waggled at his other shoulder. It was what was left of his sword arm.

Twitch didn't seem to know he was wounded. Kerry Blue slapped a med seal on the bleeding stump.

Twitch's narrow eyes went round in horror, as if just now realizing his right arm wasn't attached to him. Tried to turn around, gabbling, "Get m'arm! Get m'arm!"

Reg Monroe yelled at him, helping to drag him up to the deck. She was half his size. "Grow a new one! That one's gone. Leave it. *MEDIC!*"

"ARM!" Twitch bellowed wildly.

Kerry Blue suddenly understood. Twitch was famously bad at putting words together. "He's not saying what he means! He's only torqued about his frogging arm because he's got to be holding onto *Carly!* Where's Carly!"

"Oh, jeez!" Reggie cried. She whirled with her sword and sent pincers flying.

Dak Shepard jumped into the maintenance pit.

Up on deck, Twitch mumbled, eyelids fluttering. "Get m'arm."

"Dak is getting," Kerry assured him. She spun round and almost stabbed Reggie.

Twitch murmured, *"No me gusta. No me gusta."* He didn't like this at all.

"Stay with me, Twitch," Kerry yelled at him. "You're not deading on me, *hermano*. I won't let you." Heard the whine of an approaching medibot.

Dak lumbered up from the pit clutching an unconscious Carly Delgado to his side. Twitch's arm came along, dangling. Twitch's broad hand was locked fast onto Carly's suit, not letting go for anything.

*   *   *

Augustus cut through monsters with inhuman speed and machine precision, coldly efficient. No wasted motion. No wild strikes.

Until he stopped. Froze with his sword upraised.

His head turned dreamlike slow. Unfocused eyes directed toward John Farragut.

"Augustus!" Farragut shouted into Augustus' blank face.

Augustus' sword lifted, winding up for a strike. His eyes were vacant.

Jose Maria darted behind Augustus and yanked his patterner cables out of his neck.

Augustus swayed in place.

Jose Maria cut down the alien that reached between them.

Detached pincers twitched and dissolved through the deck grate.

Awareness returned to Augustus' face. He grunted. Might have been thanks.

There were too many monsters. He swung at the nearest.

More razors were forcing themselves in.

A sphere just like this one had crippled *Merrimack* in the Myriad. But the stage was different here. This was Earth space. *Merrimack* couldn't run.

And *Merrimack* was not alone.

Sounds like ripping metal tore through the ship with screaming heat.

"Cavalry's here," Farragut said. No one could hear him over the noise, as many decibels as the ship's sonic filters allowed through.

Outside, the battle cruiser *Rio Grande* strafed the length and breadth of *Merrimack* with a flamethrower.

Fleet Marine Swifts from *Rio Grande* darted through the vacuum, hunting down surviving razors, picking them off one by one.

✳ ✳ ✳ ✳ ✳

26 February 2444
U.S. Space Battleship *Merrimack*
Solar System
Near Space

Merrimack licked her wounds. Repair crews and technicians tended to the ship. The hospital was over full. There had been no deaths, but the wounded numbered just about everyone.

Captain Farragut visited every one of them. Augustus last.

"It overtook you," Farragut said. "The Hive."

"It did," Augustus croaked. He pushed at his temples. "I got the Hive harmonic."

John Farragut's mouth dropped open. He sputtered, "That's outstanding!"

"No." Augustus opened his eyes. "I had it. It's gone now. I knew it while I was a part of it."

"Just—*tell* me."

One hand caged Augustus' face. He peered out between his fingers. "First, you tell me how you translate a thumbprint into a rutabaga."

"You mean there's no correspondence."

"None. Our expression of harmonics has no counterpart in Hive existence or awareness."

"We use numbers."

"The Hive doesn't."

"Everyone uses numbers."

"The Hive doesn't." Augustus' face creased in pain or concentration. "Even while I was part of the Hive I didn't define the harmonic because I *was* it. I was Hive. The harmonic was my existence."

"You said you had the harmonic."

"I did. I don't."

"Can't you rerun your thoughts?"

"There wasn't any thinking being done."

"Do you remember the Hive wanting me dead?"

"Oh, that wasn't the Hive," Augustus said.

✳ ✳ ✳ ✳ ✳

28 February 2444
U.S. Space Battleship *Merrimack*
Solar System
Near Space

"Bogey," Tactical reported. "Someone is out there. We have a ghost."

"Hive?" Commander Carmel demanded.

"Not Hive. It's stealthy. Too massive for Romulus' Xerxes. Can't tell you much about the bogey except it's there. It's a gravitational whisper. He's close. He's here."

"FTL jump! Jump now! Random vector. Execute!"

"Balk," the pilot reported.

You felt the drag. Heard the strain in the engines. The space battleship refused to jump.

"We have an anchor."

A drag on *Merrimack*'s mass prevented any escape to FTL. Calli looked through a porthole. Didn't believe it. "It's *Gladiator*!"

Caesar Numa Pompeii's battlefort.

Commander Carmel called for siege stations as Captain Farragut barreled onto the command deck. "All hands, Personal Fields! Prepare to repel human boarders!"

Calli surrendered the com to the captain. "We're arrayed against Hive. Not against a conventional enemy."

Farragut nodded. He knew that. "Son of a bitch."

They watched on the ship's internal monitors as an opening formed in the inertial shell, an air lock giving way—someone opening the ship up as though he had keys. Shouts sounded from below, with the buzz of Roman stun sticks.

"Where's Augustus?"

"I am here," Augustus said from the place where he usually lurked when he was on the command platform.

"Are you taking over my ship, Augustus?"

"Not I. Had Numa consulted with me—and he didn't—I would have advised him that opening up a second front in this war is fantastically stupid."

"War? Numa calls it a wildfire."

"You and I know that's *merda*."

"Colonel Augustus. Step outside an air lock."

"May I suit up first?"

"If you have to," Farragut said, angry. He drew his sword and charged below to meet the boarders.

Marines lay in the corridors, immobilized, swords in hand. Farragut prayed that his men were only immobilized. He didn't see blood.

Unlike swords, stunners didn't need to touch you.

An interior air lock was open. Farragut heard Romans stomping in cadence inside his ship.

Farragut ran toward the sound.

They were big, the legionaries of Rome. *Mack* was nobody's yacht. Her passages were only as wide and high as they needed to be. Max height to serve on a U.S. spaceship was six foot eight. None of these boys would pass muster. And Numa Pompeii was doublewide. His legionaries filled the corridor. They were marching away from Farragut.

Farragut broke into a run and yelled at the Romans' broad backs. "This way, dickheads!"

They turned as a unit. They were carrying shock sticks.

Numa Pompeii pressed between his men to face Captain Farragut. His gaze found the sword in Farragut's hand. Numa's deep voice was flat with disgust. "Swords. Really. Swords." He looked down at the immobilized Marines, clutching their swords. "We thought we were being fed disinformation." He spat. "Swords."

Farragut spoke into his wrist com to the command deck. "All hands. Hold present positions." Then to Numa, "Didn't Augustus tell you?"

"Aug—?" A deep crease appeared in Numa Pompeii's craggy face, genuine-looking confusion. "No. I don't use patterners. Is that abomination on board?"

"No. He deserted. He's probably on your boat."

"That thing will not get on my ship. *This* Caesar doesn't use patterners."

"I missed your declaration of war. Does this mean Caesar Romulus speaks for you?"

That rippled Numa's all-holy smugness. Numa's voice rumbled up from his vast chest. "That is not Caesar! The Empire and the United States are not at war!"

"*You're on my boat!*" Farragut roared.

"It was necessary to show you mortal. You have an invincible reputation you don't deserve. I require information," Numa said. "I shall have it. I need to know your secret to fighting the Hive."

"You boarded me to ask me that? I'm fighting for my home. I don't expect to be back-doored by Caesar-fornicating-Numa-you-bastard-Pompeii!"

Numa demanded, impatient, "How did you survive what sixty-four imperial Legions did not?"

"Swords."

"I heard that rubbish story. I am not here for fairy tales. Tell me how you survived the Hive."

"Is that it?" Farragut cried. "You came here looking for a magic key. The magic key is the Hive harmonic. Romulus has it. But you didn't board

Romulus. You stormed in here to make it look like you're doing something. You boarded the wrong boat, because it's the one you could! You're a bigger fraud than Romulus is. I told you my secret weapon. It's swords. Get out."

Numa's eyes flicked toward an attendant. The attendant must've been reading biometrics by which to judge Farragut's truthfulness. The attendant gave Caesar a small nod.

Numa's small eyes widened. "*Increditus*. You have nothing."

"I have Americans. Go fight your own way. It's working so well for you."

Numa spoke, witheringly. "Swords. One at a time."

"That's how it's done."

"I am a triumphalis. I am not an exterminator."

"Yeah? Romans are no good against the Hive. Just make for fat gorgons. You go ahead and feed your surviving troops proudly to the Hive. Flush another sixty-four Legions and the rest of Rome down the crapper. Get off my boat. Take your patterner with you."

"I do not now and never have had a patterner. But I will take the creature's Striker."

"Go get it. Augustus' Striker is in the Myriad. Two thousand parsecs *that* way. Augustus is outside. Pick him up or let him drift. I don't care."

"I leave you to your game of toy soldiers," Numa said and strode away. Caesar's entourage closed behind him.

Farragut spoke at Numa's back, urgent, "Just so you know, a gorgon will eat its own weight in thirty seconds, then do it again. They burn dirty. If you open up half the body sack it usually dies, but the mouths don't get the message for another minute."

Numa turned slowly, looked back scowling. Listening.

"Gorgons dodge beam fire and antimatter. And now it looks like they dodge flamethrowers too. Did you even watch that last battle? Tactics don't work twice. The Hive learns. They'll just get out of the way. If you meet a can opener, go for the joints. Anything you teach one gorgon, you've taught all of them. All the swarms that killed your sixty-four Legions? They know everything these swarms are doing here. They know the way to Earth. All of them do. Nothing you know of conventional warfare means spit against the Hive. Throw out your playbook, there's no strike zone. They're coming. They're here!"

Numa moved slowly, assessing. "Were you really a Boy Scout?"

"I *am* an Eagle Scout."

Numa shook his head, and turned away muttering, "Who made you up?"

When the Roman battlefort *Gladiator* vanished into FTL existence, Calli advised Captain Farragut, "Sir. Numa's contingent didn't collect Augustus. Augustus is still outside. Should I have him picked up?"

"Ask me again when he's out of air," Farragut snarled. Then. "No. Belay that. Pick the son of a she-dog up."

Lieutenant Colonel Steele returned to the command platform, holstering his sidearm. His head was boiled-lobster red. He pronounced the ship clear of Romans other than Augustus.

Farragut nodded. "Casualties?"

"Minor."

Farragut turned his gaze pointedly toward the red spatter on Steele's sleeve. "That's blood."

"Roman," said Steele.

"Caesar wasn't here to kill us," Farragut said. "He's the enemy of our enemy."

"Doesn't make him our friend, sir."

"No," Farragut agreed, still vibrating anger. "It doesn't. When we kill the Hive—and *we will kill the Hive*—be ready to eject Numa Pompeii from the game."

Augustus reported to the command platform. Calli spoke across him. "Captain. You know that Colonel Augustus is a mole."

Augustus looked very cross. "How can I be a mole? I'm a bald-faced Roman."

"*Romulus'* mole," Calli said. "You were in Romulus' captivity, aboard his Xerxes. Romulus restored your health and returned you to us."

"Romulus didn't return me. I escaped. But yes, I do see the grounds for suspicion."

Captain Farragut faced Augustus. "Are you loyal to Numa Pompeii?"

"I do not recognize Numa Pompeii. I'm loyal to Caesar Magnus and to Rome. But I will kiss the ring of anyone who kills Romulus. I take orders from John Farragut so long as your interests align with Rome's. After that, you'll need to neutralize me."

"Kill you," Farragut translated.

"Are you sure you could do that, John?" Calli asked.

"If I had to, yes."

"I know," Augustus said. "You did."

"I . . . did what?"

"It's something Romulus remembers from his future life. You did. You killed me."

Farragut was left without words for a moment. Finally, "I'm sorry."

"Not looking for an apology."

"Wasn't an apology," Farragut said. "I'm just not happy that it could come to that."

Captain Farragut opened up the bar. He stood drinking with the only man on board not subject to his command. He confessed, "Numa's right. We're bailing out an ocean with teaspoons. And I'm keeping hold of a company and crew who really want to run home and defend their own homes."

"No one is deserting, young Captain," Jose Maria said.

"No, God bless them. But we haven't begun to see gorgons."

"I had a thought," Jose Maria began. "If—when—we become coated with monsters again, we could take your *Merrimack* close to the sun. The monsters must let go or die."

"I had that thought," Farragut said.

"Ah. Then you also saw the problem with it."

Farragut nodded. "If we head for the fire, we're saved but the gorgons will jump ship and take their mouths right back to Earth."

"Still, it could give us some breathing room. Unless we allow ourselves to become overwhelmed."

"Jose Maria, you don't need to be on the front line. Take your yacht to Terra Rica. Go home and be with your family."

Jose Maria let his gaze drop to the deck. "No. And I confess altruism does not hold me here. You saw the video Romulus gave me. When Romulus is sure he has my attention and I am home with my family around me, my world will end."

"Then you and your sword arm are welcome to stay here," Farragut said.

2 March 2444
U.S. Space Battleship *Merrimack*
Solar System
Near Space

"Rome has a new training recruiting video," the com tech advised. "You're in it, Captain."

"Rome does? Which Rome?"

"Numa Pompeii's Rome, sir."

"Let's see it."

The video on the main tactical display showed Caesar's hulking Praetorian Guard boarding *Merrimack*. Farragut hadn't realized he was being recorded. Last thing on his mind at the time.

Farragut watched himself giving Numa a quick and dirty, heavily edited guide to fighting the Hive. *A gorgon will eat its own weight in thirty seconds, then do it again. They burn dirty. If you open up half the body sack, it usually dies but the mouths don't get the message for another minute.*

Farragut was astonished. "Numa listened to me. Son of a cur listened. This is a training video? That means Numa is taking on the Hive. *Rome is in the war.*" His excitement dropped a little on a following thought. "When this is all over, Numa is going to be dangerous."

Found Augustus gazing at him strangely.

"What?" Farragut demanded.

"You think we're getting out of this alive."

"I do," Farragut said. How could he think else?

Augustus stared at him. "You're either an idiot or . . ."

"Or?"

"You see patterns I don't."

"Major displacement event," Tactical reported. "Hive sphere. Magnitude four. Thirty thousand miles out."

That shocked everyone on the command platform.

"That puts it on the front porch," Farragut said.

The gorgons could easily make planetfall.

"Yes, sir." Tactical kept reporting, "Hive sphere. Magnitude three. Altitude twenty-one thousand miles.

"Hive sphere. Magnitude four. Altitude twenty-two thousand miles.

"Hive sphere. Magnitude four. Altitude twenty thousand miles.

"Hive sphere. Magnitude undefined. Altitude twenty thousand miles."

The low band was pounding. The tactical display was thick with splintering Hive spheres.

"Glory, glory!" Farragut breathed. Didn't matter now if Rome was in the fight.

Calli murmured, "This is the Alamo. It's the Corindahlor Bridge."

Farragut looked to the rear of the command platform. "Augustus, why are you laughing?"

Augustus wore a bright graveyard smile. "Why the hell not?"

27

10 March 2444
U.S. Space Battleship *Merrimack*
Solar System
Near Space

THE FIGHTING WAS NONSTOP NOW. Kerry Blue dosed herself to sleep at mid watch, then hopped herself awake at reveille. She killed gorgons with a sword. Then she did the whole drill again.

Didn't get to eat. Wore her food pack plugged in. Hydrator too. She thought her hydrator must be spent. She was shaking.

The monster spheres kept arriving, splitting open, raining a million more gorgons down on Earth and throwing a million more razors against *Merrimack*. They clotted thick on *Mack's* inertial shell. When the coating of monsters got so thick that the engine containment fields burbled, *Merrimack* tore off to the sun again.

Close to Mercury's orbit, it took only a few minutes to burn the burrs off. Still, every time *Mack* ran for the sun, it felt as if they were abandoning Earth.

You gotta be alive to fight.

The ship got hot fast. The surface of the sun looked grainy and crawly through the filters. Gorgons either jumped ship on the way here or they burned here.

Each time the Hive interference lifted, *Merrimack's* atmospheric controls returned. Kerry Blue felt her thoughts making connections. She could breathe. Inhaled hugely. She smelled gorgons. Coughed.

She didn't know what brimstone smelled like. Figured this was it.

The boffins said people couldn't detect resonance. Bull skat. When the gorgons got thick on the ship's hull, Kerry Blue felt like she was drunk or missing three nights sleep. She had orders to sleep through the mid watch, and she did. It wasn't doing any good. She was pretty sure something about the gorgon mass scrambled everything her—her what? What was she just thinking?

Wasn't just her. No one was all right.

And here we go charging back into it again. Left the sun behind. The ship cooled down on the way back into battle.

She didn't know what keep her fighting. She just did it.

A pincer punched through the bulkhead right at Kerry Blue's eye level. She jerked back, sliced the pincer off. The hard black claw melted before it could hit the platform.

Another claw point poked through the bulk. Kerry shaved it off.

She'd lost contact with Cole Darby. Heard him yelling somewhere. "One two! One Two! And through and through! His vorpal blade went snicker snack!" Darb must've gone mad.

One level down from Kerry Blue, a whole cluster of pincers punched through the bulk. Kerry slid down the ladder to the lower landing. Mowed off the claws.

The claws clattered all the way down the hundred-foot fall to the bottom of the lower sail. They splashed down. Gorgons and razors and their severed parts melted into brown sludge on dying.

There was lot of sloshing down below. A lot of oily brown rain coming from above.

Another claw punched through the bulkhead. Kerry swung at it. Connected. It was reflex by now.

The whole shaft was sprouting appendages.

Kerry Blue slashed off pieces of pincers as they stuck through the metal. She kept swinging.

Heard her mates calling her name. Sounded farther away than they ought to be. They ought to be right here. Or she should be right there. She'd gone and got herself separated. Her adrenaline rush dribbled away. What was she thinking?

Thinking was hard. She was out of hoppers, and she'd waited too long to reload. She hauled herself up the ladder a couple of rungs. Felt like she was carrying Dak. Her limbs felt thick. What was she even doing down here?

A deep metallic groan sounded from above. She looked up dully. Something wide and metal up there—a platform or a hatch—gave way with a tumbling clatter. It was on her before she could move. Swept her down with it. She landed flat. Chest, chin hit with a woof.

Trouble breathing. No idea what happened to her sword.

It was dark down here. Chemical lights were spotty. She couldn't call. Couldn't whimper. Couldn't move her rib cage. Breathing felt like folding daggers. She could only sip in shallow breaths. Her wrist com was fugged. She whispered, "Help?"

I'm going to die here.

How had she let herself get separated from her team?

This is reallio trulio all ucked fup.

Sounds of battle boomed throughout the ship.

She thought she was suffocating. Not sure. Could be the platform crushing her, or the gorgons making her think she wasn't breathing. Not sure of anything. Couldn't string two thoughts together. Couldn't hold one thought for more than a panicked heartbeat.

She wiggled her toes to find out if she still had a spine. Right toes, okay. Left toes? Left leg not responding. Couldn't see what was happening back there.

A shadow fell over her, darker in darkness. She knew, just knew, it was a can opener come to finish her. She stayed still. Didn't have much choice.

A scritching of claws. Then a clang of something dropping down a level. Shuffling. Another clang, it dropped closer. More scritching. Another drop.

Clang. It dropped closer still. Claws clicking at every drop.

The thing descended, snuffling.

Hive razors don't snuffle.

Clunk. The dog landed on her shaky perch. Rapid panting breaths drew near.

A tickle of whiskers and a fuzzy muzzle as she managed to turn her head. A damp canine nose. It was God—Godzilla, the rat terrier—licking her cheek in between salvos of yips. The dog couldn't talk, but it was smart enough to sound off specific calls for different scenarios. Godzilla recognized this situation and sang out the call to indicate man down critical. It sounded like *here here here here here here!* Not the words. The tone told you to get a medic down here here here here! Now now now now!

Godzilla paused to give Kerry's face more licks. She was crying. Didn't want anyone to see her tears.

Thank you, God.

The rat terrier was back to barking its big doggie heart out. *Here here here!*

Rapidly moving shapes made the light flicker up above. Something way up there made an unhealthy creak.

Everything that fell from the upper sail dropped through the main fuselage and picked up a holy hell of a lot of momentum by the time it dropped into the lower sail.

Something way up there let go and came falling, bashing and tumbling. It halted. Stayed that way for a long minute, hung up on something.

Kerry grimaced as a rain of debris pattered on top of her. She tried to shut her nostrils. Closed her one working eye. Opened it. Blinked grit clear.

O God, don't make me cough. She thought a cough would kill her.

She heard God, speaking for her. A different bark this time. No words, but the meaning of the barks sounded pretty clear. *Watch it! Watch it!*

A structural groan.

A snap. The thing in the overhead lurched, dropped downward, fast. Kerry squinted her face shut. As if that would stop anything from falling on her.

Heard a slam, a flexing screel of metal hung up on metal, and opened her eye. Above her head, a piece of shorn sheet metal dangled edgewise by shredding cable. From this angle it looked exactly like a guillotine blade.

The dog huddled against her face. Godzilla's warm side moved against her cheek with his quick panting breaths.

Was this a death vigil?

This can't really be it.

She tried not to cry. It was painful--crying, trying not to. She kissed the dog. Shut her eye.

Sense of floating. Was this death?

She still hurt. And the dog was still there, his mouth holding her sleeve so he didn't float away from her.

Her hair, her clothes lifted slightly.

The ship had lost artificial gravity.

The platform on top of her chest wasn't floating. It was jammed. She was stuck. Her leg was a solid mass of pain.

The guillotine blade was still there, hovering lazily, more or less over her neck, deciding where exactly to fall.

Artificial gravity could reengage at any instant. She had to get out from under that blade.

She lost the light above her. A big living shape descended. She knew that silhouette, knew the way he moved.

It's the Old Man. Lieutenant Colonel Steele. Moved as easily as if he were swimming. He pushed the floating blade out of his way. Descended. Moved the dog out of the way, kinda gently actually. He gave it an upward push. The dog rose straight up the shaft, stubby legs moving as if paddling.

Steele took hold of the metal platform that had Kerry pinned down, and he pulled. It was jammed in place.

Steele regripped, crouched, and lifted. The metal gave a tooth-shredding scream as he peeled it back.

Kerry felt air on her back. Didn't feel any less crushed.

Steele crouched down close to her. His arms slid under her, carefully. He knew better than to squeeze.

His hands—they were real warm, and she was real real cold—his hands closed on her carefully. She melted into his warmth. He smelled good. She'd smelled a lot of men. Liked this one a whole lot more than she was allowed.

"Gonna hurt."

"Huh?" she said, thick.

Then she saw it. She had a fixed stanchion harpooned through her thigh. No wonder that ached so bad. Must've missed the femoral artery. That woulda been a geyser.

The stanchion was fixed in place. Steele got a grip on her, positioned to lift her off it. "You ready?"

She answered with no breath, "Yep."

She braced for the pain. Tried to leave her body. Be somewhere else as *Fargo! Frodo! Fuck! That hurt!*

She came free.

There could have been a whole lot more blood.

Feeling queasy, heavy, she looked up. Her guillotine blade was back.

The sheer metal sheet had lazily caromed off another piece of wreckage and drifted back right over her head. She tried to talk. Couldn't find a word. The thing—! Look out! Heads!

Gravity abruptly returned.

The blade dropped.

A sudden wrench yanked her to the side with a stab of pain. Steele had jerked her hard against him. The blade chopped down. It split the platform and kept going, then stabbed into a lower platform and stuck. The scaffolding of the entire sail sang with the reverberation. The blade had opened up the side of Steele's deck boot.

His hands loosened their hold on her. Her eyes watered with pain. She didn't want him to think she was crying.

Steele snarled, trying to get a grip on her that wouldn't cause more damage while he carried her up the ladder. He lurched up the ladder, one lumbering rung at a time, like King Kong.

He had to stop. Set her down and drew his sword to cut down the razors that came for them.

He sheathed his sword and crouched to pick her up again, muttering.

She said, "Colonel, I know you don't think much of me, but—"

The look on his face stopped her. Blond brows rose in jagged arches. His mouth hung open, angry or astonished or both. She stared into his eyes for an eternal moment. They were ice blue and burning. A lethal growling whisper started somewhere way down deep in his broad chest. "I *what?*"

Kerry opened her mouth. Shut it before something stupid could come out of it.

Oh.

The intensity in his gaze made her writhe inside.

Steele's breath seethed. He snarled a whisper, "You are *all* I think about."

His face got real red.

She stared at him, amazed. Then afraid.

She touched his cheek. It was rough, bristled. She lifted her fingertips to his lips. "Are we dying?"

"*No!*" he bellowed, like an order.

Gravity quit as if he'd startled it.

Quickly, Steele made her grab onto the back of his suit. She grasped his suit and held tight in case gravity kicked in again. Steele stormed up the ladder.

They made it to the main fuselage and onto a firm deck. Hospital level. A triage bot came out to assess her.

Kerry felt a change in the air. She could think. The sickening sounds of insinuation tapered off. "Are we running to the sun?" Kerry asked.

"Must be," Steele said.

But they weren't. The lights returned. The engines didn't sound to be straining.

Kerry heard some cheering, then a triumphant screeching *"Yeah!"*

Word came around quickly. The enemy were jumping ship. It was a retreat—the Hive's.

"Are we *winning?*" Kerry asked.

Steele's face looked grim. He wasn't a trusting man. He didn't look ready to celebrate. Something was wrong here.

News spread through the space battleship. The Hive spheres were changing direction, all of them, lifting away from Earth. The gorgons were running.

✳ ✳ ✳ ✳ ✳

Captain Farragut wore an expression of alarm when Lieutenant Colonel Steele appeared on the command platform. "TR. Hospital. Now. You look like crap."

Steele shook his head. "Unable to comply. Triage says I'm a priority five." Kerry Blue was a two. "What's our situation, sir?"

"The Hive is moving."

"They're running away?"

"Not exactly."

The captain frowned at the sounds of his ship, at the images on the tactical display. "It's like the Hive is chasing something else. Tactical. Tell me what's out there."

The kid at tactical, Jeffrey, couldn't identify the thing, but he pointed out a distinct pattern in the paths of all the monsters. They all converged on a single moving point, heading away from Earth.

"We've seen this before," Jeffrey said.

Steele recognized it. Farragut said it. "Someone out there has the irresistible harmonic and is luring the monsters away."

Systems said, "Thank God."

"Nothing to do with God, son. And thanks are not in order. It's another monster."

As the Hive presence thinned around *Merrimack*, the ship's atmospherics came back to life. Gravitation steadied, as much as it ever steadied on the space battleship.

A newsfeed from somewhere showed amazing images—images of Romulus walking among gorgons. He casually brushed fanged tentacles out of his way with the back of his hand, completely at ease among his fellow monsters.

Romulus wore his customary black shirt, black trousers, and black boots. His short red cape was edged in gold. A golden oak wreath sat on his dark curls. He posed for the recorders.

To anyone watching he said, "Now that I have your attention." And left it at that.

Systems couldn't stay quiet. "What's he doing? What's that mean, sir?"

Commander Carmel answered that one. "Romulus is waiting for a bigger audience."

At last Romulus announced, "I require the unconditional surrender of the human race. Know, people of all worlds, that Claudia is queen of the universe. Any disrespect toward her is your request to be removed from the universe. I am your Imperator, your Romulus. I invite the nations of Earth to bow willingly to me. Except for the United States. The U.S. must earn our mercy. The American military must walk in Subjugation through a gauntlet of racked spears before they may be admitted back into the fold.

"This is an easy choice. You will join my Roman Empire and submit to my rule, or my Hive will consume you."

The com tech spoke, urgent. "Captain! Tight beam from Rear Admiral Mishindi and Captain Forshaw!"

Tight beam was old technology. It was redundant. Tight beam didn't attract Hive attention. And it was adequate for connecting the rear admiral at Base Carolina with his two space battleships in Earth orbit.

Matthew Forshaw was captain of *Merrimack*'s sister ship, *Monitor*. A hard, lean man, Matty Forshaw looked as though he'd been carved from an oak timber. Matty Forshaw and John Farragut exchanged quick nods.

Admiral Mishindi looked grave. He'd aged decades in the past year.

Farragut started first. "Sir! Romulus is a monster. How can anyone follow him? There can't be anyone left in the civilized galaxy who doesn't want him dead."

Mishindi sounded tired. "Making Romulus dead requires targeting him. His Xerxes ship makes that impossible. And the brutal fact remains that if Romulus withdraws his hold on the Hive, Earth cannot survive."

Farragut and Forshaw started like runners jumping the gun. Objections rose. And immediately stopped inside their throats. Farragut grunted.

Mishindi's voice remained steady. "President Reed is facing Romulus on a galactic broadcast at 0800 Greenwich Time. We expect Romulus will make a formal demand for the unconditional surrender of the United States. President Reed will refuse." Mishindi's eyes dropped briefly. He rephrased, "President Reed intends to refuse."

"Sir!" Matty Forshaw there. "If the President surrenders, we don't have a country!"

Mishindi waved a forefinger side to side. "Not so. Whether Romulus recognizes it or not, the President does not have the power to surrender. The Constitution of the United States does not allow for its own dissolution or suspension. President Reed cannot surrender the United States."

Farragut was looking beyond Mishindi. Behind the rear admiral, images from other locations were visible on many monitors. One caught John Farragut's attention. On it, somewhere, Romulus' soldiers were assembling with spears in preparation for a Subjugation.

Farragut pointed. "Sir, I'm not doing that."

Mishindi had to turn around to see what Farragut was talking about. He turned back to face the captains. "Then it's a good thing those aren't your orders. John, Matty, take your ships and go somewhere FTL. Disable your res chambers. *Rio Grande* is already in the wind. I'm tight-beaming you Captain McDaniel's touch points separately.

"Do not let yourselves, your ships, your crews, or your Marines be captured. We have the beginnings of an underground. I'm sending a bouncing bubble with the galactic coordinates for ammo dumps, spare parts, tools, and rations. We have been organizing a resistance in case the worst falls. I don't know what our mole situation is, so be aware that any of these drop sites may be compromised. That's it, gentlemen. If this be treason, make the most of it. Do not surrender even if your Commander in Chief does."

"You said he can't surrender," Captain Forshaw said.

"Reed can surrender himself—not the nation. But it would be a propaganda opportunity for Romulus. You need to get gone."

"Sir!" Farragut cried. "If we run and hide, that leaves Earth defenseless!"

"Actually, Earth is safer without you right now, John. Romulus wants something left intact to rule. He wants a mighty empire, not fields of devastation and famished people. The best way for you to defend Mother Earth is to abandon her for now. Don't say anything. You know I'm right, and we have little time.

"This won't be forever. Eventually someone will discover or steal the Hive harmonic. Romulus has it. We will get it. We will see the end of this. Just hang on. Romulus can't locate you as long as you don't resonate and you stay at FTL. You're safe at FTL."

"We're not here to be safe," Captain Forshaw said. It seemed the kind of pronouncement one should make at a time like this.

"You had better be safe, sir," Mishindi said. "You're no good to anyone dead or captive. Now disappear."

Before *Merrimack* jumped to FTL, Captain Farragut asked Colonel Augustus, "*Quo vadis?*"

Augustus showed no emotion. "Is that the only Latin you know, John Farragut?"

"Just about," Farragut admitted. "Where are you going?"

"As I have no means of transport, I'm with you."

"I can't give you a spacecraft. I can set you ashore somewhere."

"The last order I had from a legitimate Caesar was from Magnus. Magnus gave me to John Farragut. I was never here by choice. Sad to say, you are my best shot at keeping Rome alive. I vowed to protect Rome. I'm stuck serving you."

"Where I come from, vows made under duress are not binding," Farragut said.

"That is the difference between us. When a Roman gives his word, his word is given. The duress invalidates nothing."

11 March 2444
0800 hours
U.S. Space Battleship *Merrimack*
Asteroid Belt, Solar System
Near Space

President Sampson Reed refused to seek refuge in the emergency continuity of operations center underneath the White House. So it happened that Romulid Legionaries were able to lay hands on him. They sat President Reed down in the Oval Office and activated all the cameras and news links. Romulus ordered the President to surrender the United States to Romulus.

Farragut needed to drop *Merrimack* out of FTL to view the newscast in real time without relativistic gaps. The space battleship lurked inside the Solar System, on the surface of an asteroid, reflecting a light return that mimicked the asteroid's surface.

Lieutenant Hamilton couldn't watch. She shifted her eyes away from the tactical display and stared off into nothing.

When Romulus' demand came, President Sampson Reed refused to surrender.

Hamster heard the shot. She flinched. It had the sound of an old-fashioned handgun.

Marcander Vincent reported coldly: "The President is down. The Speaker is up next. Congressman Sol Roythemd. Democrat. Connecticut."

Glenn peered at the display and caught a glimpse of Roman legionaries dragging Reed's body out from behind the blood-spattered Resolute Desk before she looked away again. She heard the legionaries seating the Speaker of the House. Heard the voice of Romulus demanding surrender.

Glenn Hamilton jerked at the pistol crack.

Marcander Vincent: "The Speaker is down."

Glenn Hamilton looked to Captain Farragut.

Farragut's eyes were downcast, his gaze fixed on the deck.

"Oh, no." Lieutenant Hamilton put her hand on the captain's shoulder, just for a moment.

She never thought they would go this far down the line of succession this quickly.

Tactical sounded as though he were checking program notes. "Up next is the President of the Senate Pro Tem. Who is that?"

"Catherine Mays," Glenn snapped at Marcander Vincent. More softly, she asked the captain, "Do you know where she is?"

"Under the White House," Captain Farragut said, trying to look stoic. "She's in the bunker."

Glenn asked, scarcely audible, "Does Romulus know she's your sister?"

"I have no doubt that he does."

*   *   *

Romulus signaled Senator Catherine Mays on a public broadcast channel and invited her up to the Oval Office.

"The President's place is in the White House," he scolded. "Not hiding underneath it."

"I am not the President," said Senator Catherine Mays.

"Yes, yes, Senator. I do understand that you need to resign from your current position as President of the Senate Pro Tempore before you become President of the United States," Romulus said.

Captain Farragut roared on his command deck, "Get me a firing solution on Romulus!"

"Searching, sir," Targeting said, reluctant. The Xerxes' stealth was perfect, and it was probably moving, probably close to Earth. *Merrimack* was fourteen light-minutes away.

Romulus had access to an imager inside the secure bunker. It was focused now on Senator Catherine Mays.

Romulus' voice sounded, "Very well, then, Senator. Resign from your position."

"I do so resign."

Farragut shouted uselessly at the tactical display, "Cat! What are you thinking!" No one could hear him except his command crew. "Where's my shot!"

"Negative target."

"Augustus!" Farragut was near pleading.

"If it were in my power, I would have taken the shot long before now."

They were searching for a hole in the vacuum.

Romulus spoke sweetly for all the civilized galaxy to hear. "Very good, Madam President."

From here, a swearing-in wasn't necessary. Catherine Mays was already President.

Romulus' imager cut in another scene from a second location, where Roman legionaries waited, arrayed in full ceremonial armor with spears.

Romulus commanded the legionaries from afar, "Rack 'em."

A centurion repeated the command for the assembled troops. In a single motion, the Roman legionaries hoisted their spears to form an arch over a long gauntlet. The legionaries were all young. The centurion relaying Romulus' orders to the men was terribly young.

Glenn Hamilton gasped in sudden recognition. "That's—"

She stopped talking.

The centurion was John Knox Farragut Junior. John John. Brother to Captain Farragut. Brother to the President of the United States.

"That has to be an imposter," Glenn said.

Captain Farragut shook his head.

No. It doesn't.

John Junior wore a belligerent expression that was trying to show pride, but it read more like wounded anger, as someone getting even after a grave insult.

Under John Junior's direction, Roman guards herded captive men-in-uniform into a column in preparation to walk in shame under the spears.

Calli Carmel looked up from a data station. "Captain! None of those troops are U.S. military personnel. I ran their idents. They're not even American citizens, and they're no one's military. They're colonials dressed in U.S. uniforms. Romulus has pressed a few thousand stand-ins for this show."

Farragut nodded. The truth wasn't necessary here. The appearance of truth was all Romulus required.

John Junior was real.

As more and more people from all the settled regions of the galaxy tuned in to watch the U.S. be subjugated, Romulus lined up a beam shot into the underground Presidential Emergency Operations Center. The bunker was well fortified.

Executing the President down there required Romulus to plot a firing path through all the layers of the bunker's inertial shell that was every bit as adamant as a space battleship's fortifications. He could make those calculations. They were intricate but not beyond his power to resolve.

His beam drill waited, ready to hit President Mays in the forehead when she tried to defy him.

She would defy him. Romulus already knew that. She was a Farragut. Groveling would be good, but he couldn't expect it.

President Mays was young, a famously stodgy dresser. Her only jewelry comprised a wedding band and a plain locket on a thin chain around her neck. Romulus knew the locket contained pictures of her two boys and her husband.

She was ridiculously ordinary.

Catherine Mays made a prosaic figure seated at the broad desk, a faithful replica of the Resolute Desk that stood in the Oval Office above ground, but without the fresh blood on it.

Romulus detected some reluctance in his Xerxes to acquire the target. The damned diplomatic ship kept asking him to recalculate his line of fire, pointing out the risk of hitting a human being.

Just in case his beam drill failed to fire, or in case Catherine Mays hid under the desk, Romulus had a resonator standing by in his displacement chamber. The resonator was prepped to transmit the irresistible harmonic. He made the necessary calculations to displace the resonator intact and functioning through the CONCOM bunker's formidable jammers.

What that death lacked in immediacy, it would make up for in terror.

Romulus saw the President on the imager. She had taken a seat at her impressive desk. She looked straight ahead. Her posture made sighting the beam easy.

Romulus gave the order over the public broadcast. "Madam President. The civilized galaxy is watching. Surrender your nation to the true Rome and to me as its Imperator."

President Catherine Farragut Mays spoke clearly for all the news outlets and for Romulus' imager to carry. "My fellow Americans. This day, speaking as Commander in Chief, I order all U.S. armies and all U.S. military ships in port and in space to carry on. No surrender. Not ever. God bless America."

She made it a point to keep her eyes open.

Romulus stood up, vibrating. Anger tasted rich. He ordered his Xerxes: "Fire."

28

EVENTUALLY THE PRESIDENT had to blink. She appeared unsettled.

Catherine Mays assumed a posture of dignified waiting, becoming perplexed. Her eyes flicked to one side. She asked tightly, "Mister Julius, are we done here?"

Captain John Farragut pounced on the tactical station. "Status! What's Romulus doing? Someone tell me what just happened?"

"Nothing to report, sir."

It was like waiting for a UXB.

At last, on the feed from the CONCOM bunker, John Farragut saw President Catherine Mays stand up. "We're done." She walked out of the picture.

Romulus scrambled to make his beam drill fire.

He sent the order again.

But the Xerxes' firing system had shut down altogether.

No. No. No.

He commanded his ship: "Diagnose system failure."

The ship replied: "Unauthorized use of a Pacific product against a sovereign governmental institution resulted in system termination. If you believe you have received this message in error, please contact the manufacturer. Pacific apologizes for any inconvenience. Agents are standing by to assist you."

Romulus proceeded to his backup plan—to displace a res chamber transmitting the irresistible harmonic into the presidential bunker.

But the displacement failed. The failure wasn't an issue of the bunker's defenses. The Xerxes' displacement controls were not responding.

A yelp from Claudia on the upper deck told him that her fantasy habitat had gone dark.

And now all the Xerxes' systems were shutting down.

Targeting was dead.

The Xerxes wasn't even apologizing anymore. The ship didn't like the target. Romulus had given it an illegal order. On his second attempt to breach the U.S. continuity of government bunker, the Xerxes decided it had been taken over by terrorists. It was sending a report to the manufacturer, shutting down, and erasing programs. Life support remained functional. Little else did.

This was infuriating. Romulus would just shut the whole ship down completely, restart, and begin again.

Farragut bellowed: "Find Romulus!"

Tactical responded with some surprise. "I think I have him! I *have* him! There! Unidentified spacecraft on the grid." Marcander Vincent brought up a visual image. He turned around from his station. "Is that what a Xerxes looks like?"

The image of an elegant yacht-sized ship appeared on the monitor.

"Acquire the target! Confirm identity!" Farragut ordered. "Hold your fire until I know for damn sure who that is."

The elegant ship was quickly collecting a coating of gorgons. They were clotting onto the ship, rapidly obscuring its graceful lines.

Calli said, disgusted, "Now Romulus is shielding himself with gorgons."

Augustus spoke from the rear of the command platform. "You think that is shielding?"

Romulus worked quickly, aware that the res chamber, which he'd tried to displace into the Presidential bunker, was still inboard. It was inside his displacement chamber, and it was resonating the irresistible harmonic.

He needed to get down below, shut the res chamber off, and eject it.

The Xerxes' inertial field was down. Gorgons flocked to his unshielded ship. He heard them moving on the hull, scratching and thumping. He bellowed to Claudia to get a spacesuit on.

In an attempt to reestablish control of his rogue systems, he plugged into patterner mode. He made the last connection to his Xerxes.

The data bank was not there.

Immediately, he was lost in a vast resonant consciousness, nebulous, infinite, hungry, angry, urgent. He was in the Hive. The Hive's mindless mind overwhelmed. He was trying to form a thought, struggling to keep hold of himself.

I?

He was attempting to put words to things without definition. He was losing . . . losing what?

The Hive detects the enemy Other inside a hard shell. Hardness of shell doesn't deter. The Other inside must be destroyed.

Gorgons chewed through the Xerxes' hull. They squeezed the oily brown sacks of their bodies inside. They sprouted mouths.

They touched an alien awareness.

The Hive pressed on Romulus' consciousness.

I am—lost.

I am all. I am everywhere.

Am.

What does am mean? Am has no meaning.

Two things Romulus must do.

He must keep hold of his singular self. And he must blend into the Hive totality. Romulus must do both. Neither allowed the other.

Gorgons milled. They were inside the ship. They prodded with their mouths. Jostled him. Searching for the enemy Other. They sensed the Other. It must not exist. Imperative to kill the Other.

This self was different. Incongruous. Is it I? Am I food?

Romulus thought quickly. No. Not! I am not food. I am Hive!

I am hungry.

I am Hive. I am the infinite self. I am I. Single but not separate.

The whole was still aware of difference. Romulus insisted: I am. I am All. I am One. I am *Hive*.

Finally the whole resolved: You are Hive.

Romulus: Yes! Yes! I am Hive!

Hive: *I* am Hive.

Romulus: Yes.

Hive: You are You. You are Hive.

Relief. Understanding. Romulus: Yes. I am Hive.

Hive: I am Hive.

Yes. The Hive understood now.

Hive: I am Hive. *You are OTHER Hive!*

The gorgons swelled. Their skins split open. They turned inside out. Translucent blue whiteness extruded from the gorgon husks. The new beings pushed and curled in on themselves into overlapping double loops.

The empty gorgon husks shriveled. The skins' dead flat stalks collapsed.

Within the loops of each of the new gluies, a single large orifice, ringed and ringed with stubby milky teeth, undulated.

Romulus swung a knife. The blade stuck in the gelatinous body.

The orifice clamped onto the blade and sucked it in, along with Romulus' arm. The stubby teeth were visible within the body, tearing his suit, chewing him.

Burn stench stung his eyes. Smelled like death. Heard a sucking with the sound of chewing. Saw red.

Heard Claudia. Screaming.

Claudia wore her protective earring, and the protective harmonic ran in her bloodstream. The gluies scarcely noticed her moving among them. They had no ears to hear her screaming.

She disintegrated at their acidic touch. The gluies consumed her organic remains.

Gluies used more energy than they provided to the Hive. Now, without the rival Other to combat, the Hive let their high-maintenance cells disintegrate.

The gluies gave off black smoke as they melted.

Merrimack's tactical displays gave visual images to the sensor readings. The command crew saw the gluies that clung to the Xerxes were now losing cohesion. Their remains slowly sloughed off the ship's hull on the inertia of their last motions.

"Get a drone in there!" Farragut ordered. "We need to preserve Romulus' data bank and get his res chamber! Get it done yesterday!"

He crossed the command platform with long strides, back and forth, bouncing off the bulkheads. Caged.

We won the battle. We're about to lose the war.

*   *   *

The Xerxes put up no defense against the drone's approach. The Xerxes had no inertial shell and no stealth properties. Its hull had been breached in many places.

Wraith Raytheon, the drone wrangler, cringed as he piloted his drone in through a ragged hole in the Xerxes' hull. Black ash and oil coated the interior surfaces. Small remnants suggested that the ruined space inside the ship used to be beautiful.

"Any sign of Romulus?"

"Negative presence," Wraith reported. Flinched at a drop of his own sweat. "Possible remains. Here."

Wraith's drone hovered over what looked like a patterner's cables on the deck.

"The gluies got him!"

"Mister Raytheon. Locate and access the Xerxes' data bank."

"Control center located, aye. I'm in, sir. Nothing to retrieve. The data bank has been destroyed."

"There has to be a trace read," Farragut said. "Retrieve the ship's data cells."

"Nothing to pull, sir."

The image from the drone showed fused and scorched masses that might once have been components. Melted trails burned across hard polymer surfaces. The drone found on the deck what might have been an earring in a patch of black residue.

"Can you get the Hive harmonic off the ship's res chamber?"

"I can't find the res chamber. This might have been it." The drone hovered over another amorphous plastic mass. The melted heap was of a size and in a position where one might expect to find a ship's res chamber.

"Mister Raytheon. Get a drone inside the Xerxes' displacement chamber. Determine if anyone displaced out of that ship."

Wraith's drone found the displacement chamber blackened and scored with a special fury. There was nothing to inspect. Nothing to retrieve.

Romulus was dead, and he'd taken his secrets with him.

TR Steele's Fleet Marines had a word for this situation: BOWASS.

Bend Over We Are So Screwed.

All the Hive spheres renewed their assault on planet Earth. More spheres arrived. No one alive knew how to stop them.

Augustus glanced from the ship's chronometer to his own.

Farragut noticed the glance. "Are you waiting for a shuttle, Colonel Augustus?" Farragut asked, cross.

Just as Tactical sang out, "Striker on the grid! Sublighted inside the Solar System, heading ten by three by sixty-six."

Augustus' black and red Striker now appeared on the tactical display. Its hatches hung open to the vacuum, exactly as they had when *Merrimack* abandoned the little Roman ship in the Myriad, a half year ago and two thousand parsecs away.

"You told me your Striker was heading to the galactic hub," Farragut said.

"So it was. At the time," Augustus said. "My Striker got far enough and turned around. Here it is."

Tactical sang out again, and he brought up another display. "See the gorgons."

The gorgon swarm nearest to Augustus' Striker moved toward it. Already the gorgons were turning themselves inside out, breaking out their gluies. They mobbed the Striker with the frenzy reserved for the irresistible harmonic.

"Colonel Augustus. What are you doing?"

"Not my doing," Augustus said. "But it's not unexpected. I knew Romulus wouldn't just leave my Striker unsecured in the Myriad. He would either destroy it—he didn't, obviously—or he would rig it with a booby trap against its possible return to Near Space."

"You were right," Farragut said. "He rigged it with the irresistible harmonic."

Translucent white gluies quickly obscured Augustus' red and black Striker, and kept piling on.

A shiver roughened Farragut's skin. *Gluies.*

"Augustus, your Striker is well and truly finished now. What did it gain you to bring it here? Can I assume you brought it here?"

Augustus stayed maddeningly calm or else he was just sick to death. He said indolently, "Romulus never played enough moves ahead, and he always undercounted the pieces left on the game board. A player begins the game with two knights. I knew I might need to sacrifice one of mine."

"You're talking in symbols, Augustus. Can't you just say what you mean?"

"In terms you can understand, John Farragut, I hit a sac fly. Look for the runner coming in to home. Tactical! See the plot at ten by three by sixty-six. Same vector as my Striker came in, but two light-years behind it. There's something to be said for redundance, John Farragut."

Given the precise vector, Tactical was able to locate the FTL object and put its image on display.

The target was a small ship, sky-blue and white, recognizable as a Roman Striker by its waspish lines.

The Striker kicked down from FTL. It wasn't attracting gluies as Augustus' Striker was.

Sacrifice fly.

Augustus got the Hive to chase his own Striker while—while what?

"You're bringing it in a little close, Augustus."

"We don't have a lot of time," Augustus said. "I need to get on board that Striker."

"You know what's in it?"

"I do. I don't know if it's alive. If it's dead, so are we."

Farragut ordered Space Torpedo Patrol Boat One to be readied for immediate launch. He ordered TR Steele to report to the hangar deck with a team of Fleet Marine gunners. Full suits, breathers, swords. He invited Jose Maria to come with him, and he charged off the command deck. "XO has the deck and com!"

On board SPT 1, crossing the void from *Merrimack* to the blue and white Striker, a team of Marine gunners were seated, ready at the guns. The guns were loaded with fragmentation rounds.

TR Steele stood at a porthole, glowering intently at *Merrimack*. Kerry Blue was back there. The space battleship grew smaller with distance.

Not small enough that he couldn't see the gorgons. His heart dropped. "Captain!"

"I see it, TR. Pilot, stay the course."

Merrimack was taking on gorgons.

It took all Steele's discipline to keep from requesting permission to open fire. Only the futility of it kept him in place.

He wondered if it was possible to choke on his own beating heart.

It was killing him not to be there, with *her*, repelling boarders.

His only shot was right here. This sortie was grasping at a miracle that he just couldn't see happening.

The Striker, where they were headed, hadn't attracted gorgons yet. The Striker was visible by the forward lights from SPT 1.

Farragut nodded ahead at the Striker. He asked the monster patterner, Augustus, "Whose ship is this?"

"This Striker belonged to the patterner Secundus."

"You knew him?"

"No. Secundus died sixty years ago."

The blue and white Striker filled the Spit boat's forward view ports. The pilot pivoted the Spit boat one-eighty and closed in, presenting the Spit boat's sternside air lock forward.

At Augustus' clicking request, the Striker formed an opening in its inertial screen to allow the Marines to establish a soft dock between the Spit boat's aft air lock and the Striker's only air lock.

Steele knew, because *Merrimack* had hangared another Roman Striker for way too long, that this Striker's air lock probably accessed its living compartment.

The living compartment couldn't be much more than seven by seven by eight feet empty. It housed all the patterner's possessions. Steele's own berth on *Merrimack* was smaller, but Steele had the rest of the space battleship to move around in. He wasn't confined to his quarters for months on end.

The Marines fixed a short flexible walkway between the Spit boat's air lock and the Striker's air lock and pressurized it. Then they withdrew to stand rear guard at their guns on board SPT 1.

Augustus took the point position in the walkway to board the Striker. He shut the Spit boat's hatches behind him.

He crossed to the Striker's outer hatch in three long strides. When the pressure gauges read equal, the locks on the Striker's outer hatch relaxed. Augustus advanced into the Striker's air lock.

He grasped the handle to the Striker's inner hatch.

Farragut's voice sounded over Augustus' suit com. "What are we expecting to find in there?"

"I'm *expecting* a dead mess of aliens from the Deep End and a nest of dormant gorgons waking up to devour me. I'm *hoping* for a *Deus ex machina.*"

Saying so, Augustus pulled the inner hatch.

The hatch sucked open with a billow of dense, damp, heated air. Condensation formed on Augustus' bubble helmet.

The Striker's living compartment had been converted into a tropical biosphere. Green plants dripped. The rubbery trees were breathing. Their black-green leaves hung like rags. Their trunks bent over as they had been forced to grow across the low overhead. Where there was a bed in Augustus' Striker, there was a pond here. Creatures moved in it.

There was no fear of alien microbes. Terrestrial life made incompatible hosts for alien infection. Basic airborne poisons—carbon monoxide, cyanide, and hydrochloric acid—were reasonable fears, but they were not present here.

Augustus spoke into his suit com, "Send Doctor Cordillera over."

Farragut: "I'm coming."

Augustus: "If you must. But I need Doctor Cordillera yesterday."

Farragut and Jose Maria were already suited up.

With the opening of the Spit boat's outer and inner hatches, the heavy scent of chlorophyll and damp, heated air spilled inside. Moisture condensed on all the surfaces and fogged the portholes.

Farragut bounded out the air lock. "TR! Your boat!"

"Sir."

Farragut crossed the walkway in three bounds. On entering the Striker, Farragut resisted swatting at the insectoids. The compartment was tight and it was clogged with living things. He didn't know where to step.

Toad-skinned rays with pulsating, bristling warts trembled and spat at him.

"Friends of yours, Augustus?"

"These are natives of a world deep in the Deep End of the galaxy."

"No. That's not possible. The Deep End is plagued with Hive. Nothing lives there."

Augustus picked up a warty ray. Its lizard tail twitched. Its bristles stood out rigid from its warts. "Life emerges where it can, and it evolves to survive the conditions present. Life on this creature's world evolved to coexist with a Hive swarm. All the life in here is resonating the Hive harmonic."

Augustus passed the wart ray to Jose Maria as he stepped in through the air lock. "The Hive mistakes these creatures for part of itself. Doctor Cordillera, you may get the Hive harmonic off of anything in here."

"You think that can be done?"

"It's *been* done. The patterner Secundus did it. It needs to be done again, very, very quickly."

"Then plug into patterner mode and analyze these creatures," Farragut ordered.

"No."

"You're refusing an order, Colonel Augustus?"

"Yes. If I get the Hive harmonic in my head, I *will* join the other side. I can't allow that to happen."

Jose Maria regarded the wart ray in his gloved hands. "Young Captain, I believe I can analyze the shape of the natural res chamber of this creature, and, from that, perhaps, derive the harmonic."

"You sound reluctant, Jose Maria."

"This is so, young Captain. It requires my taking a resonant sounding."

"Can you do that?"

"Understand that a resonant sounding entails *resonating*," Jose Maria warned. "This *will* provoke the Hive."

"Odds of success?"

"Better than not doing it," Augustus answered for him.

Jose Maria nodded assent.

"Go," Farragut said.

In the instant that Jose Maria took the res sounding, all the creatures inside the chamber made noises of protest. The creature under Jose Maria's direct observation shrieked. Its warts spat.

"Now what?" Farragut demanded.

Jose Maria wiped the viscous spit off his res reader. "There is a new harmonic in my chamber."

"Is it the Hive harmonic?"

"I do not know." Jose Maria stepped carefully over the pond creatures and crossed back to the Spit boat at a run. TR Steele stepped away from the air lock to let him board.

Jose Maria wiped condensation off a porthole to give him a view out.

Through the clear spot, TR Steele could see *Merrimack* out there, covered in gorgons and razors.

Jose Maria announced loudly, "I am resonating the harmonic that is currently lodged inside my resonator *now*. And—"

Steele watched the gorgons. Held his breath.

And?

And nothing.

There was no change in the behavior of the marauding gorgons out there.

Farragut barreled through the air lock. His heavy footfalls sent the flexible walkway bouncing in his wake. "Any reaction out there?"

Jose Maria's answer fell on Steele's ears like an epitaph. "Negative response."

Steele glowered out the porthole, his brows lowered, his jaw set.

So this was it. Negative response. End of the world.

By the light of the sun he could see gorgons continuing to clot onto *Merrimack*.

This really was the Alamo now. Kerry Blue was in there, in that living tomb. And he wasn't with her. Was she alone? Were her mates around her? Kerry Blue loved her team. *God, if I can't save her, if I can't be with her, please don't let her be alone.*

He was dumbfounded to hear the captain shouting with a sound like hallelujah. "Jose Maria! You *mean* it?"

Steele was bewildered. Farragut sounded *happy* about it. Joyous. Was negative response a good thing?

"Yes, young Captain," Jose Maria confirmed with a fragile smile.

Farragut bellowed, crowing now: *"We are singing with the choir!"*

Jose Maria looked to be trembling. "We have the Hive harmonic." It was the end of a long dark ordeal.

Farragut ordered, "Send the complement of the Hive harmonic. *Yesterday!*"

Jose Maria made entries into his handheld resonator. As he did, he warned Farragut, "Know that resonating the complement of the Hive harmonic will cause both harmonics to cancel each other out. Neither will exist."

"That means the Hive will cease to exist?"

"Yes."

"You're sure?"

"Near to a certainty. Resonance is the nervous system of the Hive. The Hive is a resonant entity. It cannot exist without its harmonic. Resonance knows no distance. All the Hive swarms on this harmonic, everywhere in the universe, will cease. The ramifications are far reaching. For example, what the absence of the harmonic could do to those creatures in Secundus' Striker, I could not say."

All the strange creatures from Constantine's Deep End world—the bristling little wart rays in their shallow pool, the weeping stalks, the rag trees pushing at the overhead, and the pulsing sponges—all of them were resonating a harmonic that was about to go extinct. Might they die? Might all life on their home world die?

Steele struggled to keep from bellowing, *So what!*

To Steele's huge relief, Farragut said, "I'm not doing an impact study, Jose Maria."

Merrimack was now coated with gorgons so thick there was no making out her spearhead shape anymore. *Merrimack* was dying.

Farragut said, "If anyone has objections, keep 'em to yourself. I'm destroying the enemy."

Jose Maria took a breath. His voice came out shaky. "I have it. I have the complement to the Hive harmonic."

"Kill it," Farragut said. "Kill the Hive."

"In my lifetime, if you please," Augustus added.

Jose Maria paused over his resonator. He looked to be praying.

Captain Farragut reached around him and activated the harmonic.

In the next moment Jose Maria cried, *"Dios! Dios!"*

PART FIVE

The Ends of a

Lemniscate

29

THE ALIEN CREATURES INSIDE the Striker's living compartment shrank, withered, and closed. The plants turned dull and curled into their mud beds.

Part of Steele died. He stared out the forward viewscreen. His heart pounded. It wanted out.

Merrimack was visible only as a gorgon tomb. Nothing of the space battleship herself showed. She looked like a mountain adrift in space.

But something was different. The surface of the mass wasn't crawling. It wasn't moving.

Then, like a slow shrug, a crack appeared in the mass. A great sheet sheared off, split. Pieces, they were gorgons, slowly crumbled in the vacuum. Tentacles lazily broke off and drifted.

Now part of *Merrimack*'s hull showed through the crust of gorgons. The space battleship's running lights were on.

The American flag broke surface, furled, but still there.

The motions of all the individual gorgons in space changed. Their tentacles dreamily detached and drifted away from their bodies.

Inside the Striker's swampy compartment, the alien creatures from the Deep End stopped contracting. Slowly, they expanded again, unfolding. They thrust out bright stamens and spread their fins to the compartment lights. The wart rays shed their dull skins. They chirped. They were alive.

The Hive was dead.

✳ ✳ ✳ ✳ ✳

Black grit like volcanic ash fell to Earth. Meteors streaked across the skies. Dead gorgons clouded the atmosphere. Earth was facing a climatic nightmare.

Most people considered themselves blessed to be alive to have the nightmare.

Cleanup efforts started immediately. It was a different sort of battle, another scenario for the U.S. Fleet Marines to train for. New equipment was installed on *Merrimack* to turn back the new threat.

President Catherine Mays publicly thanked Caesar Numa Pompeii for all his assistance during the recent crisis. Numa had given none. She declined any further assistance from Rome and privately advised Caesar that should Roman troops attempt to occupy Earth during the reconstruction, she would personally stab him in the heart with a sword.

Kerry Blue and Alpha Team waded in the little swamp on board the Roman Striker. They crated up the aliens and hovered them as fast as they could to an identical hold on board *Merrimack*. Orders were to move everything. Slime. Ooze. All. They needed to get it done before Caesar Numa Pompeii could demand the Striker be returned to Roman custody. Numa could lawfully do that. The Striker was Roman property.

The aliens inside it were not.

They got the compartment battened down. Twitch and Dak stood in the hatchway and took a last look inside to see if they'd broken anything in transit.

Nothing floating belly up. A couple of leaves were a little crinkled, but they may have already been that way.

As the Marines turned to go, a wart ray, wallowing in the shallow pool, made a break for the hatchway. Carly pointed, cried, "Get it!"

Twitch and Dak grabbed for the slithery wart ray.

It went airborne.

"I didn't know they could fly!" Carly cried.

The wart ray came down on Kerry Blue's head and held tight with its rubbery sides.

"Get it off! It's peeing down my neck."

"I don't think that's pee, *chica linda*."

The creature was flapping, its warts pulsing.

"Aw! Nah! Come *on*! Really?"

*   *   *

Captain Farragut opened up the ship's bar to toast *Don* Jose Maria de Cordillera, Colonel Augustus, and Commander Calli Carmel. He would have invited Lieutenant Colonel Steele, but that wouldn't be doing Steele a favor. Steele was a plain soldier at heart. You'd never find him in an Officers' Mess unless commanded to be there.

Farragut said, "Someone—that would be you, Augustus—explain Constantine to me. Was he actually the same historical megalomaniac who supposedly died decades ago?"

"That same Constantine, yes. Constantine Siculus arranged his own death to stop the hunters from searching for him."

"You knew he was still out there?"

"I only became aware of his continued survival when I was on board Romulus' Xerxes. One of the first things Romulus did on arriving back in time—stop wincing, John Farragut—was send an assassin missile to the Deep End to kill Constantine. I thought it strange that Romulus found it necessary to kill a dead historical figure. After we left the Myriad, I sent my Striker to follow the assassin missile."

"You told me you couldn't contact your Striker," Farragut said. "You lied to me, Augustus."

"I left off half the truth. I couldn't contact my Striker by resonator. But Strikers talk to each other by tachyon clicks. It's slower than resonance, but clicking doesn't attract Hive attention.

"Secundus' Striker transmitted a continuous warning on the tachyon clicker for any other Striker who might come out that way. It told us that Constantine was alive and intent on coopting any patterner who came there."

"Us? Who is us?"

"Me and my Striker."

"And yet you sent your Striker into the Deep End."

"It was a risk worth taking."

"And your Striker killed Constantine?"

"No," Augustus said. "Romulus' assassin missile killed Constantine. My Striker ordered Secundus' Striker to follow it back to Near Space. It was a long trek."

"And what was Secundus doing while his Striker was running away with your Striker?"

"Being dead."

"You're sure? The patterner Secundus is dead? Death doesn't seem all that permanent these days."

"Secundus has been dead for sixty years. Patterners don't live that long."

"And Constantine?"

"Dead."

"You're sure."

"Secundus' Striker sent confirmation to my Striker by tachyon clicker. Romulus' assassin missile successfully connected with Constantine. Constantine is finally, truly dead."

Augustus' Striker was also dead. Farragut knew that. To the extent that Strikers could be considered alive in the first place, Augustus' Striker was now thoroughly dead. The gluies had eaten into his Striker's antimatter chamber.

Secundus' Striker—the little ship that had served as an ark for its cargo of alien creatures from the Deep End—that Striker was still functional. The possession of Secundus' Striker was hotly contested now.

"Caesar Numa Pompeii has the lawful claim to the Striker," Augustus said. "The Striker is a Roman vessel. It must be returned to Rome."

"Okay," said John Farragut.

Okay?

Farragut had never known Augustus to blink.

Now Augustus looked cross. "John Farragut, you are the most transparent being in the known galaxy. You've already offloaded the aliens."

Farragut didn't deny it.

"That could be construed as piracy," Augustus said.

Farragut's broad shoulders lifted. Dropped. "My sister granted the aliens asylum."

Augustus' face was an impenetrable mask. Commander Calli Carmel flashed a dazzling smile. She had to be envisioning Numa Pompeii's reaction. She laughed out loud. "Why were all those creatures on board the Striker in the first place?"

Jose Maria de Cordillera answered that one. "Constantine Siculus intended that Striker to be his life craft out of the Deep End. The creatures mimicked the gorgons' resonance and passed themselves off as part of the Hive. The resonance from the creatures could have given Constantine safe passage through the Deep."

Farragut made an exasperated noise. "What makes men like Constantine and Romulus think they can rule the universe? They're not real. They're megalomaniacs. They shouldn't be real."

"Constantine and Romulus are not unique," Jose Maria said. "As much as one might want to believe that the madman who sets himself up as a god in the jungle is the stuff of fiction, the heart of darkness is real. History is populated with genocidal maniacs with delusions of invincibility, from Caligula to Hitler, to His Excellency President for Life, Field Marshal Al Hadji Doctor Idi Amin, VC, DSO, MC, Lord of All the Beasts of the Earth and Fishes of the Sea, and Conqueror of the British Empire in Africa in General and Uganda in Particular.

"As late as this third millennium there was also Glorious General descended from heaven, Dear Father Guiding Star of the Twenty-First Century, Great Defender, Savior, Great Sun of Life, Shining Star of Paektu Mountain, Ever Victorious Iron-Willed Commander, Highest Incarnation of the Revolutionary Comradely Love, His Excellency Kim Jong-Il. No one needs to make these men up. They *are*. The Pacific Consortium, who created the Xerxes ship, were well aware of the existence of such men. 'Unleashing a weapon without a failsafe is the dumbest godforsaken thing in the world.'"

John Farragut winced, nodding. "I said that, didn't I?"

The Pacifics already knew better than to give their products the ability to kill a world leader.

Calli asked, "Why didn't Romulus detect the failsafe in his Xerxes? He was a patterner."

Augustus answered. "The failsafe is not in the Xerxes' specifications. It's entirely passive. The failsafe doesn't exist until it's triggered by a grossly forbidden command, such as an act of war. The Xerxes expunged its operating system when Romulus tried to use it to kill the U.S. President."

Farragut: "Would you have detected the failsafe?"

"Detect it? No. But I knew there had to be one. It's common sense."

"Why didn't Romulus know? You said he was a superior patterner."

"Have I ever told you that being able to see doesn't make you *look*? The ability to see patterns doesn't curb the human tendency to kick unwanted data under the rug to get desired answers." Augustus leaned back, his eyes shut, brow creased as if in pain.

"Can I do anything for you?" Farragut asked.

"Tell your sister to surrender the U.S. to Rome."

"I don't see that ever happening."

Augustus snorted. Mistake. Got blood on his mouth and chin. "*Merda.*"

"Are you dying?"

"Technically we're all dying," Augustus said. "I just also happen to have a nose bleed."

* * * * *

The space battleship *Merrimack* reverberated with a colossal ship-wide 'cuss jam.

Company and crew were dancing, clanging, clubbing, and stomping.

A massive unglamorous reconstruction effort awaited them. But now was now. They'd won a big one. The ship was dancing.

A resonant hail came in on Farragut's private harmonic. He withdrew to the relative quiet of his cabin to take the call. The image that came up stunned him.

"Captain Farragut," his brother said.

"John!"

"My name is Nox. Call off your search. I won't be found."

Captain John Farragut had people looking for his younger brother. Captain Farragut was wealthy. He could mount an interstellar manhunt. He needed to find his brother—find him before anyone else did. Everyone else wanted him dead.

"Nox," Captain Farragut started over.

John Junior blinked at the sound of his own chosen name. He may have expected his older brother to ignore his demand for a separate identity.

Captain Farragut got the idea that his brother was trying very hard to hate him and not quite getting the job done. "Nox, come home. We can work this out."

"*Work this out?* Are you stark raving? I am wanted for treason. They will fry me."

"Nox? Our sister is the President of the United States."

Nox gave a graveyard laugh.

So what if Nox didn't get the death penalty? So what if he got a full Presidential pardon? He'd backed the wrong horse. He was a man without a country. There was no life for him back home.

"Let me go. You're making it hard for me to disappear. Just stop. John? Can you do that for me?"

Captain Farragut's throat felt thick. Nox had made himself one of the most despised men in the galaxy.

Captain Farragut wanted to be a big brother to him. It was the dead last thing Nox wanted.

Captain Farragut bowed his head. "I will."

The resonator went dark and silent.

Farragut turned his gaze upward, the direction heaven was imagined to be. Maybe in another life things turned out differently for his brother.

But, even after everything he'd seen, John Alexander Farragut still didn't believe in that stuff.

Eventually the 'cuss jam silenced. Everyone went back to work or back to sleep.

Captain Farragut caught up with the Hamster before the change of the watch. "A moment of your time?"

"Of course." Lieutenant Glenn Hamilton pushed back a lock of hair that wasn't loose, a nervous gesture. She looked down at the deck. "I'm sorry about your brother, John."

Captain John Alexander Farragut gave a small nod.

Glenn asked, "Have you heard anything about Donner?"

The Archon of Arra. Another dictator. Not a terrible one. A fair one, in fact. Donner had been Glenn Hamilton's benefactor when *Merrimack* had been at the planet Arra in the Myriad.

Farragut nodded. "Arra came out of this in better shape than Earth. Your buddy, Donner, is now giving orders to the LEN relief missionaries. I think they enjoy it. I've approved your leave."

"Oh," Glenn said, a descending note. Not enthusiastic. She hadn't requested leave. Her husband Patrick had requested it for her.

Captain Farragut stopped walking. Glenn stopped with him.

He turned to her. Cradled her face in his hands. "Hamster," he started. Shook his head. Started over. "Glenn. I want you—"

He got lost in her eyes.

She held her breath, expectant.

He found himself again.

"—off my boat."

All the muscles in her face let go.

She recovered quickly. She always did.

Lieutenant Glenn Hamilton inhaled. Exhaled as if she'd been running. "Okay. Yeah. Right. Okay."

Patrick was taking her to a planet the farthest point from anywhere.

It was an unflaggable world. The scientific expedition there needed a xeno-linguist. Patrick was excited about it.

The planet was called Zoe.

"I guess I'll either remember why I married him or—"

Or. She let that hang.

"You're not coming back here," Farragut said. "With or without Pat-rick."

That hit her deep. "It's not fair," she said. Immediately winced; she couldn't believe she just said that.

It didn't need to be fair.

"I'm recommending you for an independent command," Farragut told her. "You figure out what you want. There's no road that has you and me on it."

"I think I always knew that," Glenn said. "You were always a fantasy of mine, John." She could swear his face looked pink.

"Fifth amendment," he said back.

It was the change of the watch. TR Steele heard quick light footsteps behind him in the corridor. He picked up his pace. He knew the sound of her footsteps.

She sped up. Caught up with him.

She had recovered completely from her ordeal in the lower sail. He had been able to avoid her since then.

He didn't want to acknowledge anything that happened in the lower sail.

Here she was, asking, "Did you mean what you said?"

TR Steele hadn't thought he would be alive to face down those words. He'd thought they were both going to die down there when he said them.

You are all I think about.

"I didn't say anything," he growled.

He was taking big strides. She skipped to keep up with him. Swung her arms. Did she have to skip? Marines don't skip.

Kerry Blue was not what anyone outside the service would call beau-tiful. Steele thought she was beautiful. She filled his dreams. Her big heart, her toughness. She could get scared, but she never let it make her give up her ground. She was shameless. She lived in the moment.

There was no one so alive as Kerry Blue. She was a life force. She owned him.

She was smiling at him. "You gonna go back to being mean to me?"

He pressed his lips into a straight line, chin pushed out. Didn't intend to answer her. Heard himself talking. "Meaner."

"Yes, sir." She got herself in front of him. He either had to stop or else walk into her. She stood up on tiptoe, kissed him on the mouth, then twirled—Marines should not twirl!—and she skipped away, ponytail swinging.

He watched her go. He wasn't watching the ponytail.

And he imagined things that were never gonna happen in this or any universe.